SWOON

SWOON

NINA MALKIN

SIMON PULSE

NEW YORK   LONDON   TORONTO   SYDNEY

SIMON PULSE

An imprint of Simon & Schuster Children's Publishing Division
1230 Avenue of the Americas, New York, NY 10020
First Simon Pulse paperback edition May 2010
Copyright © 2009 by Nina Malkin
Also available in a Simon Pulse hardcover edition.
For information about special discounts for bulk purchases, please contact
Simon & Schuster Special Sales at 1-866-506-1949 or business@simonandschuster.com.
The Simon & Schuster Speakers Bureau can bring authors to your live event. For more
information or to book an event contact the Simon & Schuster Speakers Bureau at
1-866-248-3049 or visit our website at www.simonspeakers.com.
Designed by Paul Weil
The text of this book was set in Adobe Garamond.
Manufactured in the United States of America
2 4 6 8 10 9 7 5 3 1
The Library of Congress has cataloged the hardcover edition as follows:
Malkin, Nina.
Swoon / Nina Malkin. — 1st Simon Pulse hardcover ed.
p. cm.
Summary: In rural Connecticut, when seventeen-year-old Dice tries to
exorcise a seventeenth-century man who is possessing her cousin Pen, she
inadvertently makes him corporeal—and irresistible.
ISBN 978-1-4169-7434-5 (hc)
[1. Spirit possession—Fiction. 2. Supernatural—Fiction. 3. Cousins—Fiction.
4. Psychic ability—Fiction. 5. Conduct of life—Fiction. 6. Love—Fiction.
7. Connecticut—Ficiton.] I. Title.
PZ7.M29352Swo 2009
[Fic]—dc22
2008040679
ISBN 978-1-4169-9801-3 (pbk)
ISBN 978-1-4391-6436-5 (eBook)

To AMR, who wanted something darker

PART I

THE TREE

I

Love at first sight must be glorious. I wouldn't know, since at first there was no sight. Smell, yeah—the tangy, salty scent of horses. Plenty of other sensations too. But I'll get to that. The point I want to make up front is that by the time I laid eyes on Sinclair Youngblood Powers—in the flesh, that is—I was already in love with him. Nothing could change that. Not even the fact that he was dead.

Sinclair appeared—in this dimension, this century—on the autumnal equinox, but he'd been with us since late July. That's right, us. Pen's been involved, intimately involved, from day one. Which was, as I mentioned, late July, the second half of summer like haze across a field, and us by then thoroughly indolent, twitchy, bored.

"Dice, I've got to *do* something."

Dice—that would be me. Everyone goes by a monosyllable

here—reference Pen, née Penelope—so this past spring, having been plucked from the companionable misery of NYC and dumped in the Connecticut countryside, I took mine. It's fine. Candice never fit; too fancy. Candy, either; too cute. As it turned out, Sinclair adopted a tidy truncation too. Can you guess? I'll give you a hint: It wasn't Clair.

But I'm jumping ahead. Let me focus, let me feel it—that fervent midsummer afternoon in the village green, Pen and me, free and idle.

"Watch this." She jumped up, stubbed the joint we'd been sharing onto the stone fence (never would the potential consequences of smoking pot in plain sight even occur to my cousin), then took off at a trot. Me, toasted, I just want to loll, let my mind go off while my body indulges inertia. Pen, no—she had the remarkable goofball gusto to go climb a tree.

Physically, the girl could do anything. Throw and catch with agility and accuracy. (I could duck.) Dive and swim and water-ski. (I could . . . not drown.) Even in flip-flops she scrambled up that tree like a monkey, hoisting herself onto carbuncles that stuck out from the trunk like mutant broccoli. Pen knew the tree, had grown up with it, and must have scaled it countless times. Still, it's huge, a handsome, ancient ash. Grabbing at branches, strong of grip and sure of foot, she was soon half lost in foliage—saw-toothed leaves and clusters of purple-black buds. I got off the fence to stand below, admire her ascent. Pen was high, literally. Then, with a rustle, she changed course from vertical to horizontal.

"Dice!" she called from her limb. "Can you see me?"

A patch of tan skin, a swatch of blue shorts. I saw her. Apparently I wasn't the only one. There, across the village green, lounging legs splayed on a bench with some cohorts, was Kurt Libo, his antennae up. He'd picked up that Pen Leonard—*the* Pen Leonard—was going out on a limb. Not that Pen has to do much to capture the attention of any sentient being, especially if male. With those breasts and that silken bolt of blond hair, all she has to do is breathe. And what did she do with this embarrassment of rapt male riches? Not much. Banked it, maybe, in case she wanted a favor later, or gave a groan that turned into a giggle. The way guys behaved in her presence, Pen thought it was funny.

Further on she crept, hands and knees, fingers and toes. Then she cursed, and one of her flip-flops swished down. The limb she'd picked was thick, but it bent with her weight.

"Pen, you are a cuckoo bird," I said, more to myself or the universe than her.

"What? Louder!"

Hmm, so—she'd noticed Kurt had noticed her. That was to be my role, then. Fine. I could play emcee, no problem. "Pen!" I shouted. "Pen, you're crazy! Oh my God, you'll kill yourself!" Overwrought lines from some soap opera script. I didn't have to turn to know that Kurt's radar for girls gone wild was in full blip. I hollered some more, waved my arms. I didn't have to look to know that Kurt was on his way, friends in his wake, with their slouchy, gas station saunter.

At some point during my theatrics I felt a prickle of fear, the plain and simple fear that Pen could get hurt. Yet before I could fix on how unfair that was—I wasn't supposed to know such fear, not now, so soon, not here, in Swoon—there came a familiar, tingly foretaste. That anticipatory tremor, that distant thunder roll. There wasn't a thing I could do about it. There never is. So I let it course through me with secret not-quite delight.

Right about then Pen wrapped her legs around the branch, emitted a shriek, and let go. The bough dipped, and she dangled like a lantern, ankles locked, hair a cascade, bra threatening to disgorge out the scoop of her T-shirt.

"Holy crap!" from someone.

"Nice!" from someone else.

Hooting, whistles, applause. Kurt, his boys.

Pen may have been laughing, too, but it sounded strangled— it must be hard to laugh upside down. But oh the ease and grace of her swing, like she could do it and eat a sandwich; I was impressed. Only the awe got shoved aside, diminished by a second, stronger tremor that didn't seem related to Pen at all.

Not even as she fell.

Talk about buzz kill. Energy versus gravity. Arms and legs pawing at elusive leaves and then the utter emptiness of air. Torso twisting like a cat righting itself post-plunge. Only Pen's no cat. She body-slammed onto the ground, hard. The impact reached the soles of my feet while a cranial choir sang hosannas of *"Stupid! Stupid! Stupid!"* I dropped to kneel beside her. Pen was on her back, eyes closed. She was very, very still. My mouth was open, but her name hid behind my tonsils. Kurt and company hovered nervously, wondering if somehow they could be held responsible. Them. Yeah, right.

Then, the third tremor—a steamroller with thorns this time—and with it, the equine smell. The world folded in and out like accordion bellows, and suddenly none of this was here. No, it was—but it wasn't the same. The tree wasn't nearly as mighty. The day was different, too; drizzly, the sun off duty. Pen, Kurt, et al were absent, but there was a crowd. This was . . . an event. A spectacle. The atmosphere was thick with it. Every one of these people had something to feel, and none of it was good.

Then, with a time-wrenching twist, I was back again, kneeling by Pen, and her eyes shot open. Except they weren't her eyes. Pen's eyes are indigo, same color as mine—her mother's eyes, my mother's eyes. These were shards of onyx, sharp and black.

"You put to death this day an innocent man!" cried Pen, who was not Pen.

"What the . . . ?" wondered Kurt, or someone, a distant insect.

"You convict me of murder—what a cowardly lie! In truth you condemn me for doing in life what you all dare do in dreams! It festers there in the sweat of your beds, expunged now as this poisonous righteousness."

The voice spilling from Pen was her own, but as I began to grasp that the cadence, the eloquence, the unadulterated wrath could never be, the cosmos convulsed again, and I was once more part of the angry throng.

"Mark me, oh town of Swoon, oh great Connecticut colony, I shall be avenged."

I couldn't see him for all the people in front of me, who crushed forward and howled back. I could feel him, though, his rage and his terror. The onslaught of his oath seized me from the inside, held my heart like a shipwreck victim clings to flotsam.

"So warn your children's children's children and beyond— warn them well!"

The assembly roared scorn, and tightened together as fibers on a loom. *They're going to do it,* I thought, all at once comprehending. *String him up on this very tree.*

It takes a while to hang a man. He must have been strong; he must have fought. But at last he was well and truly dead, for the knots and clots of the crowd began to unravel and disperse.

For me, the world flexed in and came out the other side. There was sunshine. And there was Pen.

"Dice . . . ," she said weakly, her eyes—they were hers—on mine. "Did I do something dumb?"

Relief was oxygen, brisk and blessed. "Yeah . . . no," I told her. "You fell. You probably shouldn't try to move right now. I think you lost consciousness or something."

"Whoa . . . really?" She blinked. Tickly shards of hair covered her face. I smoothed some away with a finger. "I think I'm okay," she said. "Nothing . . . really hurts."

Me? I was burning up, but it would pass. I studied Pen. The position of her body was normal; nothing stuck out at odd angles. My cousin is one of those indestructible people. One of those lucky people nothing bad or weird ever happens to. A bouncy rubber ball of a girl. Except something about the way Pen's glance flicked to Kurt's—the way she seemed to suspend him for a second with an almost sexy smile—made me wonder if such people genuinely exist, or if they're just a legend we hold to so we can feel safe.

II

THE DIAGNOSIS, DELIVERED WHEN I WAS THIRTEEN, WAS EPILEPSY. A rare form (wasn't I special?) that might or might not respond to meds. But at least we *knew*.

"At least we *know*," my mother had said, tension draining from her spindly frame. She'd lost ten pounds on the sick kid diet—call it a perk.

"At least we *know*," my father had echoed, smiling the reassuring lawyer smile. Daddy's not a lawyer; he just plays one on TV. Peter Moskow, hardly a famous actor but a working one; he's hooked up with the whole procedural crime-drama circuit. He's been on all sides—prosecutor, D.A., mobster, vigilante (yet never a cop; Daddy says he's too Jewish-looking to be cast as a cop). Momster's in the business, too, sort of: Lesley Reagan, executive editor for *In Star*, number one in tabloid trash.

"At least we *know*," they'd said and held my moist hand as I nodded bravely and the doctor went on about how my symptoms would most likely continue to be mild. No tongue-swallowing, no thrashing spasms at inopportune moments. Just these little lapses. "To the rest of the world, it'll look like you're spacing out for a second," he'd said, skin crinkling around his doctor's smile.

At least they *knew*. Trouble is, I knew different. Epilepsy, my ass. The seizures, fits, spells, trances, space-outs—"episodes" is my parents' preferred term—are something else entirely. Physical manifestations of the simple fact that I, Candice Reagan Moskow, am a teensy bit psychic. Oh, gosh! I said it! What will the neighbors think?

Bottom line, I've always been this way. Not that I could give you the answers to a math test or pick winning lottery tickets. It's not at my command or within my control. Mostly it's a matter of unbidden cognizance—which can suck when you're reading a really good book and midway through know how it ends. Other times my dreams come true—random stuff, like I'll dream about shaking a cow, and the next morning at breakfast, the milk will be spoiled. And then, the hard-core instances, frightening enough for my parents to drag me up to every neurologist on Park Avenue.

The visions.

They came with puberty. Some girls get C-cups; I got previews of coming attractions and trailers of moldy oldies. Visions isn't the best word, since I more than see things; I hear things and smell things and taste and touch things; I go places and sometimes come back changed (that rosy birthmark I wasn't born with, the small scar shaped like half a heart on my left shoulder). Yet evidently these let's-call-them-visions mimic the brain patterns of a mild epileptic seizure. Ergo, I have epilepsy. MRIs don't tell lies. Fine. So what's a girl to do?

Deal, that's what. Shut up about it. My parents are a united front on the epilepsy issue. For an actor, Daddy's sternly logical about "real" life, and Momster, well, the sturdy, resilient, sniffle-resistant Reagans simply don't *do* paranormal. My Nana Lena, Daddy's mother, is up to speed, since apparently her mother (referred to in family lore as that crazy Romanian) was similarly afflicted. But it's not a topic of conversation. It's more like an accord between us—she knows, and I know she knows. For outsiders I enact a program of clairvoyance avoidance, and keep it on the low, in general. Let other kids make like a walking dartboard or human canvas; there's no constellation of piercings or ink on me. Dress somberly. Speak softly. Downplay drama. I know, I know, I'm a cliché—the reluctant psychic, but you fly that freak flag you're asking for trouble. Let's just say I have a funny feeling about that. Only Ruby ever suspected something extra-sensory was up. Poor crazy, beautiful Ruby. No need to worry about her outing me. Not anymore.

Fortunately, the visions calmed down some. At first they were frequent, violent, plus sometimes I puked or ran a woozy temperature afterward. Then I got used to them, learned to crunch ice cubes afterward to quell the nausea and fever. They're not even a regular occurrence anymore—months can go by. My theory is they were rocket-launched by an initial blast of female hormones, PMS as ESP. Four years later they're far more sporadic, and I still hope the whole telepathy thing will burn off like baby fat—I've no ambition to compete on *Last Psychic Standing.* Till then, I have management techniques.

Such as the vision return policy. That's right, like a sweater you bought on a whim and decided looks stupid. I close my eyes and imagine myself in Macy's Herald Square. I have a shopping bag with the vision inside, tags still on, and my receipt, and a matronly woman with puffed-up hair and bifocals who's been working the return counter at Macy's for half a century takes it away, and I say thanks. This helps me move on.

Except that time with Pen and the tree, it didn't work. The woman peered in the bag, inspected my receipt; she looked at me. "Sorry, honey." She had one of those gravelly voices, as though she needed a lozenge. "You can't return this."

I didn't want to make trouble, but I had to ask. "Why not?" Behind me, people shifted and shuffled, packages crackling. "I've never had a problem before."

The return-counter lady gazed at me over her glasses. She was not unsympathetic when she said, "Well, honey, you do now."

III

Swoon is segregated—only not how you think. There're maybe a dozen minority families in town, and while I don't know the total head count I do know the Latin lady has her own network cooking show, and the father of one of the black kids in school runs a multinational bank. Since Swoon is a town of courteous smiles, these people of color (the color of money) do as they please. The segregation I'm talking about is self-imposed and applies to leisure preference—you can see it in action down at the lake. There are sailing people and fishing people and water-skiing people, and everyone respects each other's space on the five hundred or so acres of perfect, placid water. And if all you want to do is nothing, as far from prying eyes as possible, there's a spot for that, too. It's called The Spot.

Pen drove. She'd gotten the car as a sweet sixteen present,

the ultimate in chunky luxe, age-restricted license be damned. Nobody worried about Pen behind the wheel.

"Oh, crap," she swore mildly, braked, and backed up. "I always miss that turn."

It's easy to miss—it isn't marked and not really a road. That's the point. We bumped along the path, the bushes so close and the tree boughs so low as to brush us on three sides. I played an inner game of jungle explorer—I'm good at suspending my disbelief. Pen sang along with a rapper on the radio, thuggish threats in her squeaky soprano, vaguely off-key.

The Spot is secluded but renowned; cars stood among the trees like slumbering beasts. Some fancy foreign ones like Pen's. A couple of heaps. Mostly trucks. New trucks. Lovingly restored vintage trucks.

"Dice, grab the cooler, okay?" Pen slung some towels around her neck and collected her enormous tote as I hefted snacks and drinks. Following my bikini-clad cousin down the narrow trail, I couldn't help but note she hadn't a mark on her. Two days after her tumble from the tree and the girl was unscathed, her swingy gait bouncy as ever. If it had been me, I'd have been in traction.

It hadn't been me—yet still I felt effects of that day on the green. Having failed to return the vision to Macy's Herald Square, it lingered like a stubborn hangover, my head cloudy and my mouth full of dust. Oh, and my dreams. How spectacular, how disturbing, how twisted my dreams must have been, since I woke up sobbing once and again laughing; only as I reached for my journal to record them as I dutifully do, I couldn't remember so much as a flicker. Which *never* happens. I've got total dream recall, reverie instant replay. Even that week they had me on flurazepam, I dreamed hard and could recite them back like nursery rhymes. Yet those last two had been eradicated by some cosmic CIA. Musing on that, I tripped on a root and crashed into Pen, and the two of us made our undignified entrance onto the lake shore.

People waved. We waved back. No one removed sunglasses. A full one-eighty from my New York friends. In the city, we kissed. Girls, guys, transgender; gay, straight, undecided. We kissed hello and we kissed good-bye; we kissed if we'd just seen each other at lunch. Too touchy-feely for Connecticut, where kissing is for family members, if even. And, of course, someone you're hot for.

Pen was hot, in her way, for Burr Addams. So, naturally, we ignored him, setting towels down beside Kristin Marshall and Caroline Chadwick. Both were friends of Pen's, and now, by association, friends of mine. I'm not sure I would've chosen Wick, who can be a bit callous and vain, but Marsh, yes. Marsh I genuinely like.

"I don't know why I'm slathering all this lotion on," Pen said, slathering. "Soon as I'm done, I'm going in."

It was another gorgeous afternoon. The lake sparkled. The tucked-away clearing was pristine—got to give Swoon party animals props for carting off beer cans from prior bashes. I envied the bumblebees sucking up to every flowering thing. Urbanites thrust into the country react one of two ways—with fear and loathing or giddy delight.

"Have you been in yet?" Pen asked the girls as she wiped her hands with a towelette. The robust tint to her complexion, the glint in her minnowy eyes—if anything, she looked better than usual. A brush with death will do that, apparently.

"I don't want to get my hair wet," complained Wick, whose hair, like Pen's, is blond, thick, and naturally, perfectly straight. "I washed it after riding this morning, and I refuse to wash it again." Wick flipped her hair to show it who's boss.

Marsh has long, straight, blond hair, too, though hers finer, faintly oily, swept off her pimply forehead with a plaid band. Ah, life in the land of blondes. My dark curls, if ever blown out into taut obeisance, would rebel at the slightest hint of humidity with an audible *boing!* Between those unruly ringlets and my mooncast pallor, not to mention a tush with the acreage of Wyoming, I was a sore thumb in Swoon. Only it wasn't the sticking out that irked, but the absence of human variety. I missed the Upper West Side, where different is in demand, celebrated, de rigueur. Here, even Angela "Gel" Burton, the black chick whose father runs the bank, wears her hair below her bra strap, smoothed by some chemical process and lightly flecked with gold.

"I'll go in," said Marsh. "Though I'm sure it'll be like ice." That's one of the things I like about Marsh—she's a pessimist.

Call it her way of sticking out, here in cheerleader country. Then again, Marsh had reason to expect the worst. Her father was . . . she used the word "strict." But I'd met Douglas Marshall, looked in his eyes, and I think she meant "psychotic."

"Me too," I said.

Pen stood up. "Good." She grabbed my wrist, hoisting me to my feet. I shed the madras button-down I wore as a cover-up.

"Oh, all right," Wick said irritably and gathered her locks into a quick top knot. "But I'm *not* going underwater."

It wasn't as though one of us had to stay behind to watch the stuff. Cash, credit cards, car keys, and assorted gadgets sat secure in open bags. We made for the lake. There would be no toe-testing, no getting used to it. Lake water is notoriously cold; the only way in is the charge. Besides, running in, with its requisite squeals and splashes, is a mating call in Western Connecticut. Soon, Pen and Burr Addams were racing each other with long, clean strokes.

Burr was an exemplary suitor, a true Connecticut Yankee. The Addams lineage dates back to the original colony. His father, a judge on the state Supreme Court, had greater political aspirations. Burr had been captain of the high school's victorious lacrosse team; he'd be a freshman at Yale come fall. Having spent the first half of the summer traipsing through Europe, he was now home to while away the rest in lazier fashion. How did I know this? Pen was a Burr Addams encyclopedia. She'd told me all that, and also that she was saving herself for him—she'd used those very words, "saving myself"—since she intended, with a certainty that bordered on grim, to marry him one day. Today she was working toward the goal.

Some guy I didn't know had swum over to chat up Wick. No one with a penis had yet approached Marsh and I. We paddled in place to maintain blood flow in the brutally glacial milieu. "Good thing we're not guys," Marsh said. "Our testicles would have shrunken to tiny little peas by now." Another thing I like about Marsh: She's funny.

"Come on, Dice, I'll teach you to backstroke," she said.

"Yeah?" I said, panting slightly. "You think? That *would* require me to lie on my back." I couldn't conceive a more vulnerable position in the middle of a freezing lake.

"Oh, come on. It's easy, I promise." To convince me, Marsh arched at the belly, then flicked arms and fluttered feet. A corona of thin blond seaweed stirred about her head. Then she rolled over and sidestroked my way. "Trust me," she said.

What the hell—treading water was proving strenuous. Marsh laid a hand at my lower back, another on my shoulder. "That's it," she said, soft but not tentative—she knew what she was doing. "Just relax; quit craning your neck like that."

The hand moved from my shoulder to cradle the base of my skull. I let my eyelids meet and listened to Marsh's gentle murmur, so close to me, an aural hypnotic.

"There you go," she said. "You've got it."

For a second there, panic struck—a ripple, urged by a not-too-distant splash, threatened to go up my nose, and I heard Pen giggling nearby. At least it sort of sounded like Pen. And I didn't so much hear as feel her, a probing inner tickle. Then the moment passed. Rigidity drained away as I heeded Marsh, sure and quiet. My legs parted of their own accord. My breathing steadied and lengthened. Marsh kept her hands on me. I trusted her. The sun on my cheeks felt glorious.

"See?" she said. "It's just like taking a bath . . ."

I was going to say, "Yeah, if your bathtub's in an igloo." Except the sarcasm wouldn't make sense since the water no longer felt so cold. Just refreshingly cool, like lawn dew on bare feet early in the morning. I could have lain there forever.

"Okay, Dice, I'm going to float next to you," Marsh said. "I'm letting go, okay?"

Rather than fully release me, though, Marsh took my hand. And as we floated together, hand in hand and feeling sublime, I began to give in . . . to thoughts . . . a particular kind of thoughts . . . fantasies. I fantasized about kissing, and being kissed. Not making out with Marsh—it wasn't lurid like that. Only the idea of turning my cheek onto the surface of the lake and having my lips met with other lips. My smile spread like honey. Other sensations stole through me, other fantasies, amorphous yet intense, and I found myself responding in all the usual places and uncharted zones as well. My temples, lapped by the water. The fleshy part of my palm that pressed against my friend's.

It was just . . . so . . . *nice*. Maybe too nice. Prolonged pleasure tends to feel like something I don't deserve, so by instinct I kicked out of the float. Only it was still all good. In fact, I wasn't the only one blissing. Color me astonished, but off a ways in deeper water Pen and Burr were wrapped around each other like a tan, wet, two-backed beast. *Go, Pen,* I thought, almost whimsically. *About freakin' time.*

We'd talked about sex, Pen and I; it was one of my favorite topics. True, I'd never had a "real" boyfriend, but I'd fooled around— no, "experimented" is the better term, since my forays with guys had been geeky like that: Hey, can I do this? Come on, let me touch you there. What does it feel like? Yeah? You like that? Cool. Okay, now you do me . . . come on, please? Chemical reactions, one sensation triggering the next—yeah, human beings are wonderfully made. Yet often I'd wonder, after a session with some boy, what it would be like to throw actual love into the mix. Spontaneous combustion? Orgasmic avalanche? When I'd babble about this, Pen would moue and call me a freak. Pity, really. On the surface, a centerfold, but inside the girl just didn't get it.

Well, she was getting it now. No, wait a second. My smile lit up a notch. She wasn't just getting it. She was *leading* it. Everyone at the lake seemed similarly . . . stimulated. It was nuts— Swoon could hardly be mistaken for the PDA capital of the world—but there it was. Off on the shore, with that boy she'd just met, Wick was getting dirt in her hair and wasn't remotely concerned. In the water and on the bank and into the woods, a chorus of sighs and coos harmonized with the sounds of—no, really—the birds and the bees. And Pen was the epicenter, the focal point of a collective erotic surge. I knew this as surely as I knew my own name, the way I sometimes just know things. *Bizarre-o,* I thought. *How not like Pen.*

"Hey, what's going on?" Marsh got vertical and squeezed my hand.

"Yo, Marsh, I'm a voyeur!" I gave her a shining look.

"Really? What are you voyeuring?"

"Check out the wonder couple." They were a few yards away. At this point we could only see Burr. He had Pen's bikini top tied under his chin, giving him a silly set of mouse ears, and he tried to tread water in a state of sheer ecstasy. Which put Pen below the water line, the source of said ecstasy. Suddenly she sprung up, glistening like a naiad, and flung her arms around Burr. Then with the heels of her hands pressed his shoulders. Apparently, Pen believed in give and take. It was Burr's turn. He went under. And Pen emerged a bit, her head back, her breasts surfacing.

"Oh, my goodness," said Marsh. "Burr Addams is a bad, bad boy."

"Uh, I don't know. I'd give him an A for effort at least." The two of us giggled conspiratorially. And then I said, "I don't know about Burr, but this is *so* not like Pen." *So not like Pen . . . not like Pen . . . not . . . Pen . . .*

Fast as the click of a TV remote, thunderclouds rolled in from the north, blemishing the sky with flint-colored peril. There came a crack of lightning; it made Marsh leap.

"Dice, come on, we should swim in." She didn't want either of us electrocuted. Other people were making for shore, the heady spell broken. A few fat raindrops fell. "Dice . . . ," said Marsh. But I was transfixed. I was watching Pen. She was upright now, and doing . . . something. Something strange. Something strong. Something wrong. I felt it like a punch. Pen would not let Burr up . . . she was holding him underwater somehow . . . she was . . .

I began to paddle toward them. "Pen!" I tried to scream, but my mouth filled with water. I choked; I thrashed. Still I struggled on. Then Marsh was with me. Then she was ahead of me, slicing toward Pen and Burr. She was on it, on them. Burr came heaving out of the water. There was some shouting— thunder obscured the words. Then we all broke for shore. Not till the soles of my feet found the slick lake bottom would fear lose its grip on me. Gasping, I reached the pebbly sand. And the rains came down.

IV

THERE WERE FOOTSTEPS ON THE STAIRS. THIS IS AN OLD HOUSE, among the oldest in the area, a white clapboard former farmhouse built in 1748. Fart on the porch and it rattles a floorboard in the attic. I could hear a spider coming up those stairs. Alone in the house—or so I thought—I sat very still. It tripped me out initially how no one in Swoon locks their doors; me, who'd kept a bulging set of keys in my pocket since third grade. Here, it's a point of pride. Here, it's safe. And since our house is directly across Daisy Lane from my aunt and uncle's, I figured it had to be Pen. Which ordinarily wouldn't have rattled me.

"You'd better be decent; I've got Jordan," she called out, giving a compulsory tap to my bedroom door before coming through, littlest blond brother in tow.

I was decent indeed, cross-legged on my bed, reading the tarot—or trying to. It might as well have been Lithuanian. The spread before me proposed a dozen interpretations. Every answer begat a question. The longer I pondered, the more baffled I became. Since I don't have the best relationship with my psychic side to begin with, you know it had taken some serious brain block for me to channel it, and here it was adding up to a big fat zero. I smushed the cards into a heap.

"Why'd you do that?" asked Pen.

"The vibe of a six-year-old is not conducive to communion with the astral plane. No offense, Jordan."

"Can I play with the bugs, Can . . . Dice?" Jordan was fascinated by my scarab collection, a gift from Daddy when I was ten or so and going through a mystical-mythical-spiritual phase. Momster didn't approve, but she didn't object, either. Agnostics both, they were raising me without religion.

"You can *look* at them, Jor," I said. "You can't *play* with them."

"That's what I *meant*." Carefully the towhead took the glass case off my desk and situated himself on the floor with it.

Pen sat on the edge of my bed. "Do me."

What she didn't know—and what I wouldn't tell her—is I *had* been doing her. I hadn't seen much of the girl since she'd sought to drown Swoon's most eligible bachelor. The incident at the lake was on Friday; my parents had made it to Swoon for the weekend and, since Daddy wasn't on a show and Momster conceded to take a few vacation days, on Monday we drove to

Newport and stayed at a seaside inn. Which was nice—I saw little of my parents lately.

The whole move to Connecticut had been a folly, although of course they'd meant well, believing it the solution to all our (read: my) problems. This idyllic place, so close to Momster's sister and her impeccably adjusted offspring—what better tonic than fresh air, sunshine, and Aunt Lainie's homemade muffins. They just hadn't thought it through. Hadn't considered how Momster rarely leaves work before eight p.m., and there's no direct train or bus service to Swoon. Or how Daddy needs to be on set at six a.m. when he's shooting. Not to mention the fact that he's allergic to virtually every strain of pollen and must spend his waking moments in the country doped up on hardcore antihistamines. Ah, but they'd gotten carried away with the quaint old house at the bargain price, and their lofty notion of how *good for me* this would be. Next thing they knew they were the proud owners of an eighteenth-century former farmhouse they'd spend hardly any time in. Oh, sure, the first month Momster bravely hopped the train to Brewster every evening, then drove another hour to Swoon, but the commute made her surly. So she became a weekender, and Daddy, with his insane schedule and poor rapport with greenery, around even less.

Fine with me. I wasn't about to *do* anything. At seventeen I was capable of fending for myself. And when I didn't feel like fending, I was welcome at the Leonards'—Pen's mother would pop a pork loin in the oven at the slightest provocation. In fact, that's probably what brought Pen over now, the ostensible premise of a dinner invitation. I steered the conversation that way, evading her request for a reading. "What's Lainie got on the menu tonight?"

Pen fingered the jumble of cards. I swept them up casually. Not to be mean, but you don't want someone else's energy contaminating your deck. Especially Pen's energy at present. "We're grilling," she said. "Some kind of fish kebabs; mahimahi, I think. But we also have steak, if you'd rather."

"Sounds good, either one, whatever." I looked at her, trying to make it look like I wasn't. She looked fine. Not in the least like a fledgling murderess.

"How was Newport?" she asked.

"Fine . . . nice. Daddy doesn't sneeze at the beach."

"Oh. That's good."

"Yeah." Stalling, I bit a cuticle. "So . . . what's been going on around here?"

"Nothing, nothing at all." Pen's posture stiffened, and she jutted out her jaw. This time when I looked at her, she knew I was looking. "You're not mad at me, are you, Dice?" she asked.

Mad? Me? Why, no—she hadn't tried to kill *me*. I was . . . concerned. Except that would bug Pen, to know she'd raised any ruffle of alarm. Pen was responsible. Pen was reliable. Pen had a good head firmly affixed to good shoulders. Pen shared her mother's belief that no matter what she did, it would come out okay. Now, maybe she had doubts. And didn't care to confront them. For damn sure she didn't want them reflecting back at her from my eyes.

"No, of course not," I replied. I put my tarot deck on the nightstand, and gulped at the lump in my throat. This was the mother of awkward moments, our first meeting since that day at the lake.

That day at the lake, the rain had changed to hail. We'd raced back to Pen's car, flinging our things and ourselves inside, and she'd taken off like a maniac. That was unusual in itself—Pen was not an aggressive driver. She just drove and drove, aimlessly tearing up the curvy roads while the sky threw stones. When I said her name, she didn't respond.

There I was, a sensitive person, an extra-sensitive person, yet I couldn't get a handle on how she was feeling. She wasn't crying. She wasn't cursing. She didn't say a word about Burr. Just stared out the windshield and sped through the storm, around and around as if to whip up further frenzy. Finally, I reached out and touched her elbow. She didn't ignore that. She turned to me, and I watched her eyes go from black to blue. It took about twenty seconds, during which time Pen (or whoever) narrowly missed a row of mailboxes. As luck would have it, we had come to Daisy Lane. Pen pulled up to my house. Oh, she looked just like Pen again—sweet and pretty and composed—when she smiled and said, "I think I'd like to come in for a while."

Maybe she wanted to talk things over, get my take on what went down. Which I had probably completely misinterpreted and which was probably utterly innocent, a little horny horseplay refracted in the lake, the way a stick appears bent in a glass of water.

That's all.

Silly me.

Yet in my head I screamed at her, *Not without an army of ninjas behind me am I letting you into my house.* Out loud I managed, "Oh . . . sorry . . . can't. My parents are coming, and the place is a shambles," before darting from the car and through the front door of 12 Daisy Lane. Which I locked. Resoundingly.

And now Pen was asking if I was mad at her. "Look . . . ," I began. I'd been wrestling with my thoughts for nearly a week, and I was not a wrestling fan. "I feel like you know my secrets . . ."

That wasn't total bullshit. True, Pen wasn't up on my telepathic tendencies, but I was referring to the epilepsy, which she did know about and certainly wasn't public domain. Alluding, also, to the trouble that landed me here in Swoon—I'd fed her a few scraps of that miserable mess. And Pen had been more than cool, never pried, never treated me like a leper or a mental case. It made me feel a little guilty at the way I'd left her in the car, all alone as hail battered the roof.

"But you don't trust me with yours," I continued. "And that's okay; I mean, I know I was foisted on you, your brain-damaged cousin."

At this, her eyebrows shot up, and she tilted her head toward her brother—that *little pitchers have big ears* look. "Dice, that's not—"

I glanced at Jordan, still deeply absorbed in the scarabs. "Wait, let me finish," I insisted, but lowered my voice, pulling a pillow onto my lap and punching it once for emphasis. "I'm not like you—I don't look like you or act like you or dress like you. Or your friends. Yet you've been great to me, Pen, you have. Above and beyond the call of duty. And I don't know, I'm an only child, and you have brothers . . . I'd concocted this idea of us as sisters, sort of. Close, you know, like our mothers. So I want you to know I would never judge you, Pen. If something's . . . if there's anything you want to talk about, I'm here. And I'm sorry about . . . during the hailstorm . . . when I just took off. That was wrong. I'll never do that again. Abandon you. I mean it."

Pen looked at me openly. "Really?"

"Yeah," I said. "Really." What stopped me from hugging her? Simply that Pen was not the huggy type?

Content with my promise, Pen grinned and clambered all the way onto the bed to sit beside me, her back against the headboard. "Thanks . . . *Sis*," she said.

"Don't be stupid," I said. *"Sis."*

Then she was quiet again.

"I'm not saying you have to say anything." As we sat side by side, my voice dipped further, as voices do for secrets. "I mean, I know how tight you are with Wick . . ."

"Oh, please," Pen said. "Wick. I couldn't tell Wick I chipped my nail polish."

We laughed over that. She drew her knees up to her chin, turning to me and laying a cheek upon them. "If anyone would understand what happened with Burr, you would—you being a superfreak and all." She said that kindly, then righted her head again and gazed away. "But it's all bits and pieces, like a puzzle, and even though I *lived* the puzzle, I can't fit it together . . ." Still staring off, she began to absently stroke herself from kneecap to anklebone. "You know that expression: It must be something in the water?"

I nodded. She paused again, resumed. "I mean, okay, when Burr swam over to me, I *wanted* him. And that was weird. Usually, I want boys to want me, but *I* wanted *him*. Wanted him . . . everywhere."

Should I have interrupted, remarked that whatever was going down—with and to everyone at the lake—I knew she was the core? That the something in the water was Penelope Amber Leonard? I opened my mouth and shut it. Pen lifted her chin and went on.

"When we were swimming, I wondered how I didn't sink—I was so weighted down with wanting. And then we were treading water, just talking, you know, in that sassy way you flirt with someone when you're being a little insulting—"

"Bantering," I said. "It's called banter."

Pen smiled. "Yes, we were bantering, and I wondered how I managed to make these flip comments when I really wanted to say things . . . things I couldn't possibly say without cracking up. Porn star things."

She blushed, replaying the scene. Those puzzle fragments were snapping together at warp speed. Then all of a sudden she blanched.

"That's when the snakes came out," she said, her voice flat. She turned and looked at me again, her eyes filled with a kind of retrospective shock. "I felt one, then another, slither against my ankles. And I didn't jump. Dice, they were *snakes,* and they didn't bother me one bit. And then there were more, dozens of snakes, hundreds of snakes, swimming in and out between my legs. I didn't mind at all. I . . . I liked them. They were, I don't know, *inspiring* me. So I said, 'Burr Addams, would you like to kiss me?'"

Talk about an offer no boy could refuse.

"God, Dice, it was incredible. I mean, you kiss with your mouth but you feel it between your toes. I remember . . . I took off my top—*I* took it off, not him. And I felt so free, and the fact that other people were around, that . . . added to it. I waved my top above my head like a flag, and then I tied it on Burr's head, and we laughed and kissed . . . and then, when I reached for him, too big and swollen for one hand, I thought: *I did that, I made him like that,* and it flooded me with power. I wanted to lead . . . you know, not just follow. . . . Oh, and Dice, do you know what it's like to be licked underwater? You're already wet, so the tongue doesn't feel wet, it feels kind of rough, and oh my God, he was licking me, just the way I'd been licking him. . . . The difference was, when I was underwater, it was like I could breathe . . . or no, like I didn't *have* to breathe . . . but when he went under, it was so good, and I . . . I just didn't want him to stop. Only he wanted to stop . . . he wanted to breathe . . . but I guess . . . somehow . . . I wouldn't let him."

Pen stretched out one leg, and then the other. And then she shrugged. "That's all," she said. Her face wasn't red anymore, or ashen, but that tawny perfection provided by a mix of defied UVA/UVB rays and a sweep of bronzer. "God," she said brightly, "when it was all bottled up inside me, I felt just terrible, but now that I've gotten it out of my system, I feel so much better."

"Oh," I said. "Good." I was glad she felt better, unburdened by the telling. Except there were a few things I had to tell her, weren't there?

"Thanks a ton," she said. Then, "Jordan, stop that." Her scolding was placid, without a hint of harsh.

I looked over. Jordan was shaking the case that held my scarabs—which, by the way, are replicas, in case you thought I was harboring genuine museum pieces.

"Come here," Pen said.

With clumsy Vienna-sausage fingers, Jordan returned the case to my desk and walked obediently to his sister. Pen took him onto her lap. Jordan leaned against her. His thumb wandered into his mouth, and his eyelids lowered as he sucked. She kissed the golden crown of his head. *What a natural nurturer,* I thought, so good with kids. Seniors, too—she'd laugh when I quipped about her gig at "the senile center," but she was such a boon to the crusty set. Mm-hmm, that was Pen: A big, blond, totally beautiful, vaguely bovine, very good person without a single evil bone in her body.

V

Weird shit happens. All the time. Here's a for instance: Driving with the Leonards to Torrington (a big town, replete with mall), and on one side of the highway it's pouring rain and on the other side the sun is out. Or how's this: Daddy on the phone, reporting how he landed a killer part in this Mark Wahlberg cop thriller because the casting director remembered him from elementary school. And what about the day when Ms. Brinker, Swoon librarian, showed up to work clad in this . . . *dress,* pastel pink, with a pattern of tiny interlocking hearts. You'd have to know Ms. Brinker, queen of khaki—know her and see her almost daily as I, her dutiful unpaid assistant, did—to understand that this was not merely monstrous, but very, very weird.

"Do you feel all right, dear?" She had caught me gaping.

"Huh? No! I mean, of course, Ms. Brinker. I'm fine."

"I hope so." Her face pinched. A germ-a-phobe, Ms. Brinker was forever rubbing her hands with antibacterial goo. She had a squirt right then, my claim of "fine" clearly unconvincing. "I need you to tidy up the children's section, Candice. We had storytime this morning."

I did as I was told, musing on how in the course of an average, ordinary day, so much weird shit can occur—meteorological phenomena, improbable coincidence, unfathomable fashion statements—it can be hard to weed the weird from the normal. So my cousin fell from a tree and started babbling about injustice and revenge. So a few days later she decided she could breathe underwater . . . no, what had she said? She didn't *have* to breathe. What's so weird about that?

And what of events later that same afternoon? I'd had a message from Marsh, saying one of their mares had foaled that morning, and did I want to see the baby. By message, I mean she called the library and spoke to Ms. Brinker, who wrote a note on a slip of paper. Cell phone towers are incompatible with the Swoon countryside, so service is spotty, and texting, forget about it. Still, I got the message. Did I want to see the newborn horse, to me as exotic as a newborn dragon? Damn skippy I did.

"Marsh has a new baby horse," I told Pen when she swung by the library.

"Yes? And?" She failed to share my enthusiasm.

"Pen, come on," I wheedled. "A baby horse. I've never seen a baby horse before. We have to go by there."

She regarded me as though I'd asked for a lift to Bhopal to witness the unveiling of a dust mote. "I didn't realize I was a counselor at the Fresh Air Fund," she said. Which was pretty snarky for Pen. "What's next, Dice? The petting zoo?"

"Pen, did I or did I not spend two hours in one store with you at the Torrington Commons while you tried on fifteen pairs of jeans?" I countered. "Two hours, one store, fifteen pairs of jeans—you do the math."

She fiddled with the radio dial. "You did, you did," she conceded. "I just . . . I really hate going to Marsh's."

I assumed this a symptom of spoiled brat syndrome. Marsh didn't come from money, and her house wasn't the sort of well-appointed palace most Swoonians take for granted. Her mother toiled in some Torrington office every day, while her father was "on disability." Whatever this "disability," it didn't prevent him from running a small horse farm on their property at the end of Stag Flank Road in what no one ever calls the slum of Swoon. "Oh, come on," I cajoled. "We won't stay long. Just a quick hello to baby horsey, and we're out of there. Please?"

A giving person, Pen gave in. Marsh greeted us with a scrub brush. "Do me a favor and wait in my room," she said. "I'll be done in a minute."

The smell of ammonia chased Pen and me through the

hall. We had a cleaning service at the Daisy Lane house twice a month, but I kept up appearances in between, so I knew there'd been advances in housekeeping since the invention of the scrub brush. But maybe Marsh liked to hunker down on that shabby linoleum. In testament, her room was spectacularly neat, not much in the way of knickknacks aside from horse-show ribbons. Her two younger sisters, Charlotte and Willa, shared a room across from Marsh—they peered out, mewed hello, and returned to their little-girl affairs. Pen was perched on Marsh's bed, impatiently organizing her purse, when Marsh came in, sooty crescents of fatigue under her eyes.

"You okay?" I asked.

Pen glanced up from her portable belongings. "Really, Marsh, you're death warmed over." It was an expression Aunt Lainie used. In regard to me, on occasion.

"And I love you too, Pen," Marsh said with a wan smirk. Then she sighed. "I'm just fried. The mare took forever to deliver, and then, you know, with my chores and my job and everything."

I was incredulous. "Wait—you were there? When she gave birth?"

"Oh, I've done it lots of times." Marsh aimed for blasé but couldn't fully hide her pride. "Let's go see him, you guys. He's absolutely gorgeous." She called to her sisters, "I'm going to the stables for a minute. Char, you're in charge."

"I wish I knew we were going to do this," Pen bitched. "I would've changed shoes. Then again, I don't believe I own a pair I'd want covered in horse poop."

Pen's wedge sandals made for endless legs under one of those Lilly Pulitzer print skirts girls and their mothers bond over here in the Constitution State. Striding through the yard, her hips couldn't help but switch left to right. The blouse she wore was a thin white cotton, simple yet feminine. I didn't worry about getting my Cons and dragging jeans dirty, psyched as I was about seeing the foal.

First we had to get past Douglas Marshall, though. "Dad? I'm here with a couple of friends . . . okay?" Marsh announced. The scent in the stables was strong—sweat, salt, leather, and straw, and horse shit, of course, which smells cleaner than the human variety, I guess because horses don't eat Doritos. Still, I expected Pen would wrinkle her nose and bitch some more, but she actually seemed to like it. She stood with her legs slightly spread, hands on hips. Then she sort of threw her head around, and as she did, some of the horses did the same.

Douglas Marshall emerged from a stall. He was a lean, sinewy man, but his brass belt buckle was notched beneath a bulge of gut. *A wifebeater,* I thought. That's what you call those ribbed, sleeveless undershirts like the one he wore, but I took unpleasant umbrage at the term, what it might really indicate in his case. He pulled off a Patriots' cap to expose a receding hairline, swabbed his brow with his arm, and replaced the cap. You couldn't help but wonder what Marsh's mom saw in him— her being so neat and trim in her secretary's suits and tailored blouses. "You finish in that kitchen?" he asked.

"Of course, Dad," said Marsh, meeting his eyes, then flitting them away. "The laundry's all done, too."

"What about the girls?"

"They cleaned the bathroom, and now they're playing paper dolls."

Mr. Marshall grunted. "They'd better not be making a mess."

What did this man have, children or chambermaids?

Finally he deigned to acknowledge Pen and me, his mouth curling like a strand of wire—I assumed this was his smile. "So I guess you fillies want to see the foal."

Fillies, I thought. *I could barf.*

"Hi, Mr. Marshall," Pen said.

I said hello, too, quietly, examining my shoes.

"Well, Penny Leonard." Mr. Marshall's wire mouth twisted into something more twisted. "Oh, but it's Pen, these days. Aren't you a sight." He looked at Pen—too long, I thought— and then he looked me, his eyes growing flinty with suspicion. "Who're you?"

"That's Candice," said Marsh.

"That's my cousin," said Pen, at the same time.

What was I supposed to say—"We've met"?

"Candice, huh? Never heard a name like that."

Good to know I was expanding his horizons.

"Well, you got a nickname like the rest of these girls?"

"Yes . . . sir." I felt pinned. "I'm Dice."

"Is that so? Wait, now, you were here before, weren't you?" He squinted at me. "You're the one from New York."

"Yes, sir. I . . . I live here now." Why was I giving this cretin personal data? Would I next provide an invitation to tea?

Mr. Marshall folded his arms. "I got some fuzzy dice over the rearview in my truck." The twist of wire contorted further. Clearly he found this clever. I could feel my hair get frizzier by the second. "Go on and look, then," he said, but took a pinch of Marsh's arm and held her that way. "Just be quick, girl. Your ma's clocking overtime since that pinstriped dickwad she works for can't wipe his own ass, as usual. That puts supper on you, and I mean I want a man's meal, no more of that Rice-A-Roni."

The creep was begging for a pitchfork tracheotomy, but Marsh merely answered with a tense nod, and her father released her. Quietly, then, we neared the stall where the mare nursed the baby. He was amazing. Not twelve hours old and already standing, with a full mane and tail and everything. Mother and son matched, both that shiny brown of a chestnut shell.

"Hey, Brandy . . . hey, mama-mama," Marsh cooed in her comforting singsong. She reached to pet the horse's nose, and the animal snuffled gently. Then the baby peeked out as if to say, "Hey! Look at me!" and a spontaneous "awww!" gushed out of me. He had eyes like wet black plums, lashes a supermodel would envy, and a white diamond splotch along his snout. He waggled his rubbery lips at us, then nuzzled back against his mother.

I ached to come closer, to touch them, but they made me oddly shy. Pen, however, who'd scarcely contained her irritation earlier, approached to stand on the other side of the big beast. She placed her cheek against the mare's curved, muscled neck. Eyes half shut, she proceeded to whisper, which made me grin—*Pen's gone horse whisperer*. It was a side of my cousin I'd not seen before. I never thought of her as an animal person; she had little to do with Peanut and Popcorn, the Leonards' two rambunctious dogs. Yet Pen was spellbound in the stable. She even went so far as to lay her lips against the mare's hide.

"Come on, Dice," Marsh beckoned. "Brandy's totally mellow right now. You can pet her."

I wanted to; I really did. Yet I felt . . . I can't explain it, unworthy somehow.

"Maybe Fuzzy Dice is scared of horses."

The coarse, mocking voice behind me socked the miracle right out of the moment.

"City people are scared of horses," Mr. Marshall said. "Jews, especially. I never saw a Jew on a horse." He spat the word as if it were rot in his mouth, then put a hand on my shoulder. "You are a Jew, right, Fuzzy Dice?"

I felt like I'd been punched. I had to confront this ignoramus, yet I was fused to the spot, horrified. It would take all my will to turn around, swipe off that filthy paw, and as I sought to summon it, Pen lifted slowly away from the mare.

She cocked her head. She smiled broadly. "You are *so* smart, Mr. Marshall," she said, walking toward him, that hip-swishing walk on those endless legs. "You really know people."

His hand slinked off my shoulder, and as Pen passed me, I could finally pivot. Briefly, our eyes met. Hers, black as the foal's, held a different species of glimmer.

"And you call them like you see them," Pen said with corrosive sweetness. "That's one of the things I admire about you."

As Pen kept coming, I could only imagine the menace in her face that made Mr. Marshall's snip of wire tighten, then slacken. She laid a hand on the man's chest. He took a stumbling step back. She held him at arm's length for a moment, her head at that amused angle. Mr. Marshall made a sound, the garble of confusion, objection, and submission. Sort of a groan. Kind of a plea. And Pen took another step forward. And another. All the while she kept up the toxic flattery, smattering him like pinpricks, until the grotesque tango moved them into the stall across from the nursing mare.

A loud, agitated noise came from in there, and the stomping

of hooves. Marsh was next to me; she breathed the name, "Black Jack!" Together we closed in to see the massive stallion buck and rear. Mr. Marshall bleated frustration and fear. He was trapped— wood slat walls, a kicking horse to his left, and something maybe more dangerous still coming toward him.

"It appears to me as though you're as good with horses as you are with people, Douglas Marshall," Pen declared. And all at once it came to me when I'd last smelled horses.

With one neatly manicured finger, she poked the contemptuous bigot, and he staggered back against the stall, hands in front of his face. His Patriots' cap was knocked askew. "I know little of the beasts myself," the person inside Pen seethed facetiously. "But I do get the impression that this one is rather agitated. It might be best if you stayed very still, and very quiet, until he comes to calm."

Then she turned on her heel and sashayed from the stall. "Thanks for having us over, Marsh," she said serenely, batting lashes over slate-blue eyes. "But come on, Dice, we've got to go. My mom's making a genuine English trifle for dessert tonight, and we wouldn't want to miss that."

While in the stall Black Jack thrashed with unfettered fury.

VI

MARSH WAS FIRST TO UTTER THE *P* WORD. WHEN I CALLED HER THAT night, her mother answered, harried, hurried, and wouldn't put my girl on the phone. The next morning, before library duty, I got on my bike to stalk her at the Kustard Kup. Marsh was a soft-serve slinger.

"Hey, Dice!" my hair-netted friend bubbled behind the counter. "Give me a second, okay?" She decanted pearly liquid into a machine and pressed a knob. The device came humming to life, and Marsh bopped over.

"Did your mother tell you I called?" I asked.

"You did? Oh . . . no. She was . . . distracted."

"What about you?" The smudgy half moons were gone from under her eyes.

"Never better," she said. "So, isn't it a little early for ice cream?"

I gave her a *don't play oblivious* look. "You think? Because I came in for a double dip of real. So why don't you get it, huh?"

Marsh scanned for snoopy coworkers, then leaned on her forearms and got extremely real. "You know how many visits we've had from the county social worker and children's services and all those other bureaucratic departments of bull dookie that added up to squat? Well, my dad's been a cotton ball since you guys left. Mom's afraid he's on the OxyContin again— whenever he's remotely nice, she gets paranoid—but we know the score, don't we?" Marsh was downright perky. "Whatever possessed Pen, I owe her a great big thank-you."

Possessed! The word pealed and then echoed while Marsh rambled on. "I intend to enjoy it as long as it lasts. There's a party tonight at the Williams boys', and I'm not even asking permission. Crane Williams is adorable, and him and his brother, Duck, have a band. Not From Connecticut. Pen knows them. It'll be fun, and . . . um, Dice?"

"Huh? What?"

She showed ersatz irritation. "*You* come to see *me,* and then zone out on me."

"I heard you. A party . . . a duck . . . some band." My mind could multitask. "Sure."

I pedaled like a crazy person. Ms. Brinker (back in familiar drab) had little for me to do, so I took advantage of the reference section. Which was useless—gardening manuals galore but not much of an occult collection. So I went online, plugging "spirit possession" into a search engine. Tons of stuff, some data eerily on target, some way off. On one site I saw that possession is often partial, at least initially—possessee intermittently pestered by ghost/demon. That fit Pen's behavior. Elsewhere I read that the more psychically sensitive you are, the more prone to possession. If so, wouldn't the spirit have picked me over Pen? I mean, I love the girl, but she's shallow as a saucer.

Then again, this had been no arbitrary invasion. If Pen had become host for a ghost, the entry point must've been her crash from the ash. When her soul checked out, *his*—the dude from my vision—checked in. He'd been lying there in wait, watching the seasons turn. Was it possible? Could a tree give refuge to the unsettled dead?

On impulse I bookmarked the possession sites, typed in "ash tree" and . . . uh-oh . . . mm-hmm . . . it was all over Greek and Norse mythology . . . sacred to Wiccans, Druids, and Celts . . . a tree of prophecy and divination . . . its wood the traditional material for the handle of a witch's broom—

Wait, whoa . . . fascinating, but I digressed. Determining if Pen was indeed experiencing "unwelcome intrusion or interference by a spirit into one's thoughts, will, and/or body" was the matter at hand, but when I returned to it, I hit a wall. There were symptoms of possession aplenty, but nothing on how to prove it. And if Pen truly was possessed . . . then what?

"Candice?"

I clicked off the site so fast Ms. Brinker had to think I'd been perusing porn. "Yes?"

She took a step away in her librarian lace-ups. "Will you sit at the checkout desk while Miranda has lunch, please? And then I have a rack of books that need to go back on the shelves."

I slapped on a helpful smile. "Of course, Ms. Brinker. That's what I'm here for."

Harrumphing, she withdrew, and I was glad for the busy-work. It filled the day, and when it was done, I rode hard to Daisy Lane and threw my bike on the Leonards' lawn. Peanut, the golden retriever, and Popcorn, some kind of fancy, nervous terrier, tore out, barking hysterically.

"Do *not* let those dogs in, Candy!" Aunt Lainie's warning was equally shrill.

I pushed Peanut from the door, avoiding his sad eyes. My aunt entered the foyer to ensure I hadn't allowed a single pet hair to infiltrate her home.

"Would you like something to drink?" she asked, baring many teeth. For a brief period in the 1980s, Lainie had been a model-actress—a career the family outwardly frowned upon but secretly feted. Her greatest claim to fame was a TV commercial for a prototypical tooth whitener called Dazzle Drops, during which she would lick her top row of teeth for the camera and promise: "You'll be dazzling with just a drop of Dazzle

Drops!" That smile remained Lainie's pride; she'd passed it, along with other attributes, to her new and improved version, otherwise known as Pen. "There's lemonade, iced tea, apricot nectar, although you *know* you should have plain water . . ."

It was Lainie's duty to watch the weight of the world.

"Oh, and I did some baking, three kinds of cookies."

Only she didn't watch it very well—the poor, conflicted woman, torn between Betty Crocker and Jenny Craig.

"And I think there's a smidge of trifle left over from last night . . ."

Lainie often used words like "smidge." Swoonisms.

"Nothing, thanks," I told my aunt. "So where my girl at?" Ghetto grammar gave Lainie hives. Hence, my use of it.

"By the pool, *laying out,*" she said, as though sunbathing were on par with shooting heroin. "Candy, convince her to cover up, won't you; the way she courts premature aging is tragic. The sun is still deceptively strong after four."

So Pen was not completely faultless in her mother's view? Would wonders ever cease? I found her in a chaise, wearing shades, her iPod, and a few shreds of fabric. I tugged at an earbud.

"Hey." She took off her sunglasses, yawned and stretched and smiled.

I parked myself on some faux wicker, posing casual. "Are we going to a party at Crane and Duck Williams'?"

Pen shot up an eyebrow. "How do you know them?"

"I don't," I said. "Marsh does. Oh, she said to tell you thank you." She hadn't, actually, but I needed to gauge Pen's reaction. Which was quizzical—or possibly cagey.

"Thank me for what?" She was all innocence.

I wasn't buying. "For that stunt you pulled in the stables yesterday. According to Marsh, Cuckoo Pops is being markedly less of an asshole." Considering how the whole thing started, I added, "I should thank you, too . . . for having my back when racism reared its ugly head. So thank you."

Distaste marred her face. "Oh, come on, I didn't do anything, really." Pen watched the sky, as if for an oracle. There was only a jet. Her lip poked out. "Except maybe tease him a little. Which he had coming. He is so gross."

Tease? If that was teasing, the Sphinx is made of Play-Doh.

Pen pulled out her other earbud and stood. "It's this heat," she said. "It's making me antsy, and it's making your imagination work overtime." With that, she headed for the diving board, performed a flawless jackknife, and swam the length of the pool in one breath. Pen kicked the wall, rotated, and stroked languidly to the center.

Maybe she was right. Or, maybe, just because you've got a hyperactive imagination doesn't mean sinister forces aren't afoot. I got up, started out.

"Where are you going?" Pen's head bobbed in the blue.

"Home."

"Do you want to borrow an outfit for tonight?"

I'd already turned away.

"I insist that you look ravishing!" she yelled after me.

As if anything in Pen's wardrobe would approach my definition of ravishing. Which is this: bright red bra, black net top, low jeans, big boots. I like a plunging neckline to display my peaked clavicle. Pants that ride my hips to show off my belly, which is round, not flat, and won't get me on MTV anytime soon, but I like it. My hair did what it does, formed its river of roiling coils to the middle of my back. We have a pact, my hair and I—I don't bother it and it doesn't bother me. But I did deign to apply some makeup—a sweep of kohl, a slash of scarlet. I viewed the results. Not from Connecticut, huh?

The Williams boys are not, in fact, from Connecticut. They're British. Swoon's transient bohemians, the Williamses are tolerated or adored, depending on whom you talk to. The father invented something, or invested in something; I don't know, but he made a mint. The mother's a renaissance woman: artist, activist, and—the saving grace as far as Swoon's concerned—aristocrat, a genuine duchess.

Since the Williamses' residences dot the globe, the family only lives here when the mood strikes, which is why I hadn't met them yet. Having Crane and Duck (real name: Simon) around was a novelty. The party, when Pen and I got there, was packed, spilling from the house to the grounds, or vice versa.

"Hullo, hullo, a pleasure!" Duck swooped down to greet us. Beefy, ruddy, and blond, he fit in with the rest of the crowd—although he did have a British accent and purple boa draped around his neck. "You're Pen, yes? Lovely to see you. And you are?"

"I'm Dice."

"Oh, very nice." Duck tickled us both with his plumage. "Look here, I'm a terrible host, so grab yourselves something." He waved an arm to indicate a banquet. "Tell me, have you seen my brother? Probably off snogging in the pantry. And we're supposed to play . . ." He pouted and took off, in pursuit of the feckless Crane, I surmised.

Pen and I mingled. Alcohol was in abundance. The Williams parents must be cool with minors drinking, very continental of them. Mm, champagne—my pleasure. We sipped, we nibbled; we laughed at the peacocks on the lawn, honking and harassing the guests. We talked to people. Kurt Libo, who cleans up okay, wanted to know if Pen had climbed any trees lately. He had a friend with him, who was being flirty. I placated him—something to do.

Other people we didn't talk to. Anderly Addams, for instance, younger sister of Burr and high priestess of the local abstinence cult. No huge fan of Pen's, she went into a spastic goose-step retreat upon seeing us, trio of primbots tagging behind. Pen and I shook our heads, but then she spied Burr. "Well," she said merrily, "better go check on my future fiancé." She drained her bubbly. "I'm off."

I let her go. Wandering around, I found Marsh, who'd been drinking steadily. That meant I'd be babysitting. Fine, all right—Marsh deserved to cut loose. A spliff came our way; I ensured she only took one hit. I didn't mind babysitting but didn't relish the thought of holding her hair later, either.

"Let's go dance or something," I said.

"Ooh, yes! Let's dance!"

The music was throbbing, and I'm a pretty decent dancer. A skill I'd honed hanging with Ruby. "You only got to understand rhythm in two places: your coochie and your heart," she'd counseled. And she was right. I checked my brain, forgot my feet, and showed C-T how we do it, West Side style. Marsh flailed like a demented windmill, which kept her from knocking back more beer. It was fun, although after a while the stereo had competition. Out on the patio, Not From Connecticut were tuning up.

"I want to see the band!" Marsh yelled, belched, and yanked my arm. "Come on, Dice. They rock!" We detoured for a bathroom first, Marsh making many minute adjustments to her headband, which I found pretty meticulous for someone that drunk. Satisfied, she thrust a fist in the air and with a howl of "N! F! C! Whoo!" clomped off toward the music.

The twang and clang of guitars, the lupine aggression of

drums, and what was that? A fiddle? Yep, uh-huh, someone was definitely jamming out on fiddle.

We wove through the throng, and I saw that someone was Pen.

She stood on a patio table, her shoes cast aside. Bare feet stamping. Cornsilk ponytail whipping. Fingers a blur. People flung their bodies around. The Williams boys—Duck on bass and Crane on guitar—took a worshipful stance below Pen, not minding one bit having a bombshell steal their limelight. Especially since she was wailing, really ripping it up. The boys had trouble keeping pace as the notes streamed from her bow. That fiddle was on fire, and so was Pen.

Except Pen couldn't play the fiddle.

Pen couldn't even play the triangle.

Weird? Decide for yourself. I'd made up my mind. So when Pen leapt off the table, still sawing back and forth, I got in her face, grabbed her by the bow arm, and hissed: "Who *are* you?!"

That made her stop. And when she stopped, the drums and guitars stopped, too. The bodies stopped, limbs and torsos and heads. The drinking and the smoking stopped. In the woods and fields around us, a consortium of creatures stopped. Above us the moon stopped and the stars stopped, as did the earth beneath our feet.

I looked into those onyx eyes. "*Who* . . . the *fuck* . . . *are* you?!"

Pen smiled. It was not her mother's Dazzle Drops smile, but a wider, wilder, crooked one. With exaggerated care, she placed the fiddle and bow on a chair. Then my cousin who was no way my cousin leaned into me with a whisper thick and warm enough to melt my insides, bones and all: "Oh, my lady, I thought you'd never ask!"

And, in a flash, we were running.

The world responded, activity in overdrive again. Clouds pursued us, cloaking the three-quarter moon and then setting it free. A chorus of crickets provided the soundtrack. Where we were going? I had no clue; I only knew we had to be alone. Ultimately, the where became obvious. The Williamses' house, a historic landmark, is "in town," a scant quarter mile from the village green. Which was deserted and dimly lit by gas lamps when we got there. By the tree—that tall and ancient ash—it was even murkier. The clouds engulfed the moon once more, and the darkness was complete.

"Come, then!" The command was not the least bit breathless.

But I could not come.

"You wish to know me, so come." It was half taunt, half entreaty, and complete purpose. "In all this town, in all this world, it's you who'll understand."

I wanted to understand, I did. Only there was a problem. Fear. You learn about fight or flight, but no one ever mentions the third alliterative option—freeze.

"All you need do is touch me. Hold my hands . . . look in my eyes and . . . *know* . . . me . . ."

The air was calm now. A faint hint of fall infiltrated the night, but it wasn't the chill that rippled my skin. Fear of knowledge had me in its grip. What are the clichés? Ignorance is bliss? Curiosity killed the cat? Don't ask, don't tell? I raised my eyes to the canopy of leaves, all the movement I could muster. No force flew down to propel me forward; I could only drop my head and close my eyes.

Here was the stillness of stalemate, and then these words, in a voice defiant and definitively male: "You leave me no alternative than to *take*."

Taken I was. Seized, lifted, pressed against the tree trunk. Then my hands, clasped and claimed.

"Look at me." The voice softened. "Please."

I would, I would, I would.

"Look . . . at . . . *me* . . ."

I would. I could. I did. Moonlight split the clouds once and for all as I opened my eyes. And there he was. Holding my hands, raised like a bridge between our two hearts, the most beautiful boy I had ever seen.

VII

Everything you think you know about ghosts is wrong. Dead wrong. Here stood no ectoplasmic transparency, no wavering will-o'-the-wisp in a cotton sheet. He looked . . . substantial. But seeing isn't believing. Feeling is. And oh, I felt him. Hard, callused, long-fingered hands with a potency only hinted at held on to mine as if life, or something like that, depended on it. The energy of his touch shot straight into my blood.

"My name," he spoke, "is Sinclair Youngblood Powers, and I was put to death on this very spot in the year of Our Lord 1769."

Which would explain the outfit. Tan frock coat and a collared shirt of coarse linen, neither one manufactured in China for Abercrombie & Fitch. I could appreciate a fashion risk, but was still, literally, spooked. *Fine,* I told myself, *he's a ghost . . .*

but he's also a guy. I knew how to talk to guys, flippant and flirty or matter-of-fact.

"I know," I said, levelly as possible, him being a convicted murderer and all. "I was there . . . recently."

That threw him—the way his head tilted, eyes darkening further—but he played it off. "Indeed?" His tone formal, the civility seeming to war with a savage kinesis that scared but also stirred me. "Extraordinary. You are quite the witch, my lady."

The word—witch, not lady—made me wince. Pesky psychic affliction aside, I never dabbled in any craft more formidable than crochet. "No . . . ," I said, but with little conviction, since there was no denying I had just conjured him, firm and steadfast in his own frame—six feet, maybe six one. Since I'm pretty tall, I only had to angle my chin to study those eyes, finally in his boy's face, large, heavy-lidded, with uncharted depths.

"Oh, but yes," he refuted, upper left quadrant of his mouth lifting higher than the right as he revealed that white, wide smile—fitting, finally, in his boy's mouth, full on the bottom and carved on top. His teeth tilted slightly toward and away from one another—orthodontia a couple of centuries down the pike—which lent that wolfish quality. "I hear they expect a bountiful harvest in eye of newt this year."

What the . . . ? Great—a raised-from-the-grave comedian. "You are so funny," I deadpanned. It was the terror talking.

"And you, Miss Dice, are ravishing."

After our sprint I had my doubts, but I know how to accept a compliment. "Thank you," I said, not surprised he knew my name; he must've picked up a few things hanging out with Pen for a month. "But just Dice will do." Then I narrowed my sights. "So what's your deal? You make a habit out of squatting in unsuspecting jock chicks?" He looked at me like I spoke Martian—he hadn't picked up that much. "Let me rephrase: Is it your common practice to send your soul into the young ladies of Western Connecticut?"

"No, not at all," he said at once, earnest as an arrow now. "This has been my sole opportunity in . . . tell me, my lady, exactly *when* are we?"

How would he know? Pen was no avid newspaper reader. I gave Sinclair the day, the date, the year, and let it sink in.

"*Whoa* . . . ah, is that the expression?"

"Mm-hmm," I said. "'Whoa' would sum it up." Ghost Boy was a quick study.

"I knew I'd come far but, again, whoa. Your manners in this age . . . the way you comport yourselves . . . the way you dress." He gazed at me appreciatively. "I shall enjoy it here . . . now."

There was a sense of entitlement to his tone. "Welcome to the twenty-first century, Sinclair Youngblood Powers," I told him archly.

"Forgive me, my lady." He was suddenly humble. "You mustn't think I take advantage of your good grace . . ."

"Hey, it's not *my* body you've moved into. It's Pen's."

"Yes," he said quietly. "Pen." I checked to see if he'd glaze over with lust or turn all puppy-dog—the two ways guys generally respond to mention of Pen. Instead he grew somber. I guess he knew the girl differently; his predicament when it came to her was, to say the least, unique. His lips pressed thoughtfully, and his brows, which were thick but not bushy, drew toward each other. A lock of black hair fell forward on his forehead. How human he seemed just then, how almost vulnerable.

"Hey . . . ," I said. "Sinclair? I didn't mean to be rude. When you said I would understand you . . . I want to, I do."

Just then came a muted flapping, and I turned to watch an owl soar from a catty-corner tree and snatch from the open green some piece of prey—a mouse, a blind mole, a chipmunk. It was so fast, so perfunctory, so cutthroat, and so purely natural, it made me gasp, and as the intake of breath snapped my lungs, Sinclair pulled me closer. He, too, saw the night hunter make off with supper struggling between its talons. I turned back. His eyes were unreadable. I wondered what he saw in mine.

After a bit, he said, "It's something of a saga. My story, that is."

One of the benefits of largely absent parents: no one to enforce curfew. Although what Aunt Lainie and Uncle Gordon would say when Pen failed to appear at the appointed hour, I could only imagine. If I cared to. Which I didn't. "I have all night."

"Yes, but we can't very well stand about all night," Sinclair reasoned. "I'd like to remove my coat, lay it on the ground so you might sit. Which would require us to . . . you see, I believe it's vital that we touch, if I'm to—"

"No problem," I said with sudden assurance. "We can let go one hand, if we hold tight with our minds."

And so we commenced this crazy minuet. We disengaged (my left hand, his right), and as I helped him lose the coat on one side, I noted the breadth of his shoulders and back. Then we re-engaged (my left, his right) and disengaged (my right, his left) to free him fully, laughing haltingly all the while.

"Very well, let us arrange the garment here on the grass . . ."

We nearly bonked heads with that maneuver, but we got it done, took both hands again, and knelt.

"Are you comfortable?" Sinclair asked.

"Reasonably," I said.

"I could move this way—"

"Or I could—"

We laughed again. And then we were quiet. Until I said, "All right."

And Sinclair Youngblood Powers proceeded to tell me everything.

VIII

No native son of Swoon, Sinclair Youngblood Powers was born in the year of Our Lord 1751, some hundred miles east, near the town of Talverne. Specifics are scant, documents nil, though sage assumption is he entered this world in a wigwam. Facts were few but whispers legion as to the assignation between landowner Q. Thomas Talverne and a Mohegan maiden called Kisoma. Both were bold, but it ne'er did well for a woman to be bold, especially if she were red-skinned and aroused the name-sake of the white man's village. If anyone mourned the maiden when she disappeared, it was with silent tears. The child she bore might have vanished with her, but Kisoma contrived to circumvent that fate.

"John! John! Do come quickly!" cried Amelia Youngblood Powers that glorious summer day. So glorious, she'd removed her boots and hitched up her skirts to wade the crystal river. But what she discovered there made her call for her husband in alarm.

John leapt from their picnic along the bank to heed his wife. Amelia was headstrong—what sort of woman leaves her man to set up the meal while she wanders off to get her feet wet? But John loved Amelia, from her strong head to her wet feet, and when she shouted again, he doubled his pace.

There she was, crouched in a thatch of reeds, skirts ballooning, more than her feet wet now. "John! Come here and help me . . ."

John Powers worked with his wife through the thick river growth, where there was trapped a tiny canoe and, swaddled inside, a wide-awake infant with deep black, seeking eyes. The couple freed the vessel and from it, the child, whom Amelia cradled in her arms. "Like Moses . . . ," she whispered.

Her mind was set—John would not seek to change it. For their five-year marriage had been one of miscarries and still-births, agonized labors and sweated, bloodied bedclothes. John stood behind his wife and embraced her, peering over her shoulder into the eyes of the babe in the colorful blanket, the boy who would be their son.

"Moses, huh?" I had to interrupt. His tale and the way he told it—sonorously, with embers in his eyes and more than a touch of ego—were already working me like a spell. Teasing him seemed my only defense.

"*I* didn't say I was like Moses; *she* did," Sinclair said. "And she didn't mean in the prophetic sense; she simply—"

"I get it, I get it. Basket-in-the-bulrushes, yeah, uh-huh." I doubled my pressure on his hand. "I'm just giving you a hard time. Go on . . ."

Where there are horses, there must be a blacksmith. So John Powers had firm standing in Talverne. No matter what pious folk might have muttered with glances askance.

"One would think our neighbors' hearts would be kindled by our charity," mused Amelia Powers after a snubbing.

"One would think," John Powers agreed, though doubtfully.

"Perhaps they will come around," said Amelia.

"Perhaps," said John, more doubtfully.

The foundling's inherited Talverne traits—distinctive broad forehead, thin, straight nose—did him no good, nor did his prominent Mohegan cheekbones and sienna-tinted skin. Yet he had a way with the world—an inherent compassion for his fellow beings and beasts, an uncanny knowledge of what was wanted, needed, yearned for. Sinclair had communion, and people drew toward his glow.

At the same time and in definite counterpoint was the boy's bearing. Half Mohegan, that he was. Brought up by a humble blacksmith, that he was. Yet nonetheless a Talverne. Raised, too, by an educated woman—Amelia Youngblood Powers, a Hartford schoolmaster's daughter. So Sinclair owned the demeanor of a gentleman. He read everything he could lay his eyes on. He learned to play and appreciate music. His wit and opinion were sought. And he did not suffer fools.

"Ooh . . . ouch . . ." We sat face-to-face, still hand in hand, legs tucked under—and I desperately needed to shift my hips. "Sorry, my foot fell asleep."

"Your foot . . . ?"

"You know, pins and needles." It was like talking to a foreign exchange student.

"Pins and needles . . ."

I got literal. "It's just what you say when you cut off the circulation and you get all tingly."

"And are you . . . all tingly?"

I could have told him, "Just my foot, dude." Instead I mimicked his mode of speech: "Beg pardon, sir, but I really must—unh!—whack it." I extended my leg and, freeing one hand to punch my awakening shin, felt Sinclair intensify his hold on the other one. On my mind, too. He didn't want to let go, that boy.

That boy! Q. Thomas Talverne had a nettle in his side, a pebble in his shoe, an itch that refused to diminish no matter how he scratched. With each passing year, the nagging grew worse. What if the boy were to discover the truth, demand his birthright? Talverne's wife had been kind enough, canny enough, to turn deaf ears to gossip. Talverne's son and heir had a governess—there'd been no risk of taunting from local youths. But still . . . that boy. That half-breed bastard. So appealing to behold. So popular in town. Sinclair Youngblood Powers was approaching manhood. Something needed to be done.

Talverne had ways. He had means. A fire. With manufactured evidence, Talverne could impel the lad to leave. Ultimately, the right time presented itself, when Amelia Powers's mother took ill, and John Powers traveled with his wife to Hartford. The youth was left in charge of the smithery—at fifteen, he was adept with the forge, the chisels, and the tongs. And so it was set—indications of arson pointing at Sinclair. A northeast wind picked up the fire in the blacksmith shop and turned it onto the Powerses' home, Sinclair fighting the blaze at both ends. Seven horses screamed in the night; three survived. As to the property, nothing remained but cinders.

"You tremble, Dice. Yet not with cold."

True, that. Chills, mm-hmm. Cold, uh-uh.

"And you aren't . . . it mustn't be . . . please say you're not afraid of me."

"Don't be silly, Sinclair. I'm not afraid of you." A big fat lie, of course. Still, it wasn't fear making me shiver.

"Perhaps some fever," he conjectured. "Are you prone to fevers?"

Actually, I was, but only post-vision. Otherwise, sturdy as an ox. Nor was this the pre-vision tremble, which runs over me from the outside. This tremble came from within. How come he didn't know the cause—he who was so sensitive, he who had communion? Maybe he did; maybe he was simply pointing my condition out to me. I shrugged, but couldn't shrug it off. "No . . . not really," I said.

I wasn't being coy. I don't do coy. I truly had no clue what was going on. It had never happened to me before—that trembling on the inside that feels like dancing and dreaming, melting and flying, living and dying, all at once.

With home and business in ashes, and Amelia's mother not yet improved, the Powerses elected to remain in Hartford. No charges were brought, so the landowner's trickery ne'er came into play. Sinclair had suspicions, but done is done. He was finished in Talverne. He saddled up—first, for Hartford.

"You will stay here," his mother said. Amelia had always thought Talverne a provincial town. Here her boy could complete his education, live up to his potential.

"No, Mother, I will not."

His father stayed clear. John Powers had given his son skills and honor; that was all he had to give. Now it was up to Sinclair.

Westward, ho! The frontier was vast, and the eager Sinclair

set off with dreams of triumph. Reality, however, prevailed. He had no money. He had no compatriots. He had to ply his trade. And so his exploration took him only as far as Swoon—a place with plows, carriages, and wagons, with riders and passengers, but no blacksmith.

Yet who was this young man with the tawny skin and unrelenting eyes? Swoon being wary of strangers, Sinclair met an uneasy welcome. He was needed, but not wanted. And once set up and settled in, he became aware that he was despised . . . but also desired. The good wives and daughters of Swoon were intrigued by him. Beguiled by him. Some would say, bewitched.

"Shall I regale you next with how I lost my virginity?" Sinclair said languorously as we rose to our knees to stretch. I bent back while he gripped my wrists; then we reversed it, yoga à deux.

"Golly gee, let me guess," I said as he arched. "Was it in the hayloft with the buxom milkmaid? Or maybe the stern mistress of the grandest house in Swoon?"

Sinclair laughed as we raised our arms, reaching in tandem for the lightening sky. "There was indeed a milkmaid, but she was not to indoctrinate me. That honor fell to—"

"Spare me the details." It bugged, the notion of him in another girl's bed—or hayloft. Which was nuts. Imagine being jealous of events almost two hundred and fifty years in the past, involving a boy you barely knew, whose very existence lay beyond the realm of possibility. "Just paint the picture in broad strokes."

No half-breed Indian could make a suitable match for any good daughter of Swoon. So Sinclair was left to woo and be wooed in shadows. Yet shadows run rampant from dusk to dawn. Shadows, yes, in haylofts and stables. Shadows, yes, in the lace-tatted chambers of refined ladies. Shadows, plentiful shadows, deep in the woods. It was all a game to the lusty blacksmith, a gambol, a romp. If an act felt right and very, very good, there could be no harm in it. May it also be stated plainly that he was the son of his father, and Q. Thomas Talverne was not one to deny himself. Like father, like son, Sinclair fed his desire as any other hunger, fed it fully, sans apology, and, sated, slept well.

Until he fell in love.

"You've been in love?"

"I have."

A bunch of questions rushed me. Like, *With who?* And, *What's it like?* And, *Are you still?* They all got stuck between my larynx and the air. I didn't have to ask, though. Sinclair went on. . . .

Her name was Hannah Miles. Hair like copper, laugh of silver, heart of gold, and will of iron.

"Oh, to hear you, Sinclair Youngblood Powers!" Hannah

would say. "You are such a smithy, you have a metal for every part of me."

"Not so, my darling Hannah. There is no metal for this spot," Sinclair would say, and caress her there. "Nor here . . ." Place a kiss. "Nor here . . ." And plumb. Hannah would sigh. And there they would be, not in the shadows but by daylight, in an open pasture, with stays and waistcoats loosened and the world rolled out before them.

Although sometimes Sinclair would brood. "They will not let us be."

"They have no choice," Hannah would counter. "We already *are*."

Yet resistance to their union stole in like obstinate fog. When Hannah's parents wouldn't sanction marriage, she rebelled by instinct. Talking sass. Skipping church. Promenading in town without her cap, waves of persimmon rivaling the sun. The farmers and townsmen of Swoon said nary a word, but cut off the Mileses like rot on fruit. Even the minister turned away Hannah's mother when she came seeking counsel—his acolyte smiled thinly, said the man of God was engaged, and shut the door. Hannah's mother took to silence. Her father took to drink.

Hannah, however, had her Sinclair. And when proof of their love began to show in her belly, Hannah carried it proud. Sinclair acquired some gold and forged a band for her finger—she needed no wedding. Sinclair had made her with child—they would start their own family. Yet her pride was to prove fatal. Hannah was found, her gown in tatters and the life beaten from her, one ordinary morning near Swoon's main street.

"Murder!" cried the distraught lover and father-ne'er-to-be.

"Murder!" echoed the good people of Swoon.

Yet as they did, they pointed at Sinclair Youngblood Powers.

"You know the rest."

"Wait . . . no! Wasn't there a trial?"

He sneered the word back at me. "In the upstanding community of Swoon? In His Majesty's great Connecticut colony? Yes, certainly. A trial. A sentencing. A charade! They couldn't wait to see me swing." I followed his eyes to the ash. "Didn't even build a proper gallows." His voice had fallen to a murmur. "The carpenter, apparently, was down with the croup."

What a moron I was. There were no CSI units back then, no DNA testing. Not that forensics can guarantee truth when the powers that be prefer a lie. Still, I had to ask him one more thing. "So . . . you never found out who killed her?"

"No," was all he said.

IX

It was time to face the music, and Pen was front-row center.

"I swear, I can't even remember what happened." It was a little after sunrise in the Leonard breakfast nook—she'd made me come in with her, of course—and her plaint sounded spent, as if she'd been talking all night. "But I doubt you would've wanted me to drive if I was . . . if I didn't feel up to it." Outside, the agitated chatter of eight thousand finches, jays, and sparrows rallied. Pen pulled off a hunk of coffee cake and popped it in her mouth. Some parents pace in worry mode; my aunt baked.

"That's no excuse, Penny. You could have called!" Lainie was literally wringing her hands. "We would have come for you. It's too—"

Closely shaven and crisply suited, Pen's father bustled in. "As long as you girls are all right," he said, giving Pen a quick hug as a ruse to sniff her for remnants of booze, or some dude's cologne mixed with the smell of sex. All he could pick up was grass and dew. "You gave us quite a scare." Satisfied, he turned to his wife. "But we're sure you did the right thing." There was a briefcase to collect, affairs to attend to—Uncle Gordon's a prominent estate lawyer, a partner in a Hartford firm. Administering a peck to Pen, then Lainie—he even had a pat for me—he was out the door.

Pen started for the stairs. The aroma of Lainie's icing-drizzled treat held me in olfactory thrall. "Where do you think you're going?" my aunt demanded.

"Please, Mom, I just want to crash."

Clearly, Lainie was flummoxed—she'd never had to punish Pen before. "Yes, right, go to your room. And stay there!" Pen winked at me, though wearily, behind her mother's back; then she, too, was gone. I, however, had not been dismissed. "Well, Candice. Haven't you got anything to say?" Lainie glared at me, convinced to her core that Pen's all-nighter was my fault. Which, in fact, it was.

"I don't know." I hate to lie and wasn't about to let Lainie wedge me into it. "It was a good party, a lot of people." That was true. "I wasn't with Pen the whole time—we're not shackled at the ankle, you know." Also true, though it was probably in my interest to curb the snippy. "I'm sorry, Lainie, I can't say what was going through Pen's head, but I was having fun and didn't think to call you." True, true, and true.

God*damn,* I had to pinch a piece of that cake! Sensing this, Lainie swept the platter out of the nook and marched it to the kitchen counter. Was this her plan—to starve me into confessing I'd corrupted her precious offspring? She spun to me again.

"Listen to me, Candice," she said. "I want to help your mother. She's my sister, and I love her. I want to help *you,* too. I agreed that having you up here would be beneficial. I agreed to look after you when your parents couldn't be around. I believed we'd rub off on you, that Penny would be a positive influence . . . not the other way around. Do you know that she's never broken curfew before?"

I hung my head, assuming the question rhetorical.

"I haven't called your parents yet," Lainie went on. "I didn't want them driving up here frantic in the middle of the night. But I will, and when they get here on Friday, I will make it clear that I won't permit you to . . . when I think about—"

Lainie thwarted tears with an embroidered handkerchief. Which must have calmed her; she handwashes them in essence of chamomile. "Meantime, I want you to go across the road and think, really think, about your behavior and your future and . . . and I believe it best if you and Penny don't communicate for a few days." She stuffed the hankie in her apron pocket.

"For her to do this, I just . . . she's hasn't been herself lately."

That was an understatement. "All right, Aunt Lainie," I managed, adding the "Aunt" for remorseful good measure. I didn't argue. I was wiped.

So home I toddled, and in the shower, as I lathered and lingered, rinsed and repeated, Sinclair Youngblood Powers ruled my thoughts. His story. His voice. His face. His touch. The longer I'd spent with him, transfixed by his tale, the more my fear eroded. At the end I wanted to fold myself around him like a quilt. But now . . . was I nuts?! He was driving Pen wild, dangerously wild. Still, the poor guy: cursed from birth, forbidden love, and finally executed for a crime he didn't commit. Who wouldn't feel for him? Only it wasn't sympathy sparking my mind and other anatomical aspects. Those trippy inner trembles I'd felt with him continued to pull on me like tides. I toweled off and tossed on an oversize T-shirt, then closed the bedroom shutters. Hitting the mattress, sure I'd be too wired for sleep, out I went as if someone pulled the plug.

And woke to the scent of sweetness.

"Can-*deee*-da! Can-*deee*-da! Yo, Ms. Moskow, yummy-yummy for the tummy."

Ruby Ramirez sat on the edge of my bed. Her hair was blown out—this must be a special occasion—her side-swept bangs dyed acid green. On her lap sat a box of candy, the heart-shaped kind. I pushed up against the headboard.

"Ruby," I said.

"Hey, Candy."

"Call me Dice, okay. Everyone does . . . here."

Ruby took a chocolate from the box, bit into it. "Butter cream." She showed me the filling. "You do butter cream, don't you, *Dice*?"

"Sure," I said without hesitation, even as the last time Ruby and I shared a bite sped through my brain like an uptown express. That impromptu, infamous soiree, this past February 13. I opened my mouth. Which was courageous of me. Or if not courageous, stupid, or possibly insane. Down went the bait, like sweet, hot satin.

"Where'd you get Valentine's stuff?" I asked. "It's practically Labor Day."

She bit into another, made a face, and returned it to the box. Must've been jelly. Neither of us cared for jelly. "Where I'm at, baby, I can get anything I want, any time I want. Chocolate at every meal, and check me out, I'm not fat or nothing."

Ruby stood, did a little Electric Slide. Tight slit skirt, sky-high heels. Stilettos, always a staple; still she'd keep up with me, me in Adidas or Cons, when we barreled down the subway steps to catch a train or trailed cute boys on Columbus Avenue. Now, boogeying on my pine bedroom floor, she looked amazing. When she sat back down, her banner of bangs had changed from granny smith to fuchsia.

"I miss you, Ruby," I told her.

"I know, baby." Ruby wasn't much older than me, but she called me baby. She'd call all of us "baby," our group of friends, gently lording all the sorrow she'd known in her seventeen years. "I miss you, too."

Mish you. Ruby had a little lisp, the chink in her armor. Hearing it, I missed her more. I also craved more chocolate but couldn't seem to move toward the box. "Here," she said, and fed me. Only the candy had changed from chocolate to something that wasn't quite candy. It was sweet, still, very sweet, and very . . . squishy. I chewed. I swallowed. It took effort. The lump was large.

"That was a weird one," I said.

"I know," said Ruby, bangs now bleached-out white. "It's funny, right, you think something's so good, and then you find out, unh-uh, not so good, and then it turns out you were right in the first place. And you wish you would have savored it more."

I wasn't sure what she meant. I searched her eyes, almond-shaped, amber-colored. "Ruby . . . ?" I started.

"Have another piece, baby-girl."

I opened. She fed. This one was still alive when it spurted against the cavern of my mouth. It was still alive, alive and kicking, as it slid down my throat.

Ruby crossed fishnet thighs. "Look, I just want you to know

I'm here for you," she said abruptly, and I tried to push the *yeah, right* away soon as it occurred. "All you got to do is call me, okay?"

Call her. Mm-hmm. Too bad I didn't have her new area code. "Okay, Ruby."

"Okay. Ooh, this one's going to be cherry." She held it aloft between glossy nails. "Want to share?"

Cherry was her favorite. "No, you have it." Suddenly I wasn't feeling so good.

A drop of sanguine fluid escaped the corner of her mouth. "Oh . . . Dice?" she said, licking it, "in case you were wondering, it's better this way, really. I'm good, you know? Nothing hurts anymore."

And suddenly my face was wet. "I'm glad, Ruby. I'm glad you told me."

When I woke again, it was stuffy in the room. I got up, parted the shutters. The sun slanted over the hills like a trellis to heaven. I ransacked a dresser for sweatpants—it was chilly enough—and padded downstairs, onto the porch. Though under house arrest, I considered the porch part of the house. Rocking in the rocker, I spied something furry scamper across the lawn. Before I could utter a "here, kitty, kitty," she was in my lap.

"Mew!" mewed the kitten, front paws planted on my chest. "Mew! Mew!"

I took this to mean: *Hey! You! Pet me! Wait, feed me first—I'm famished. Thirsty, too. Then pet me. Come on, come on, what's the delay? Let's go!*

"Yes, ma'am," I said aloud, shifting the kitten to my shoulder. A calico—white and orange and black, with a hint of brown and an almost mauve—she weighed about as much as a pair of socks. I dropped her to the kitchen floor; she played spelunker up my legs. "Okay! Ouch! Watch the claws." I opened a can of tuna. Her entire body rumbled with purr as she ate, tail like the aerial of an old car.

Perfect timing. Now I'd have company while serving Aunt Lainie's sentence. When the kitten was done—she couldn't even wait for a dish, just licked the can clean, then lapped some water I'd put in a cup—she looked at me and mewed. Which I took to mean, *That was very nice; and now I'd like to be cuddled.*

I carried her to the sofa. I didn't know much about cats, but instinct instructed me, and the little furbag conked out in the crook of my arm. "RubyCat," I murmured, hitting the sweet spot under her chin. "Ruby, Ruby, RubyCat."

The feline, for the moment, had nothing else to say.

X

IT WAS ONLY A BARBECUE. THE LEONARDS HAD ONE EVERY YEAR. Well before my abrupt relocation to Swoon, C-T, my parents would pile me, along with assorted hostess gifts, sunscreens, and pharmaceuticals, into the car to attend the annual fete.

"It's only a barbecue!" Daddy bellowed jovially up the stairs. "Come on, honey, you know how irritated Momster will be if she misses a round of Tom Collinses."

To which I dimly made out my mother's snappish, "Oh, Peter, do shut up."

I grinned. So they weren't the Reverend Eric and Annie Camden; they had a rapport. I was feeling extra kindly toward them, since, for one thing, they didn't give me shit about staying out all night. We'd discussed it, of course, "as a family." And according to them I'd been "sociable and outgoing" by attending the party, and showed "good judgment" by not getting in the car with a possibly intoxicated person. Although it would have been "more prudent" if I'd called my aunt, they understood that Pen probably wasn't "the perfect angel" her mother liked to believe she was, and they were glad I wasn't the type to "fink on a friend," even if said friend was "roaring drunk."

"Be down in a minute!"

It was only a barbecue, so whence my stress? Because I hadn't seen Sinclair, I mean, Pen, either one, both, whatever, in five days. Now Lainie's campaign to keep us apart had reached its expiration date, the Leonard Labor Day gala, and I needed to look . . . not ravishing, ravishing is by definition post-sundown style, but good. Because I'd come to a conclusion: I dug the dead guy. Me, who'd scoffed at the futility of friends' celebrity crushes, fiending for a ghost.

So there I stood, surrounded by virtually every garment I owned. My regular gear, plus new stuff my parents had brought. Another reason for my benevolence. Judging by the shopping bags, Momster had bought out half of Manhattan. Funnily enough, while she'd spearheaded the move to Swoon, she didn't want me turning into a Stepford kid.

"Candice, right *now*!" It was Momster's turn. R.C.—short for RubyCat—chose the moment to pull a coup on an island community of clothing, plastic, and tissue paper. "What are you, nuts?" I scooped her up and detached something silky from a front paw. "Half this stuff is going back to the store, sans puncture wounds, if you don't mind." I marched her to the mirror. "Want to see the pretty kitty? Let's see the pretty kitty!" I held the feline up to her reflection; she couldn't have cared less. So I scoped myself. Massive hair in a messy bun; one of Daddy's shirts tied at the waist with a paisley scarf; reliable peg-leg jeans, once black, now faded to a scuffed charcoal. It'd have to do.

The Leonard property isn't lakefront—there'd be no Jet-Skiing off a private dock—but they had a healthy turnout for their official sign-off to summer. The Chadwicks, the Emersons, the Turners, the Cliffords. All these adults in plaid and pastel, grumbling over interest rates while guzzling tall cocktails. They were so chummy, so clubby, and it struck me that more than half of them were descendants of Swoon's ruling class back in Sinclair's day. Taking a lemonade, I mused on how Pen's great-great-however-many-greats-grandfather would freak knowing that the loathed and practically lynched half-breed was sharing bodily quarters with the family's prized female.

"Dice, what *are* you wearing?" Wick said when I approached Pen's clique, rounded out by Marsh and Doll (a.k.a. Kendall Turner), just back from vacation in California. "That looks like your dad's shirt."

"Ding, ding, ding! It is my dad's shirt." I take to heart no fashion commentary from anyone outside the five boroughs.

"Dice, Doll met a guy in Marin." Marsh filled me in. "A surfer."

The blather was frothy and incessant, as if generated by a battery-operated fountain. As the girls droned on, I studied Pen. One minute she was chiming in with syncopated burble, the next she seemed disinterested, though it was hard to tell behind her oblong Oakley shades. I was only able to tell that she'd fully checked out and Sinclair had checked in when things started moving. Little things. Here and there. Somebody's high-ball tipped itself off a table. Somebody else's purse took a dip in the pool. Mustard mamboed with ketchup. A Frisbee soared up and up and out of sight, like a flying saucer in a low-budget sci-fi flick from days of yore. Nothing like a little telekinesis to liven up a dull affair. The look on Pen's face—upper left lip quadrant higher than the right—told all. The two of us cracked up, much to the offense of Doll Turner.

"I don't see what's funny." Doll sniffed. "I may never see him again!"

"Really. Harsh." Marsh snickered under lowered lashes, which made me think she'd had enough of Doll's drama.

"You're awful!" cried Doll, taking off in a huff to seek refuge among her parents.

At which point the rest of us went off to seek burgers and Aunt Lainie's blue-ribbon potato salad. As we assembled with our designer disposable plates, Pen removed her glasses, and

I saw no trace of Sinclair. Just as well. Marsh wasn't all that convinced by the lame idiot savant story I'd concocted after my cousin's recent fiddle display at the Williamses' party. If Sinclair were going to keep popping up, I'd need to improve the quality of my lies.

Wick's parents summoned then, and she and Marsh left. The Chadwicks were barbecue-hopping, Marsh tagging along since her parents were not exactly part of the Swoon social set. Once in semi-private, I asked Pen about Burr. He wasn't among the guests—everyone knew the Addamses did Labor Day on Nantucket—and she hadn't brought him up since attempting reparations at the Williamses'.

"Oh, we're fine," she said. "Nothing a little al fresco fellatio couldn't fix."

"Pen!" All right, she shocked me.

She examined her manicure. "I don't know; I think I'm over Burr anyway."

Shocker redux. Pen had been strategizing Operation Burr since he first tweaked her pigtails. But what did I care—me, with Sinclair on the brain. "Hey, my parents brought me a ton of new clothes from the city. You want to come over, help me separate wheat from chaff?"

Pen slid her shades in place, going enigma again.

We didn't say anything to anyone. We just crossed the road. Went into my house. Up to my room. Pen tossed the Oakleys and perused closet candidates, traipsing fingers over this and that. Momster had done good: deconstructed skirts, politicized T-shirts, touchable fabrics, heavy on the black, smoke, and magenta—colors I like that look good on me. Pen extended a wrap top with long bell sleeves. "Try this."

"Okay." I untied my sash. Unbuttoned Daddy's shirt. Let it slip off. And, as the bell-sleeved blouse fell to the bed and a darkening entered those eyes, I reached out. . . .

This time I watched the metamorphosis. Subtle yet manic, it was like two invisible artists at work on the same piece—one destroying, the other creating. Hard planes replaced soft slopes; straight pale hair surrendered to dark whorls. The medium was animate—length, width, and depth . . . flesh, blood, and bone. As my fingers tightened and my pulse went quick, he took form with greater urgency. That's when I realized I was no mere observer, but participant. I made the man manifest—a terrifying, thrilling, inescapable onus. The more I wanted him, the more he would be. And then, there he was.

"Hello, Sinclair."

"Hello, Dice."

We smiled at each other; I don't know for how long. A while. Then I said, "Can we talk?" Like talk was what I craved.

"I don't see why not," he said. "I can admire you and converse simultaneously."

Maybe *he* could. To me, being half naked and in full custody of my faculties were diametrically opposed. "Actually, I'd prefer to put something on."

"Of course. It's not merely your body I admire."

We went through the awkward rigmarole of dressing me while maintaining contact, then settled on the hook rug, backs against the bed. Palaver from the party across Daisy Lane filtered through open windows. There my parents were pacing themselves—they couldn't get plastered; they'd be driving. Daddy was flying out that night to start the Wahlberg picture in Toronto. Momster would take him to the airport before heading for the city. Sire and dam would soon be gone, leaving this little lamb up to her own devices again. I felt my smile turn wicked—but I had to get my priorities straight.

"So, Sinclair, I need to know: Do you want to hurt Pen?"

Tough question. It's not like he popped in and out of people on a daily basis. He had to ponder, and I could sense him trying to make sense of it all. Then, moving to his knees before me, he pressed my hands to his heart. "Try to understand, my lady—this is all new to me," he said. "There I was, an ordinary fellow; I worked a forge, paid taxes to good King Georgie, was about to become a father. Then, murder most foul, my dearest one torn from me, and in the midst of my mourning to be accused, executed—"

I knew this, I did. Yes, yes, yes, I was nodding along.

"Could it be any surprise that my spirit knew no rest? That

given the chance, it sprang into the first unwary form that came along?"

Now I was shaking my head. No, no, no, it wasn't his fault, any of it.

"So here I am." He drew me brusquely to my feet. "It's not malevolence I feel, toward Pen or anyone, but . . . alive I was a natural man. Now I'm a natural spirit. I do what I do, because . . . it's what I do." Were those tears welling in his eyes? They were the color of coffee—ghost tears.

"Oh, Sinclair . . ." I felt for him, fell for him, felt and fell for fathoms.

"Please. Oh, my lady, please embrace me."

The eighteenth-century equivalent of "I need a hug." And I obliged. Stroked the bristly tufts at the back of his head. Urged his cheek against mine. Surrendered my softness, made myself his pillow, his bed. Yet still I was afraid of him—who he was, what he was—the fear kept in balance by the sheer excitement of being in his arms. And swirled into that, another state of fear and thrill: come tomorrow, the first day of school.

XI

OKAY, I EXAGGERATE. HIGH SCHOOL IS HIGH SCHOOL IS HIGH school. Sure, the roles in Swoon were more defined than at my Upper West Side alma mater with its thousands of students and global atmosphere. If the kid next to you lugged around a didgeridoo or had baba ghanoush in his lunch bag, no biggie. Plus, the junior intelligentsia I hung with was particularly accepting. One day you were in an emo mood, the next you felt hip-hop, or boho, or gender-bender—it was all good.

The only thing exotic about my C-T school was its name: Swonowa. Sounds Native American, huh? Yeah, well, combine the three towns of the school district—Swoon, Norris, and Washington—and that's what you get. I entered the acronym in the middle of last semester; now I was merely a mildly oddball member of the herd. I couldn't even cull much status by proximity to Pen. Three mornings a week she was up at dawn, delivering bread to the elderly—a campaign of her mother's I called "Crusts for the Crusty." I biked it instead of riding shotgun in Pen's pimped ride. Plus, we had exactly zero classes together. Coincidence, or Lainie's impassioned plea to the scheduling office? The only remotely scary aspect turned out to be my chem lab partner, Anderly Addams, sister of Burr.

Considering her expression when the teacher announced who was with whom, Anderly found me scary, too. Had I worn a leather bustier with demi bra and nipple clamps to Mr. Winchell's fifth period class?

"Hiiiii!" The syllable seeped through her clenched wall of teeth. And oh, that smile. The kind of smile common in girls who aren't anorexic, just very, very, *very* careful about what they eat. Her garrote of ponytail contributed to the skeletal effect.

"Hey." We'd never technically met before, so I added, "I've seen you around."

That was so, although we traveled in separate circles. The girl's preeminence at the local chapter of Pure Love Covenant was legendary. Only I couldn't see why she troubled herself; no one would try to deflower the gaunt and brittle Anderly Addams for fear of breaking her in half.

"I'm Pen Leonard's cousin," I added for no reason.

"*Really*? You *are*?" As if she didn't know. "It's *so* nice to meet you." Anderly said, fake and perfunctory, then got busy taking notes. I did the same. We'd be determining molecular formulas and identifying chemical activity together, no more. Death mask aside, she seemed harmless.

Still, I was eager to amuse Pen with news of my Bunsen-burner buddy. She had cheerleader practice after school, and I watched for a while—I couldn't get with the sis-boom-blech, but the squad was hot, fairly funky choreography and tumbles straight out of Cirque du Soleil. Then I went inside for chorale tryouts, which I hoped to ace with my buttery, bluesy contralto. When they called my name, though, I felt a twinge of stage fright and didn't look up till I knew I'd nailed it. In the last row sat a familiar figure. How sweet of Pen to come lend support. I hustled up to her.

"Hey, you didn't have to—" What the . . . was she sleeping? Her chin dipped, a blond blind across her face. "Pen?"

"Oh . . . hey, Dice." She clicked on, blinking to get her bearings, and while she'd figured out where she was, she clearly had no idea why. She pressed the pads of her fingers against her cheeks. "I must have nodded off for a second. God, I hate getting up early." Then she shook her head, and as the silken strands settled, she composed herself.

We left the building, and I told her about the lab partner I lucked into.

"That means you'll have to work, then. Anderly's kind of a dum-dum," Pen said as I loaded my bike in her trunk.

"Proof that prolonged chastity rots the brain," I opined, and we giggled, even though we were both technical virgins.

Pen didn't start the car. Instead, she looked at me all cat-that-ate-the-cream. "Dice, can I tell you something? Last night I figured out how to . . . do for self."

Do for . . . ? I smirked. "Congratulations. A crucial life skill. I'm proud of you."

We high-fived, all grins and giggles, and she exited the parking lot. "I swear, I was convinced it was strictly a guy thing. Only now . . ."

"Now you know better."

"I certainly do." She stuck her head out the window. "Yes! Yes! Yesssss!"

Laughing, I put my head out the passenger side. "Oh! My! God!" I shrieked.

We hammed it up that way, her banging the horn and me smacking the dashboard for percussive punctuation, the whole way home. Then Pen pulled up to 12 Daisy Lane. "The truth is, Dice, I never even *went* there before."

I could guess what came over her.

"I can hardly wait to have one with another person in the room." Her smile was impish.

"Whoa, Grasshopper. One step at a time, huh?"

She didn't reply. "Hey, what do you think of Trap?"

Who? Oh, Kurt Libo's friend, from the Williamses' party. Blond (what else), rainy-day eyes, sort of a baby face. Nice, though; not a moron. "On the short side," I said noncommittally. "Why?"

"I'm seeing Kurt tomorrow night. He told me to bring you for Trap."

"What am I, a six-pack?"

Blasé, no pout, Pen said, "It's cool. You don't have to go."

"No, no, that'd be fine." Fine? The whole thing sounded hinky. A lowborn grease monkey seemed an unlikely replacement for Burr, who'd barely had a chance to crack his first kegger at Yale. Yet here was Pen, eager to hang with Kurt and his bud to boot. "I assume they're not picking us up at your house."

"You assume correctly. We'll meet them in the green, and then just, I don't know. Anyway, I've got to go help Silas with his homework now. Jordan too. Can you believe he's in real school already?" Pen marveled.

I marveled that she hadn't mentioned my audition. The next day I learned why. *She* hadn't been there. The note in my locker read:

> My Dearest Lady,
> What a pleasure to hear you sing. Wit, glamour,
> kindness, and now, I find, the voice of a drowsy
> thrush. There seems no end to your admirable
> qualities, and how I hope to continue uncovering
> them. Perhaps a private performance soon?
> Yours,
> S.

You couldn't scrub the smile off my face with a Brillo pad. I wafted from class to class on a breezy delirium and would not let so much as a sprinkle of pessimism or common sense weigh me down. "Drowsy thrush." How poetic! And the way he signed it, the simple intimacy of "Yours." If only! After school I read and reread the letter out loud for R.C., but the kitten only licked herself.

"I love you too, Ru-Beast," I said, and proceeded to do things I never do. Like take a bubble bath (dish detergent works in a pinch). Dab on perfume (Momster kept D&G on her dressing table). Twine my hair into a real French twist, carefully loosening tendrils around my temples and nape. So immersed in these feminine pursuits, I nearly hit the ceiling when Pen walked in.

I whirled from the mirror. "You scared the shit out of me!"

With hands on hips and a twitchy little smile, she said, "That's an awful lot of primping for a midget."

Oh, crap. Kurt and Trap. "Don't be stupid. I'm not even putting on makeup."

"Well, how about some clothes, then. And hop to it. Slight change in plans."

I tilted my head.

"I told them to come over here. It's time we started taking advantage of the fact that your parents are never around."

A short spate of heat rose through me. "Pen, you had no right to do that!"

"What's the big deal? If we make a mess, I'll help you clean up."

"That's not the point," I countered. What *was* the point? That more could potentially "go on" here than the village green? "You just should have asked."

"You're right, I'm sorry. I'm just so restless lately, and it's like I'm not thinking straight. But Kurt has some killer weed—"

I pulled on jeans. "Like that's going to screw your head on?" A long-sleeved tee with a graphic of a rose shedding its petals.

The knock at the front door startled me; I hadn't heard a car pull up. Pen had no doubt told them to park elsewhere. Should Lainie be inclined to snoop, she wouldn't see Kurt Libo's cherished vintage Chevy in my driveway.

"They're here," Pen stated the obvious.

Thus began another long night of weirdness. Which was fine. Weirdness I was cool with. Criminal activity I could've done without.

XII

HELLO, MELLOW. KURT LIBO BROUGHT NOT ONE BUT TWO KINDS OF killer weed—the kind that puts you in a nice, cushy stupor and the kind that transforms you into a mad genius. We smoked the former to get friendly. Kurt, Trap, and Pen were no doubt deeper in the haze than I, since they each had a beer (the boys brought their own six), and I can't stand the stuff. Basically, we just sat around the living room, talking. R.C. made the rounds, mewing at each of us in turn, then perched on the arm of the sofa like a stone griffin.

"That is hilarious," Pen said. "I didn't know you guys were cousins."

There was little resemblance, since Trap is fair and Kurt's on the swarthy side, with a wide face and fleshy features too rough cut to be called handsome. "Second cousins," clarified Kurt. He wore a T-shirt with the name of some band I didn't know, and thick-treaded work boots that made my Adidas look dainty.

"Dice and I are firsts—our moms are sisters," said Pen. "But, come on, isn't it crazy? Cousins going out with cousins?"

Trap grinned. "Isn't that kind of like incest?"

Which was absolutely the funniest thing anyone had ever uttered in the history of mankind.

"Only if Dice and I make out," Pen said. "If you want to get technical."

"Or if you two make out," I added.

The boys grimaced and made smoochy faces at each other.

"Or," said Pen, "if we have an orgy. That would probably count."

Shut up, Pen, I thought.

"Now, there's an idea." Kurt gave a lazy leer.

I smacked my thighs. "Who's hungry?" I popped up from an armchair. What the hell was in the pantry? The fridge? Momster usually does a major grocery run before coming up on Fridays; this was Wednesday, so supplies had dwindled. I did a mental inventory. Cocoa Puffs. Peanut butter. Marinara sauce.

"You need help?" Pen was sitting very close to Kurt on the sofa, her offer genuine as a Chinatown Fendi.

"I'll help," said Trap from the other armchair. He trailed me to the kitchen and leaned against the counter as I ransacked cabinets. Though he and Kurt were both nineteen, Trap looked younger. "I bet you really miss New York."

"Of course I do," I said automatically. He couldn't conceive how much. Or how inside out and upside down I felt about the city now. "But I also like it here. It's like I never had a real bug phase. You know, like in that old White Stripes song, where they're chasing all the ants and worms? Now I'm in my bug phase. Better late than never, right?" I was officially babbling. "So . . . Cocoa-Puff-and-peanut-butter sandwiches?"

I turned around, and there was Trap. I mean, *right* there. His pale gray eyes, a little bloodshot from smoke, looked gentle, curious. He had nice skin, and from this perspective I could see every pore. And he wasn't really short. "I like that song," he said. "I think it's cute."

That took me aback. Something about a guy using the word "cute." I guess I must have smiled at him. Encouragingly.

So he touched me. His hand reached for my hip—just touched, didn't tug.

I said, "Oh . . ."

He said, "I think *you're* cute."

I said, "Oh . . ." And thought, oh, about seven million things. I thought about Trap—what *did* I think about Trap? Did I think he was cute, too? Did I want him to kiss me, because he was going to, any second. I thought about Pen and Kurt, who were awfully quiet in the living room. And I thought about Sinclair. No, I didn't want to kiss Trap; I wanted to kiss Sinclair. But Sinclair wasn't here; Sinclair would never, ever, really, be here.

I didn't take Trap's hand off my hip, but I raised my hand, close to my body at shoulder level. A stop sign? Potentially. But Trap placed his hand against mine, palm to palm. Applied slight, even pressure that somehow made my head angle and my lips part and my lashes lower. And the hand on my hip went around to the base of my spine and—

"What are you *doing*?" Pen's voice—mostly playful, but with an undertone. "I thought you were getting us snacks . . . but lo and behold, what do I find?"

Mm-hmm, I knew that curve of lip, those shining shards of obsidian. Trap had his back to her; he half turned—and Pen pounced. Laid one on him, right on the mouth with a slurp more cartoonish than carnal. Then she—*he*—gave me this look I'd need about a decade to decode. Kurt, in the doorway, was equally perplexed. Like one minute he'd gotten *the* Pen Leonard horizontal on a sofa, and the next she was on the move, swapping spit with his second cousin and so-called friend. Opting not to deal with any of it, Kurt stomped to the fridge for another beer. He cracked the can, took a swig, and sat at the kitchen table to break out the mad genius weed.

As Pen sashayed back to bachelor number one, I tried to parse out what exactly was going on here. Sinclair was swinging in and out of my cousin's consciousness like there was nothing but a flimsy screen between them—yet how much of this was his purposeful will, and how much the chaotic propulsion of their coexistence? Pen appeared every inch Pen again as she arranged herself on Kurt's lap, but a Pen in whom Sinclair still lingered. "Soooo," she purred, and had a hit of his beer. "What do you say we take a spin in that Rolls-Royce collecting cobwebs in the Williamses' garage?"

In other words, grand theft auto, anyone?

"This is *crazy*." I said it first at my kitchen table as the pipe went around to fuel the scheme. I said it again as we trotted down Daisy Lane and turned the corner to where Kurt's truck awaited. I said it finally, futilely, as we snuck up to the Williams place.

This being Swoon, and the Williamses being off in Andalusia or the Caymans or wherever, and off their collective rocker as well, we assumed the garage would be unlocked and the cars free of alarm systems. The only prospective kink in our joyride was Jameson McDaniel, whom the Williamses employed as caretaker. That's Jameson McDaniel, a.k.a. the boogeyman, to any Swoonian of a certain age. Trap, originally from Chapin, a few towns down the turnpike, was as clueless as I was, but Pen and Kurt had grown up creeped out by the Vietnam vet with the blighted eye and cue-ball head. Officially, he lived in a trailer, out along the same road as the Marshalls, but McDaniel had free reign at the various part-timer properties he was contracted to watch. It was the boogeyman's reputation, deserved or not, that got him gigs.

"They say he wiped out a whole village in Nam, with just a

machete and a wild dog he'd trained to go for the jugular," Kurt said. "Women, babies, everyone."

Thanks, Kurt, I thought.

"Do you even know how to hot-wire a Rolls?" Trap asked, a little anxious, or maybe with mere annoyance—I got the impression he would've preferred to remain in the house with some kind of kissing going on. "I mean, it's an English car."

"Shut up, Trap," Kurt said as he slid up the garage door. We filed in. There were two vehicles inside, a powder-blue Cadillac big as a yacht, and the black Rolls-Royce that dwarfed it. "Come to papa!" Kurt stroked a fender. Then he started taking out tools and giving Trap orders, and I don't know how long they were at it, but in the midst of the operation I got an irrepressible urge.

"Pen," I whispered. "I have to pee!"

"Oh, God, Dice! Why did you have to say that? Now I have to."

"Shhh!" Trap shushed us.

"Sorry . . ."

"But we have to pee . . ."

"So pee!" snarled Kurt, who was finding British engineering more of a challenge than he'd thought.

"But . . . where?" I said.

"Jesus H. Christ!" Kurt swore. "Go outside . . . find a freakin' tree!"

A tree? Surely he jested. "A tree!"

Pen snatched my sleeve. "We'll hide behind a hedge or something; don't worry."

Just goes to show what a city girl I was, because as I squatted in the open air, nothing happened. It just wouldn't come out. An anatomical impossibility. Pen had done her business in an instant. "Come on, Dice!" she moaned. "Come on, come on!"

Cheerleader she may have been, but this was no football game. She was so not helping.

"Who's out there!?" I heard a grizzled shout. Followed by a grizzled bark. Right on the other side of the hedge. "I'll shoot you in the belly, you bastards! Feed your guts to the dog!"

Forget peeing. I might never pee again. I pulled up my pants and dashed after Pen, toward the driveway, just as the huge black metal behemoth came careening out. Someone screamed. It might have been me. The car screeched.

"Get in! Get in!"

Pen hurled herself at the open door as if fleeing a bomb blast, and I followed, but not before catching by headlights' glare a glimpse of Jameson McDaniel in his khaki flak jacket, spittle flying, good eye riveted on me, rifle in one fist and the leash of a slavering German shepherd in the other.

XIII

This had to stop. Before someone got maimed, killed, or grounded for life. Since Sinclair's arrival, Pen was beginning to rival the Hollywood wonderbrats my mother's magazine splattered on its pages. Plus, we'd had, what, two attempted murders (one by drowning, one by horse) and the lively little felony with the Rolls.

High on adrenaline, we'd sped down the lesser-used lanes of Western Connecticut, outmaneuvering McDaniel and the cops, if the caretaker had even notified them. The car was incredible—the floor mats were probably mink—but around two a.m. we denuded the sumptuous ride of our genetic material and ditched it, hiking over fields and through backyards to make our way home. The caper had been exhilarating, I admit, but crazy. Too crazy. And similar antics were bound to ensue, especially if Pen kept seeing Kurt Libo. Together those two—those *three,* let's not forget their ethereal third wheel—were lethal.

Pen had already begged Lainie to let her sleep at my house that night, laying on the whole "we're like sisters" spiel, and ultimately my aunt had relented. When we got in, I looked for a flash of Sinclair in her face but saw none.

"That was so fun," she said.

"Yeah . . ." I didn't even add a "but." There'd be no reasoning with Pen. "You can take the bathroom first."

"Thanks." She paused in the doorjamb. "You know, Dice, I can't imagine Wick or even Marsh going for what we did tonight. They're so . . . not you." She flicked on the light. "I don't know if I ever said this outright, but I really am glad you moved here."

Smiling weakly, I bade her good night, then skulked down the hall. And the next day awoke resolved. It was time for Sinclair Youngblood Powers to move on out. Exorcism. Except . . . how? I'd never even been bat mitzvahed, much less ordained. On a positive note, being Catholic wasn't a requirement; most major religions deal with possession. Islam has its jinns, and in Judaism the evil spirit of the dearly departed is called a dybbuk. I could even become—online, no less— a minister of the nondenominational Universal Celebration Church, the hookup to perform baptisms, officiate at weddings, and banish bugaboos. Only there was a catch: As

I gleaned from my research, in order to successfully oust a spirit, you'd better want it gone 100 percent. I had feelings for Sinclair—how could they not interfere?

Was I truly, fully in love with him? Did he care at all for me? Were ghosts even capable of love? From my journal I drew Sinclair's letter. Would it survive as a souvenir, or turn to dust with him? One thing was certain: I wasn't letting him go without letting him know what he meant to me; I wouldn't be cheated out of good-bye.

Opportunity knocked about two weeks later. The Swonowa history department had planned a field trip to the newly restored Royal Mohegan Burial Ground in Norwich. The tribe had been trying to reclaim and preserve the land since the late 1870s; now, flush with casino funds, they were able to do so. To bid adieu to Sinclair in a place sacred to his ancestry—what could be more fitting?

Autumn in New England is all it's cracked up to be. Crisp air, clear light, and leaves gone lunatic with color. There's a sentiment to it, too—a yearning to hold on to what's already slipped away, a primordial desire to nest colliding with an opposite pang, to stay up and stay out and stave off. The day of the field trip was like that, and as we were led among the markers, I sought to sort out the messages my heart, brain, and probably even kidneys were shooting off inside me.

Ultimately, the peace of the place relaxed me. I was doing

the right thing. I'd say good-bye to Sinclair my way, and then, on the weekend, ride my bike to a convent I'd seen on the Post Road. Someone there could surely steer me toward the person qualified to handle my . . . situation. I'd have some explaining to do, but by Halloween, maybe, everything would be back to normal.

Now, where was Pen? In my meditative state, I'd fallen behind. Which of those sleek blond heads and cheerleader jackets was hers? I hastened my step to catch up to the pack and picked out my cousin.

"Hey," I said. "Interesting, don't you think?"

"I guess . . . I don't know . . . not so much." The cemetery seemed to disturb her.

"Sort of seen one gravestone, seen 'em all. You want to go exploring?"

Pen gave a glum sigh, then brightened under her fading tan. "Sure, why not."

We lagged, and when no one was watching, went off toward a copse of hawthorn and witch hazel. "Wow, the trees are so thick here," I said, luring her into the sheltered spot. "It's so pretty!" I felt like a fairy-tale character, though I didn't dwell on what the Brothers Grimm would dub me. I hid further in the thicket.

"Dice?" Pen called. "Hey, where'd you go?"

"Come find me!"

I could hear Pen kicking up leaves. "God, Dice, I get enough hide-and-seek with Silas and Jordan." She floundered one way, stopped, went the other, and then . . .

"Boo!" I cried.

"Ha. Ha. Ha. I'm *so* scared."

But she was—a little. I twirled like a top. This enchanted place was getting to me.

"You're nuts," said Pen. "I'm going back."

"Wait!" I had to do this. I had to do this *now*. I grabbed her hands.

"What's wrong with you?" she demanded.

"Sinclair! Sinclair, please, I need to see you."

"Who the—Dice, what *is* your problem?" She tried to wrench free; I tightened my grip.

Where *was* he? Her eyes were her eyes. Her lips were her lips. I crushed her fingers desperately. "Please . . . please . . ."

Now alarm crossed with repulsion came into her face. "Oh my God. Dice, are you having . . . whatever they are . . . one of those epilepsy things? Shit, what should I do?"

Drastic measures were called for. Like . . . what? My mind raced. Only one thing occurred to me. So I went for it: stuck my foot between Pen's and, yanking, tripped her good. Together we hit the carpet of spongy leaves, her on the bottom, me on top, and I shut my eyes and did it: Kissed her. Kissed her hard. Kissed her long. Kissed her till she damn well wasn't Pen anymore.

Sinclair's arms encircled, and he rolled us easily, exchanging our positions. I fluttered my eyes to a heady, heavy-lidded gaze.

"Well, well, well," he said. "What the devil has come over you, my lady?"

There it was! That insolent, impish, higher-on-the-left-side, lower-on-the-right, irresistible grin.

"Oh, I see," he went on. "It is *I,* is it not?"

Had he been hiding all along, using me like a yo-yo? He was so . . . *ugh*! I struggled, only to feel his muscles tense around me. His breath was warm—no icy, ghostly tinge—and the scent I'd come to know as his made me weak, the way you feel when you sleep late and just want to sleep some more. But I fought it. I did.

"Oh, but good sir, I have prepared something for you," I mocked right back at him. "Alas, I need to *breathe* to bestow it."

"Can it not wait? I like you as you are just now—"

"No, I'm afraid it can*not* wait." Saying this, I realized I had a few fingers free. Which I put to good use, just below his ribs. Sinclair, I discovered, was ticklish.

"Yahhhh! I must . . . insist . . . you stop that. Dice, now, don't. Stop. Please. All right. Very well. You win."

He seized my hand and fell onto his back, still gasping. I straddled him, took both his hands and laid them on his chest, then placed my hands atop them. I looked up at the orchestra of leaves, then down into his eyes, and began to sing. The mother of all breakup songs: "Greensleeves."

Right away, he caught on. Of course he was familiar with

the courtly ballad—it's been a standard since the late 1500s. And although it's a lament from a scorned lover to the one who cast him off, "Greensleeves" amounts to the last rites for any relationship.

"Why?" Sinclair broke in before the second verse. His voice was thick and somber, his eyes bottomless. "Why sing me such a song as that?"

"I didn't know how else to tell you . . ."

"Tell me?"

"That this . . . this is . . ." What a simple word—four letters, two syllables—yet I couldn't say it. Over. "I can't stand it, how unfair this is, how . . . cataclysmic, emotionally, but . . . this can't . . . it just can't, Sinclair. You. Me. Pen. I—"

"Dice, Dice, my dearest lady—"

"Do I have to go down the list for you? What's been going on since you got here?" One fat tear fell onto his chest. Then another. It was cruel to blame him, since the whole spirit-flipping upheaval had been a fluke to begin with. Yet it *had* happened, and all signs pointed to disaster unless I slammed the brakes, pulled the plug, insert your preferred full-stop metaphor here. "I can't stand by and let it continue," I vowed. "I love Pen; she's like my sister. If anything bad were to happen to her, or to other people because of her, it'd kill me." Concern rose to his expression. "And, wait, no—don't say it, don't say you'll be good because we both know you *can't* be good. And . . ."

"Hush, now. Dice, please, do not weep. I—"

"I can't help it, Sinclair. It's the injustice, but then how dare I speak to you of injustice? My petty little feelings are nothing, *nothing*, compared to what you've had to bear, but here I am, all sorry for myself because I—I—I—"

I tumbled off him (but still held on), pulled my knees to my chin (but still held on). He held me, rocked me, his face in my hair and his mouth in my ear. "You mustn't cry; it hurts me so."

I wouldn't cause him pain. I sniffed, gulped, made it stop.

"There you are, my dear, my dear," he soothed. "Now listen to me. You mustn't fret. Dice, I knew this day would come."

I swiveled slightly to see him. "You did?"

"Yes, I did. You are a noble woman. A noble woman takes care of her own."

But oh, he was "my own" as well. Could I tell him? His eyes had found a point in the distant hills.

"And the truth of the matter is, you're absolutely right. It has to stop."

Wait, whoa—he agreed with me? Not exactly what I antici-pated. An argument, yes. A con job, maybe. But compliance? It would take a while to wrap my brain around that. And while I was working on it, Sinclair threw me for another loop, leaning into my ear to murmur, "And I know how it must be done."

XIV

THERE WAS SO MUCH I WANTED TO TELL HIM. THE THREE JOKES I knew by heart. About my favorite books, my favorite bands. My secrets, all of them. So much to tell, so little time. The autumnal equinox was in three days. Per Sinclair, unlikely source of info for his own exorcism, that's when the ritual had to commence. He'd been pretty explicit—when to, where to, how to. The ceremony was among tidbits he'd learned at the feet of a shaman when the progressive Amelia brought her boy to visit the Mohegan camp. I'd jotted it all diligently in my history notebook.

After which I asked, "So this is good-bye?"

"Ah, well, difficult to say. It's all speculation at the moment."

I hate when guys do that—get all clinical and distant when the emo-meter tips toward the red zone. We stood, hands in hands, of course, but at arm's length, Sinclair's face sculpted stone. "There's a chance it shan't be successful."

"If I screw up, you mean."

"Oh, I highly doubt you'll screw up, my lady. You're motivated, and your abilities are extraordinary—much as you wish to deny them."

I didn't wish to go there, debate the extent of my "abilities." I'd just follow his instructions, which were fairly simple and made as much sense as any other exorcism schemata I'd dug up. Hindus, apparently, burn pig excrement to vanquish evil spirits—was this any weirder?

"So let's not muddle through mundane good-byes," he finished.

Mundane! Turnips were more emotionally available! Sinclair shifted his gaze, and when it returned to my wounded one, he softened slightly. "The universe is a strange place," he said. "Perchance we will meet again."

"Yeah," I said, equal parts pissed and wistful. "Perchance." I would *not* cry. Nor launch myself onto the lean, tall strength of him, let the scratchy fabric of his coat abrade my cheek and the heft of his breath be my burden.

"Penelope Leonard! Candice Moskow!" The chaperones had turned search posse.

So much to tell him. Not the least was, "I love you." Instead, we just let go. And as I watched, the beautiful boy faded away and the beautiful girl replaced him.

"Ugh!" Pen scrunched her eyes tight and opened them wide.

"They're looking for us," I told her flatly, and headed toward the buses.

Three days till my astronomical imperative, a.k.a. the Rise of the Eighth Moon (there are thirteen in the Mohegan calendar). Hurdle number one: persuading Pen that she was possessed. Red-and-gold scenery streamed past while I mused on broaching the topic. I could try capturing Sinclair's transformation on camera—one final excuse to invoke him again—but I'd seen my share of unconvincing ghost videos on YouTube. Technology and spiritualism just didn't jibe.

The last thing I cared to do while sorting this out was watch the Swonowa Lancers take on the Torrington Trailblazers. But this was Swoon; if you weren't in a coma, you went to the game. The Leonards invited me, but I begged off to go with Marsh, who'd scrimped and saved enough to buy herself a car. The used Toyota wasn't nearly as nice our other friends' vehicles—in fact, it was a brown four-door box too dowdy for your grandma—but Marsh was so psyched she'd drive to the mailbox.

"You haven't given me your take on the cat fight between Pen and Brie Atwood."

Huh? Pen and Brie were squad cocaptains, but cheerleading was Brie's reason for being, while for Pen it was just something you did. When Brie got bossy, Pen usually gave her the *whatever* wave. "Cat fight?" I said. "What cat fight?"

"How could you not know? According to Wick, there was actual hair pulling."

The CliffsNotes version revealed that a scuffle had broken out at practice. No one knew why, but it got ugly. "So then Brie said something, and Pen said something back, and Brie made a rude comment and then Pen, well, Wick says Pen laid into Brie."

"Yeah, well, I don't know anything about it."

"Look, don't think I'm awful, gossiping like that," Marsh said. "But your cousin has definitely been smoking something lately."

I regarded her sharply. The urge to spill climbed, peaked, and passed as Marsh pulled into a parking spot. "Speaking of which," I said. "Want to fire this up?" Kurt Libo had left a lovely parting gift on the table at 12 Daisy Lane.

"Ooh, goody!" said Marsh.

The first time our fingers met, passing the joint, I felt a trembling tingle. The back of my arms, the perimeter of my scalp.

The second time, I felt it more insistently, all over.

The third time brought the distinctly homey aroma of apple pie . . .

And then . . . I was in Alaska somewhere; no, *I* wasn't there, Marsh was. With her two little sisters. All alone in this frozen tundra rimmed by forbidding woods, no shelter in sight. Did I say alone? They wouldn't be for long. Something was coming . . . something with a long snout and sharp teeth, low to the ground and hungry, matted, rank. And the Marshall girls in a chattering huddle, no place to hide . . .

Then Marsh giggled. The Marsh who sat beside me in the car. "I think you're good, Dice," she said, still giggling. "I know I am."

"Yeah," I managed, snuffing the ember in the ashtray, putting the roach in my bag, searching for gum.

"Wow—where'd you get the Wonder Weed?"

I figured it best not to share the association with Kurt Libo. "You know, I don't even know," I non-answered, proffering Doublemint. "Gum?"

"Mm. Mm-hmm," she said.

Taking a piece myself, I eyed Marsh sideways. I thought to inquire if everything was cool—do a little follow-through before returning the vision to customer service—but as we got out of the car, her thoroughly un-Marsh-like outfit distracted me. "How cute are you," I said. The flouncy mini and patterned tights were a far cry from her usual jeans and shit-kickers.

"Oh, Dice, thanks!" She pirouetted, struck a pose. "You know I left the house with Levi's on. My dad's back to his strict old self again, and if he saw me in a short skirt he'd call me . . . he'd make me change."

Marsh rambled on as we scoped out the bleachers; she shouted happily and waved to friends. I triple-twirled my woolly scarf and hunched in my seat, fussing over the encroaching equinox as the game got under way. Maybe I should raid Momster's medi-cabi. Half a Valium and a Xanax ought to make Pen pretty malleable. Then I caught myself, horrified. You never know how someone will react to pills. Besides, drugs would affect the purity of the ceremony; sobriety, I sensed, was crucial if this was to go off without a hitch.

There I was, back to square one. The score was . . . who knew? It barely registered when the Prancers—the Lancers' official percolation committee—took the field. Whoo-hoo, halftime already. Yet it would wind up the most jaw-dropping, pearls-clutching moment in cheerleading history. For on this auspicious occasion, a member of the squad chose to flash a pom-pom of a biological nature, busting her moves—high kicks, cartwheels, somersaults, and all—sans a stitch of underwear.

XV

BEDLAM IN THE GIRLS' LOCKER ROOM. PEN — WHITE-HOT AND WAILING.

Brie Atwood—trying to get a wail in edgewise. Ms. Beard, squad advisor—bobbing and weaving between them. Aunt Lainie was there, too, part lioness defending her cub and part ostrich hiding her head. As the screech rose in pitch, I prayed it would enter that range only dogs can hear.

"You *psycho*!" from Pen.

"You *slut*!" from Brie.

Their latest beef concerned Pen's uniform bottoms—specifically, Brie's thievery thereof. Which made no sense. Brie wouldn't electively embarrass the squad, and even if she had, what about the panties Pen rode in on? As usual, in the absence of sense, I knew who was stirring the pot. I pushed to the front lines.

"D-Dice?"

I took a step toward her. Everyone took a step away. Even

Aunt Lainie. "It's okay, Pen," I said. "It's going to be okay," I corrected.

At which point Pen collapsed on me in full sob. Which was problematic. I had to console her, right? Yet might such contact summon Sinclair to this chicks-only refuge—and hadn't we scandal enough for one night? I patted, I stroked. I swept errant wisps and checked her eyes—indigo blue, tears clear; she was 100 percent Pen.

"All right, girls. Show's over!" Ms. Beard announced, clapping to disperse the flock. "Come on, everyone, back on the field. Now, please!"

Someone warbled a weak "Let's go, Lancers!" as Pen sucked back snot.

"It'll be okay," I repeated. "I promise."

She got a hold of herself, let go of me. Lainie put her arms around both of us. "You girls ready to head home?"

The ladies Leonard exchanged a look. No judgment, only love. For a former model/Martha Stewart wannabe/control freak, Lainie was a pretty decent mom. "Penny, you and Candy go to your car," she said. "I just want to call Dad real quick."

Lucky for Lainie, she got a cell signal, as did Pen's father, still in the bleachers. She kept her voice low. Not that we cared to eavesdrop.

"Dice, I'm losing it," Pen said. She hugged herself as we traversed the parking lot. "Like I'm having a nervous breakdown."

"Mm, I don't think it's that."

"No," she said. "I don't, either." She turned silent, testing her trust. "Dice, I *like* it," she confessed. "I don't want it to stop."

"*Shhh!*"

Lainie had caught up. Again, I gave her credit for putting maternal angst on pause. She asked if Pen wanted her to drive, and when Pen said no, she got in back. The whole way home there was no reproach, nor did I sense her stare burning holes in my back. Lainie was being cool. She was being quiet. Until she said, "Well, I for one thought it was a boring game." The tension broke, all of us emitting a crippled kind of laughter. At 9 Daisy Lane, we trooped in through the side door, the family door.

"How about some cocoa?" It was so Lainie.

"Sure, Mom, awesome," Pen said, and I echoed along those lines. "Dice and I are going up to my room, okay?"

"Sure, honey," Lainie said. "I'll bring up the cocoa. What kind of cookies would you like? I baked oatmeal-raisin this morning, but there are peanut-butter bars and—"

"Whatever, Mom. I mean, surprise us."

Pen's spacious domain was not-too-messy, not-too-neat, and high-end feminine—teak sleigh bed and patchwork quilt, eyelet curtains and a vintage vanity table with an apron of tulle. She slid into velour sweats, balling up her cheerleader uniform and flinging it away. She sat on her bed; I stood on her rug. We looked at each other.

"Come here, will you?" she said.

"All right." I toed my shoes off. Vertebrae to the headboard, we appraised the needlepoint samplers Lainie had crafted, framed, and arranged along one wall.

"So you don't think I'm crazy?" she asked at length.

"No."

"Well, what, then?"

She'd have to drag it out of me. Reverse psychology. Plan-wise, I was winging it, but it felt wrong to gush. "I don't know," I said.

"No, no, you know—you do. I don't know how you know, but you know." She spoke like a machine gun shooting soap bubbles. "Even if it's just a theory, you'd better tell me before I really do lose my mind."

"Since when am I the go-to girl for mental health?" A salient point, I thought.

"Since you're all I've got." She had a point as well.

"All right," I said. "It has come to my attention that you are possessed."

"Possessed?" To Pen, the word meant ownership. You possessed a pair of pearl earrings. "How do you mean, possessed?"

"Like *possessed*-possessed." I began to do-do-do "Tubular Bells," the theme from *The Exorcist*, and waited for her to crack up, call me nuts, kick me out.

Instead she said, "By . . . what?"

"Not what. *Who.*"

Enter Lainie, steaming mugs and chewy goodness on a tray.

"Mom, Dice is going to sleep over, okay? I just . . . really want her to."

Lainie started to frown but her face changed its mind. "Of course," she said. "I'll put towels and a fresh toothbrush in your bathroom. That sound good . . . Dice?"

"Mm-hmm, thanks, Aunt Lainie. And thanks for the cocoa and everything." By "everything" I meant "being chill, not meddling." Lainie seemed to get it. She left the room. Closed the door. Let us be. Pen and I took our mugs, inhaled the sweetness, still too hot to sip. And all at once I wished she *would* crack up, call me nuts, kick me out. Since to tell her was to share him, the first step to losing him, forever.

Only Pen said, "Dice . . . *please.*"

"Okay—fine." I would tell her. In broad strokes.

The just-the-facts version (omitting any personal interest on my part) took over an hour. We heard Pen's dad and sleepy siblings come home, and welcomed the boys when they begged to say good night. Later we endured Gordon and Lainie's stilted but well-meaning warmth in stereo. Interruptions were tolerable. What I'd hoped to avoid was an onslaught of questions from Pen. Mostly she shut up and listened. But then she asked the big one.

"So, wait, you're telling me you *saw* him?"

Saw. Heard. Smelled. Touched, touched, touched. Once, briefly, tasted. "Yeah," I admitted. "A few times."

"What did . . . what does he look like?"

"I don't know, just some guy," I lied uncomfortably.

Snuggling down amid the bedclothes, she peeked over at me. Her pupils were dilated. Through parted lips her teeth shone. "He's beautiful, isn't he?" she said, and cooed, *"Sinclair . . ."*

"I wasn't exactly sizing him up as a homecoming date. Too busy being terrified, you know." Tell one lie, the second and third flow more easily.

"You know," she said, "it's because of him I had that orgasm."

Talk about TMI. And how dare she claim they had any kind of bond. All she was to Sinclair was a body, a bag of flesh he could hang out in until I—*I!*—called him forth. He appeared to *me*. But I made my face blank. What Sinclair and I had was ours; I wouldn't be disclosing it to Pen. "It's possible." I forced a shrug. "Or maybe your hormones just kicked in. May I continue?"

When I got to the part in the burial ground, and how we'd agreed it was time for Sinclair's final curtain, Pen gave a snort. "I don't think so," she said.

"What does that mean?"

Pen righted herself in bed. "It means that when you and Sinclair made this decision, you failed to consult a very interested third party. Me. He's in *me*." She thrust her chin. "And I like him there, thank you very much."

This was not good. "Pen! You do not!" At this decibel level I'd rattle the rafters. I brought it down to a desperate whisper. "He almost made you drown Burr Addams. He wound you up at the Marshalls' so bad, our best friend could've lost her dad, and, granted, he's a complete asshole, but he's still her dad. And what about flashing your poonany to a healthy portion of Western Connecticut?"

She reveled as I itemized, sapphire eyes glittering. "That's because I didn't know what was going on. Because you were keeping secrets from me." She wagged a finger. "Bad, Dice. You're lucky I'm not mad at you."

Lucky, lucky me. "I don't see your point."

Pen jumped out of bed. "You don't? You don't see that I have this amazing source of power inside me?" She assessed herself in the full-length. "Now that I know the deal, I can harness it . . . him. I'm the one in charge."

Silly, silly Pen.

"Look, check it out!" She did a handstand. Then she saluted with one of the hands. Then she switched hands, for a nanosecond suspended in midair. A spinning helix, she leapt back to standing, face flush, eyes manic, hair, as usual, perfect. "What a rush!"

"Uh . . . I don't know about this, Pen . . ."

She wasn't listening. She was opening her window. She was climbing onto the ledge. The Leonard home was a big, brick Tudor with ivied walls, and Pen—barefoot, blissed-out—was using strands of vine as a ladder to the roof. *Shit, shit, shit!* The girl would *not* have a fatal accident, not on my watch.

My choices were slim. I could alert her parents, which would land Pen in the mental ward, and even if for a brief observation period, we'd miss the equinox. Or I could go out the window and climb the ivy and hopefully not plunge to my death in borrowed pajamas. But that would accomplish what? I couldn't stop her shenanigans.

The only other option? Simply trust Sinclair.

I leaned out. The moon was waxing, nearly full. I craned and contorted every which way but couldn't see Pen. It sounded like squirrels up there. What was she doing, a balance-beam routine on the mansard? I paced the room. *Think!* I thought. Not like me. Like *him.* Pen believed she was in control, but Sinclair pulled her strings—what reason would he have to bring her to such a dangerous brink? Right, to remind me how crucial it was to stay in my exorcism lane. As if I was about to detour! Just then came a muffled thud. I got to the window again as Pen came hurtling down, grasping blindly.

"Pen!" I screamed, though it came out a mew, and stuck my upper half out the window. Still clutching ivy, Pen gained a precarious toehold on the tip of the shutter below. I reached down. "Grab on!"

"I—I can't. I'm scared!"

"I can pull you up." Or so I hoped—I'd been doing my yoga

DVD faithfully; all those *chatarangas* had to amount to something. I withdrew again to drag a chair to the window, braced my feet for better leverage. "Come on," I said. "Before someone sees and you'll be in a straitjacket for homecoming."

That struck a chord. We grasped each other by the wrists. I heaved; she clawed. And just when our faces became level, I saw black eyes and a certain smirk. "Hello, my lady!" Her voice, his words. "We've got to stop meeting like this!"

One more yank and Pen toppled over me, a clumsy vault hinting at none, absolutely none, of her earlier grace. She landed on her ass. Her hair, finally, was wrecked; I even detected a bit of ivy-induced frizz.

"Okay," she said. "Let's get it done."

XVI

REPERCUSSIONS? SURE, THERE WERE REPERCUSSIONS. PEN GOT suspended from the squad for three games, but then the suspension was suspended, since the games were *so* important and Pen *was* cocaptain and everything. Voluntarily and, I suppose, sincerely, she apologized to the Prancers for her "brain fart" and to Brie Atwood, specifically, for slander. To her parents, Pen was duly remorseful as well, citing early-onset senioritis and guaranteeing a marked and virtually immediate improvement in her behavior.

To wit, we got to work, cutting fourth period to collect provisions—though Pen's priorities seemed askew.

"I think I should wear white, don't you? Something floaty . . ."

"It's an exorcism, Pen, not your red carpet debut," I said, marching purposefully through the green.

Pen trotted to catch up. "You don't have to snap my head off."

I mumbled an apology, hoping it came out insouciant. I didn't want her noticing how nervous I was. Not to mention conflicted. But this had to be done. Here, now, at the ash tree. Dig. With a soupspoon—a shovel was too cumbersome to get between the roots.

"How much do we need?" Pen asked.

"He didn't say." I kept my eyes on the earth till she reluctantly got down to help, tossing dirt into Jordan's beach pail. When it was nearly full, we gathered leaves, twigs, and ashkeys—the oblong seedpods that hung from the branches in ample bunches. We scoured the ground for black buds that failed to develop into pods, used a steak knife to pry off bits of bark. Smacking dirt from my hands, I told Pen, "I think we're good."

Later that afternoon we reconvened at the picnic table behind my house. Pen had swiped a cookie sheet from Lainie (my mother wouldn't know what a cookie sheet was), and as I blended water into our rarefied dirt, she kibitzed over my shoulder. "Watch it, not so much. It ought to be like clay."

I gave her a look. "Like you've done this before?"

"Actually, me and my mom took a pottery course."

Well, I asked. Ignoring her, I focused on the task at hand. On Sinclair. His tragedy. Which segued into a tragedy of my own.

"Hey, watch it!" Pen barged in on my reverie.

"What?"

"Dice, you're crying into it."

So I was.

"I don't know what you're getting so emotional about," she said. "I'm the one being exorcised."

Right. I was merely a service technician. Knowing my place, I proceeded to mold him—a mud mannequin, a miniature Sinclair Youngblood Powers, created from the earth of the very tree where his soul departed, and re-entered, and would soon again be sworn to oblivion. With twigs for fingers and leaves for hair, black bud eyes and a seedpod for . . . We both cracked up. Proportion-wise, Sinclair's penis was a bit outsized.

"What's funny is the pod is actually an ovary," said Pen with the authority of someone who earned a B in earth science.

"It's cool, though—the magical properties of the ash enable it to balance masculine and feminine energy," said I with the authority of someone who'd trawled a few Wicca websites. We studied Mister Mud. "We ought to bake him."

"Did he say to?" Pen countered.

Why did she insist on second-guessing me, snooping into privileged communication between Sinclair and I? "No, but I don't want him all mushy when the time comes."

The oven was set at three hundred—safe for the twigs, though it crisped the leaves a little—and when he was done, we pulled him out, let him cool, and draped him, solemnly, with a napkin shroud.

"What about dinner?" Pen asked. "It's goulash or stroganoff or something."

"I think I'll pass." I had butterflies. Butterflies with combat boots.

"What about me? Should I be on an empty stomach?"

I gave her a wry smile. "Not unless Lainie's serving pea soup as an appetizer."

She smiled back. We were in on this together. Something about conspiracy made me feel strong, and something about it made me feel sick. "Just don't do anything out of the ordinary," I said. "Then tell them we're going to Wick's to study."

"Okey-doke!" Damn, she was perky. "See you in a few."

The sun would go down lazily, in her late September way, with gaudy splashes of lavender and flame. There'd be no rushing her descent, so I took a shower. Pulled my hair into a tight bun. Slicked a little Vaseline on my face—boxers do this, street fighters, too. I had no clue what might come flying my way, and no desire to be scarred for life. Dressed in basic burglar (black turtleneck, black jeans, black Converse).

Pen came in, called out. A vision in cream chiffon. "You look like meringue."

"Thanks." She took it as a compliment, plucked at the hem. "I got it for the winter formal last year."

I felt so butch beside her. As it should be—our roles were clear-cut. Pen was the damsel in a dress; I was the badass ghostbuster. So before we left her car, parked unobtrusively a quick sprint from the green, I levied this little speech on her: "Okay, Pen, look, once we start, you can't be arguing or correcting me, or making suggestions or whatever. You may be the star of the show, but I'm calling the shots, all right?"

With a single mum nod she agreed, and I wondered, fleetingly, what really went on in that blond brain.

At first everything proceeded like a chem lab experiment proven countless times before. I positioned Pen against the tree, facing east. Then, to consecrate the area, I walked a pentacle, drawing the sign and the circle with spilled salt.

I entered it. Easy enough.

The Eighth Moon had risen, yet still hung low. It was orange—a harvest moon—big and round as the belly of an any-minute mom-to-be. It made the moon benevolent, not just a chunk of rock. That doubled my resolve. Tough as this was, I'd keep my eyes on the dual prize: Pen un-possessed, and Sinclair at peace.

"Great Spirit of the Eighth Moon, hear us . . . ," I began.

"Great Spirit of the Eighth Moon, hear us . . . ," Pen repeated.

"Bless us . . ."

"Bless us . . ."

"Help us . . ."

"Help us . . ."

And then it was all on me. I told it straight up, with conviction: "Great Spirit of the Eighth Moon, we need your help. This past July, Penelope Amber Leonard, who stands with me tonight, had an accident. She fell out of this tree, and we think she might have actually died for a second. That's when the spirit of Sinclair Youngblood Powers, who also died here, a long time ago, invaded Pen's body. And it's been nothing but trouble ever since. Plus, it's getting worse. So, basically, we ask that the soul of Sinclair Youngblood Powers leave the body of Penelope Amber Leonard, and we enlist the forces of heaven and earth to align with us and make it so."

At which point—carefully, carefully—I laid our primitive earthen effigy on the roots of the tree and—carefully, carefully—removed its shroud. How fragile it was, how crude. "Great Spirit of the Eighth Moon, we make this offering as a gift to the forces of heaven and earth, and as a vessel for the soul of Sinclair Youngblood Powers."

Then I said the prayer. Or what I thought was a prayer. It was in the Mohegan language. Sinclair had recited the words, and I'd written them phonetically, memorized them easily (later, after everything, burning them with any and all other damning evidence). It sounded beautiful, and I felt better, having something sanctioned to say. I'd never thought to ask what it actually meant.

Did it matter what it meant? No. What mattered is I said it.

Once I did, the timbre of our ritual changed. Drastically. The napkin went up between my fingers in a spark and plume of smoke. And the moon grew till it filled the sky—a glowing nectarine night was upon us. A gasp and then a moan came out of Pen as she levitated, but not like in the movies, stiff as a board; she went fluid, a breeze inside a body, wafting up toward that hot-colored void. With her hair all mermaid-like as if the air were water. And a gentle smile on her lips, belying that her eyes had rolled completely back, a milky blank staring out of their sockets. How lucky she was to loll, idle and blind, on atmosphere, since right about then the tree roots got busy. They twined around my feet and ankles, an attack of tentacles with a thirsty rasp. Swarming and slurping, constricting and consuming, up and up till they got what they wanted.

With that, the world drained as rapidly as it had surged. The moon shrank, and the sky went its same old dark. Pen alit, hair in place, eyeballs, too. The roots of the ash returned to their stoic spread across the ground.

And the little boy made of mud? He was gone.

PART II

THE TOWN

XVII

I WOKE UP NAKED. THE DUVET NOT JUST OFF THE BED BUT HALFWAY across the room, the top sheet crumpled as though I'd tried to murder it. My whole body felt sticky-damp—I must've thrashed and stripped in my sleep. Some virus coming on? That would suck. There was a chorale performance on Monday— not a proper recital, just a "pre-rec," but a big enough deal for Momster to stay an extra day and Daddy to fly in from the set. On the tail end of a cold I'd sound like a stricken frog.

Only . . . no. No tickle in my throat or threat of sneeze as I padded down the hall. It wasn't me. It was the day—seven a.m. and at least seventy degrees outside. Even the bathroom tile felt warm to my bare soles. Un-PC though it may be, Indian Summer had crept in.

I was pouring Cocoa Puffs when the first pang struck. *Sinclair.* I barely knew him. Technically, he didn't exist. So how come it felt like low-budget surgery, all these essential organs hastily, sloppily removed. Errant innards aside, I functioned—washed uneaten cereal down the sink, grabbed my pack, got my bike, headed for school.

I made it ten feet. Wondering if Pen was feeling some hundred and sixty pounds lighter this morning, I glanced toward 9 Daisy Lane to see her car in the drive. She should've been on her "Crusts for the Crusty" rounds. Some post-exorcism ailment, maybe? I pedaled up the driveway and let myself in.

The mingling aromas from the Leonard kitchen were a bit much, even for Lainie. Coffee, fine. The buttery aftermath of scrambled eggs, sure. Some kind of baked thing, okay. But bacon *and* sausage? And were those remnants of pancake batter? Also odd: The breakfast nook was barren. Faint voices trilled from the dining room. Were the Leonards entertaining royalty?

Further weirdness: Peanut and Popcorn, inside, dozing on the furniture! Popcorn played it cool, but Peanut lifted her head with pleading eyes. I called out a querying hello. No response. I called out again. But only got as far as "Hell—"

Lainie presided over the table, pearlies harking back to her Dazzle Drops prime, teapot from the silver service in one hand, pinky extended. "Oh!" she trilled, as though trying to recall who I was. Pen swiveled in her chair and wouldn't quite meet my eye, though her face glowed like a billion-watt bulb. Silas and Jordan did pogo-stick impressions by the head of the table, usually their father's seat, but of course Uncle Gordon would be halfway to Hartford by now. The boys paid me no heed at all, but the Leonards' guest was not so rude. He chided the children, pushed back his chair, and got to his feet. The way a gentleman ought greet a lady.

"Good morning," he said, and damn if he didn't bow—not low, just enough to show the top of his dark, wavy head—then stood erect and did his best to keep his expression even. For an instant that left quadrant of mouth traveled north, but then he widened his smile, deepening the dimple. The black eyes were filled with mirth.

"Candy!" All at once it occurred to my aunt who on earth I was. "Oh, my goodness, Candy. Come in." She put the teapot down and flitted toward the handsome figure in her husband's place, taking his arm. "Candy, this is Sinclair . . . Sinclair Youngblood Powers. Of the Westport Powerses . . . and the New Canaan Youngbloods."

Oh, was he really.

"His father's brother went to college with your Uncle Gordon."

Sinclair inclined toward me the tiniest bit. From the corner of my eye I caught Pen wriggle in her seat.

"Sinclair, this is my niece, Candice," Lainie continued.

"Unh . . . huh—" was the breadth of my eloquence. My body

was rigid as a Rodin, but inside my heart was acing decathlons. *What* the? *How* the?

"Hey, nice to meet you," said Sinclair, sounding every bit the typical contemporary all-American boy, raised on Xbox and ESPN.

"Gnnu . . . too," or something equally glib tripped off my tongue.

Aunt Lainie tittered. Clearly I was bowled over by the good-looking young man—after all, we hadn't any in New York. "Come, Candy, have something to eat."

"E-e-e-e . . ."

This was stupid. I'd handled myself better when Sinclair was a potentially vengeful spirit. Now here he was, a . . . what was he, exactly? He appeared the same, the only difference being he no longer required my touch to obtain three solid dimensions, and had lost the frock coat and breeches. Sometime between moon-crest and sunrise he must've raided Ralph Lauren. How was I not in his arms right now? Oh, right, I was frozen, stunned. And behind that composed, genial visage, Sinclair was enjoying my stupefaction. I rallied some semblance of composure.

"Everything looks great, Lainie," I said, casually taking a slice of cinnamon toast. "Gordon will be so disappointed to have missed this—and you, of course, Sinclair. The only reason I stopped by is I saw Pen's car and wanted to make sure she was all right. You *are* all right, aren't you, Pen?"

Pen nodded once. "Definitely, thanks, Dice. Perfectly fine. Mom got a neighbor to take my route this morning when it turned out we had company."

"Uh-huh. And what about that little thing called school?"

"Oh, my goodness, school!" cried Lainie. "Now, Sinclair, you go with the girls, and I'll call the principal right now. You do have your birth certificate and everything? If there's any other paperwork they need, we'll get it straightened out. Oh, Penny, drop the boys off, won't you, please?"

"Moh-*ohm*," Pen whined. "We're already late."

"I wish you wouldn't use that tone, Penny—it's so unattractive. I suppose I can call from the car, *if* I can get a signal." Apologetically, Lainie turned to her guest. "I often feel we're in colonial times around here." Then, to her little ones, "Boys, get your things. Quickly!"

With that, a flurry of activity as everyone hustled from the room at once. Outside, Sinclair went directly to the driver's side of Pen's horseless carriage to open the door for her. Chivalry, apparently, was not dead.

"Thank you, Sinclair," she oozed.

Next, he held the back door for me. "My lady," he murmured.

"What?" Add another layer to my disbelief. "I'm supposed to ride in back?"

"Ahhh . . . is that a problem?" Sinclair seemed genuinely

mystified, but I wasn't sure. How much had he managed to absorb about teen culture? Had he any idea what an all-access pass it was, riding up to Swonowa High next to Pen Leonard?

"Really, Dice. With his long legs?" my cousin reasoned.

Stumped for a reply, I got in the car. Sinclair claimed the shotgun spot, and Pen helped him fasten his safety belt. Took her damn time about it, too.

"Okay," I said steadily, remembering to breathe. "Will someone please tell me what's going on?"

Laughter from the front.

"Oh, Dice, you should have heard him—it was priceless!" Pen said giddily. "He's like the parent whisperer, had my mom eating out of his hand. Of course I knew—just *knew*—who he was the instant I laid eyes on him."

She knew who he was. But did she know how he was . . . or what?

"Sinclair, how *did* you do it?" Pen asked. "My mother's just awful to telemarketers and stuff."

"Oh, yes, Sinclair," I said. "Pray tell!"

He turned in his seat. "It appears my current incarnation includes a talent for persuasion. First I fabricated a connection to Gordon Leonard, then told of my great-uncle in nearby Norris who'd suffered a stroke—that I'd come from Westport to be of use during his recovery, that I wished to enroll at Swonowa, and that since Uncle Edmund was so out of sorts

I thought to introduce myself to the Leonards of Swoon and see if they could assist me. Which dear Lainie was happy to do. Beginning with that breakfast." He patted his stomach. "I cannot tell you ladies just how much I've missed bacon!"

No doubt he was counting on plying those persuasive powers at Swonowa—he'd pass off some blank sheets of paper for his birth certificate and transcripts. "Is that how you charmed your way into those clothes?"

"Ah, no, these I had to borrow. Courtesy of the Williams house."

"Really? I've never seen Crane or Duck dress preppy," remarked Pen, ever the arbiter of Swoon's sartorial habits.

"I believe it's their father's clothing." Sinclair plucked at the purloined polo. "Nothing of theirs quite fit."

"Well, don't get it into your head to 'borrow' the Rolls," I said. "I know you're feeling like you could sell dental floss to Daffy Duck right now, but you should probably think about keeping a low profile in Swoon."

We'd reached school, and even though Pen was late, no one had parked in "her" spot. As we all got out, I faced Sinclair, searched his eyes. How strange it was not to be touching. "We need to talk," I said.

"Yes, indubitably. This evening, perhaps."

"This evening, definitely."

"Very well. Till then."

The three of us began to cross the campus. Students and teachers who ought to have been in class paused unwittingly mid-sprint. Heads turned. Hair flipped. Smiles flashed. The sun shone a little bit brighter; the air got a fraction fresher. Pen was back on her babble, explaining where the office was and who to ask for, blah-blah-blah.

"By the way, ladies," Sinclair said before we split up. "In regard to what Dice counseled about my profile. I do want to fit in around here." He smiled at us, that smile you want to get eaten alive by. "So please be so kind as to call me Sin."

XVIII

ONE THING I MISSED ABOUT MANHATTAN: A DOZEN CUISINES ON speed dial. Pizza? Mexican? French-Asian fusion? Here in the wilderness you established a rapport with pots and pans. Biking to the Stop & Shop after library duty, I riffled through my repertoire. Rice and beans? Lemon chicken? Ooh, yeah: mac and cheese. With a cool garden salad to offset the day's weird simmer. I got dinner going, then whirled around tidying up, scarcely having time to primp before sensing Sin's footstep on the porch.

"Good evening," he said. It was a murky dusk when I met him at the door, but light from the house spilled through with clear, bright welcome. "These are for you."

Queen Anne's lace grows prodigiously as summer segues into fall. Yet this handpicked bouquet, long grasses and purple thistle thrown in, was special.

"Thank you," I said. "Please come in."

We were being so proper, so polite. After all, everything was different now. I located a vase, hit the tap, arranged the flowers. They made a pretty centerpiece on the pine table, set with plain white plates.

"I know this house," Sin said. "A farmer lived here, Farmer Howe, if I recall. He raised . . . cows . . ." Poised in the middle of the room, hands clasped behind him, there was no hint of slouch to him. Mm-mm-mm, to trace a fingertip from shoulder blade to shoulder blade, then along the length of his spine.

"Uhh, I hope you're hungry." Food was a ruse to cover my urges.

"Yes, very much so!" he said, so enthused, so alive. "The way my appetites have been rushing back . . . all my appetites . . . I think that's positive." A flash of desire lit his face, and then subdued. "Don't you, Dice?"

"I don't know." I folded my arms, surveying him openly. "When it comes to you, Sin, I really don't know what to think."

In two strides he closed the space between us. *Whatever, whatever,* I told myself, high on his proximity. He was here; the how and why ought to be irrelevant. Except they weren't. I was crazy about him. That didn't make me crazy.

"My poor Dice," he said, and I suffused myself in his scent. "You mean so much to me." He lifted his hand to my cheek but stopped short of caress. "And I—*zounds!*"

Out of nowhere RubyCat leapt on the table, all puffed up to intimidate.

"Ru-*Beast*," I said. "What's your problem?" Although I thought it cool, like she was my guard cat.

Sinclair collected himself. "How like a feline to sneak up on you." He extended a finger. Whiskers twitching, R.C. sniffed.

"Her name's RubyCat; a.k.a. R.C. I named her for my best friend in New York."

"New York! You've been to New York?"

How little we really knew each other. "I'm *from* New York," I said. "Ruby, chill. Be nice to Sin."

"Truly? Wondrous!" he said. "But I should have known. You're not like these country girls."

R.C. flattened her ears and gave Sin's digit a swat. "She's not usually like this," I said. "Come on, furbag, off the table." Swishing the kitten, I looked at Sin quizzically. "I thought you were good with animals."

He coughed into his fist. "Cats are territorial, about their places and their people. Perhaps I threaten her," he said. "She'll come around eventually."

He wasn't being cocky, just matter-of-fact. No one, regardless of species, could resist his allure. "Hey . . ." In the oven, cheese segued from bubbly to burnt. "Why don't we eat?"

"Excellent idea!"

Conversation came easier, Sin and I comparing notes on

Swonowa. As it turned out, we had a class together—American history, hilariously enough.

"I did as you girls suggested, telling classmates I'd been home-schooled," he said. "But everyone reacted as though I were extremely devout."

"Ooh, yeah—forgot about that. Most homeschooled kids are seriously Christian."

"Is that it? That explains their faces when I told them to call me Sin!"

He drained his iced tea. I refilled his glass, ladled some more mac and cheese. The boy could eat.

"A few of the fellows recommended I go out for hockey," he said. "That's a sport you play with sticks on the ice."

"Yeah, Sin, I know what hockey is. And don't call them 'fellows' unless you want your ass kicked. Call them guys."

"Guys, right, I knew that." He patted his lips and leaned toward me with his signature smirk. "But you needn't fret about my ass."

I blushed. "I didn't mean . . . I'm sure you can take care of yourself."

"Indeed," he said.

The mood shifted. Avoiding it, I rose to clear the table, yet felt oddly adrift in my own kitchen. Unable to avoid it, I turned to Sin. "Let's go hang out on the porch awhile."

Certain things are best discussed in darkness. Crickets made desperate plans around us. We took the swing, but didn't swing. We listened to the night. We breathed.

"Dice, thank you," Sin said at last.

"Oh, mac and cheese, no biggie."

"Not for making dinner. For making . . . me."

"Say *what*?" I aimed for humor. I doubt it came out that way.

"It's what you want to know, the reason you invited me to dine."

True enough. "Okay, Sin," I said, resigned. "Go ahead. Explain yourself." I wanted to know what I didn't dare know.

"Are you familiar with the Bible at all? Old Testament? Genesis, specifically?"

Basic stuff, even for me. "Adam and Eve, right?"

"Let's leave Eve out for the moment. More like Adam and God."

"Okay, you're losing me already."

He stood up abruptly to execute an exaggerated bow. "Madam, *I'm* Adam."

Palindromes? He's giving me palindromes?

He dropped to a knee and took my hands. Our first physical contact since . . . "Which would make *you* my creator."

Oh, that was crazy. And I knew from crazy.

"You made me, Dice. You did. You dug the earth, you mixed the clay, you shaped me with your own two hands."

Me, me, me? No, no, no!

"You implored the forces of nature," he went on . . . and on. "Made the offering, delivered the incantation. You did it all. And now I'm here." He brought my hands to his lips and then showed me his eyes: dark, controlled, unreadable as ever. "Nice job."

"I—I don't understand." Because I was an idiot, maybe?

"I think you do."

A gullible, besotted fool?

He rose to lean against the porch rail. "I only cite Genesis as a point of reference," he said. "The concept that man is made of clay is a common principle to many faiths. Ashes to ashes, dust to dust, yadda-yadda-yadda."

It was impossible. I believed in the big bang theory, in evolution. Besides, I was no god, or goddess, witch, whatever. Except Sin was there, in flesh and . . . what, mud? Leaves? That extra-special ingredient of my own tears? Only he couldn't be! I did those things, yes—but for the opposite reason. "What I did"— each word was a sharp pebble from a quarry below my lungs— "was supposed to bring you peace."

Sin smiled. A dissolute, ferocious thing in his face. "It's a lovely night, my belly is full, and I'm in the presence of a beautiful woman. I couldn't be more at peace."

Fire trucks raced to the blaze in my brain. "You *lied*!" The indictment came out a whisper, but Sin heard me, all right.

"I most certainly did not."

"Shut up! You did!" My voice grew stronger, and with volume

came motion. I vaulted off the swing, while Sin kept still, so comfortable in his long-limbed, fine-tuned, accursed frame. "There in the burial ground, you agreed—you said it: 'It has to stop.'"

Sin laughed, just once, a wolf bark. "What had to stop was the damnable purgatory inside Penelope Amber Leonard."

What's the worst possible lie? A betrayal. "You . . . you tricked me!"

"Did I? Or did you deceive yourself? Did you not think it odd that I'd give you the ways and means to be rid of me?"

Oh . . . I did.

"Since if such concern occurred to you, I don't recall you positing it."

No . . . I didn't.

"Come now, Dice, be honest. Didn't you like me just a little? Didn't you want me?"

How dare he say those things, terrible things, contemptible things, true things.

"Perhaps you felt my frustration—my clever and extraordinarily sensitive girl." In a flash he was upon me. My eyes told all like tabloid headlines. I shut them, wouldn't let him see my soul.

"Dice, I had to be free." There was no scorn in his voice; he was just giving it to me straight. He needed something, he figured out how to get it, and he went for it. "Now, thanks to you, I am. I'm here." I sensed him lean into me. "And I have things to do."

XIX

SIN'S TO-DO LIST. IF EVERY ITEM ON THAT AGENDA HURT ME AS much as the first, I'd surely perish. With one stroke my interior landscape was looted, pillaged, strip-mined. Not that this was his aim; my agony was collateral damage. And I might have seen it coming, were it not for the disorienting fugue state that settled in the moment he left me at 12 Daisy Lane with a head full of muck and a sink full of dishes.

Where he went was anyone's guess. Though evidently he discovered a new fount from which to "borrow," since the next day he came to school wearing not just fresh clothes but a new style. White tee, blue jeans, black boots. The low-key look suited Sin, whose aura announced itself—at least, to me it did. Sitting in history, I could intuit him through the wall. Then he was in the room, and it was futile to fight it: He owned my attention. As he walked to his seat the *ko-chunk* of his heels was the only sound.

After class found him shooting the breeze with a couple of jocks, and I swept past. Funny how you can ignore someone outwardly while on the inside he rules every spark from every synapse, the march of every corpuscle, and every single thump of your heart. If only I had a handle on my feelings. Anger, fear, mistrust—all present and accounted for. Yet there was compassion, too. His life had been cut short, so he seized a second chance. True, he'd played me like a tin kazoo, but wouldn't I benefit? Since oh, oh, oh, I wanted him so.

Friday ticked by, and then came the weekend. A girls' night out with Pen, Wick, and Marsh—Thai food and a chick flick in Norris. Now, granted, Norris is slightly bigger than Swoon and claims both an actual Thai place and a movie theater, but we all knew we'd gone there in hope of stealing a glimpse of the new guy, who everyone knew by then lived in Norris with a convalescing uncle. As if Pen's status wasn't lofty enough, it escalated further once everyone also knew she had some link to the "so hot" and "weird but in a good way" Sin Powers. Wick and Marsh pinioned my cousin with questions; I concentrated on my curry. Not easy, with Pen kicking me under the table at regular intervals. She seemed to revel in all things Sin related, including our perverse and secret partnership in his origins.

It rained on Saturday—an oppressive summer rain that refused to face the calendar facts—and Momster and I tried not to peck each other to death. She'd brought the in-progress issue of *In Star* to fuss over, and I rehearsed to my download of Mozart's "Ave Verum Corpus." We drove to fetch Daddy at the Hartford airport that evening, but his plane was delayed due to weather and the ride home was leaden.

Sunday brunch at the Leonards' was endurable, until guess whose name popped up. Aunt Lainie mentioned him, and Uncle Gordon was stymied to remember Sinclair's nonexistent father's brother. I yawned theatrically, and my mother called me uncouth, a comment I challenged with a burp. It further bugged when Lainie told Momster that Pen had been unusually sullen and snappish all weekend, too, and the sisters concluded sagely that we must have fallen into the same menstrual cycle.

"You okay?" I asked Pen as we scavenged the leftovers we were ostensibly putting away.

"Fine," she said, snappish, sullen. Ripping at aluminum foil, slapping Tupperware around. "But you'd think he'd have been in touch by now. I mean, what is he *doing*?"

Good question: What *was* he doing, this boy who had things to do? "I don't know. I haven't heard from him either."

Pen wasn't sure whether to be alarmed or relieved by this. And I wasn't sure how to take her interest in his affairs.

"Cut him some slack," I said. "He's got catching up to do. No doubt he's up to guy things." I considered that pretty magnanimous of me.

"Hmpf," Pen hmpffed. "I did see Con Emerson practically tackle him with friendly zeal. They're probably slamming Budweiser in front of the TV as we speak."

Right, Connor Emerson, heir to the Emerson Electronics chain—Sin couldn't hire a better tutor in all things fermented, football, and flat-screen. "That must be it. I bet Con's house is the Taj Mahal of high-def. Though it's hard to picture Sin—"

"I know, I know, with such a Cro-Mag!" Pen said. "Someone as deep and intelligent as Sin."

My, he'd certainly made an impression. Vaguely annoyed, I tried to dissect Pen with my stare, call on my "abilities" to illuminate what he meant to her. All I got was static. I took a knife to the unruly edge of Lainie's pumpkin loaf.

"Uch, I ate too much," Pen said, watching me chew. "If someone doesn't put a stop to my mother's fanatical baking, I'll turn into a big fat cow."

Yeah, right. The girl had the metabolism of a tsetse fly. Unless she said that to make *me* feel like a big fat cow. No, Pen wouldn't be so mean. Nevertheless, I put the knife down, leaving the loaf a little jagged.

"I should go," I said. "I want to practice for tomorrow."

"Hmm? Oh, okay," she said. "I really ought to go for a run." Instead she flopped heavily into the booth of the breakfast nook, glaring at nothing.

Miraculously, her spirits had lifted by fifth period Monday, when I found her lurking at my classroom door. "We're ditching." The gleam in her eyes was ardent.

Normally I wouldn't argue. The Swonowa curriculum was a cakewalk compared to my NYC school; I could've aced it somnambulating. But she wanted me to cut history, and I was jonesing for Sin. "Can't," I said. "Quiz."

"So what." She latched onto my elbow. "This can't wait."

Pen steered me to the exit, and we hustled to her car. Cranking sugary country pop, she tapped the steering wheel half a step behind the beat, and, as she missed a turn, braked, and made a U-ie, I realized she was driving to the lake. The Spot. Maybe our friends were taking advantage of the crazy, clinging heat with an impromptu party. But there were no vehicles I recognized when Pen put hers in park.

I flicked the Nashville nonsense down a notch. "What?"

Pen beamed at me. "Do I look different?"

In fact, she did. Pen rarely wore makeup, but her lids seemed darkly slitted and her lips, conversely, fuller and wetter. "Maybe," I said. "Is that mascara?"

A hysterical sound, something a strangled swan might make. "Mascara? Oh, Dice!" Pen lunged forward and hugged me. Her arms and chest were hot, her scent strong, and I don't know what made me more uneasy, the pure physical press of her, or the fact that Pen simply didn't do squishy. I must have writhed, because she giggled and readjusted her hold on me, leaning into my ear.

"I have a *see*-cret," she singsonged, too close and too loud.

I pushed her off. "Pen, you are on serious drugs."

"I am!" she cried. "But I'm not. I mean, I am so high right now. I still feel . . . come on, Dice, can't you guess?"

No, I could not. A very stubborn part of me had jammed my speculation mechanism. So Pen relented, telling all with the destructive swath of Mount Vesuvius, circa 79 A.D.

"He came to me."

Naturally I knew the "he" to whom she referred. Naturally my immediate inclination was to take one of her pom-poms and ram it down her gullet.

"Last night. Finally! He rang the bell around nine, chatted with my dad a while—of course, my mom had to get in on it, too—and then they just sent him to my room like we'd been together forever."

Surely he could have arranged some sneaky rendezvous, but it was so much more audacious his way. Stroll on up to the front door, get chummy with the parents, then pop in on the darling daughter upstairs.

"Dice, it was amazing. Of course, we had to be quiet—but we didn't say a single word, and that made it so much more intense. He just looked at me, and I thought I'd turn into a puddle on the carpet."

There'd be no broad strokes of this particular brush. Pen was going to relate her tale in pointillism. No way could I stop her, either, or emit a hint of resentment or offense. Pen hadn't snaked me; she had no idea that I . . . that Sin . . . that we . . .

"He'd make the smallest gesture, and I'd have to interpret it," she said. "Like when I started to undress, I knew by his expression I was right."

Dab, dab. Jab, jab. The picture formed for me.

"It was a game. I would try something—a nibble, a squeeze— and then check for his smile, his nod, to know it was what he wanted."

Uh-huh. Got it. Figured out what Pen figured out, the supreme excitement of stoking a boy.

"All I wanted was to be good, because if I was good, very good, he might reward me." She seemed to shimmer in the heat, or was that a mirage? "And, oh, it was unbearable, an eternity till he touched me. But then he did, he did."

He touched her. With those hands. Those incongruously tender and diligent hands. Alternately callous and kind, but never once tentative, as he pressed and spun her, positioned her this way and that. Until she was ready, until she was ripe.

"It hurt like crazy, like being cut with a dull knife," she said. "I thought I'd bite my tongue off, but he pushed the heel of his hand to my mouth, and I bit that instead. Then it eased, and it was . . . you'd think the first time I wouldn't . . . but I did. Me! And it lasted forever, and not just down there but everywhere. No, literally, I curled my toes!"

Would she ever shut up?

"And can I tell you the heaviest part?"

Like I could stop her?

"You'd think, after an experience like that, you'd want to rest for a minute. Take a breather. Take a bath. But all I wanted was to do it again. Immediately. Only no. I tried to make him want me again, but he shook his head, and I couldn't risk displeasing him. So off he went . . . and there I was . . . still am . . . dying for it, Dice. Dying for it."

XX

WITH THE COMPLETE AND UNABRIDGED DEPICTION OF MY COUSIN'S deflowering in the forefront of my consciousness, I was to stand before parents, peers, et al, and sing Mozart. Lucky for them if I didn't projectile vomit. A dozen girls in prim white blouses and knee-length navy skirts, we laughed off jitters in the instrument storage area of Swonowa's music room. Mrs. Welch, our plump, pigeon-chested leader, hadn't booked the auditorium—we didn't expect the masses cluttering the corridor and challenging one another for chairs.

"Standing room only!" Mrs. Welch had a wobbly warble when she spoke, but could hold a high C as long as David Blaine could chill in a lead sarcophagus. "We've never had a turnout like this for a pre-recital."

I'd have hated to bust her bubble, but the crowd hadn't gathered for chorale. Rather, it was a loosely formed receiving line for Sinclair Youngblood Powers. He must have mentioned to someone in passing that he'd be here—that was all it took. Kids who hadn't a class with him wanted a better look, and buzz about the new boy had piqued adult interest as well, although none would cop to such curiosity. They couldn't say what, exactly, had them defying speed limits to get to the high school by four thirty. And in such stifling conditions, with Swonowa's temperamental AC on the fritz.

Poking out of the instrument area, I watched townsfolk cluster to taste Sin's vibe. My dearest wish was to cleave through that human bulk with a banshee howl and a nice sharp scythe. No, screw the scythe. The way I felt, I could've relieved those handsome shoulders of their finely chiseled head with one meaningful smack.

If I believed I'd reached the summit of outrage hearing Pen's oral submission to "Penthouse Letters," I was mistaken. As Mrs. Welch led us onto risers, who did I see seated next to Momster, with Daddy leaning across to dote on his every word. That fiend! I was rapidly running out of family members for him to inveigle.

Mrs. Welch tapped baton to podium. The assemblage settled down. "Ave Verum Corpus." Translation? "Hail, true body." Mozart had a hit with his version of the hymn in the 1790s, but it actually dates back to the fourteenth century. Though we sang in Latin, Mrs. Welch had provided an English text so we'd get the gist. A gory little ditty, it concerns Jesus Christ, specifically, but if you give it a broader interpretation, it's about redemption through suffering.

How.

Very.

Apropos.

I sang quietly—the direction is sotto voce—but a whisper can cut like a scream. I sang sweetly—since I fully believe there is no bliss without anguish. I sang to him and him only. And with every note that issued, the temperature began to fall. Not like the AC kicking on or a breeze blowing through, but a smooth, steady phenomenon. Cold. Colder. Okay, really cold. At first the freaky freeze was welcome relief. Soon enough, sleeves were rolling down, buttons got buttoned. Had the hymn inspired anyone to weep, by the final measure, the last line: *"In mortis examine"* ("In the trial of death")—tears would have turned to icicles.

We finished to silence—then the audience broke from its cryonic state to applaud. During our second number—the rousing spiritual "Do Lord"—the atmosphere moderated to tolerable, then pleasant. A cookies-and-cider reception followed, Mrs. Welch clucking over not having near enough. Momster and Daddy loaded on the accolades—"Honey, you were wonderful!" and "You sing like an angel!" and "That's my girl!" Mrs. Welch stammered through an introduction, telling Daddy how much she enjoyed his work on *Law & Order*, while he slung me into a clinch and proudly pointed out how the apple doesn't fall far from the tree.

There's just so much of that a person can tolerate, so eventually I began to scope for Sin. Shouldn't he be holding court, stealing chorale's thunder? After all, he drew this confederacy, though that seemed forgotten by now. I extricated from my parents' clutches, did a once-around of the room, then wandered the halls a bit. No sign of Sin. Evidently, he'd pulled an Elvis and left the building.

After a quick meal at a roadside diner, Daddy and Momster shuffled off to their respective hustles. The house was a haven—*my* place—and I hoped to revel in the emptiness, sort out my junk drawer of emotions. Which is when the phone rang.

"I'm coming to pick you up." It was Pen. "We have to go to Marsh's."

From her clipped tone I could tell something was wonky. I slipped on a sweater against the new chill just in time for her honk.

"It's so awful," Pen said. "Marsh will explain when we get there."

My cousin's liaison with her paranormal paramour didn't come up on the way. Maybe she was preoccupied with concern for Marsh. Or else believed I lacked enthusiasm for the topic. All I'd managed to mutter at the lake was "Congrats on disposing of that pesky hymen," then paraphrase a safe sex PSA. As the car ate asphalt, we kept our thoughts to ourselves.

The smell of fresh apple pie hit us the instant we entered the rundown but spotless Marshall place. A golden brown deity sat in the middle of the Formica table with Marsh sitting rapt before it. She turned to us with swollen eyes.

"She's gone," was all she said. Then she handed us the note.

Dear Kristin,

I don't expect you to understand or to ever forgive me, but I've taken all I can take. Now I have a chance for happiness with Mr. Sorensen. It may be hard at first, but things will be easier for everyone this way. I have to believe that. Kristin, I've done my best to raise you right, and I know you will look after your sisters. When things settle down, I'll be in touch. Till then, please know that you girls are forever in my heart.

All my love,

Mom

"Holy crap," I said, and placed the note beside the pie. Mrs. Marshall's last stab at maternal instinct.

"Who's Mr. Sorensen?" Pen asked.

"Her boss," Marsh said without bitterness. "I wish I could say something bad about him, but he's nice. She deserves to be happy. But . . . I just . . ." Her head dropped, her shoulders crumpled, but her sobs were silent.

"Oh, Marsh, I'm so sorry," I said, truly, ineffectually. Inwardly I cursed the pre-game vision I'd blown off in the Swonowa parking lot. I'd foreseen this and, so immersed in my own drama, done nothing—although I couldn't imagine how I might have prevented it. The rank and matted creature that had menaced Marsh and her sisters in the scary movie of my mind? His name was Douglas Marshall.

"Where's your dad now?" I suddenly wanted to know.

"Out getting wasted, probably," she said. "They'd had a huge blowup last night. Started out quiet, nasty-quiet, like gas escaping. Then he was hollering, calling her everything in the book. I just stayed in my room, figuring he'd slam out, come back later with convenience-store roses—you know, the ones that are already dead when you buy them. We'd all pretend like nothing happened, and the whole stupid cycle would start again. Only . . . I guess she'd made up her mind. I don't even know if she told him. And of course Charlotte and Willa don't know, although on some level they do, they must. I mean, she baked a *pie* . . ."

The soundless sobs began again.

"What are you going to do?" Pen put a hand atop our friend's. So Pen—kind and caring. Still, the gesture seemed empty, and I caught her glance at the clock on the wall.

"I don't know," Marsh said.

"What can *we* do?" I fidgeted straight through to my brain. "Pen, your father's a lawyer. Does he handle this sort of thing? Or what about Burr's father? He's a judge, right? Maybe—" I shut up. Uncle Gordon, Mr. Addams—white-collar professional types in the same league as Mr. Sorenson—involving them could set Marsh's dad off on some proletariat rampage. "Are the girls in their room?" I changed tacks. "Maybe we should all go back to my house. There's enough room and—"

"No," Marsh said firmly. "I can't disrupt them any more. They need stability, and . . . they love Dad. He wouldn't . . . he won't . . ." Her voice got shaky. She pulled her hand away from Pen, wiped her nose with it. "I just have to keep it together."

"We'll stay with you," I said.

Marsh looked at me, thought it through. "No," she said. "No, thank you. You guys are great; I appreciate you coming over. But this is my thing." Steeling herself, she rose from the table and opened the fridge, shut it, went to the cupboards. The baggy jeans were back, sweatshirt big enough for three. "I ought to fix something for dinner. God, it's so late. The girls haven't eaten, and when he comes home, if he's hungry . . ."

"Are you sure?" I said. Because I wasn't.

"Positive," said Marsh.

Pen sat at the table, absently admiring her manicure. Dragonlady red. Beyond bizarre. Pen's nails were always done, but always a subtle mauve or pale pink. She and her mother had them done together, a matching shade; it was their weekly bonding ritual. They must have gone that afternoon. I wondered if Lainie went for red as well.

Marsh got jumpy. "You guys should go," she said. "I don't want him to think I've told anyone."

"But you'll call us, if . . . anything."

"Yes, yes. I'll call. But it's fine. Really. Just go, all right. I'll see you in school."

I didn't see another option, so I said okay. Then I said, "Pen."

No answer.

"Pen?"

"Hmm? What?"

"Let's go. We're going."

I wanted to give Marsh a hug, but she'd shrunk down so small inside her clothes, inside herself, I couldn't find her. In her place, a robot made Hamburger Helper. Driving out of "that part" of town I noticed the Wolverine, a neon-lit tavern built like a log cabin. What was a wolverine, anyway? A rank, matted sort of beast, low to the ground, with a long snout and sharp teeth. I tightened my sweater around me.

"You think she'll be all right?" I asked Pen.

"Oh, sure." She was so blasé. "Her father's a freak, but she knows how to handle him."

"Yeah, but what if he doesn't come back—and they're all alone out there?"

"I wouldn't worry about that, either." Pen shot me the slightest smile. "There's a gun on the premises, and Marsh definitely knows how to handle a gun."

Pen pulled up to 12 Daisy Lane. "So was it fun before?" she asked pleasantly.

"What?"

"The chorale thing. Did it go well?"

"Yeah . . . ," I said, like it took place months ago and I had to remember. "It was fine."

"Sorry I missed it. Next time. Promise!"

It had to be some WASP thing, the switch you flip to make everything okay. Clearly my Jewish genes—encoded with impending disaster around every corner—were dominant on this. I wanted out of the car. "See you tomorrow," I said, and bolted.

"Night!" she called.

I sprinted up the driveway as if chased.

"Good evening, my lady." Sin sat on the porch, big boots above the rail, one finger gently rubbing RubyCat's chin. The fickle feline didn't even deign to acknowledge me.

Now, I had to get this right. Clarity was key. No euphemisms or modernisms he might not comprehend. "You fornicated with Pen."

"Yes."

I repeated the statement, using another word beginning with *f*, dropping the preposition, substituting a pronoun, and adding an exclamation point.

"Yes. That disturbs you?"

I literally stamped my foot—it was a reflex. "Damn skippy it disturbs me, Sin. But you know what? Right now I have other things on my mind that make who you screw not so much a priority."

"Ah, do you wish to talk about it?" His voice rubbed gently across my cranium, coaxing me, confusing me. "People place so much importance on being open nowadays. Communication . . . validation . . ."

As if I needed him to validate me. What nerve. And I wished he'd get his paws off my cat. Yet I seemed incapable of either utterance or action; I just stood there.

"See?" Clunking down his feet, he took R.C. from her curled-up position to lay her supine in one palm, head cradled inside his knuckles, tail dangling off his wrist. "I told you she'd come around."

"Yeah," I said. "You've got the touch."

He didn't respond, just tucked R.C. in the crook of his arm and teased her with the tip of her own tail. She batted it lazily.

"Sin, what are you doing here?"

"I wanted to see you," he said, and stood. "Tell you how much I enjoyed your performance, and meeting your parents."

This was prime opportunity for me to demand, "Not what are you doing here on my porch—what are you doing here in Swoon?" To offer all the weirdness that had begun with his arrival. Such as why the parents of people who weren't even in chorale would attend a piddling pre-rec. Or why Pen would polish her nails a garish red. And if that seemed inconsequential, how about

Marsh's mother running off with her boss? Sin seemed responsible somehow—but as I ran it over in my mind, I knew how paranoid it'd sound coming out of my mouth.

"I also wanted to ask you something," he said.

Ko-chunk, ko-chunk. He was close to me now. I reached for R.C., and he gave her easily. She nuzzled my neck. The furry little slut. "So ask it."

"It's gotten so cold," he said. "A neat trick, by the way. Brava."

Was he inferring that *I* made the Fahrenheit fall? And, in fact, had I?

He held out his hand. "Shall we go inside?"

How easy just to take it, let him lead me through the door. Then maybe he'd build a fire, and we'd stretch out before it, and he'd explain everything away, make even his seduction of Pen reasonable, forgivable. And once in that clichéd romantic setting my lashes would flutter, overwhelmed by the day's tumultuous events, and I'd sink into Sin, his kiss . . .

"No."

Why couldn't I just hate him? Pure, clean, simple loathing. What flaw in my wiring kept me from kicking this aberrant, inhuman excuse for a boy to the absolute, ultimate curb? How many more tricks would it take to set my head on straight?

"I'm tired," I told him. Resting against the whitewashed clapboard of the house, I realized how true that was. "You want to ask me something? Make it quick."

"Very well," he said. "Homecoming. A momentous occasion, I've gathered. Particularly the dance at the end of next week. I'd like very much to escort you."

Homecoming, as a concept, didn't jibe with my urban experience. Even senior prom is a bourgeois affair city kids begrudgingly acquiesce to for the kitsch factor. But he was right—in Swoon, homecoming was critical. To snag Sin Powers as my date would be a social coup. "What about Pen?" I said.

"Pen? Yes? What about her?"

Was he kidding? "I'd think in light of recent amorous activities, you'd want to escort *her*." I glanced across the road. Behind my cousin's bedroom curtain, the lamp threw a soft glow. "I bet she's up there right now, waiting for you to ask."

"Why, you make it sound as though Pen and I are betrothed or some such."

"Yeah. Uh-huh. You're just friends with benefits."

The term was new to Sin. But he approved. "Yes, that's it precisely."

I shook my head. It was all so nuts. But Swoon was turning into crazy town, so it made sense. Ergo, I offered an insane proposition. "How 'bout this: I'll go with you to the homecoming dance if you ask Pen, too. You know, make it a merry threesome."

The notion planted itself in Sin, as I heaved myself off the wall and went inside. Alone.

XXI

CRIMSON MANICURES WERE ALL THE RAGE. EXCEPT FOR MARSH, WHO worked with her hands too much to fuss with them, and me, who bucked trends just to be obstinate, everyone had one. Even Ms. Brinker collected overdue fines with glaring nubbins. Aside from that, everything was normal—or as normal as a sports-obsessed small town in the throes of homecoming madness can be. People went bonkers prepping for the parade, and of course there was a pep rally for the game against the Bristol Bobcats. Brie Atwood was a shoo-in for homecoming queen, which didn't irk Pen in the slightest.

"Everyone does homecoming, but only geeks care about it," she explained as we sifted racks at the Goodwill Superstore off Route 84. Much to my cousin's chagrin, that's where I chose to shop for a dress. Typical of Pen to turn up her nose at the previously owned, she'd nonetheless conceded to assist my rummage.

She'd been her usual cheerful self all week, and completely cool with our three-way date. Go figure.

My Sinclair situation was complex as ever. The fury had mellowed. The attraction, however, had not, so I took the path of most avoidance—I didn't trust myself around the boy—while mining Pen for information. Those two had several classes together and were often seen strolling the quad à deux. It was she who imparted, for instance, that his actual place of residence was a studio apartment atop Libo's Gas & Lube. Sin and Kurt had hit it off, and I presumed them engaged in some nefarious for-profit enterprise. Like burglarizing the better half of Western Connecticut, or investing in hydroponics. Whatever they were up to, Sin now had at his disposal a 1972 Cutlass Supreme convertible that Kurt had rebuilt and was hoping to sell.

Pen put a hand on my arm. "Ooh, Dice," she said. "That's actually hot."

A slinky number in emerald charmeuse, sleeveless, cocktail length—fifties vintage. I loved the fabric and the cut, but the color? "I don't know; can I wear green?"

"Oh, absolutely. With your pale skin and dark hair, that'll look great on you."

The dress fit as though custom-made, and I began to feel optimistic about the dance. What the hell; if it sucked, I was only out $14.99.

The second Saturday of October rolled around, and Momster

arrived with her wacky friend Mally Shagberg, hairstylist to the stars. Lainie was invited to the primp session, and the women swilled Cristal while Mally coiffed Pen and me.

"I did this for Scarlett Jo at the Golden Globes, but you've got better hair—of course, so does a scarecrow," Mally told Pen. "And you, *bubeleh,* I think we should go big."

I shrugged, winked—and boosted Mally's champagne.

"I saw that!" said Momster.

"Oh, don't be such a pooper," said Mally, extending her flute for a refill. Momster caved, administering a whole half glass each for us under-agers.

When our escort arrived, one bottle was empty, a second had been popped, and the three women were semi-drunk. Their greeting was thoroughly Shakespearean—they the witches, he Macbeth.

"Ooh, Sinclair—you look so dashing!" gushed Lainie.

"Yum-mee!" howled Mally. "Like a young Daniel Day-Lewis. Only duskier. And studlier. Let me tell you, darling, you could make me reconsider men!"

"Don't mind her," said Momster. "But you simply must pose for pictures. And if Candy and Penny are good, we'll take some of them, too."

Because he was Sinclair Youngblood Powers, he obliged them with a bow. I thought they'd collapse in a sputtering, peri-menopausal heap.

Blech! I scowled at Pen. Although, in truth, he couldn't have been finer if he were confectioners' sugar. His suit was charcoal gray, single-breasted, tapered to perfection. The engineers' boots and classic white shirt, no tie, gave the look an edge. And the smell of him—simple soap, leather, something else, that new facet to his essence, something earthy, woodsy, rich. Plus, he'd brought us corsages—Pen's pale yellow and mine so deep a purple it seemed fashioned from a raven's wing. The tipsy trio followed us out, oohing and aahing over the Cutlass, that black leopard of a muscle car. Pen, uncomplaining, got in back; I rode beside Sinclair. Which was nice, I guess, though I wondered if they'd agreed in advance to placate me.

Virtually the entire Swonowa student body turned out for the shindig at the Kendall Wynn Inn (heaven forbid the posh burgs of Swoon, Norris, and Washington hold the affair in the banal environs of the high school gym). Semiformal, males mostly in jackets and ties, females favoring little black dresses. Ironic in white, Pen stood out, as did I, in my slinky green. It appeared that my first high school dance would prove a positive experience. The deejay definitely knew his shit, and the sound system was excellent. Nearly everyone was out on the floor.

"Shall we?" asked Sin, holding our hands, smiling his ravenous smile.

"We shall!" I said definitively. The threesome had been my idea, and I'd play it to the hilt. Pen reached for my hand, gave it a squeeze, shook her shimmering tresses. Electric pulses tingled my palms. Our circle was complete.

Soon as we hit it, the music segued into a track unfamiliar on the surface yet known to all as if by ancient memory. Hypnotic beats, throbbing bass, the vocals a sort of grunted chant interspersed by wails. Dancers responded accordingly, and within minutes there was serious juking going on. The rump-shaking got competitive, everyone trying to out-freak one another. Everyone sort of smoldered together, and it reached the point where you couldn't tell where one person ended and another began. Once Sin, Pen, and I had bumped to the center of the floor, everyone began to orbit around us. No, not around us. To us. To *him*. Part Bacchus, part Balanchine, Sin silently, smilingly stoked his minions. For his pleasure. For ours too. Everybody's. Every body's. I closed my eyes to find I could dig even deeper into the groove.

And someone was kissing my neck.

I arched, to allow easier access.

Someone—someone else?—slid a hand between my thighs.

I twirled, teasing away my prize.

Slitting my eyes, I found various aspects of human anatomy on display at the Kendall Wynn for the first time in the stately inn's history. We were an entity, a thrusting, jerking thing. It was all so gloriously out of control, and I rode the wave, all juice and jump and lovely lady lumps.

Until the screaming started.

It sounded like a flock of gulls following a garbage scow.

Yet remarkably, it all issued out of one person.

Anderly Addams.

Anderly had not worn black to the homecoming dance. She had worn blue, the color of the sky on a sunny day. She wasn't wearing much of it anymore. It had been ripped from her spindly frame, which now staggered through the Kendall Wynn Inn, white bra and cotton briefs exposed. Her updo had come undone, hair-sprayed strands sticking up in tenuous spikes. Her nose was bleeding. In one hand she clutched a swatch of blue taffeta—a scrap from her pretty party dress. And she was screaming.

What she was screaming, over and over, was: "Rape! Rape! Rape! Rape! Rape!"

XXII

THE TATTERED GIRL SOON HAD ACCOMPANIMENT, HER SHRIEKS IN harmony with an ambulance, and as she was whisked off to be swabbed and probed and scraped, every cop in the county seemed to descend on the Kendall Wynn Inn. The media came out in force as well. Sunday papers were to stop their presses for such lurid headlines as Homecoming Orgy Shocks Community, but the local TV news broke the story, training its cameras on Swonowa students. One particularly striking couple appeared in all reports.

"We were having a good time. We had no idea what was going on with that poor girl." Sin was succinct, his expression somber, Pen at his side, her movie-star coif undisturbed. Presumably, I was taking a pee or something when this snippet was shot.

According to Anderly's SAFE kit (that's Sexual Assault Forensic Evidence), there had been no penetration, and seminal fluid was absent. Swoon's poster girl for chastity by choice was proven pure—her dress shredded but her precious maidenhead deemed intact. Yet Anderly would not return to school in the days or weeks that followed. Rumors were rampant. She was catatonic in a mental ward, being force-fed through a tube. She had cited seven Swonowa students (the Swonowa Seven) by name, and they'd be arrested at any moment, her father the judge calling for castration. The whole thing had been a hoax—no one had touched Anderly; she'd spun it to pimp the ideology of Pure Love Covenant.

Everyone had a theory. No one really knew. And as we waited for either charges to be filed or the whole debacle to blow over, each person present at the Kendall Wynn Inn that night had to decide for himself or herself what went down. It took a while for me to render my conclusion. Whatever had happened to Anderly Addams, Sin was the catalyst. He had an effect on people; the boy couldn't help it. Or could he?

The day after the dance, I got my answer.

The wee hours after, Momster and Mally had been waiting up. All they'd wanted were girl-gab details, but once it got super late, worry mode kicked in.

"Oh, Jesus Christ!" My mother bulldozed me on the porch, hugged me so hard it hurt, then held me away from her for inspection. "You're all right!" she pronounced. "I should kill you!" She clenched me to her bosom again.

"Please . . . don't . . ." I begged for my life through the vice grip, and she let up. Inside, the kitchen table was a wreck, with ravaged takeout containers from Manhattan's finest gourmet grocery. "Some kids were juking, and it got out of hand," I explained, toying uselessly with the clasp of my satin evening bag. "One girl claimed she was assaulted, and the cops came, and it was a huge mess."

"Juking—that's dirty dancing," Momster translated for Mally, who lounged bleary among the rubble.

"I know what it is, Lesley. God."

"What about you? Nothing . . . no one tried to . . . ?"

The evening's events were already receding, as though spat on and smeared with a rag. I recited the company line. "I was having a good time. I had no idea what was going on with that poor girl."

Momster scrutinized me further, then gave Mally a look to convey that I was to blame for her Botox habit—a daughter like me *aged* a person. "Let's all go to bed, then," she said.

Great idea. Miraculously I coped with matters of undressing and makeup removal, unpinned my cathedral of hair, and laid my bleeding violet corsage to rest on the bureau. A ball of fluff between my pillows, R.C. readjusted herself when I hit the sheets, cuddling up to my belly. Near dawn, I woke to find her namesake in bed with me instead.

"Hey, baby."

"Ruby?" I squinted in the thin light. The tiara she wore had been pushed off-kilter by the pillow.

"No, Paris Hilton. Who'd you think? God, I am so mad at you right now."

"Why? What'd I do?"

She sat up, squinching the pillow behind her, readjusting her rhinestones. "Because what'd I tell you last time? Call me if you need me. But do you call me? No!"

"I . . ." There was good reason not to call Ruby. "I didn't realize I was in need."

"No," she said. "Of course not. Because of him." She made a face—part disgust, part commiseration, a little amusement thrown in. "Your dirt devil."

"You mean . . . Sinclair?"

"You mean . . . Sinclair?" she imitated. "You are such a dope, Candy."

"I'm not a dope. And call me Dice. Look, I know Sin is . . . trouble."

"Trouble? Baby girl, you don't know the half, no, you don't know the freakin' millimeter what you're dealing with."

"Oh, and you do?" Who died and made her the authority on all things supernatural?

"No. Not really," Ruby conceded. "But I know what he's not. He's not a ghost."

"Clearly. He got his body back." And what a body it was.

I flashed on the way we'd danced with him, Pen and I, and a ripple ran through me, a lascivious aftershock.

"It ever occur to you that that's not the only way he changed?"

Of course it had. Just with all the homecoming hoopla I'd found it possible to backburner that. I tossed in bed, but Ruby was right there, same position, other side.

"Because change is inevitable," she said as though imparting the wisdom of the ages—and then had to illustrate. Her eyes became putrid black holes, the skin puckering and blistering around them. Maggots crawled from the pits with a slithery sound.

"Yeah . . ." Now it was my turn to make a face.

Ruby got regular, except for the larvae trapped between her fingers. Which she promptly ate. "But not all change is good. Like with your boy."

We were quiet for a moment, and she said it again, with emphasis: "*Your* boy."

"You think I'm responsible for him?"

"Aren't you?" When I didn't answer, Ruby sighed. "You're a smart cookie, Candida, you might want to explore this a little. I'm just saying."

She was probably right. Only I was still so tired. I gave her a disintegrating shove and fell back to sleep. Hours later I arose famished and cranky, glowering at Momster for culinary ineptitude. The woman could make three things: coffee, martinis, and reservations. I gave Mally a wounded look as well—she'd helped decimate the goodies they'd brought. I binged on Cocoa Puffs while Momster and I conversed:

Her: Do you want to talk about last night?
Me (crunching): No.
Her: Because Penny and Sinclair were on the news this
    morning.
Me (crunching): How nice for them.
Her: Do you know the girl who got attacked?
Me (crunching): What part of "no" did you not understand?

Is it ever okay to be mean, especially to someone you love? I grappled with that. It distracted me. As did the pore-cleansing mask I applied to my face. And checking out colleges online (although I'd set my sights on Columbia practically since birth). I pouted at my pores, my computer, emerged from my lair to be nice to Momster and Mally. Once they took off for the city, I'd run out of diversions.

It was time to delve the Sin thing.

The place to start was the beginning. As in: "In the beginning . . . ," the Bible's opening line. Which Sin had, after all, cited for me. Procedurally, the way I made Sin compared to how God created Adam, but for two major discrepancies. First, God knew what He was doing. Second, God gave Adam a soul.

My one major omission. Obviously, it hadn't occurred to me (see "bumbling," above), and even if it had, I would've figured his original soul sufficient. In fact, I assumed Sin was making do with his same old soul right now. Since the other possibility— that he had no soul, no soul at all—was unthinkable.

Except I *had* thought it. And couldn't unthink it. So I perused myth and legend for the attributes of soil, yes, soul, no. Lo and behold, such a creature exists—in Kabbalistic folklore, no less. Name? Golem. Purpose? Unpaid manual labor. Help around the house, mind the store, protect members of the tribe from marauding invaders or evangelical inquisitors. Basically, he lives (and I use the term loosely) to serve.

Unless he gets too big for his britches. Then you're in deep shit.

XXIII

WAIT, WAIT, WHOA. INHALE. EXHALE. OKAY. FIRST THINGS FIRST. To test the validity of my research, I channeled my inner bitch and summoned my servant. It was not a request. I dispensed with politesse, such as "please." Rather, I sat on the porch and deliberately directed brain beams: *Sin, get your ass over here—stat.* I made it a mantra, compelling the gutsy rumble of the Cutlass up Daisy Lane. So I was sort of rattled when Sin took the driveway at full gallop astride a snorting Black Jack. He dismounted, tied reins to porch rail, leapt the stairs, and stared me down with bewildered obedience.

"My lady?"

"What up with the horse?"

"I—you—Kurt has the car," he managed finally.

"Oh." The corners of my lips twitched. "You didn't have to rush."

"Didn't I?" Since of course he did.

I got to the point. "I know what you are, Sin. You're a golem. It's a Jewish thing, but evidently you're the Native American version." He voiced no objection, so I went on. "According to the literature, a golem is required to do the bidding of the person who creates him."

His next words spouted like a hiccup: "Your order is my honor."

This was interesting. Very Aladdin. R.C. collected her nerve to check out Black Jack while I assessed a big dark animal of my own. "How about a lap dance?"

Sin had to process that. Then he made a face that said: *Come on.* I gazed at him impassively. So he began to swivel his hips . . .

I cracked, of course. "Oh, cut it out." He looked relieved. "Sit down." I tilted my chin toward a chair. He sat. "So, not only did you con me into creating you, you also forgot to tell me that your entire raison d'être is to be my personal assistant."

"It's true," he said. "I can deny you nothing."

"Well then, here's my first official command: Never lie to me."

He grew petulant. "I never have," he insisted. "There are rules to our relationship, and that's one of them."

"Rules, huh? Good to know. So how about you bring me up to speed and tell me what, exactly, you're capable of. Leaping tall buildings in a single bound? Invisibility on demand? X-ray vision?"

"I know not until I try. Do you need a tall building leapt?" He regarded the roof. "A silo, perhaps?"

I didn't reply.

"I believe it's more subtle than the slapstick attributes you mention," he went on. "As far as I'm able to ascertain, I have the same skills I had as a man, only heightened. As a man, I was intuitive. Now, X-ray vision, no—but I sense, dear lady, I *sense*."

Could he sense I was holding down the Fort Knox of fear?

"Furthermore, I was once considered charismatic; now I am exceedingly so."

Could this porch sustain the two of us plus Sin's burgeoning ego?

"Invisibility may elude me," he continued, "but I can convince someone he cannot see me, which is surely as good."

He ran a contemplative hand across his chin. Stubble grew there, and I had the urge to touch it, find out if it felt like moss.

"And . . . what else. Oh, yes. Permit me a demonstration?"

I bid him go on with a wave. Sin removed a flowerpot from a nearby plant stand, hefted the pedestal. "As a man, I worked dawn to dusk forging in fire. I was strong." He snapped the legs off and began bending them like a party clown makes balloon animals. "Now I'm stronger." Ta-da—a wrought-iron bunny rabbit.

He returned to his seat, and we watched each other levelly. Meanwhile, Black Jack craned his great span of neck to where RubyCat stood her ground. Snout to snout, they sniffed. The horse I'd once seen menace his master turned meek in the face of a pint-sized kitten. And the boy so adept at clouding his eyes no longer sought to do so. I looked in them and saw . . . so much. Intelligence. Intensity. Humor. Hunger. Anger. Honor. Pride. Yet so much was missing, too.

"Okay . . . moving on," I said. "Chances are you've got a leg up on the garden-variety golem." Sin was a mutant—his own brainstorm but my brilliant, inescapable mistake. "This makes me doubt that your main objective is to be my valet. That's more like a downside you've got to contend with. So pray tell, Sin, what brings you to Swoon—specifically?"

He had no alternative but to answer. "It is my mission to ensure that the people of this town have their comeuppance. As to my means, it ought be easy: I'll simply point them toward their inherent proclivities and let nature take its course."

Uh-huh. Wind 'em up and watch 'em go destroy 'emselves. Only if revenge is a dish best served cold, Sin's would have serious freezer burn. I almost laughed. "Look, dude, I know you got a very raw deal around here, but that was practically two hundred and fifty years ago," I said. "Remember? Hello, twenty-first century?"

"I cannot see what difference the passage of time makes," he said stubbornly.

"Let me break it down for you, then: The people you want to extract justice from are stone-cold dead."

He shook his head dismissively. "I may never know who murdered my Hannah, but I do know who persecuted us, and their families still hold much sway in Swoon."

As he said this, I recalled the oath he swore that certain summer's day in the village green. "Warn your children's children's children . . ." Oh, damn.

"The Addamses, for instance. An Addams was the judge at my travesty of a trial. How royally it must suck to be his descendant at present, with a precious daughter publicly humiliated and now unable to do anything beyond gibber and drool . . ."

So Sin *had* orchestrated what went down at the dance. And the catatonia theory won.

"And then there are the Emersons and the Chadwicks."

Wick, no! She was an elitist snob, true, but she was my friend.

"And lest we forget the Leonards."

That did it. "Sin! The Leonards had nothing to do with what happened to Hannah and you."

"I beg to differ. My lawyer was a Leonard, the case he presented grossly inadequate. Pen's father is a lawyer, is he not?"

"That's just a coincidence."

"Perhaps; perhaps not. But I have a Leonard at my disposal now who'll prove far more useful than her forebear."

"You mean Pen."

He extended his legs full length, with each boot heel a

distinct thud. "I've awakened Pen in a way that suits my purposes. And soon my sweet, insatiable succubus will seduce one Mr. Lawrence Chadwick, Western Connecticut's most prominent realtor. Word of their illicit liaison ought demolish the Chadwicks handily."

Wick's dad? In a word: *blech*! He was old, and wore Dockers. Pen wouldn't . . . she couldn't. But of course she could, would. Why, Sin was no better than a pimp!

"The wheels are already in motion. Pen won't get much rest at Caroline Chadwick's upcoming sleepover, I assure you."

Wick, having a sleepover? What were we, twelve? And where was my invitation, lost in the mail? "No, Sin. I . . . I forbid it."

"Ah, but you have no dominion over Pen, my lady."

"But you do. She'll do anything for you. "

Sin shrugged. "I think you'll discover limitations to your dominion over me, as well. No garden-variety golem, indeed."

I glanced away. Already he'd built up resistance to my sway and was recruiting soldiers: Pen in place, Kurt Libo surely; who else had he tagged? The moon had waned to a crescent; it lay against the sky like a slim blade in a velvet box. "What about me?" I asked him. "How do I figure into your plans?"

There was something akin to kindness in his gaze. "Ah, Dice, now that is the question." He ruminated on it with a weighty sigh. "May I tell you my dream?"

I would've thought a soul prerequisite for dreaming, but clearly I was a nincompoop. "Go ahead," I said.

"Well, to preface: The way we are entwined, we two—I believe that is providence. That day in July, Pen was a handy vessel, but it could have been anyone. Kurt Libo. Ms. Evans." The thought of Sin moving into our history teacher, all five-feet-zip, almost made me smile. "But you were—you *are*—my destiny. It didn't matter whose body I entered, as long as you were around to deliver me."

Deliver him. So I was FedEx now.

"You know I have long admired you, and not the least for those abilities you abjure. I see you as my equal, Dice—my match, the way no woman has ever been."

"Oh, really?" I said quietly. And asked what begged. "What about Hannah?"

"Hannah." Sorrow and resignation softened his features. "Hannah was different. *I* was different." Internally he inventoried the many, many ways. "Hannah was . . . immature, frivolously impulsive. Whereas you, I've never known a girl so . . . competent."

Competent? Great. Well, what had I wanted to hear?

"And at times I dally in the notion of you and I united. First, in bringing this town to ruin. After which . . . who knows? You could show me New York, your New York. Or we could go to London, or Paris, or Constantinople—"

"Istanbul."

"It's *not* bull; I mean it." His eyes were adamant.

"No. Istanbul. Constantinople is called Istanbul now."

Sin smiled. "Ah. But you see? The ways we could enrich each other? The things we might share, the worlds to conquer. We'd know no borders, no limits . . ."

It was a lovely dream. Fraught with hubris and inhumanity, maybe, a cutthroat, mendacious sprawl of a dream. But lovely, so lovely, and tempting nonetheless.

XXIV

HAVING REDUCED THE RULING CLASS OF SWOON TO RUBBLE AND freed the citizenry to revel in simple rites of joyous abandon, SinMan Superstar and Diva DiceTruction retreat to their tree-house fortress on high in the wild, wild woods.

"Looks good," says she, sipping from a victory goblet. In the clover-laden valley below, mortals scamper with the innocent glee usually seen only among furrier animals.

"Looks great," counters he, taking her crystal cup in order to fully embrace her. "Inspiring," he adds, his voice a flooded growl, drawing her up for a kiss.

Which she returns with equal ardor. But before their kiss proves a gateway drug, she arches away. "Hold up, my love," she says, a Euphrates of black curls roiling across the crest of her scalloped bodice. "This is but one battle won. In a nation of hypocrite moralists, many more walls must fall before we two can cop a cuddle."

Releasing her by feint and then snatching her up anew, he reluctantly agrees. "True—yet to think I once needed to cajole you into accepting the mission, dear lady!"

"Cajole? More like bully—"

He clinches tighter . . .

"Strong arm tactics!"

She struggles . . .

"Torture! Torture! Torture!"

No cause for alarm—it is how they play, beings such as this.

SinMan Superstar. Diva DiceTruction. Just a couple of avatars I devised for my amusement as I stood roadside, thumb extended. I should've worn a sweater under my hoodie. Mittens, maybe. Pedaling to Norris, I hadn't noticed the nip, but after ditching my bike to take up position a few miles from the highway, I could feel the north wind.

Where was I going? No clue; I just had to get out of Swoon. Hitchhiking was new to me—it sure as hell wasn't hailing a cab—but in due course a car pulled over, snapping foliage. Sedate maroon sedan, Connecticut license plate JSS1015. I memorized this, lest I be found later in a gully, half alive. White male, grandpa type, mottled hands, wedding band, taupe raincoat with sparse hair to match. He looked harmless—whatever that means. I got in.

"I won't give you a lecture," he said, lowering the stereo a notch.

"I appreciate that." I liked him already.

"I suppose you're headed to the station in Brewster."

Was he telepathic? Doubtful. Any teenager hitching out of the boonies must hope to hop the next train to New York. "Yes, sir," I realized. "I am."

Nodding, he turned up his music again. Classical—cool with me. Minutes later we hit the highway, my taciturn chauffeur zooming for the HOV lane. Maybe that was his purpose in taking on a passenger. Or maybe he was my personal Hermes, god of speed and deliverance. Either way, I lucked out.

The next train to the real world came through soon enough. Nose in Flannery O'Connor, I rode the Harlem Line to 125th, then changed for the subway. Downtown a few stops would bring me home. Only, oddly, I went uptown. Way uptown—the Kingsbridge section of the Bronx. Hardly part of "my" New York, the New York Sin would have me show him. I'd only been there once, a few days after I turned sixteen. Ruby had given me a tarot deck for my birthday but insisted it be officially blessed before use. Her Tía Anaisa was the woman for the job.

Technically, Kingsbridge hadn't been Ruby's turf since her mother's marital upgrade, but she'd still claimed stomping rights. Without her, I was rudderless. Boys bounced by in puffy jackets, whispering offers for cell phones, cigarettes, gold chains. Girls my age trundled along with baby strollers, dreamy one second, fiercely attentive the next. There were bars, bodegas, and botanicas, numerous hair salons and ninety-nine-cent stores stocked for Halloween. A white stone church on one corner. Narrow restaurants and bakeries flaunting Latin and Caribbean flavors beckoned—I'd left Swoon an hour before school to sneak out under the radar, but it was lunchtime by then. It had been eons since I'd had a beef patty—I craved one now. As I bit the crumbly yellow crust and spicy sweet meat oozed into my mouth, I once again felt on a path.

Feet and faith led me off the main drag onto residential streets that cut in and out in a Pythagorean pattern. The apartment buildings were grave, gray towers with trash cans in the courtyards and pigeons on the cornices. On a span of telephone wire a dozen pairs of sneakers dangled, tied at the laces and lofted by kids—a popular urban sport. Up and down I wandered till I felt Ruby so hard she might as well have punched me. Lo and behold—the residence of Tía Anaisa.

"Candy, yo." The boy who answered my buzz was unfazed at the sight of me. Ruby's cousin Alexis, he'd dropped out of high school junior year and still lived, to Ruby's eye-rolling dismay, with his *mami*. Damn if he wasn't cute, though, with his scant mustache and run-amok afro. He'd come down to hang with us sometimes—I'd even debated exploring his mouth with mine—but it had been a while. "What up?"

"Not too much. How are you?"

"All right, all right." His lanky frame angled across the doorway.

"I came to see your mother." I didn't say why. I didn't know why.

"Yeah? Not me?" He was obliged to work it.

"Oh, Lexi." Thrusting my hip, tipping my head, I worked it back. "You're a what-you-call-it, a perk. A bonus."

He liked that. "Yeah? I could show you my bonus."

I was done. "Mm-hmm, I bet. You going to let me in or what?"

Lexi shrugged with effort. "She's busy right now, but you can wait."

I followed him at a distance to imply I had no interest in catching up with his sorry ass. The apartment was vast—rambling, drafty, high-ceilinged. Tía Anaisa ruled this roost, using the front rooms to conduct business. Spiritualism. Her own special brand, an open-minded olio of Santeria, Wicca, Thelemic Law, et al. She was no joke, no charlatan. Extreme psychic. I could tell, in that "takes one to know one" way.

I lingered in what I'll call reception. A pair of couches, histrionic telenovela on the tube, magazines on a scarred coffee table. Incense burned, yet under it stank the anxious sweat of woe and trepidation: Will my lover betray me, will my child survive, will my money hold out. It was almost too much to bear, but when the revered *curandera* appeared, trailed by a crusty in a tracksuit—a client, I presumed—the space lifted and lightened.

However you envision a spiritualist, I doubt it would be her. Forget gypsy skirts and bandannas, forget the bright-colored island gear, forget yards of diaphanous fabric. More like skinny jeans, oval-toed pumps, and an aubergine turtleneck, the simple outfit serving as backdrop for bangles, crystals, crosses, and a pair of hoop earrings with the circumference of saucers. Her mahogany hair was cut in a blunt bob, and she wore glasses with rectangular Lucite frames. The look was more artsy-chic gallery denizen than Dominican-born, Bronx-based shaman, but her figure— curvaceous, regal, some might say imposing—was one indication that she'd take no mess, be it on the mortal plane or the astral one. And her essence, that of a queen and a sprite and a siren.

"Ah, Candida!" The hug she administered made me feel like a cherished niece instead of some girl she'd met exactly once. "Connecticut agrees with you," she said upon inspection. "Only why am I picturing you in Las Vegas?"

I pondered that briefly, then chuckled. "Probably because up there, everyone calls me Dice."

"Hmm. So, Candida, you see much of Ruby?" Like Ruby, she would call me what she pleased.

"Oh . . . some." At last I could admit to the uninvited visitations.

"Well, she comes around here constantly with chocolates

and wine, and I am all, 'No, no, baby, your tía's got enough junk in her trunk!'" Anaisa smiled. It was one of Ruby's smiles, the goofy, gummy one.

"Anaisa, I need a reading." So that's what I'd come here for. Laying the cards for yourself is futile—you just can't be objective. "I mean," I said, "if you're not booked."

She patted my arm and went to see out the geezer in shabby Sean John. Then she led me into the shaded chamber where she plies her craft. Votives cast flickering light, making shadows of statuaries dance against the walls. We sat at a round table, and Anaisa brought forth the carved wooden box that held her deck.

"Will you tell me what you want to know?" she asked. It can help when the reader knows your question, but it's not mandatory—some people prefer secrecy.

"I would," I said, "but here's the thing: So much has been going on, I don't even know what to ask." Frustration surfed my sigh.

"That's all right," Anaisa reassured and handed me the deck. "Let's just see what the cards have to tell us."

Classic Rider-Waite worn to a powdery finish, her cards bore the hopes and fears of countless inquiries. I shuffled, I cut, and as Anaisa began to arrange them, just perceptibly chanting the positions of the Celtic cross, we both grew amazed. Not a weepy three of cups or painful nine of swords in the bunch. Every card was major arcana.

"This is . . . significant," Anaisa allowed.

"Like I said, a lot's been going on."

The *curandera* sat up tall, pushed at the bridge of her glasses, and steepled her fingers. "Well, all right." She surveyed the spread. "There is a boy . . ."

Isn't there always?

"And a girl . . . and tsk-tsk, *chica,* you have the whole world on your shoulders."

Nah, not the whole world. Just the whole town.

"Now, this boy, he's something else." She inhaled deeply as if to absorb him. "Very sensitive. Very intense."

There he lay in all his cardboard glory, the Hanged Man. Representing rebirth, sacrifice, and staunch devotion to a cause. Sin in a nutshell. Intense? The seer was about to discover how on target she was.

"But I must warn you—*oh!*" Anaisa sprang as if goosed. "Excuse me." She tugged her turtleneck as a flush pinked her cheeks. "Where were we? Oh, yes, this boy . . . *eee!*" A smile tried to infiltrate, and as she fought to keep it at bay, it blossomed into a pout. "*Ay, Dios mío!* Candida, I apologize . . . I seem to be—" At which point she dipped her head, tulip petals of bob enfolding her face, and threw it back, glasses askew.

Man, just when you thought it was safe to go back to the Bronx. Evidently, Sin was not to be bound by Connecticut's borders. He was here, having his invisible way with the woman as I sat transfixed. It was a peep show. It was a train wreck. Had he interrupted so Anaisa couldn't caution me? Or was he just showing off, flexing his muscles, proving himself ahead of my game, no matter that I was across state lines, in a grave, gray sanctum, under the protection of what I'd believed to be a one-woman SWAT team of spiritual reckoning. Yeah, right. Anaisa had been reduced to a puppet, squirming and spouting, "Oh my God" in Spanish. Toes pointed in their pumps. An orchestra of jewelry jangled. Perfume reached its zenith. Finally Anaisa went rigid from head to foot for a few endless seconds before slumping, spent, in her chair. Delicately, she righted her Lucite frames.

"Candida, excuse me a moment?" Her voice was kitten fluff and far away.

"Sure, of course." I was embarrassed for both of us. "Take your time." After her hasty exit in the afterglow, I glared at the emptiness around me. "You know what, Sin, you can be a real dick sometimes." I said it aloud, whether he was still there or already gone. Then I appraised the spread before me. All those pretty pictures. All those portentous interpretations. The Moon. The Devil. The Tower. Damn, couldn't the Sun make an appearance? Or the Lovers would be nice. Still, a chief axiom of tarot is: The future is molded in warm wax. You can affect your own fate. You can be a force for change. You can alter events with action. Why dabble in divination if there isn't that chance?

XXV

LEAVE TOWN ON ANY GIVEN WEDNESDAY, AND YOU CAN MISS A LOT.
So bespoke the messages on the old-school answering machine
at 12 Daisy Lane.

From Pen: "Dice? Good dish—well, terrible, actually. Boz
cheated on Wick. What a tool. So of course she's a basket case.
I feel *so* bad for her. Anyway, are you coming for dinner? Mom's
chicken and dumplings, not to be missed."

From Marsh: "Dice, I have to talk to you. You won't believe
it in a million years, but the Williamses are back in town, and
I'm dying—Crane Williams asked me out! Sort of. I am so hot
for him. Oh, did you hear about Wick? So sad! Why weren't
you in school today? Call me!"

From Wick: "Dice? Wick. I don't know if you've heard or
not but it's true: I broke up with Boz, and I really need support from my friends right now. So I'm having a girls' night

in on Saturday, and I hope you can come. BYOPJs."

Pen, redux: "Hey, Wick's going to call you. She's having a slumber party like we're twelve or something, and you have to say yes because I did. What are friends for, right? And listen, where are you? You better not be sick or anything—I've got to take the boys to the corn maze after school tomorrow, and I'm making you come along."

Corn maze? Mm-hmm. Corn maze. Any farmer with a few extra acres and access to GPS technology can turn a tidy profit transforming his cornfield into a labyrinth. The Corny Conundrum, this one's called, on the Gladney Farm off Heritage Pike. Halloween marks the season finale for the maze, and the Gladneys hoped to gross all they could, with a pumpkin patch and a pony trail and a sweetshop selling pie and preserves.

"And we're here because . . . ?"

"Don't be so negative, you New York snob," Pen scolded. "So it's not the MoMA filled with Picassos—it's fun."

She pronounced the modern art museum's acronym "moo-ma" and added an extraneous "the"—errors I didn't point out. Fun? Whoo-hoo! I could use some. Pen fastened the boys' jackets and had Jordan blow into one of Lainie's freshly laundered hankies. With their corn-colored heads together, they plotted in whispers, then broke the huddle to chase me through the maze. Growing up on a uniform grid of streets left me with a nonexistent sense of direction—I was completely disoriented in thirty seconds flat.

The first thing to strike me as strange was the absence of other people—judging by the packed parking lot, I should've been bumping into half the county. Then the silence, which wasn't silence but the white noise of steadily rustling stalks. Despite the lack of audible footfalls, I knew the Leonards were on this lab rat's tail. Still, it *was* fun to run, just run, leaves brushing against me with a saturated sunny smell.

After a while, the row widened, and I thought I'd found an exit. Only, no . . . what the? . . . Crap! I'd blundered into some kind of corny—literally—jail cell. Hoots and giggles as Jordan and Silas slammed the gate.

"You're in jail, Dice! Ha, ha! You're in jail!" shrieked Jordan.

"Yeah, you're our prisoner. You have to stay in there forever till you rot and die and the worms eat you." Clearly, Silas had entered a morbid phase.

Playing along, I grabbed the bars of this hokey pokey. "Oh, please, please let me out! I'm innocent!"

By then Pen had approached to lead her brothers in a squeaky round of "the worms crawl in, the worms crawl out." Soon as the worms were spitting guts, my jailers were joined by the warden.

"Exactly what atrocities has this dusky maid committed?"

Sin demanded, brow furrowed and arms akimbo. "State her crimes for the record."

The boys went nuts at the sight of him, jumping and jabbering. Predictably, my internal thermostat cranked up of its own accord.

"Dice is bad, Sin! She's really, really bad!" Jordan sold me out. "She didn't put her toys away and then she made juice come out her nose!"

"And then you know what? You know what?" Silas wracked his brain for heinous behavior. "Then she laid a fart! A really loud, stinky one! And she didn't say excuse me."

Sin shook his head. "Disgraceful!" he said, as I burned beneath his stare, and hated myself for burning, and hated him for making me burn, and loving him for it, too, which is the most hackneyed way to describe the feeling, but that's how it was.

"Ooh, if you think that's bad . . ." Pen had found a way to usurp her siblings and attach herself to Sin. "That nasty girl in there has confessed to me some of the things she dreams of doing . . . and they're so dirty I can't say them out loud." Getting on tiptoe, she leaned into Sin's ear.

"What?! What?!" clamored the boys.

"Never you mind, lads," Sin said. "What's important is her punishment. Do you think a good spanking will do it?"

The Leonards roared approval as they stormed the Bastille,

cornering me against the stalks. Then Sin got me by the wrists, his fingers flesh-sheathed manacles.

"Bad girl, Dice," he said, all apple breath and brilliant teeth, swinging me around as if I had all the heft of a scarecrow.

Onlookers had shown up to gawk, and I flashed on the Roman Colosseum, the sort of entertainments presented there. Humiliating . . . so why was I was laughing? Gasping and gulping at air and hungering for another whiff of that boy's crisp breath. I loved and hated it all, the gasping and gulping and struggling, the laughter and even—especially—the fear.

"We should pull her pants down," Pen suggested with something like a snarl.

And the boys went "Whooooo!" as a unit.

"You wouldn't dare!" I yelped and twisted and laughed.

"This wicked maid? I'd wager that's just what she wants," Sin said as he toyed with me, holding both wrists with one hand and using his other arm to fold me at the waist. He dropped to one knee, hauled me over on his half a lap.

And I heard Sin say, "Go to it, lads!"

Silas and Jonas followed orders—slaps and smacks and then hard little fists. All I could do was take it, with exaggerated cries of "ouch!" and "please, stop!" like a good sport. Until Sin said what I'd been hoping and dreading he might.

"All right, my turn!"

The childish game was over.

Up went a chant: "Get her! Get her!"

There was a pause, my chance to scramble and flee or to ask—nay, command—that Sin desist (whose golem was he, anyway?). But I did neither. And the flat of his palm came down. Again and again. Sharp and blistering. As every whack resounded, I felt the heave of his exertions, making it impossible to tell where I left off and he began. It was physically surreal—how clenched I was yet how relaxed, how present in my body yet part of his. Each spank brought another firecracker explosion inside me until the final firecracker, more like a bomb, releasing and suspending me with a dopamine surge the likes of which my prefrontal cortex had never known before.

I do believe I emitted a squeal.

Sin knew just when to stop. Since I could feel what he was feeling, it made symbiotic sense that he experienced my every sensation as well. So I slid to the ground, throwing my mad, tangled tresses behind me. Sin had both knees in the dirt now, perched on his heels. His face, so close to mine, was placid, but he didn't bother masking the mischief in his eyes.

"Are you all right?" he asked.

All right? My hair had to look like Helen Keller styled it, and I tasted salt (I must've bit myself), and my ass cheeks blazed, and I was radiating a post-orgasmic beacon bright enough to land planes at JFK, but sure, "all right" was a fair assessment.

"Yeah," I said, and licked the blood off my lip.

XXVI

RUSTIC AUTUMN RITUALS WERE TO CONTINUE. THE VERY NEXT NIGHT, in fact, would bring us back to Gladney Farm for a hayride. My first. Marsh, naturally, had been on such excursions before, but on this one she'd be nestled next to Crane Williams—their first date, her first date, period. Although depending on your definition of "date," it was or it wasn't. Crane wouldn't call for her at the Marshall home or meet the Marshall parent-in-residence. But coordinating to be at the same place at the same time was the outcome of the dialogue between Crane and Marsh at Letters Unlimited, the chi-chi stationery shop in Swoon's town center—her gig since the Kustard Kup closed for the season.

"What was he doing there, anyway?" Marsh and I were in my room, me dusting her eyelids with shimmer. "The boy felt a sudden urge for prissy writing paper? I think not. I think he saw you in the window and was spellbound by your beauty."

Like the rest of her, Marsh's ego was underfed—my take on the encounter made her beam. "Actually, he was with Sin Powers, who bought a stick of sealing wax. Ooh, Dice, give me those smoky eyes like in all the magazines."

Dramatic maquillage couldn't possibly jibe with the dress code for a hayride, but what did I know? Doing Marsh's makeup was a welcome reprieve—my mental energy otherwise monopolized by what had gone down in the corn maze. What Sin had done, how I'd succumbed—it was mortifying, amazing, the best and the worst at once. Next on *Oprah:* Dominance, Submission and the Teens Who Love It!

Now I could focus entirely on Marsh's situation. Her grandmother had moved in to help (read: keep Psycho Dad in line) while Marsh worked her butt off between the stables, the stationer's, and school. If anyone deserved a little romance, it was her.

"You'll have to curl your own lashes. See? Like this." I demoed, then handed off the medieval device. "Try not to pull your eyelids off."

Tentatively, Marsh secured her cilia. Two coats of mascara later, all Lancôme and cheekbones, she could pass for one of those fledgling models you see gliding through Manhattan. When Crane spotted her among the crowd at Gladney Farm, he strode up and took her hand, and I thought she'd turn into a flock of doves and fly away. I knew that feeling—that fluttery, breathless feeling. Grinning, I said hey to Crane's brother Duck, who launched into a travelogue of his family's recent trip to Guatemala.

"Our mother's helped build a hospital there—literally, with her own two lily-white hands. Such a do-gooder, Mum is. Whilst I preferred to lounge around Lago de Atitlán. Utterly gorgeous—the deepest lake in that part of the planet."

Pen strolled over around then, representing with fellow cheerleaders Doll Turner and El (Eleanor) Daley, plus El's twin sister Em (Emma), whom I knew from chorale. It was cold enough for our breath to appear in puffs, like we were smoking, and before long we *were* smoking, a pungent spliff going around, and a bottle of something strong and sweet as well. As I got my glow on, I realized that I pretty much knew and pretty much liked all these people. I'd been living in Swoon about six months, and these were my friends, maybe not my best friends, but they were all right.

I even got a little misty over the conspicuous absence of Wick and Boz. What a shame to be licking wounds on a night like this—brisk, beautiful, sonically heightened by sleigh bells as two wagons drew up. A stout man in overalls helped preceding hayriders disembark, then clapped in our direction.

"All right, kids!" he called. "No dillydallying."

Just as we began to load in, I heard a familiar, "Whoa!"

"Better late than never, dude," someone said.

"Heyyyy!" said someone else.

A quick flick over my shoulder confirmed who led the late-comers. There was Sin, with Con Emerson and some guys who may have been on the football team, or the hockey team, or both. I had to give him credit—tonight he rolled with a jock contingent, but yesterday it was two guys with fitted shirts and carefully mussed hair—as close as Swoon got to art geeks. Not only did Sin have a variety of retinues, he was always himself. Stuck to his basic tee-jeans-boots ensemble (now topped by a gray hoodie). Spoke in his hallmark modern-meets-archaic ver-nacular. Yet whatever company he kept, it was always he at the center, everyone gravitating to and then radiating from him.

Pen and her girls made a beeline for the laggards, funneling with them into one of the wagons, while Duck and I trailed Marsh and Crane into the other. Crane had a beat-up guitar with him, and I decided the music wagon was the one to ride in anyway.

"Hay, huh?" I said dubiously to Duck.

"Yes, well, it shouldn't be too bad. Unless it's infested with mites or lice or what have you."

Just what I wanted to hear as I plunked ass first onto the nearest bale.

"Ah, it's lovely!" Duck settled beside me in the pliant com-fort of dried grass.

"Like a beanbag chair," I agreed. "Except no beans . . . or bag."

With a rattle of reins, we were off. Duck was an indefatigable conversationalist, but at least he wasn't boring. I could comment on his prattle while stealing glances at Marsh and Crane, shy and crush-struck and cute. Lacking his brother's gift for gab, Crane went for his guitar—an old Martin, among the finest acoustic instruments made. The boy knew lots of tunes, and a sing-along rapidly ensued.

"Isn't he awesome?" Marsh whispered, and squeezed my arm.

"Totally!" I enthused, and squeezed back.

I was buzzed and in the moment. I'd stay that way till, oh, about the second verse of a Beatles classic. That's when the wagon ahead of ours veered toward the right of the path and I saw Sin, on his feet amid the hay, beckoning the horses pulling our wagon with clicks and clucks of equine-only comprehension. Neither driver seemed to care. It wouldn't occur to man or beast to hinder the whim of Sinclair Youngblood Powers.

When the wagons were side by side, Con Emerson—linebacker, loudmouth, all-around blowhard—stood up, wobbling awkwardly.

"Go on, man," Sin said. "Go!" He gave Con a little shove.

"I'm going, I'm going," said Con, and with a shout of "Banzai!" cannonballed from one rolling wagon to the other, while kids shouted and jeered.

"There's not enough room, you 'roid raging moron," came a grumble.

"Get bent, asshole," said Con, crawling around clumsily.

"Oh, it's all right, we'll find space." This from the affable Duck, who squinched closer to me, and Con forced his way in. Both big guys, they made it a tight fit all around.

"*You* get bent." A lacrosse player with inherent disdain for football players got up, maneuvered to the side of the wagon, and jumped into the other.

It was on. Extreme hay diving, soon to be huge on ESPN. Not everyone took part, just basically a few jocks. Though throughout the contest Sin remained standing—coaching, refereeing, running the show. Which meant the reshuffling wasn't random; he'd instigated it for a reason. I pondered that reason as Duck transferred his interest to Con. Then Sin, apparently pleased with the new seating arrangements, leapt to the rim of his wagon. He balanced with the poise of an acrobat, lingering to illustrate how easy this was. Finally, he stepped off.

"Beg pardon, ladies, is this seat taken?" One big black boot after the other, he lowered himself between Marsh and me like a king to his throne.

I stared ahead and hugged my knees. Then I looked at him. And felt . . . the litany.

"Cozy, isn't it?" Sin said, asymmetrical smirk in place.

"Yeah," I said. "Quite."

One wagon pulled ahead; the other followed. Sin leaned left to exchange a handshake with Duck, then right to salute

Crane. "I believe this was to be a music cruise," he said.

"Yes. Well. All right." Crane reached behind to where he'd found relatively safe harbor for the Martin during the athletic portion of the evening's amusements.

Sin shifted his hips, his thigh pressing mine, so he could go into his jeans' pocket. "Check it out," he said, withdrawing a shiny, rectangular object. "We can jam."

Okay, I looked this up online later: The harmonica hadn't even been invented till 1821. Sin not only had one, he could play it. I'm not talking "Frère Jacques," either. Sin could play the blues. As for me? I could sing the blues. My father's favorite genre, I was weaned on the stuff. And it's not like I was trying to compete with Sin or anything, but when Crane went into a number I instantly recognized, I couldn't resist. Lifting my chin, I sang to the sky, and when I was done, people wanted more.

So what the hell. With the moon as my spotlight, I sang. From a fountain of sad and a sea of confusion and a full-on Niagara Falls of inarticulate emotions, I sang. And everyone was feeling me. Because the blues I sang were love blues, deep, sick, simple songs of longing and losing, bending over backward and being made the fool. When I'd run through my repertoire—my Billie Holiday, my Bessie Smith—and they still wanted more, I did what any blues diva would do. I improvised.

"Give me a twelve-bar in D," I told Crane, snapping the

beat with my fingers. No big deal to take the standard theme of love gone bad and put my stamp on it. Like this:

> *"You throw the dice, baby, you just throwing me away.*
> *Yeah, you throw the dice, baby, nothing I can do or say.*
> *You worry and mistreat me, every night and every day.*
> *There's an aching in my head, boy, there's a riot in my*
> *   heart,*
> *There's a story that needs telling but I don't know where*
> *   to start*
> *Because I love you, baby, and all you do is throw me*
> *   down.*
> *You been running me ragged ever since you came to*
> *   town."*

I sang for everyone who'd ever been screwed over and dragged under and messed up by love. And I sang to everyone who'd ever done the screwing and the dragging and the messing. And I sang to and for everyone who'd some day be on one side or the other, probably both. In other words, the whole wide world.

> *"You throw the dice, baby, because you're a gambling*
> *   man.*
> *You throw the dice, baby, because you're a rambling*
> *   man.*
> *You throw the dice, baby, just because you know you can.*

There's a needle in my skin, a machine gun in
    my soul,
You went and pulled the trigger—now I'm all full
    of holes
Because I love you so much, baby, but all you do is
    do me wrong.
You throw the dice, baby—all I can do is sing this song."

Only let's be honest: I sang for *me*. The lyrics came easy, as if already scribed on the tablature of my subconscious. I went from sitting in my bale of hay to standing astride it. I sang with my arms thrown open and my eyes half closed. I sang from my belly, from my intricate system of female parts, and from those sacs inside me that wouldn't show up on an ultrasound but held all the rocks and stones and broken glass of want and need I'd managed to collect in seventeen years.

"You throw the dice, baby, and the boys all yell and
    scream.
You throw the dice, baby, and the girls all spill like
    cream.
It's a nightmare for me, baby—I can't wake up from
    this dream.
There's not a woman in this place who doesn't know
    your name,
Who doesn't know your number—oh, but they don't
    know your game.

Only I know it, baby, I know what you're all about,
And if the knowing doesn't kill me one day I'm going
to lay it out."

All at once, in singing, I found my strength, my mojo. Blues music *is* strength, that's why it was invented. The blues is alchemy—a golden hammer of might forged from the mean ore of sucky situations. So then my eyes went bold and my finger was wagging. Around me, girls and boys were "whooing" and "hooing," those loud, primordial sounds of understanding and agreement. They were with me, listening now not because I could sing, but because I could testify.

"You throw the dice, baby, you throw it like my love
is free.
You throw the dice, baby, you want to make a fool of me.
You throw the dice, baby, and that's a tragedy.
It's all about you, baby, you're living like a king.
A hundred girls think you're the world, but that
don't mean a thing
Because I made you, baby, so you better just think twice.
Keep on playing me like you play me, you're going to
have to pay the price.
Oh, you better watch it, baby, you don't want to
throw this dice."

That was it—I was done. And they all clapped and said nice things, and I said thank you and sat back down on my bale of hay. Which is when Sin leaned in to me like I was his birthday cake, candles lit, frosting just a blow and lick away.

"Oh, my drowsy thrush," he said, his voice molten. "You slay me."

The heat of his words on the heat of his breath were treasure. Still, I thought, *no,* as I leaned away to look at him evenly. *Not quite. Not yet.*

XXVII

"So what's the deal with you and Sin Powers?"

Marsh was asking. I was checking my look in the ladies' room of the Yankee Diner. Various responses came to mind. Such as, "Deal? What deal? There is no deal." Or, "Oh, he's hot but kind of a jerk, don't you think?" Or simply, "I don't know." All reasonable. All rejected.

Rather, what popped out was, "I'm in love with him." Remarkable, how easy it was, how good it felt. Because it was true. Impossible, ludicrous, insane, maybe. True, true, true.

"You—*what*? Shut up!"

Clearly, not what Marsh expected, and she got so excited she knocked me into the towel dispenser. It's pretty small, the ladies' room in the Yankee Diner.

"I'm in love with him." This time I said it deliberately, and it felt even better.

"What do you mean, you're in love with him?" Marsh grabbed both my arms with both her hands while jumping in place. "I didn't know you were even going out with him. *Are* you going out with him? Or is it just a crush? For a while there I thought he was with Pen, but I guess that's over. Does he know you're in love with him? Oh, God, is he in love with you too?"

How cute was she, burbling like that, my typically plaintive, pessimistic Marsh. "Calm down, okay." I put my hands on her hands. "It's . . . complicated. We have . . . history."

That really unhinged her, jaw dropping, brows climbing. "I knew it! The way you look at each other, I could tell. The connection you have with him is almost spooky, like you know each other from a past life or something."

Hmm, I thought, *yes and no.*

"How *do* you know him? Oh, from New York, of course. His people are in Westport, that's like a minute from the city. But . . . oh, I get it. You don't want anyone to know, because of Pen, right? She's crazy about him too." Marsh let go of me to fish around her purse. "Although who knows what's up with that girl lately."

Who *did* know, besides me? So far, everything Sin had accomplished around here was readily assimilated, as though it had always been this way. Naughty little nuances like red nail polish, skyrocketing condom sales. Pen, of course, epitomized Sin's effect on the town, with her 24/7 nipple erections and, I suspected, an ongoing antipathy toward underpants. I'd thought I was the only one who noticed. Maybe that wasn't so.

"Pen?" I queried noncommittally as Marsh ran bristles through lank locks.

"She's just, I don't know, different." Marsh threw her brush back in her bag. "But I don't want to talk about Pen. I want to talk about you, and Sin, and what's going on."

I gave her an ambiguous grin. "I bet you do," I said, though in fact I preferred to talk about Pen. Marsh's comment on my cousin's altered character stirred something hopeful in me. I wasn't sure what, but sex and the superficial versus love and the eternal were part of it. Only the Yankee Diner ladies' room was hardly the venue for such dialectic. "But don't you have a call to make?"

Marsh grimaced at the mirror and sighed about her plight— a life led in increments. When her father wasn't busy boozing, he was micromanaging her existence. She had to report in between one activity and the next to obtain clearance, which was our primary purpose for stopping at the Yankee—the pay phone in its lobby. I'd offered my cell, sure we'd get a signal this close to the main highway, but Marsh didn't want my cosmopolitan area code revealing itself on caller ID.

"Hi, Dad. I'm at the Yankee Diner."

Zero psychic skills required to quote Douglas Marshall's side of the conversation.

"What are you doing there? You had supper at home."

"We're not eating, Dad. I'm just checking in. The hayride was fine, and now a bunch of kids are heading to Conner Emerson's house. Can I go?"

"To do what?"

"To watch a DVD or play video games. It's the Emersons, Dad—they have all that equipment, so no one has to waste money on the movies."

"[Hairball noise] Those spoiled brats you run around with don't give a shit about money. Who are you with, anyway?"

"Pen Leonard and some other girls."

"And you want to go to a boy's house? To play games?"

"Video games or just hang out. Dad, come on. Con's parents are home; you know them. And it's not even nine o'clock. I'll be home by eleven."

"You'll be home when I tell you to be home."

"So can I go? Please?"

A series of pleases and promises later, she hung up happy. "Come on," she said, and we trotted to her car. "But don't think I'm letting you off the hook about Sin. You have to tell me everything. Or at least something. I'll keep your secret, I swear."

"I told you the important thing; I told you how I feel," I said. "There's not much else. I mean, we talk sometimes, flirt, whatever. He wrote me a sweet note once." I opted to omit the spanking session of the previous day. "It's nothing tangible, though—not like what you have with Crane."

That shifted the subject matter, and Marsh went off on a Crane jag till we got to Con's house. Make that mansion. Though of merchant rather than professional class, the Emersons were of solid standing in the area, their retail empire encompassing some twenty temples of technological consumption throughout New England. Built on old land, the house was new, and humongous. While I can't say for certain there was a TV in every room, there was one in the ground-floor half bath I used.

About a dozen kids in party mode: Pen and her posse, the Williamses, the football and/or hockey players No (Jesse Nolan) and Way (Jonathan Wayfield), Sin, Con, of course, and two middle schoolers—Con's brother Wolf and a friend. This was in the rec room, quite the pleasure pit, with furniture like quicksand and enough gadgetry to guarantee a seizure of overstimulation. Con played host, doling out beverages from an array of appliances. Girls and boys arranged themselves by some process of natural selection, Pen fielding passes from the jocks while El and Em each took a side of Sin. Which really didn't bother me. Much. Marsh sort of floated toward Crane, and I started chatting with Doll about some triviality. After a bit, Con banished his brother with a flurry of expletives and, eventually, brute force. Which is when the door was locked, the lights went out, and the porn came on.

"Oh, man!"

"Ack! Look at the size of that thing!"

"I can't look! In fact, I think I'm scarred for life!"

"Do you think those are real?"

"Real as money can buy, baby!"

"Who needs reality? Reality sucks."

"Whoa! So does she!"

"Shut up, please! I can't follow the plot."

"Plot? I thought this was an instructional video."

"Well, some of us need instruction, and some of us know what we're doing."

You get the gist. Everybody had to say something. Indeed, I was the wit who spoke of the story line. Clowning was mandatory, but I personally found the material a little disturbing. Not the content—it was standard fare, nothing freaky (a takeoff on *Lost,* brilliantly entitled *Lust*)—but the presentation. My previous exposure to porn had been on the Internet. The screen in the Emerson rec room covered an entire wall, and the "actors," oversized to begin with, loomed larger than larger than life. In close-ups, the action resembled a bout between Godzilla and Mothra. A vagina the size of a walk-in closet? Give me D. H. Lawrence any day.

But that's me. Other people were, shall we say, inspired. Not everyone, though, and a little while later, Doll reached her limit. "I'm out of here," she announced. "Anybody who wants a ride had better pull up her panties right now."

She didn't have any takers. Con showed—more like shooed—her out.

I guess I could have gone with her but felt responsible for Marsh. If she missed curfew, she'd be in deep shit, and I didn't want to imagine Douglas Marshall meting out punishment. What time was it, anyway? I left the den of iniquity to check a clock, use a toilet, maybe take an unguided tour of the Emerson abode. I'd found the kitchen when I heard a ruckus in the rec room.

Which, I supposed, had been my fault—I'd left the door ajar . . . and the younger boys had snuck back in . . . and turned on the light . . . and hollered like hell. I hurried back that way to see what they saw. Not such a big deal, really.

So Marsh and Crane were snuggled up on the same La-Z-Boy.

So Sin was stretched out prone on the carpet, getting a massage from El and Em (none of them having removed anything more gasp-worthy than shoes).

So Pen had gone a bit further—she was topless on the sofa between No and Way.

So Con had dropped trou in order to be orally serviced by Duck, who was ambitious enough to wank off in the process.

Typical Friday night for the youth of Swoon, right?

Although, oops, maybe not. Maybe the pup otherwise known

as Wolf didn't need to see his big bro in homosexual flagrante delicto, nor did Donald Emerson and his lovely wife, Tina, who came tearing into the room shortly after the outburst, missing the display itself but catching the recap when Wolf pointed and cried, "Mom! Dad! Conner had his pecker in that kid's mouth!"

Probably no one needed be privy as the linebacker and the gadabout discovered what Sin would call their "inherent proclivities." Now no one in the room knew where to look. Except for Sin, of course. Having rolled lazily into a supine position and risen up on his elbows, he was looking, directly, triumphantly, at me.

XXVIII

The Duck Williams-Con Emerson tryst wagged on every tongue. Which had Caroline Chadwick regally pissed. It was her party, and didn't she and her ruptured romance deserve their due? Holding court in the Chadwick family room, all pout and five-hundred-thread-count pajamas, she fed from a crystal bowl of Cheetos as we, four of her dearest friends, gabbed blithely.

"Well, I'm not surprised," said Doll Turner, veteran of a clinch with Con. "I'm not saying he couldn't get it up; I'm saying it never got that far."

Matching perky ponytails bobbed.

"What I don't get is what turned them on in the first place," Brie Atwood said. "I mean, it wasn't gay porn, was it?" For a girl named after runny French cheese, she really knew bupkis about sex.

"It isn't always so literal, Brie." This from Swoon's improbable answer to Dr. Kinsey, a.k.a. Pen.

"Really—gay, straight—guys are just incurably horny," added Doll, helping herself from a platter of chilled shrimp. The Chadwicks had spared no expense on sleepover treats—there was Camembert and Gouda, melon and berries, a pyramid of Belgian truffles, plus the more plebian junk. (As to Wick's predilection for Cheetos, what can I say—the heart knows what it wants.)

I mused on how Marsh would chime in—she so recently bit by the libido mosquito—but it was Grandma's bingo night and Psycho Dad's binge-o night, so she was stuck babysitting.

Brandishing a fistful of cheese that goes crunch, Wick grudgingly went with the conversational flow. "It's just awful for the Emersons. Not to mention that Con is ruined at school, that the Lancers might as well forfeit the final game." Chemical orange spittle flew. "The Broncos will slaughter us when they find out our linebacker's a big faggot!"

A chill stole over me despite the blaze in a massive marble fireplace, and I mulled over the potential fallout from one itty-bitty blow job. Each scenario involved testosterone run rampant, and somebody getting beat up. Con? Duck? Both? As long as Emersons suffered, Sin would be pleased, but I couldn't dwell on that; I was here to thwart his machination of the moment and had to stay focused. "So—who wants a reading?"

"Ooh, me!"

"No, me!"

"Oh, Dice, do me!"

Everyone, apparently, wanted her fortune told. Not that I was particularly adept at the tarot. I was a newbie, a dilettante at best. Which didn't matter one iota, since I intended to lie my ass off in order to snag Sin's plan. "Wick should go first," I said. "After all she's been through."

"Thank you, Dice." Our hostess relinquished her hold on the Cheetos. "So how does it work? What do I have to do?"

I nudged a napkin toward her—didn't want errant artificial flavor all over my deck. "It's not just what *you* do. We all have to concentrate. Stray thoughts mess with the psychic flow."

"Yes, Madame Candice!" Pen said, and I shot her a look.

I had the girls arrange themselves on the floor. "Now, presumably, Wick, there's something you want to know. You can keep it to yourself, or you can share it."

"Oh, that's easy," said Doll. "Who's the skank who moved in on Boz?"

"As if I care!" Wick retorted. "Actually, I would prefer to keep the question private."

"That's cool," I said, assuming her query to be Boz-related and laying the deck in her palm. Per my instructions, she cut and shuffled, then handed the cards back to me.

I opened an Evian, took a sip, and began to place the spread. "This is the seeker," I intoned.

Wick inclined forward, her ponytail a teapot handle, her pug nose the spout.

"This is what covers you, this is what crosses you . . ." The cards were distinctly Wick: heavy on wands and discs, action cards, money cards; little in the way of aching swords or emotional cups. "Okay, let's see. Well, for one thing, you were very well brought up. You know right from wrong."

"Oh, definitely," Wick concurred.

"And you're also a practical person. When something happens, good or bad, you want to know why—you're all about reason."

"Wow," she said. "That's so true."

"Oh? So how come you got a C in trig?" Pen said snidely.

"Pen, please! We all know Mr. Borden had it in for me!"

"Shh!" I clapped twice, an imperious swami. "Now, usually, this pragmatism works for you. But see?" I tapped a card arbitrarily. "Reason can also be your downfall. You spend so much time and energy trying to figure out the 'why' that you lose touch with what you really want."

"Ohhh," said Wick. "That makes so much sense!"

Sure it did. About as much sense as an episode of *SpongeBob SquarePants*.

"The point is, you're afraid of what you want, afraid to want it." Inane yet convincing, I babbled on. "But you shouldn't be afraid, Wick. You can have your heart's desire."

"I—I can?" She lifted her head, buying my act hook, line, and sinker.

"Wick, yes. Yes! Do it!" My smile aimed for that Buddha-like beatific thing. "Call him! Call Boz!"

"Oh, this is just stupid!" Pen spewed with a gurgle of disgust. "I cannot believe you'd tell her to call that jerk after he so blatantly disrespected her."

"Did he, Pen?" I asked coolly. "How do you know? Were you there?"

Feminine attention snapped like a whip. Apparently, I'd asked a very pertinent question.

"No, of course not," Pen said quickly. With a wave of her hand, she settled on her haunches, the hem of her baby dolls tenting her thighs. "You want to humiliate yourself, Wick, be my guest. I don't have tarot cards. All I've got is common sense."

Wick seemed to waver. She glanced at the other girls. They didn't want to believe Boz was beyond redemption. They wanted to believe in love. And so did I. More than anything, so did I.

"I will!" Wick decided.

"Now!" I urged, gently emphatic.

"Now? Right now?"

"Why not?" said Brie. "He's probably just moping around, wondering how to get you back."

"Yes, and if *you* call *him,* show him how cool you are, how understanding, God, you'll have him eating out of your hand." This from Doll—an angle the practical, sensible Wick could appreciate.

"Yes, okay—I will," she decided. "Doll, come with me for moral support."

Doll sprang to her feet, and she and Wick ran for the reliable landline.

Pen gazed at Brie, glittering like a cobra. "Brie, your turn," she said.

"Oh, no, Pen. You go."

They spoke as sweetly as only true rivals can.

"Don't be silly." Pen reached for a strawberry and bit it in half, exposing the flesh, wet and tart. "Dice is my cousin. I can get my cards read anytime."

"All right." Brie was eager enough. "What do I want to know? Let me think . . ."

I let her think. Pen selected a truffle and plopped on a cushion to consume it.

"I could ask if a certain person likes me," Brie considered. "Or maybe it should be more open—maybe I should ask when I'll find true love."

"Yeah, Brie, whatever," I said absently, then recovered. "I mean, the cards will advise either way."

"Okay, okay. When will I find true love?"

I was halfway through the spread when Pen stood up with an "ugh" of annoyance. "Now, how'd I manage to get chocolate all over my fingers?"

"Pen!" scolded Brie. "You're supposed to be concentrating!"

"Sorry. Darn that ADD," she said. "Don't let me and my scatterbrain mess with the psychic flow. I'll just go wash up."

Uh-oh—this was it. "Pen?" I said. If I were an animal, I'd have simply growled.

"Yes?" she turned to me.

But how could I stop her? "Nothing," I said.

And she was gone. So I gave Brie a speed reading: "Youwillfindtrueloveyoursophomoreyearatcollegehewillbeanastronomymajorfromagoodfamilyandhaveredhair." Then I said, "Excuse me, Brie. Got to pee."

Unlike the Emerson McMansion, the Chadwick place was old—corridors and barriers as opposed to the open space of modern architecture. Where might Pen be? I roamed. Up a staircase. Down a hall. Peeping in keyholes. Pressing against grand oak doors. Giggling, excited chatter—in stereo. Wick's room, no doubt. Downstairs again, under an arch, left, right, another corridor, another door. I listened. Nothing. The worst kind of nothing.

The brass knob was egg shaped, polished and cold. Easily and silently it turned. Lawrence Chadwick's study. A desk big enough to sail, and upon it a lamp with a green glass shade produced the only light. An angelic vision in white leaned casually against the desk, ponytail bouncing. Pen, doing her best to appear captivated. Seated before her, with a quizzical though not displeased expression, her target was saying something. It didn't matter what— Pen licked it up like batter from a spoon. Her movements were minimal but in a way magical. Arching a foot. Fiddling with a ruffle. Visibly breathing, her breasts rose and fell.

Why was I rooted there, hovering at the threshold? Waiting, I guess, waiting for something overt, something that couldn't be mistaken as innocent. Pen had known Mr. Chadwick nearly all her life. What harm was there in a little conversation about something, anything, whatever a fascinating man of the world would choose to discuss.

Pen inched closer. He wanted to show her something. She wanted to see it. Standing beside him now, she bent obligingly, then lifted her head to toss a stray wisp from her eyes. That's when she saw me. And winked! She knew I was there and didn't care, maybe even enjoyed an audience to the seduction. Pen reached toward the book he proffered, touched the page where he had his hand.

"Pen, no . . ." I mouthed an impotent plea.

"Pen? Dice? Where are you guys?"

Whirling, I saw Wick down the hall, flanked by Doll and Brie. "Over here!" I called.

"God, Dice—what are you doing? Where's Pen?"

Right behind me. The foiled escapade sizzled like a steak yanked off the grill.

"Sorry," I said. "Wrong turn on the way to the bathroom. God, Wick, this house is enormous."

"Yes, well, no—it's just that your house is so small," she said. "And of course you grew up in an apartment." If anyone could pronounce the word "apartment" like it meant homeless shelter, it was Wick.

"So you and Boz all patched up?" Pen said.

Wick beamed, grabbed Pen's hand and pulled her past me through the door. "He is so sweet!" she told Pen. "He's just so awesome—I can't believe I ever doubted him."

Upon reaching the foyer, Wick stopped, and we fell in line. "So look, you guys have to leave," she said. "Boz's coming over. And look at me, look at my hair!"

Precisely what I'd been wrangling for. Shut down the sleepover, shut down Sin's scheme. "Wick, that's fantastic!"

"I'm thrilled for you." Pen manifested the unbridled joy of an undertaker.

"Mm-hmm, cool," said Wick, all brusque "now, where's your stuff?" and "thanks for coming."

Brie had driven over with Doll; they walked to her SUV. I'd come with Pen, and as she stomped to her vehicle—furious at me—I followed, abashed. Opening the passenger door, I remembered. "Shit!"

Pen did not acknowledge me.

"My deck," I said. "I forgot my cards."

A tsunami of annoyance swept my way.

"It'll just take a second."

I raced back to the house, waited for someone to answer the bell—it was Mr. Chadwick, still a little bemused. All apologies, I hurried toward the family room, took a wrong turn, collected my cards, made a frantic search for the scarf I tied them in, found it under the coffee table, and blew out of there.

So it took more than a second.

I never imagined that Pen would drive off, leaving me there in the middle of the night, with a two-mile walk along black, country roads.

XXIX

THERE WAS THIS NIGHT, A BLOWOUT IN SOME GODFORSAKEN PART OF Queens. There were these guys; they had a car, Ruby explained, adamant, so we wouldn't have to take the train. There was this fight—the boy Ruby was into neglected to mention his girlfriend. Before any serious bitch-slapping commenced, we were out of there, on this strange street, in Friday night flirt clothes, in Queens. Queens! Men gathered on the stoop of a dilapidated building hissed at us like snakes. Obviously, we wouldn't be inquiring about the nearest subway. We walked for blocks, and then Ruby tripped, breaking a heel, so I walked slower, she hobbled, bumping up our courage, talking nonsense till we spied the green globe of the Junction Boulevard station.

Nightmare? Yeah, pretty much. But nothing compared to this. This silence. This darkness. This loneliness. I pulled my cell from my backpack and cursed every one of its useless buttons. Then I cursed the countryside, with its intermittent majestic homes far from the road behind impassive high shrubbery or an infinite stone fence. I cursed the cold; I cursed the mist that rose off Swoon Lake. Cursing, I plodded, every sound that dared breech the quiet giving me a jolt.

What was that? Some forest creature crackling twigs.

And that? A gust through the trees.

And that? Coming up behind me? Coming after me? Louder, louder, a relentless encroaching clatter. That slowed. Then stopped. Right there.

"Need a lift, my lady?" Sin, astride his stallion friend.

I got it together enough for sarcasm. "Looks like a one-seater to me."

"Alas, Kurt's courting a buyer for the Cutlass," he said mildly. "They're taking a test drive, and Black Jack's the only horsepower I could avail myself of this night."

Sin slapped the beast's neck, and Black Jack shook his mane like a rock star. Then something skittered in the grass, and the stallion reared and I gasped, my hand reflexively flying. Sin caught it, held it, and I remembered how much that simple act of connection meant to us once. And all at once my body was a waterfall in reverse, impelled to motion by a boundless heart as Sin swept me into the saddle.

"There we are," he said.

There we were. His arms about my waist, my spine pressed

to his chest, this amazing animal between our thighs. One arm still encircling me, Sin slung on my pack, then adjusted the reins. Digging heels into horse, we were off at a canter, that raw silk mane stinging my face as the boy I loved urged us forward. By the time we reached 12 Daisy Lane I'd decided I could ride like that forever.

"Whose car is that?" Sin asked as we stopped in front of the house.

Car? I wondered, for I felt whisked away to a time before such conveyances. *Oh, right, car.* "My mother's," I said. "She drives up to Swoon every weekend."

"Ah, yes. Your mother. Charming woman. How is she?"

"She's fine, thank you." The lights were on in the living room. Momster was probably enjoying some Shiraz while critiquing *In Star* layouts lugged from the office. "I'd ask you to come in . . . but—"

"But?"

"But . . . look, get me off this horse, okay?"

He dismounted first, then lifted me onto the lawn. Black Jack bent to graze.

We looked at each other.

"Well," he said. "Score one for you."

The aborted seduction a check in my column. "You don't seem all that upset."

"There'll be other opportunities to deliver Chadwick's due."

What a study in nonchalance. "I've plenty of time."

"Well, the way Pen left me, she must be livid."

"She'll get over it. She doesn't . . . retain much, that one."

I couldn't let him see me smirk. "Yeah, well, I guess you won last night. That's what all the hay hopping was about, huh? All you needed was to get Con and Duck next to each other."

"I'd told you it would be easy. And isn't it better for Con to be outside?"

"No, Sin, we're outside. Con's just out." I didn't care to explain the origins of the reference. "And better off? Well, it's not like he *came* out, he was outed, thanks to you."

At a standoff, there was nothing left to do but look at each other some more.

"Very well, then." In a split second, he was all business, his foot in the stirrup as he hoisted onto his borrowed Arabian. "I bid you good night."

"Yeah," I said. "You too." I picked up my backpack. It had three books in it, a change of clothes, my toothbrush, stupid useless cell phone, and a deck of tarot cards. Nothing I couldn't handle. My brimming tears, however, were another matter. My brimming tears were mercury, which, at 298 K, is the heaviest known elemental liquid. Yeah, I was doing great in chemistry. And failing miserably at love.

XXX

"SO YOU'RE IN LOVE WITH HIM NOW?"

Momster pounced immediately, but it was easy explaining the terminated girls' night in (mostly truth) and why she hadn't heard Pen drop me off (complete fabrication). Fact, fallacy, she didn't care—she was just glad I was back. She knew I had a life and wouldn't expect me to drop everything for her, but she didn't make the trip out of a masochistic fetish for weekender exodus traffic. She made the trip so we could bond, damn it. So I blinked back mercury tears, and we sat and talked and ate ice cream, basically had (her words, not mine) our own slumber party. Except we didn't sack out in sleeping bags on the rug. Ultimately, Momster went to her room and I to mine, whereupon an inquisition in earnest began.

"No, actually, I was in love with him pretty much from the get." I said this with a straight face. Difficult, considering

Ruby's outfit. The baby-dolls zeitgeist hadn't escaped her, but the set she wore was rainbow striped and accented with lavender braids and platform boots, platforms thick as an unabridged dictionary. An ensemble direct from the Gay Pride Parade told me Ruby was up on the latest goings-on in this burg. But it was my recent admission d'amour that had her on my case. "You got a problem with that?"

"Not especially." She took a seat at my dressing table. Poking through products, she selected a liner pencil and drew herself a beauty mark, à la Marilyn Monroe, her hair as she did so transforming into a platinum pouf. "I always get the fuzzy end of the lollipop," Ruby complained, breathily indignant.

A quote from *Gentlemen Prefer Blondes* or *Some Like It Hot*—I can't recall which but it made me smile. Until I realized how true it was. Not for the first time I wondered, *why her?* And also, *why not me?*

"Hey, I saw your aunt," I told her, pushing the wonder away.

"Mm-hmm." She said it like she knew it. "Lot of good it did you."

Damn, she could press my buttons. "What, Ruby? What? Ever since Sin and I . . . ever since we met, for lack of a better term, you've been on my ass about him. Yeah, I love him. That doesn't mean I've gone deaf, blind, and stupid. I know what he's up to, and I . . . I'm going to stop him. At least I'm going to try."

"You *are* trying." She said it sincerely. "But wouldn't you say this love of yours is a bit of a detriment?"

"No, not at all." I realized right then that love was probably the only thing I had going for me.

Ruby read me like the E on an eye chart. "Mm-hmm. Love conquers all."

"Something like that, yeah." Whatever that meant. My love was immense, it was real—but it was unwieldy, and I had no clue what to do with it.

"So, what, you think you can tame him with the sheer force of mush?"

It was an idea. A snotty, cynical idea, but an idea. At least it had a long-term goal attached, as opposed to my stopgap measures as one-woman bomb squad out to defuse the boy's diabolicals. But tame him? No, I loved him just the way he was . . . except for the vengeful coup d'etat on the town part. I was about to shoot Ruby some snark when her four-legged namesake nosed into the room. One look at the two-legged Ruby, and she puffed up all porcupine. Clearly, R.C. hadn't encountered anything quite as phantasmagoric and fabulous as Ruby Ramirez before. We couldn't help cracking. I went to snatch the funny little furbag, but R.C. did a crazed crabwalk, taking cover in my closet.

"Too cute," Ruby said.

"Yeah. Cats. Who needs cable?"

We traded smiles, and then Ruby told me, "Look, Candida, I don't want to pee on your picnic, I really don't. I've seen the dude, okay? He's gorgeous and talented and smart and knows how to work it to maximum effect. I get it."

Did she really think me so shallow? "Um, I don't remember you developing a crush on the Elephant Man," I pointed out. "And anyway, it's not just that. The thing with Sin is, I *feel* for him. He's been through a lot. He never knew his real mother, whom we can only assume died horribly, while his biological father was a major asshole who ruined his adopted family, and then he was out on his own—"

"Oh, Candy, that's so you," Ruby interrupted. "Always picking up strays."

She ought to know. Fourth grade. Pudgy new girl with a hint of lisp. I wasn't exactly Miss Popularity myself, but I stepped up the first time one of those over-styled, under-parented Upper West Side bitches-in-training tittered over Ruby's speech impediment, and I got my first and only best friend.

"He comes to Swoon to live in shadows," I continued unabated, "and then, when he finally falls in love, this whole town shows its true colors."

At that, Ruby emitted the strangest sigh. Hair now bright and shiny as a new penny, poking out from a starched white cap. Dress now of dark muslin, pleated and prim and brushing the ground. "And how do you know all this?"

"Because," I said. "Because . . . he . . . told me."

Off came the cap to release a stream of flaming waist-length waves. Lovely, as lovely as the wounds that mottled her face were vile. "I see," she said. "He told you." The words came out singsong, a lilting, mocking melody.

"What are you saying?" I croaked. Angry. Shocked. "Are you saying he lied?"

But who was I angry at? And what was so shocking? I'd devoured Sin's sob story like a cupcake. Since then had I learned nothing of the boy's ability to manipulate and betray? I took Sin on faith, but if faith were money, fools would be billionaires. What did I actually, factually, know about the tragic murder of Hannah Miles, here in the town of Swoon, then in the summer of 1769?

"I'm not saying anything." Ruby was just Ruby again, in faded jeans and scoop-neck sweater an on-purpose size too small. "It's just that I know what it's like on this side of the fence, the need that fuels you to cross back." Sin, too, had a need, and his fuel was high-octane premium. "I'm just saying . . ." And saying, she began to diminish—for that's how she goes, she fades away. "You got to watch more than your back on this one, baby. You better watch your heart."

XXXI

RAZOR BLADES SLID INTO APPLES. POISONED CANDY METICULOUSLY rewrapped. Anyone over five feet tall and wearing a mask a potential pervert. Urban legends could wreck Halloween for a city kid, but places like Swoon are supposed to be untouched by such paranoia. So I was expecting kitchen wizardry and craft projects, dozens of genuine pumpkin jack-o'-lanterns illuminating lawns and every other address converted into a harmless house of horrors. Only, no. Distracted parents forgot about the festival until the last minute, then rushed out to purchase pre-fab tricks, treats, and decorative trimmings. Adding to the perfunctory feel, Halloween fell on a Monday, much to the disappointment of the single-digit set. There'd be no abolition of bedtimes, and candy intake would be conscientiously monitored so no one might wake with a bellyache.

Fine by me. The weekend had been wild enough, thanks.

Taking my chances with the cafeteria's Ghoulish Goulash was about my speed. While poking it with a spork, I spied Con Emerson, no shame in his game. Somehow his swagger seemed less obnoxious, his vibe more laid-back, like he no longer had to try so hard. Could be Sin was right that outing Con was to the linebacker's benefit. Though surely a new, improved version of any Emerson hadn't been my golem's goal.

After school I rigged up a slapdash costume and prepared for community service. "Thanks for doing this with me," I told Pen as I got in her car. No way was I biking to the library in a tail, whiskers, and cardboard cat ears.

"No biggie," said fairy princess Pen, who, as Sin had predicted, was fully over the foiled entrapment of Lawrence Chadwick. And I was over the dump job—Pen wasn't spiteful, merely impulsive, like RubyCat trashing the toilet paper roll. Besides, I half suspected that Sin sent her off so he could swoop in with the valiant knight routine. Pen stepped on the gas. "It's an even trade," she said.

True, that. She'd help me tend to a cabal of preschoolers on a juice-and-cookies high, and I'd help her dole out punch at a geriatric masquerade. First stop, story time. Little girls encircled my cousin with oohs and ahhs, touching her tulle, stroking her wand. Little boys, equally enamored, ran up to be near her, then turned their excitement onto the girls with a pinch or slug or pigtail tug. Pen was magical, a mix of every

Disney princess with a dollop of Pussycat Dolls thrown in. Watching her with the kids buoyed me, proved that Sin hadn't totally sullied her: Pen, the real Pen, was still lovely and sweet and kind.

A paragon of patience, she hushed the crowd, and I read aloud a few favorites from *The Big Book of Spooks*. Ms. Brinker took over after a while, freeing us for our next round of do-gooding. The route we'd take to the Oak View Residential Manor went right past Wick's house. As we drew near, I pressed the issue.

"So what were you up to when I busted you Saturday night?" I presented the question slyly, hoping to imply approval.

"Busted?" Pen feigned offense. "Candice Reagan Moskow, whatever do you mean?"

"Yeah, right. As if you weren't working Mr. Chadwick."

Pen giggled. "Well, maybe a tiny bit."

"Please! You already know you could have any guy just by farting in his general direction." I played to her ego. "Only Wick's dad! How did . . . when did it even occur to you to go for him?" If outmaneuvering Sin were my aim, it'd be good to know how he instructed his agent.

"Funnily enough, I don't really know. I guess it just popped into my head."

Well, that was a whole lot of brick wall. I moved on. "What would you have done if he'd gone for it, though? Could you really fool around with some paunchy bald dude?"

"Oh, sure," Pen said with frightening flippancy. "Looks don't matter much to me anymore."

So she'd become an equal opportunity slut.

"I mean, Jesse Nolan's no Calvin Klein model," she went on, "but I'd have done him and Way both Friday night if the whole thing with Con and Duck hadn't blown up."

I let that pervade my consciousness, saying nothing.

Pen, however, wanted to talk. "It's like . . . Dice, have you ever done coke?"

"Yeah, once, but not my thing. All it made me want to do was chew gum. Crystal was worse. Although I did get my room organized."

Pen laughed. "Last year it was big around here. Guess-who-Kurt-Libo brought it to our attention. The thing is, whenever I'd do it, the first line felt amazing, but every one after that felt like I was chasing the feeling of the first. Does that make any sense?"

"Sure," I said, unclear how it related to Pen screwing her way through Swoon.

"It's kind of the same thing with sex," she expounded, offering the method to her nymphomania. "My first time was incredible, so now, whenever I can get with a guy, it's like I'm trying to recapture that." At the traffic light before the highway entrance, horns started bleating—a couple in the lane perpendicular, making out like mad, unaware they had the green. Pen sighed. "And I haven't been able to."

I forced myself to say, "Maybe that's because your first time was with Sin."

"Don't I know it!" She nodded like a dashboard doll. "And he refuses to be with me again! Can you believe it?"

I wasn't sure I could, but I was going to try.

"Fortunately, I figured out why," Pen said. "I haven't earned it yet, that's all."

If I knew Pen, she didn't give up easy. And I knew Pen. Glumly, I steered the conversation back. "But the thing with Mr. Chadwick, what I don't get is, didn't you worry someone might be hurt? You know, like his wife, or our friend, or even you, Pen. A scandal like that wouldn't do your college apps any good."

"Hmm?" Pen pulled up to her volunteer venue. "Oh, no, I never worry about stuff like that." She put the car in park and swatted me on the shoulder. She smiled. "You know what's wrong with you, Dice? You think too much!"

That was an understatement. Only how could I opt for brain dead after Ruby's last visit, the seeds of doubt she sowed? She'd hinted I was out of my league, playing a game with a grand prize of pain. Worse, her insinuations about Sin. Could he have invented the tale of Hannah Miles to stoke my sympathy? Or what if Hannah had existed, and Sin the one who—full stop! I couldn't go there, I wouldn't go there.

But maybe . . . maybe I could go back.

People like me who aren't in denial often train themselves to intuit on demand. Some do it for a living, like Tía Anaisa, or those clairvoyants employed by police departments. There was no reason I couldn't employ my sense—my *gift*, there, I said it—to take a time trip and investigate events in the year of Our Lord 1769.

As the idea began to gel, I gave an inner whoop: I wouldn't even have to fly solo. Sin was gifted, too. Together, we'd see for ourselves what had happened to Hannah. And once we found out, maybe Sin would be sated. The truth could set him free. Then Swoon could go back to normal, and he and I could have our chance. Didn't we deserve it, both of us—the opportunity to throw snowballs at each other, to bicker over what movie to see, to study, heads bent above the same book, and take long, snuggly study breaks?

I smiled dazedly around me. It was quite a place, the Oak View Residential Manor, a former estate now home to an exclusive enclave of Western Connecticut's elderly. There was indeed a view of oaks, plus gourmet dining, a stellar program of lectures, a huge gym, an adjacent golf course, the whole nine. The magnificent ballroom was the jewel in the crown—naturally, the masked gala was well attended.

So giddy was I by prospects of the near future, it barely registered that the residents were dressed in a manner more befitting a bordello. That the dancing didn't quite suit the dignity of the setting. That some naughty septuagenarian spiked the punch. All right, it was a little icky, how my boy could awaken "inherent proclivities" among the elderly, too. But I simply smiled, pouring fizzy orange substance into cut-glass cups and handing them out in a stupor. Nothing could disturb me now.

Not even once I noticed Sin, dressed for the occasion in familiar frock coat and breeches, spinning and dipping one little old lady after the next. Pen was on the floor as well, waltzing with one gent only to be cut in on by another. Eventually, inevitably, Pen and Sin were partnered, and the other dancers rimmed the sidelines to give these perfect young people space.

"Oh, aren't they lovely!" gushed a woman who appeared at my right.

"Yeah," I said. "Lovely."

"Such a pretty girl!" Another woman had come up on my left. "But he, oh, there's something about him, isn't there? Something special."

"Absolutely," agreed a third. "He's the one you reach for in your dreams."

Now I was surrounded by the sagging and wrinkled and rheumy. Talc and Je Reviens covering an acrid odor of longing. Voices impossibly girlish, frenzied in pitch.

"The one you'd do anything for . . ."

"Cuckold your husband for . . ."

"Empty your bank account for . . ."

"Stab your sister for . . ."

"Drown your babies for . . ."

"Set the house afire for . . ."

Trapped in a cluster of sparkling gems and yellow teeth, suffocated by foul and wistful vows, I watched a cut-glass cup of fizzy orange substance slide slo-mo from my hand and crash to the parquet floor. Rather than follow it to be trampled by merciless pumps, I cleaved the gaggle of crones and fled.

XXXII

THERE I WAS, HUSTLING UP HONEYSUCKLE ROAD, WHEN THE CUTLASS pulled alongside. A newly blackened window descended.

"Dice! Hey!" Marsh called and waved from the shotgun seat. "Come on, get in!"

I hopped in back, Marsh's little sisters scooting over to make room. Crane Williams was at the wheel.

"Thanks," I said, deducing that Crane had bought the car from Kurt and ordered the tint job so he and Marsh could drive around undetected.

Marsh pivoted in her seat to glow at me. "Are you okay? You were walking!"

Pedestrians are a rarity here, and I wasn't exactly dressed for a hike. "Yeah, sure," I said. "Just got a little creeped out at the Oak View."

Willa, the youngest Marshall, tapped my elbow inquisitively. "What are you?"

"Huh?" I said, rearranging my tail (the sock-stuffed leg cut from a pair of tights). "Oh, I'm a cat." I assessed their get-ups. "Dora the Explorer, right? And, Char, you're . . . Hannah Montana?" How did I even know these things?

The girls nodded happily. "We were trick-or-treating," said Willa. Both hoarded bulging pillowcases. "And then we met Crane. Isn't he nice? We think so. We really like him—Kristin especially. He can play guitar." They must've sworn a secrecy pact about big sister's boyfriend—I hoped chatterbox Willa wouldn't blow it.

"I know, I've heard him," I said. "Nice ride, Crane."

He turned to me briefly, grinned bashfully. "Ah. Yes. Quite. Thanks."

"So what's next on the Halloween itinerary?" I asked. "If you guys want to come over, I'll make witch-os," which I explained were like nachos, only with bat wings, rat entrails, and dehydrated owl eyes.

That sounded yummy to all aboard, and we stopped so Marsh could use a phone. Not long after at 12 Daisy Lane, the girls were sorting candy in front of the tube while Marsh and Crane kept me company in the kitchen as I shredded cheese. A peaceful milieu, until, "We interrupt this broadcast with a special news report . . ." alerted from the living room.

"Shortly before five p.m. today, a fire broke out at the Oak View Residential Manor," the anchorwoman said with jittery thrall. "We take you now to Duffy Bartlett on the scene in Swoon. Duffy?"

We saw Duffy and fire engines and ambulances and stretchers and smoke and flames. It was a mess.

"Oh my God," I said, still clutching a hunk of cheddar.

"Dice!" said Marsh. "You were just there!"

"Oh my God," I said again, staring at the screen.

"You're terribly lucky," said Crane.

"Oh my God." I went for the triple. And then I said, "Pen."

I dropped the cheese. Dashed across the road, flew up the lawn, Peanut and Popcorn at my ankles. Pen's car wasn't there. Lainie's was, though. Also a Mercedes I didn't recognize. "Aunt Lainie!?" I called once inside. "Hello? Lainie? Anyone?" Where were the boys? Some Halloween play date, no doubt. I started up the carpeted stairs. Music from the master suite. It might have been Céline Dion. "Lainie, hey, there's a—"

Oh, shit. Much as I tried, I could not avert my eyes—they were stuck in gape mode. And so I witnessed the spectacle of my aunt, in bed, wearing the flippy skirt of Pen's cheerleading outfit and nothing else, on top of some guy who had silvery chest hair and was definitely not my uncle.

"Oh, shit." I actually uttered it.

Lainie turned, vocalized shrilly, and hurled one of Pen's pom-poms at me. "Get out! Get out!"

Ducking behind the door, I sputtered, "Lainie, I—I'm sorry. But Pen—there's this huge fire at the Oak View, it's—"

A commotion in the bedroom—the scrambling of sheets and whispers, hisses and underwear. Lainie came out, hastily dressed in chinos and half-buttoned blouse. "Oh, dear Jesus!" she wheezed. "I must get over there!"

Following her, I didn't glance again at the man who'd been enjoying the rah-rah-royal treatment in the Leonard king-size. Lainie scuttled about, grabbing at purse and car keys. Barefoot and frantic, she darted out, nearly colliding with Pen at the side door.

"Penny! Penny! Oh my God, are you all right?"

My cousin looked rattled, ashy-white, soot-streaked, but otherwise unscathed.

"Yes," Pen said shakily. "I need . . . let me sit down." She leaned on her mother, who helped her into the breakfast nook. I went to the fridge to get Pen some water. Lainie knelt by her daughter, held her hands; I lingered nearby.

"Thank God, thank God," Lainie kept repeating, no doubt grateful that her recent indiscretion hadn't caused divine wrath to smite her firstborn. "Oh, my baby. Penny, are you sure you're all right? Smoke inhalation?"

"Yes . . . no. Really, Mom." She did seem overwhelmed, though. "They checked me out. I'm okay . . . but . . ." Pen buried her face in her arms and began to cry. "Oh, those poor people. Those poor old people!"

Lainie soothed her daughter, but I found the gush of humanity encouraging—so much of Pen's sensitivity these days seemed clitoro-centric. I turned on the small TV mounted under a cabinet. It filled with fire. We watched, momentarily mesmerized, and then Lainie remembered her other offspring.

"The boys! I've got to pick the boys up from the Reynoldses," she said. "Oh, Candy, can you—oh . . ." She gave me a withering look, like I was the most useless waste of flesh on the planet.

I spared her a withering look in return. I may not have known how to drive, but at least I wasn't cheating on my husband. At some point Lainie's lover must have slipped out and snuck off. "Some friends are over at my house," I told her. "They'll take me to get the boys, no problem."

"Thank you," Lainie said quietly. "I really don't want to leave Penny right now."

Pen lifted her head. "Dice, wait." She got out of the nook, latching onto my arm as we walked to the door. She was trembling. "Sin . . . ," she said.

The sound of his name was a wrecking ball.

Pen dipped her head, inclined toward me. "Dice, he wouldn't leave. It was crazy in there, this . . . stampede. And I screamed for him, but he wouldn't come. The last I saw he was just . . . standing there. The old people were falling down and getting up and falling down and . . . and the smoke . . . and the screaming . . . and he just stood there in the middle of the dance floor. And he was laughing."

XXXIII

The five-alarm fire at the Oak View Residential Manor would claim two and seriously injure a dozen more. Damage to the landmark buildings, erected in the 1880s, was extensive, and due to an insurance oversight, the ensuing lawsuit threatened to cripple the facility's owner, Chadwick Choice Properties. So Sin had found another way to crush Wick's family. Too bad a couple of lusty crusties had to perish in the process—as the investigation later proved, there'd been no crime of arson but a pair of masquerade ballers who accidentally toppled a candle while getting busy in a pantry.

The score was tipping in Sin's favor, the death toll mounting. Which upped the imperative to hurry him out of this century ASAP. I had Crane drop me at Libo's Gas & Lube after fetching the little Leonards, then bringing Marsh and the girls to her car. The garage was open for business, Kurt's father minding the till. I crept around the building, found an iron stair, and started up. A brick wall, painted white, the paint peeling; two windows hung with impenetrable curtains; a door. I knocked.

"Hey, kitty-kitty, you didn't say trick or treat." Kurt's greeting reminded me I still had my costume on. The way he said it—deliberate monotone, with a lead-eyed stare—implied approval of the whole tight leggings, high boots, pointy ears look. "Come on in."

"No." The first thing out of my mouth shot from my gut. "I'm just looking for Sin."

An expression of *no shit?* shaded his simian features, as if what chick didn't have a jones for Sinclair Youngblood Powers. "He's not here, but he told me you might come around. You can wait if you want."

I didn't want. Chasing my tail seemed preferable to doing nothing. Plus, I wasn't nuts about being alone with Kurt. For some reason. No, for this reason: Sin's whole modus operandi was to put people in touch with the parts of themselves they hid—the parts society would deplore, the so-deemed ugly parts, strange parts, sick parts. From what I knew, Kurt was pretty overt in a Popeye the Sailor "I yam what I yam" sort of way. If the guy had kept anything under wraps that was now on the loose, I didn't care to encounter it.

"Come on," he said. "I'll smoke you up,"

A tempting invitation—why not take the edge off? "Ohhh, I don't think so . . ." But bottom line, where else would I go? Here,

Sin crashed. Here, Sin would eventually return. And I had to see him; we had business.

"I will wait, though, if that's okay," I decided, stepping into the apartment. Passing Kurt, trying to sense him out, getting nothing but a certain bitter sharpness that made my cavity fillings ache.

It was a small L-shaped studio. The curtains I'd seen from outside turned out to be heavy-duty garbage bags duct-taped above the windows. There was a plaid salvaged sofa, torn in spots. Mini fridge and microwave. A tile floor, last mopped . . . never. In the short end of the L, a single bed with an army blanket; rolled up catty-corner, a sleeping bag. Mechanic manuals and car magazines mixed in with a stack of novels from Daniel Dafoe and Chuck Palahniuk. The table was a plank of wood atop a pair of sawhorses, with two mismatched chairs. On it, a laptop glowed. An iPod rigged to auto sound speakers bled a threatening amalgam of black metal and bluegrass.

I gazed skeptically at the couch and pondered a graceful way to remove my feline accoutrements. Kurt filled a bong made out of a camshaft or something. He took a hit, handed it to me. Again, I demurred.

"Come on," he said.

"Okay." I hit it. Just to be sociable. It was nice. Instant, all over, nice.

We stood in the middle of the room, but there was nothing weird about that. I forgot the inanities of my outfit.

"You know about the fire?" I asked Kurt.

"Figured something. Heard sirens." The boy wasn't big on complete sentences—a symptom of speaking with lungs full of smoke.

"It's over at the Oak View," I said, and then wondered, wait, when did Sin tell Kurt I might come around? Had he been to the apartment since the fire, and left again? Or did he mention some time in the last month or so that my appearance on their threshold was in the realm of possibility?

"Sucks," said Kurt. "Hey, you want to see something cool?" He walked to the computer, swirled the mouse.

"Yeah, I guess." I propped my knee on a chair. What did Kurt Libo consider cool? Monster trucks? Midget wrestlers?

"This major storm in Iowa," he said. "And all these birds, wait, here, look . . ."

A mass exodus of Canadian geese, thousands of them, tens of thousands, filled the sky, honking like a feathered brass band. It was awesome. I leaned a hand on the table, Kurt watching over my shoulder.

"Whoa . . ."

"Right?"

Forty-six seconds later it was over, and I wanted to see it again—you know how addictive some videos are—so I pressed play. I was into it. Kurt was too. Or so I thought. I thought different when he kicked the chair out from under my knee.

The way I fell—forward, banging into the table but not cracking my head open, onto that repulsive floor—set up his next move. Kurt gave out a kind of yelp, and I felt his knee between my kidneys.

Scared straight, indeed. I was stone-cold sober and hyper-aware of everything. The gritty, tacky tile against my cheek. The fumes of ganja and motor oil and last night's french fries. The breath being forced out of me. It's still crystal clear—I could offer play-by-play minutiae of our roll and tussle across the floor. Every grab he made. Every thrash and claw from me in response. Only I get enough unbidden flashbacks, why recall it on purpose? Fast-forward to the relevant moment when Kurt, glomming onto a hank of hair, ripped off the elastic headband with the stupid cardboard ears glued on and used it to bind my wrists behind my back.

"Finally," I heard him mutter.

Then he had my ankles, and a cord or rope or . . . oh, shit, he was trussing me up with my own goddamn tail. I screamed—of course, I screamed: "*Stop! Help! Murder! Osama bin Laden!*"—but my screams sank into the dead acoustic weight of the floor.

And then he was gone. Just like that. I squirmed, flipping onto my side to see Kurt held aloft, his sneakers pumping an invisible bicycle. Sin had him scruffed by the T-shirt collar, the way I'd snatch RubyCat in the midst of some kitten misdemeanor.

"Hey, man! Put me down! Come on, put me down!"

Sin didn't put him down; Sin flung him down, across the room and into a wall.

"What the?!" spewed Kurt. "What'd you do that for?"

Sin spoke, quietly vehement. "How dare you touch her."

"What are you talking about?" Kurt bleated, cowering.

Sensing the fury that quivered from Sin's every fiber, I thought he'd ram Kurt through the brick and halfway to Ohio. Instead he got beside me and deftly began to undo my bonds. My head swam as my hands and feet came free.

"You told me you were going to be busy!" Kurt cried defensively. "You said I should keep her tied up!"

"I told you, you imbecile, that I was going to be tied up, you should keep her busy!" Sin thundered, then shook his head and resumed his ministrations. "Are you hurt?" He was murmuring now. His touch was kind, but he couldn't quite meet my eye. "If you're hurt, I'll beat him senseless. I'll have him drawn and quartered. I'll—"

"Sin . . . just . . . stop." Sitting now with my knees pulled to my chest, I placed my fingers to his lips. "He didn't hurt me." I wasn't so sure of that. In fact, I flashed on Momster's stash of codeine-laced Tylenol in the medi-cabi of 12 Daisy Lane. Sin gathered me in his arms and helped me to my feet, and for a few fleeting heartbeats I reveled in the strength and heat and beauty of his body.

Then I withdrew, calling my skin onto my bones. "Let go of me," I said simply.

The golem did as he was told.

XXXIV

It's tradition for idle youth of the area to congregate at Grimley Parish Cemetery on Halloween Night. There's no defacing of gravestones or pillaging of plots. These "good kids," the progeny of "good people," wouldn't dream of such villainy. Some smoking and drinking, maybe, some exchange of rural legend—plain old "good" spooky fun. Yet Sin and I were unaware of this custom, setting out for the place with a reason of our own, a reason settled upon after a whole lot of harangue behind the Libo garage.

"So," I said, hugging myself, "you have a nice time incinerating old people?"

"It's not about a nice time, Dice. You know that."

"Oh? I heard you were laughing it up pretty good."

Sin, still in eighteenth-century garb, let his shoulders rise and drop. "There's a certain satisfaction in a job well done."

"Yeah, I'm sure the big shots at Buchenwald said the same thing." I don't know if Sin knew from Buchenwald (our history class was early American, and he was acing it) but he surely surmised by my intonation it was no Disneyland.

"The denizens of Oak View had deep roots in Swoon—they deserved what they got, as far as I'm concerned," he said. "Moreover, it's Lawrence Chadwick who'll suffer long term, and as you well know, my initial plan for his undoing was handily undone."

The implication being that if I hadn't interfered at the slumber party, he wouldn't have kindled the old folks' flambé. Logical. Exasperating. "Look, Sin, I want you to stop this shit!" I figured I'd give petulance a shot, stamping my foot and everything. "You're my golem, and you'll do what I say."

It got me nowhere.

"I think we've past that point, my lady," he said. "Look to the literature—that of your own culture has tales of golems who rebelled against their masters. Look beyond, to *Frankenstein, The Sorcerer's Apprentice,* any of your *Terminator* films."

What a popmeister he'd become.

"Keep in mind, too," he continued, "that you neglected to install a deactivation measure."

It was true. Back in the day, a rabbi would inscribe the Hebrew name of God somewhere on his golem; later, if he wished to destroy his dirtbot, he simply erased the first letter, conveniently spelling the word "death." Those Kabbalah boys were smart, but I'd made no such provision.

"I don't want to . . . deactivate you. I—" Could I say it? I could not. "I just don't happen to agree with you."

"Then it appears we belong to a most intimate debate club, in which we agree to disagree."

It was a fruitless path of argument, so I went a different way. "You seemed awfully pissed at Kurt in there."

This made Sin punch fist to palm. "That idiot! The thought of him laying a finger on you. Mark me, I'll go back in to finish him off."

"No." I put a hand on his arm. "Aural dyslexia aside, it's not really Kurt's fault."

Sin regarded me, brow raised in disbelief.

"What you need to acknowledge," I told him, "is that you can't pick and choose who you influence, and to what extent. I mean, Kurt Libo's no Quaker, but what he did to me was the natural result of what *you* evoked in him."

I let that sink in. It seemed to strike a chord.

"What you say has merit," Sin allowed. "You were attacked, you were hurt, and by my hand, albeit indirectly." He threw his eyes to the evening sky, sought salvation in emerging stars. Then he looked at me. "How can you ever forgive me?"

"Forgive you? How can I not? Sin, I can't separate me from you. I'm responsible for you. What you do, I do. If I can't forgive you, I can't forgive myself. And I don't want to feel bad about either of us. I want . . ." How to put this . . . "I want to love us."

Quick as a hammer strike he enfolded me. "You are my *life*." His forceful whisper lost itself in the crown of my head.

Life. I wasn't about to quibble over the term. I didn't know much, but I knew we were in this for keeps, lashed together by a law of our own invention, basic as blood, crucial as gravity. Time ticked along and evening thickened as we stood that way.

Then Sin said, "You are my life, but you are not my purpose."

Damn it straight to smithereens—without passing go, without collecting two hundred dollars! His stupid, persistent purpose! The spirit fuel Ruby spoke of, the essence that roars in the restive dead. If I thought I was involved in a bizarre love triangle when Sin was stuck in Pen, now I had to compete with his revenge. Sin's purpose was my nemesis; that's what I had to obliterate. Yet as I steeled my mind to the task, another notion intruded, so startling, so frightening, it made me quake: Once Sin's thirst was slaked, what then? His purpose fulfilled, he'd have no reason for being, no reason to exist at all.

Unless love could sustain him. Our love.

There'd been a time when Sin at peace was a concept I could accept. That was then. Now, could I really instigate a course of action that might tear him from me forever?

I willed myself to stillness and hugged him back. "I know that," I breathed into his body, then looked into his face. "Hence my proposition."

So I spoke to him of Hannah Miles, and how crucial it was to know the truth of her death, and how we might go about discovering it. Subdued and downcast, Sin listened, and when I was done, he took my hand and led me to the automotive masterpiece that was Kurt Libo's '62 Chevy.

"What are you doing?"

He opened the passenger door. "I believe Kurt owes me one."

I climbed into the truck. He went around the other side.

"Where are we going?"

Resting his palms on the steering wheel, Sin looked out the windshield for a place inside himself. "If we're to get to the bottom of what happened to Hannah, I know where we must begin."

XXXV

IF SOME NEW YORK PROMOTER WERE TO HYPE THIS SCENE, HE'D GO with Day-Glo flyers announcing Rave Around the Graves. Kids tranced willy-nilly in a colorful delirium, wielding chemoluminescence. True, no portable sound system was plugged in to pump out beats-beats-beats, but everyone was too blitzed to notice.

"Zounds!" Sin exclaimed, taking in the sight. "Have they no respect?"

So my iconoclastic soldier for sexual freedom had an old-fashioned bent. Then again, Sin would naturally be deferential to the dead.

The first person to come running up to us was Con Emerson, who'd eschewed a costume save two glow golf balls dangling from the crotch of his cargos.

"Dude!" he hollered, and punched Sin squarely on the

bicep, then grabbed him in an ungainly hug. "Dude, man, I love you, man!"

Sin went with it, rocking Con and ruffling his hair.

"Sin, you are so beautiful!" Con bellowed, then opened one arm and pulled me in. "You too, Dice! God, you're beautiful."

"You're beautiful, Con." I knew this script. "I love you."

"Yeah! Love! Right! I love you too!" he said with absolute earnestness, and then loped off like a distracted toddler.

Sin raised an eyebrow.

"Ecstasy," I explained.

"Evidently," he replied.

"It's a drug; it, uh, opens you up," I clarified. Considering the collective horniness of Swoon these days, phenethylamine seemed like overkill. Still, I was glad that Con hadn't blown his brains all over the Emerson rec room or run away to become the victim of some chicken hawk. It seemed like he was going with the gay thing. Smiling at Sin, I asked, "So, where to now?"

"I'm not sure," he said. "I've not been here by night before."

"Heyyyyy! Hiiiii!" trilled a girl we didn't know—a freshman, no doubt. She vaulted herself onto Sin like a gymnast. I tried to decipher her attire—my best guess was hippie-faerie-astronaut.

Gently, Sin peeled her off and sent her packing. "And I wasn't anticipating all these diversions." His scoped the boneyard. "Let's try this way."

Off we went, equipped with an unraveworthy flashlight

filched from the Chevy. The deeper we forayed, the older the monuments, which were mostly maudlin and strangely pretty. A sea captain had an ornate anchor carved into his marker. The grave of a child depicted a garden-tending cherub. There were intricate portraits, lounging skeletons with and without shrouds; a generic icon adorning many stones resembled a lightbulb skull that sprouted wings. I trained my mind on Hannah Miles, beseeching her to guide us to her earthly bed. And in her way, she did.

A warmth-of-spring fragrance on this bracing autumn night. "Lilacs?"

Sin paused, inhaled, concurred. "Her passion."

We followed the scent to an arbor of bushes in full bloom, the pale purple opalescent under the moon. The shrubs bent toward each other to arch above a plain stone engraved with nothing but a name and two terse dates that said so little yet told all. Sin fell to his knees, reached out to trace each letter and numeral. Standing back a bit, I mused on how it feels to grieve when you have no soul.

"Hannah . . . ," he called.

Hannah, I thought.

Maybe she'd appear like Ruby, in livid living color with a bag of FX tricks. Or as the stereotypical transparent specter, all sighs and moans and icy light. If she appeared at all. There was significant chance my presence would perturb her—I was, after all, in love with her man, my objective in cracking the mystery of her death entirely selfish. Might she come as a gray-cloaked banshee, railing at me for the temerity to disrupt her rest? I lay my palm on Sin's shoulder; he reached up to place his hand over mine.

"Hannah," he said. "Please . . ."

Hannah, please.

And she came trotting up. In a coppery coat. Intelligent black eyes framed by a pointed face. And a lush flame of fur trailing straight out behind her.

I gasped quietly. Very softly, very slowly, I knelt behind Sin. The vixen posed a foot away, circled the spot, and sat. Take the wonder I'd felt meeting Marsh's foal and quadruple it to imagine my awe before this creature, so beautiful, so precious, and wild as the woods themselves.

Sin didn't speak aloud; he didn't have to. Inside my head I heard him. The little fox did too.

"Hannah. So. You've come."

She watched him with bright avidity.

"You grace us by heeding our call," he said. "May I present Miss Candice Reagan Moskow. You needn't fear her—she is a noble woman."

The vixen fixed her eyes on me, summed me up, and returned her gaze to Sin.

"Ah, but then, you feared no one. I loved you for that, Hannah.

Even if it brought your demise." Remorse resounded in a minor key. "Which is why we've come."

She cocked her head. She was listening.

"For centuries I seethed over your murder. The rage kept me alive, my dying words a vow for justice. And how I thrashed in my grave, awaiting the chance."

At that, her tail swished, once left, once right.

"In truth, my thirst for revenge overshadowed even our love. The rage was all that mattered."

The little fox sat perfectly still again.

"Now I believe I must know the details of your undoing. I cannot even tell why, except I think it will . . . help me somehow. You know peace now—I can tell by the very form you chose this night. But I am lost, I am floundering, Hannah, not man, not phantom, just this . . . this thing that draws breath in order to punish."

Now the fox regarded me again, as though she understood my role in Sin's existence, and did not judge it.

"So I ask for your blessing, Hannah, and your guidance. Dice and I, we know not a whit about what we propose to do. Where to begin? How to proceed? Through what portal starts the journey toward truth? In the verbiage of this modern age, we're clueless!"

At that, the vulpine vision lifted a paw to her pert snout, the way a proper lady in another era would discreetly mask amusement with a fan. Then, to my amazement, she took two dainty steps closer. With utmost care and quiet, Sin extended his hand, and the little fox nuzzled his fingers. Incredibly, miraculously, when I reached out a tickly flicker of whiskers and that wet button nose grazed my knuckles, too.

I cast gleaming eyes at Sin and saw that he matched me. We both knew the vixen's kiss sanctioned our pursuit into the past . . . our pursuit together. Except we hadn't long to idle in enchantment. There came a change in the wind, stinging from the north. The small animal rose on her haunches and tested the air. As she picked up the scent, her fur began to bristle and a stuttering noise came from her throat, followed by a short, sharp bark.

Without realizing it, I'd mirrored her stance, sitting up on my knees, lifting my head, trying to define that smell. It didn't come from around here. It didn't belong here. Yet somehow it was here—and I knew it.

The second the vixen bolted, it came to me.

Wolverine.

XXXVI

HALLOWEEN BACKLASH BIT ME THE NEXT MORNING. BIT ME EVERY-where. Rolling painfully over in bed I found myself face-to-face with my boy. An inch nearer, my nose touched his chin, the joy this induced dissolving what ailed me like sugar in water.

And I remembered.

Returning from Grimley Parish Cemetery. Feeling near collapse. Saying to him, "Stay with me."

Nothing happened. By that I mean the universally understood connotation of "nothing happened." Some partial undressing ensued, then we got under the covers. My curves melted into his corners. It felt like dough rising. Thus expanded and enveloped, I slept. Now, however much later, I learned that golems, too, sleep—sleep like stone, a statue with a heartbeat. I lay there, counting his eyelashes till I lost count. Again, I slept.

The next time I awoke, Sin had too.

"Hey," one of us said first.

"Hey," one of us seconded.

RubyCat heard our morning murmurs. She circled the lump we made, took up position between our rumpled heads, and politely tapped my cheek.

"Meow?"

"Remain abed," Sin said. "I'll feed the beast." Yet he didn't move.

More adamantly, "Meow!"

Grumbling amiably about serving not one mistress but two, Sin threw off the blankets. Before long, he was back with a glass of juice, a big bowl of Cocoa Puffs, and twin white tablets.

"Can you sit up?"

With effort, I did, to swallow acetaminophen with a gulp of OJ. From the edge of the bed Sin spoon-fed me some cereal, then tried it himself.

"Bah!" He grimaced.

I grinned. "It's an acquired taste."

I crunched a few more bites. "I don't think I can make it to school."

"I'll stay with you."

"No, it's okay—go." I said this weakly. I didn't want him to leave. I flashed on Hannah Miles, the shape she'd appeared in. If Sin had slain her, wouldn't she have come as a grizzly bear or something equally man-eating?

His face inscrutably set, he lifted a corner of the sheet and peered beneath. "Let me stay. We can play doctor and patient."

I shrugged (ouch), expanded my smile. "With so many people E-tripping last night, Swonowa will be a ghost town today anyway." As if a clock had struck, I all at once felt self-conscious. "I should try to shower," I said.

"Ah . . . well." Either he shared my timidity or at least respected it. "That ought make you feel better."

Under the spray I examined my body. It was a map, each bluish bruise a landmass. But steamy water, combined with the meds kicking in, did wonders, and I accomplished the feat of dressing. Downstairs, Sin taunted R.C. with her feather toy. He wore socks. And tighty whities. And had somehow acquired a glow tube, now dimmed, around one wrist. The kitten went bonkers at his ankles. I could have watched them forever. Then again, I couldn't. "The bathroom's all yours," I said. "I'll scrounge around for a clean T-shirt you can wear."

I was searching through my father's dresser when the phone rang.

"Hello?"

"Honey! You're there!"

"Daddy!" I flopped onto my parents' bed.

"I had this great message all ready to recite. But hey, why aren't you in school?"

I thought fast. "Halloween hangover. Too much candy corn."

He gave me the "cool dad" chuckle. "You sure it wasn't too much beer?"

"You know I hate beer. But it was kind of a scene. It's fine, though; it's not like I'm missing a test or anything. So what's up?"

"Well, on the topic of crazy carousing, we had the wrap party last night. And this officially being November, I assume all those nasty Connecticut allergens to be dead. So I booked my flight into Hartford; I'm going to spend the week with you."

"Really? Daddy, that's fantastic!" I meant it; I did. Just that *parentis interruptus* would delay the psychic journey ahead. I filled Sin in when he found me.

"Maybe we can all have dinner," I said. "We'll go to that steak place in Norris. Or, no, I'll make lasagna. Daddy loves my lasagna."

He pulled the "Property of *Law & Order*" tee over his wet head. "I'm sure I will as well," he said, but his eyes were stormy, clouds rumbling through.

"Look, Sin, my mother will come out as usual on Friday, and by Sunday they'll be back in the city and we can . . . resume."

"Yes," he said. "Very well."

He was unconvincing. I looked at him sternly. "Till then, I hereby impose a moratorium on malicious mischief."

"I'll try to abide by it," he said. "Right now I'd best get the truck back to Kurt. He'll be apoplectic."

So Sin went and Daddy came, and everything was normal. Relatively. Con Emerson began wearing eyeliner to school, and the one kid who made a peep about it got his lights punched out. Ms. Brinker showed up to the library in her ridiculous frilly dress because she had a date after work, with none other than itinerant caretaker Jameson McDaniel. I barely recognized Swoon's own boogeyman, scrubbed and brushed, sans army jacket and German shepherd.

Momster hit town wielding prosecco, which is almost as good as champagne, and Sin joined us bearing a humongous pot of chrysanthemums, and it was just like your fondest dream of earning the parental stamp of approval for your boy.

Then Uncle Gordon showed up.

After a long day at the office, the professional men of Swoon generally transformed into a casting call for Lacoste. My uncle was still in lawyerly pinstripes, though with loosened tie and haggard face. It was past nine, but our quartet still lingered over lasagna.

"Gordon! Hello!" my parents heralded, more or less in unison.

A ripple of displeasure surged through Sin—my uncle undoubtedly reminded him of his former lawyer—but he quelled it. He was being good.

"Prosecco?" Momster tilted the bottle.

"No thank you, Lesley. Uhhh . . ."

"Oh, Gordon, don't tell me you're on the wagon," Momster

chided merrily. "Come sit down and have a glass! You look like you could use it."

"No, I—I—"

"Uncle Gordon?" I ventured. "Did something happen?"

The question made him lucid. "Yes," he said. "That's it. Something's happened. There's been an accident. It's Lainie. Her car went off the Davender Bridge."

XXXVII

THE "APPOINTMENT IN TORRINGTON" AUNT LAINIE HAD BEEN rushing home from might have been taken as genuine had she been wearing actual clothes under her prim tan trench coat. But she'd driven to her rendezvous in nothing but La Perla and London Fog, no doubt as a treat for Mr. Mercedes. So everyone knew she'd been up to salacious no-good when they fished her out of the Housatonic.

The moments following Uncle Gordon's announcement were busy ones, all of us manning our battle stations. Momster, superb in a crisis, made necessary inquiries, first and foremost ascertaining that Lainie was alive but critical at Lutheran Hospital.

"What about the children? Do they know?" Momster asked.

"Penny, yes, she's waiting in the car, but not the boys," said Gordon. "Penny is . . . very upset."

"And our parents?"

Gordon gaped blankly.

"Bert and Helen?"

"Oh, Christ!" He raked his already disheveled hair. "No, I haven't phoned them."

"All right, don't worry. We'll call from the hospital; it's early in Arizona yet." She turned to me. "Candice, go across the street and look after the boys." Then to Daddy. "Peter, you drive." And to Gordon. "We'll follow you."

And they were off. Like my mother, I moved swiftly, Sin striding after me to 9 Daisy Lane. I couldn't deal with him— not with this searing inside me that knew Lainie's plummet was another tick on his scorecard. Except, as it splintered through my solar plexus, I finally accepted that this was no game. Lainie was a human being, someone I loved; she was tight-roping between life and death because of the boy who was my blunder. This was Sin's fault, and by extension mine, yet desperate as I was to put things right, it didn't seem as though I was up to the challenge. Like when I let myself into the Leonards'—there were Silas and Jordan, antic with the blind energy of turmoil, only what did I know from tending to bewildered little children?

I didn't have to know a thing. Sin stepped up, so tender, so calm. Using quilts and chairs, he made a tent in the living room as my suspicions melted into a pool of evry-lil-thing-gonnabe-alright. After a while, the boys settled down. After another while, Sin hefted them, first Silas, then Jordan, up to bed.

When the Leonards' phone jangled, I jumped to get it. Momster.

"How is she?" All my fears about Lainie's condition—and how she got there—leapt back at me like attack dogs.

"It's touch-and-go." Her voice was strained.

"Oh . . . Mommy, how are *you*?" I hadn't called her Mommy since I was nine.

"Holding up. I just keep telling myself she'll pull through. Anyway, honey, your uncle will spend the night here. We're on our way home now with Penny."

"Okay."

"Candy, I want you to stay with her."

Sin came down the stairs. "What's the news?"

I cocked my head. "Do you really care?" I didn't fling the words; I just wanted to know.

Studying my face, his creased with injury. "What do you mean to imply?"

"I mean," I said, then faltered, "that . . . I don't know what I mean. All I know is I look at you with those kids, and you're so sweet and sensitive, and you know just what to do. But then I think of their mother taking a dive off the Davender Bridge, and you might as well have messed with her brakes, or put an oil slick under her wheels."

"Dice, that's not so!" He came toward me. "I had nothing to do with that!"

I felt my fingers clench and release. How I wished I could believe him—he was a satyr, not a sadist. "What are you telling me, that you don't want to bring the Leonards down?"

"No!" he swore. "Not this way. Your aunt . . . isn't even from here; she was never anything but kind to me . . ."

I started to pace, which is what I do when going berserk. "Oh, Sin! Don't you see? Maybe you didn't write it out in your Swoon-smashing playbook, but you . . . you have no control over what you do anymore, what you've . . . unleashed on this place."

Interrupting my tigress stalk, he took me by the forearms. I shuddered, stomped, was still. "Dice," he said. "Look at me."

I did.

"Dice, I am so—"

Pen slammed into the house. Sin let me go. I ran to my cousin, tried to hug her. She smacked my arms away.

"Get off me, Dice."

"But . . . Pen—"

"Just get away from me." Without so much as acknowledging Sin, she headed for the antique armoire that served as the Leonard liquor cabinet. Which was locked. Pen knew where the key was kept but opted to smash the glass with an angry elbow. Shards scattered to the rug and onto her cheerleading jacket. She grabbed a decanter of something brown.

"God, Pen! Take it easy."

"Easy? Cousin, easy is my middle name. Guess it runs in the family."

She lifted the stopper and swigged.

I went to her, put a hand on her shoulder. She flung me off again, eyes sparking, then assumed a façade of calm. "Really, Dice. I'd prefer it if you refrained from touching me." She drank again. I stared at her. "You seem to think I need comforting. But why? Because my mother had a wreck? Or because she's been fucking her dermatologist?"

So it was Dr. Mercedes. "You know about that?"

"I'm not as blond as I look," she said, gesturing with the decanter. The fierce fluid splashed in threat. "Let me tell you what's so ironic. She'd been going to him for years, all on the up and up of course, to maintain her stupid model complexion. Every line, every spot, she'd go running. He'd inject her with this, plane off that, sell her some four-hundred-dollar youth serum. Well, wait till he sees her face now." Pen sneered and slugged. "But I suppose he can always put a paper bag over her head. And if she comes out of this a vegetable, even better. Then he won't have to listen to her talk."

What was the source of this? Pen and Lainie had always been cloyingly close, the kind of mother-daughter combo Lifetime movies are made of. Besides, Pen wasn't one to throw stones in the promiscuity department.

"Oh, Pen, you're upset," I said lamely.

"Upset? Hardly. Bitch is just getting what she deserves, and you know why? Because she couldn't be honest about it. If she'd really fallen in love with him and went off like Marsh's mother did—you know, had some dignity—she wouldn't have been speeding home to put up her big fake front of wifely devotion. But she doesn't love Dr. Darwin; and she doesn't love my dad, or . . . or any of us. She's just a selfish pig."

Pen set down the decanter, took off her jacket, and aimed her venom elsewhere. At Sin, who stood quietly near his home-spun wigwam.

"You!" It wasn't a pronoun; it was an indictment. "What are you doing here?"

Sin clasped his hands behind him. "I came with Dice to help mind your brothers."

"No!" she cried. "You came to ruin my life! That's why you're here." Pen shook her head as if something had landed on her. "What an idiot I was. That whole ritual in the green, and then you showing up, I thought it was about getting you *out* of me so you could get *into* me. I thought you *loved* me."

A pang of guilt to the solar plexus. I'd never told Pen that it wasn't merely her life Sin had come to ruin. Naturally she'd believe his manifestation was borne of desire for her. Guys always jumped through hoops for her—why not ghosts?

"But you don't want me; you don't love me." Her keen

turned to whine as she approached him. "You won't even have sex with me again. I meant nothing to you, nothing. You took my virginity like it was a stick of gum."

Then they were an inch apart, and I couldn't tell if she was about to kiss him—hungrily, crazily, in that desperate way you'd kiss a boy you'd already lost—or slap him. I don't think she knew, either.

Before she could act, Sin began to speak—and all the gentleness he'd displayed minutes earlier was gone. "You're right, Pen, I don't love you." The weariness in his tone daunted decoding. "You're right that I don't want you. Where you're incorrect is in the conceit that I came to Swoon with the sole intention of taking your precious maidenhead, sullying your reputation, and casting you aside. What you are, Pen, is insignificant."

That made her mind up. She hauled off and struck him, digging her nails in and dragging them across his cheek. Welts appeared, but the light in the room was meager—was the yield bright red, like my blood, like Pen's, or the umber of the earth?

Sin did not falter; he went on. "You're a little girl from a small town, that's all," he said. "But lo, what's this? You're changing, Pen. You're *seeing*. For the first time in seventeen spoiled and sheltered years you're confronting the hypocrisy of your life. That's what I've done to you, forced you to face the lie under which you and your kind function, and have so functioned for centuries. That's all I've done to you, Pen; that's what I've done *for* you. And you're by no means the only one. This whole town will look into its duplicitous heart before I'm done, and let the pieces fall where they may."

Swoon, Connecticut. A painting by Norman Rockwell. Now showing the wear and tear and ugly truth of what happened to that picture of Dorian Gray.

"Get out of my house," Pen seethed. "Get out of my house, and go back to whatever hell you came from."

"As you please." He could have chucked her under the chin. He could have grabbed her and kissed her until she went to goo. Instead he bowed, bid us both a fare-thee-well, and left the premises.

Pen and I were alone.

It was my turn, I figured, and I braced myself for the onslaught. Didn't I deserve it? I'd tried to do right by her, keep her from harm, but I'd messed it up across the board. Which was nothing new. To love someone, stand up for her, and be there for her, and have her slip through your fingers anyway is like dying halfway. Only you mustn't be anything but thankful, thankful, thankful because you are so lucky, lucky, lucky that nothing, nothing, nothing happened to you.

Now, nothing was happening to me again, only more slowly. One day I woke up and Ruby was gone. Here, in Swoon, I'd wake up and a tiny bit more of Pen would be chipped away—

the sweet-tempered, golden-girl Pen I knew, anyway. And whatever I'd do to prevent it was about as solid and effective as a sigh on the wind.

I stood there, waiting. But Pen didn't scream at me. She did something worse. She looked at me. "You knew," she said quietly. "All along, you knew."

Then she turned away and walked up the stairs to her room.

XXXVIII

Sturdy, resilient, sniffle-resistant, my aunt rallied and within a week was out of ICU. Momster and Daddy extended their Swoon stay until ensured of her recovery, then beat a hasty retreat for civilization. Once her internal injuries stabilized, Lainie was okayed for release. Her external injuries, however, would require a number of cosmetic surgeries. All in all, she'd been lucky, lucky, lucky that she hadn't perished in the plunge. Another plus, in true Swoon style Uncle Gordon made no accusations of adultery or motions for divorce. Even Pen, hostile as she'd been the night of the accident, sucked it up to adopt the doting daughter role.

"I don't see why she's not back in school," Marsh remarked as she drove me home from Swonowa one blustery, rain-drenched Friday. "It's not like they can't afford a maid *and* a private nurse."

"Yeah, I guess." Call me the queen of noncommittal. The

truth is, I had no idea what really went on behind the drawn drapes of 9 Daisy Lane. Pen barely addressed me when I'd visited the hospital, and now that Lainie was recuperating chez Leonard, my cousin fully shut me out. Only right then I didn't care to think about my cousin. I rarely got to hang with Marsh these days—this was a treat. "You want to come in for a while?"

"Can't," she said. "Got to get to 'work.'"

Marsh marked the air with four fingers. Last week her grandmother had returned to her own home, upping Marsh's scullery and sister-sitting duties. Which would have left her no time for Crane. So she quit her gig at the stationer's and was allowing her rich boyfriend to pay her salary. As long as she brought in her regular contribution to the household income, Psycho Dad would be none the wiser—it's not like he'd ever set foot in Letters Unlimited. That was her reasoning, anyway. To me, it seemed she was figure skating on land mines. Sneaking around was risky enough, but Crane shelling out for the pleasure of her company was really tempting fate, not to mention icky.

Only who knows—maybe I was just jealous that Marsh's romance had launched while mine was bound to crash and burn. She evidently didn't mind kept-woman status, and it sure did agree with her. Formerly the mousiest girl in Pen's posse, she had blossomed, big time: Her skin was clear, her hair free of greasy blight, and although she was still a twig, sported a new improved (read: larger) cup size. Either the miracle of love or Ortho Tri-Cyclen, probably both.

Marsh frowned, realizing it hurt my feelings to be blown off like that. "But I can sit for a minute," she said, putting it in P in front of my house. "Fill me in on you and Sin. Any developments? You two looked awfully cozy on Halloween."

We'd run into Marsh and Crane at the cemetery, exchanged obligatory rhapsodies, but I wouldn't have called us cozy. After all, we were there on business. I gazed at the slanting rain, resisted the metronomic spell of windshield wipers.

"Ohhh," I said, heavy on an exhale, "not much to report. With all the family drama lately, I've been otherwise occupied." Which was true, but I nonetheless felt a void when Sin wasn't around, and I couldn't stanch my suspicions about what he might be up to while keeping his distance from Daisy Lane.

"Dice, you and Sin will wind up together, I just know it!" Marsh predicted with the glowy optimism of one in love for real. "Have faith, okay?"

"I will," I said. "Thanks. You know, for the lift, and the good vibes and all." Then I ran from her car through the downpour. R.C. greeted me inside, and I picked her up, then sat us both down in the gloom of the living room. Momster wouldn't be up this weekend—*In Star* was in the throes of its spectacular year-end double issue, so she'd be perusing paparazzi pics and sifting celeb faux pas round the clock. Daddy had meetings in

LA—post-production buzz on the Wahlberg picture was opening doors for him. My plans? What plans? Pen wouldn't talk to me, Marsh was "working," Wick was blissfully back with Boz. And Sin, the passion and impossibility of my life, the best and worst thing ever to happen to me, was . . . who knew . . .

"Pathetic," I complained to R.C., nuzzling her furry crest. This wasn't about being alone. I was cool with alone. I enjoyed my own company, sought my own counsel. This was different, desolate. This was loneliness. I tried to toss it off. "Look at me, a crazy old cat lady at seventeen."

Which R.C. didn't take too kindly, and wriggled away.

So I sat by myself. Turned on a lamp. Riffled through a catalog. The afternoon closed in on me, claustrophobic and damp. Mustering enthusiasm from absolutely nowhere, I practiced my piece for the chorale recital—I'd snagged a solo in an Andrea Gabrieli madrigal—but my voice sounded hollow to me. Besides, I had competition, this incompatible melody filtering through . . . my head? The air? Had I left the clock radio on in my room?

It was thin and tinny, far away. Then it grew in volume and insistency, seeming to come from everywhere. By the time it was booming—rattle-the-rafters, throb-the-floorboards, call-the-cops loud—I was scared. And excited. And, oddly, annoyed. Because I *knew* the song; it was hugely famous, one of those catchy-as-a-bad-cold hit singles that during its heyday played in every store and on every station. I think it might have even been in a TV commercial for some soda or breath mint or something. Yet the lyrics eluded me—and it was driving me nuts.

Only when the lights started flashing and a mirror ball descended from the living room ceiling did I give in, get up, and begin to dance.

"Ahhhhh'm coming up, so you better get this party started . . ."

And in shiny leather and ice-white spikes, Ruby was dancing with me, howling vintage Pink at the top of her lungs. Anyone with a pulse in the year of Our Lord 2002—even a geeked-out grade-schooler like me—knew those words, and now I was yowling, too. Twelve Daisy Lane, da hottest club in Western C-T! Whoo! Me and my girl shuffled and slid, we hopped and waved, we popped, locked, and dropped, Ruby costume-changing for every track. Lacking such sartorial skills, I could only remove articles of clothing as the temperature started to rise.

Which would have me barefoot, in jeans and bra, when we congaed into the kitchen. It was time for refreshment. Ruby put a bulbous cast iron pot on the stove. She lit the gas, and flames slapped the cauldron's bottom like blue sadistic fingers.

And I said, "Wait . . ."

But she didn't wait. She flung open the fridge. She threw back the cupboards, the ones above the counter and the ones below the sink. "Come on, Candy! Come on!" my best friend urged. My best friend, forever.

"Ruby, no . . ."

Déjà vu to the twelfth power. Rice and milk and applesauce. Cinnamon, cayenne, and Cocoa Puffs. The last of the leftover lasagna, forgotten, congealing on the bottom shelf. Pine-Sol and Windex and that scouring powder with the apropos name of Bon Ami.

"Hmm," Ruby hmmed. The junk drawer: thumbtacks, rubber bands, a spool of thread. Next, a pair of crystal wineglasses. Ruby cracked one like an egg on the cauldron's rim. Broken bits tinkled into the brew.

"Ca-nnn-deee!" Ruby wheedled and held out the other wineglass. "Come on. I miss you so much . . ."

I missed her too. I walked toward the stove. Could I do this? Why not? What did I have going on here? A fractured family. A town full of souls I'd set up for devastation and couldn't save. And a love with no future. Ruby's lashes bowed in understanding— she knew I couldn't win with Sin, that every outcome from any angle was the fuzzy end of the lollipop stick. I took the wineglass, smashed it.

"Yes, yes, oh, baby, yessss!" More like yeshhhh. Ruby had a shovel; she was using it to stir. I laughed and grabbed the handle, too; we mixed up our mess together.

"Now for the secret ingredient." The ring on Ruby's left

hand was the size of a grapefruit and set with a clasp and a hinge. She flipped the clasp and let glittery granules of some superdeluxe pharmaceutical pour into the pot.

"This will make it feel real good going down," Ruby said with a wink and one of her best smiles, the one that promised the world.

Together, together. Forever, forever. In an Eden of chocolate at every meal and no extra pounds on the scale. No bad hair days, either. A thousand and one outfits at your beck and call. And Ruby. A place with Ruby.

Once more she stirred, and then lifted the spade to me. "Hey, ma, you so fine—let me buy you a drink."

We cracked up so hard some of the stuff spilled, sizzling an inkblot pattern on the laminate.

"Quit it, Ruby. Don't make me laugh."

"Okay, you're right. This is serious. Let's be serious."

We pulled poker faces, and locked eyes. Her eyes, almond-shaped and amber-colored and always so loyal and true. My hand on her hand, we brought the smoking potion to my lips.

XXXIX

"WHAT'S COOKING, GOOD-LOOKING?"

The absolute lamest line in the history of humankind. Spoken in a hush—and in jest. Yet caught unaware by the words, I spun from the stove as if charged with some heinous crime. The spoon (just an ordinary spoon) slipped from my grasp, clanged against the pot (plain old Calphalon), and landed on the floor. And there was Sin, an audience of one for my impression of Rachael Ray gone very awry. Events of seconds earlier fragmented, then got sucked into a vortex and delegated to a vault of nether consciousness. What *was* cooking? It smelled vile, whatever it was. Suddenly I had the impulse to give him a hero's welcome, throw my arms around his neck, and thank him . . . thank him for . . . something. But I didn't do that. I just stole away from the noxious concoction and said, "Hey, you. It's really good to see you."

"You too." He said this in earnest, to my face, before drinking in my state of dishabille. "Very good. Exceptionally good."

Hands on hips, I let him look. "Shut up," I advised.

The planter of mums Sin had brought for dinner with my parents sat on the counter, wilting. He ran a finger over bronze and burgundy petals. "I was wondering what you were doing tonight."

"Me? Not much. You?"

"The same," he said. "Which leads me to think, if you're not doing anything, and I'm not doing anything, it's an ideal opportunity for us to do what we're destined to do."

How furious and frustrated I'd been the night of Lainie's accident, and how committed to stopping Sin—for good. Yet now he was prompting me. He was here; he was ready—neither of us was playing anymore. It was time to get this done.

"Let me find my shirt," I said, retracing a path I couldn't quite remember taking. There, dangling from the newel post: my fleecy sweater. I pulled it on, grabbed a jacket, and we walked out into the dwindling rain. The Cutlass sat rumbling in neutral. Sin opened a rear door for me.

"Hey! Long time no see!" Marsh chirped.

"Yeah, really." Beside me, Sin sought to fold his legs into the cramped backseat of the coupe.

"Well, we ran into Sin in town," Marsh explained as Crane drove off. "When he mentioned he was hoping to hook up with you, how could we not offer to bring you two together?"

God, she was squishy these days. "Ah. Gotcha. Sweet," I said. "So you still at 'work'?"

Marsh emitted a sound, half snicker, half purr. "Uh-huh. I told Mrs. Stevens I'd stay late and help her decorate the store for the holidays."

Unlike the rest of America, which sets up for Christmas the day after Halloween, Swoon shuns such crass commercialism and waits a few weeks.

"I'll probably be there till at least eleven. But of course I'm getting paid overtime." She leaned into Crane across the console. "Isn't that right, Mrs. Stevens?"

"Oh, indeed." Crane took his eyes off the road to kiss the part in her hair. "So where to, then?"

"Yes, Dice," Sin said. "Where?"

There was only one place. "The Wolverine Tavern." Per the vixen's terror, that would be our portal.

"Ick!" Marsh gagged. "Dice, that's just crazy!"

What was up her butt? Marsh wasn't normally opposed to getting her drink on. She turned in her seat and gave me a stern look. Which I had to ignore. "Yeah, I know it's a hole, but I bet they have a pool table," I said, winging it. "Sin challenged me to a game, and I intend to beat his ass for him."

"Fine, but you don't have to stoop that low to do it," Marsh reasoned. "Pen has a pool table; why don't we just go there?"

Sin coughed. "Marsh, hmm, you see . . . Dice and me . . . and Pen . . . in the same room . . . bad idea."

"Ohhh . . ." She got the hint. "Well, I'd say let's go to Wick's—they have a beautiful billiards room—but she's gone to Vermont with Boz's family for the weekend."

Here, Crane piped up. "This Wolverine Tavern, it's legendary, isn't it? I've heard of it but haven't actually seen it."

"There's nothing to see—it's just this nasty dive on Underhill Road," Marsh snapped, then turned back to Sin and me. "Anyway, forget it. I'm sure they card."

I glanced at Sin; he nodded encouragement. We had to keep our priorities straight, and sipping root-beer floats on a double date at Ye Olde Soda Shoppe wasn't one of them. "I hear you, Marsh, but I've got an infallible fake ID—this guy in my old school supplemented his college fund selling them. And Sin looks twenty-one. I don't think we'll have a problem. So why don't you guys just drop us off?"

"Dice, no! I thought we were all going to hang out." Marsh no doubt felt the same sting I did when she had no time for me this afternoon. Gazing out the window, I noticed we were coming up on Underhill Road. Itchy anticipation infected my palms and throat. Soon, Sin and I would bear witness to the murder of Hannah Miles. And Marsh and Crane would be safely out of the way, off to one of Swoon's secluded make-out zones. Except Crane had his own idea.

"The Wolverine Tavern, yes," he said. "I'd rather like to have a go at getting in."

At which his girlfriend expelled a sigh and said, "Okay, sweetie . . . sure."

We pulled up and piled out, and as we neared the entrance, I got the feeling we'd be able to waltz right through. The Wolverine, after all, would be just as susceptible as the rest of Swoon; any formerly rigid door policies would be lax under Sin's sway. The stocky bouncer barely glanced at us; he was far more interested in the action at the classic pinball machine—two girls I vaguely recognized as Swonowa sophomores all giggly and jiggly over a game called El Dorado.

So we weren't the only minors to venture into Swoon's token reprobate roadhouse. The Wolverine was crowded, and among the regulars—hard-looking men in flannel and mullets, harder-looking women with frosty lipstick on thin, chapped frowns—younger flesh shimmered and callow voices called out. There was sawdust on the floor, a television mounted above the bar, and a beautiful old jukebox bleating a procession of country songs—jocular laments, sappy ballads, paeans to trucks, dogs, America, trains.

Crane was clearly digging it, but as he ogled the atmosphere, Marsh gave me a jab in the ribs. "How could you bring us here, Dice!" she hissed into my ear to be heard above the din. "You always have to have your way! You don't care about anyone else!"

I was stunned, but when Crane tugged her arm for attention, I could see in her face how badly she didn't want to be here. She blamed me—I was, after all, to blame—then gave me her back.

We squeezed into the bar to order drinks; I asked for a beer—didn't matter what kind, it was a prop. Marsh clamored for Jägermeister. If she had to be here, she aimed to get good and drunk. She tossed back half a shot, chased it with Budweiser, and finished it off.

Conversation was not going to happen; too cacophonous in there, and besides Marsh seemed to hate me. With so much else at stake, I never imagined I could lose my friend, too. There was no way to quell her anger—I couldn't exactly explain to her why Sin and I had to be there. If only I could turn around and plow toward the front door, get out of this crummy bar and blow off my appointment with the past. Then I felt Sin's hand at my hip, propelling me forward.

We pushed our way to the back room, where there was in fact a pool table, but it was in use, and by now any pretense of a game was forgotten. Fine with me, since I sucked at pool and had to devote my energies elsewhere. Only how, exactly, did you trigger a psychic episode? I'd spent my life ducking them, returning them to Macy's when they did muscle in. Now I needed to bring it on and didn't know where to begin.

Already a little sloppy, Marsh clung to Crane. It wasn't just seventy-proof, herb-infused liqueur getting to her, it was the brutal, teeming stew of the Wolverine—Swoon at its most wanton. Crane's British diffidence had deserted him, too. The two of them began to kiss with abandon, bumbling blind till they found a wall. He put her back against it. He pressed his length upon her. And then they were fully lost in each other, for all intents and purposes alone.

I wasn't about to stand there and watch, but as I looked away, I smiled. I couldn't attest to other couples—how much infidelity or simply raw animal urges were being vented around me—but those two were bona fide. Absolutely, unequivocally in love.

Breaking my reverie, Sin took the untasted beer from my hand and placed it on a ledge. Then he maneuvered me toward the area between jukebox and pool table, jam-packed with jerking bodies. A honky-tonk tune blared, the sort of thing that calls for a jaunty two-step, but once we entered each other's embrace we did little more than rock back and forth.

It was enough. With our arms around each other and without the slightest warning—no tremble doing a trapeze act from neuron to neuron, no particular stink rising above beer and sweat and cheap cologne—Sin and I tumbled down the rabbit hole.

XL

Except that I was wrong.

We two touching, my head tucked beneath his chin, was *not* enough to break the tensile fabric of time and space and send us skittering backward to where we had to be.

Unbeknownst to us, a third essential element was required.

Unbeknownst to us, that third essential element had just sashayed into the bar.

PART III

THE TRIP

XLI

On a summer's morn in the Swoon village green, an entwined pair materialized betwixt the trees. The components drew apart . . . and the bickering began.

"What the—what are *you* doing here?"

"Where else would I be but with you?"

"What? You haven't even spoken to me in weeks."

"That's ridiculous! Have you taken leave of your senses?"

"Taken leave—? Oh, goddamn . . . *Sin?*"

"Pray tell, now what?"

"Uh, you better check yourself."

Which he did, to discover: a gown of fine silk, pleated and full skirted to accommodate a petticoat. A fitted cutaway robe, brocade across the bodice. All in a demure shade of celadon to set off porcelain skin, midnight eyes, and pale gold hair pinned in a complex coiffure. Familiar lockdown. Different clothes.

"What in blazes have you done to me?" Sin lashed with Pen's tongue.

"Me? I didn't do it."

"Then who did? No, more pressingly, *why?*"

As the cock in chick's clothing crowed in dismay, I got a load of my own gear: Basic black with starched white cuffs, plus no-nonsense button-up boots. Figures, right?

"Damnation!" Sin cursed, tugging at the unkind realities of eighteenth-century femininity. "I thought I was over and done with this misbegotten body. Here I am, back in it—and torturously attired as well."

Though quick to commiserate, I'd come to see that telepathic tripping would make its own organic sense—we'd just have to roll with it. "I don't know how women dealt with it, but if this is 1769, we can't go traipsing around in jeans and T-shirts," I said. "Look, Sinclair Youngblood Powers is happily inhabiting his own body right now. So for you to be here, too, you'd have to be someone else . . . at least superficially."

"Valid enough. But tell me, Lady Know-It-All, couldn't I be someone with a bit . . . less . . . breast?" Sin complained, still tugging. "Why the devil did it have to be Pen?"

Another good question I was ill equipped to answer. "Why not?" I shrugged. "She's been part of our unholy alliance all along."

Sin made a moue, then surveyed our surroundings. "So be

it. But if I must look like a Leonard, I'll be damned if I don't put it to use. Let's go." He strode off—or tried to, an assertive strut not so easy in kitten-heeled kid leather slippers.

I was at his side. "Go? Where?"

"To the blasted pettifogger's, that's where."

Uh-huh. Glad I asked.

Dotting the landscape, simple structures native to New England known as saltboxes—two stories in front, one in back, with a steep, sloped roof and a single chimney. Sin sallied forth, knowing his way, as homes became larger, more lavish. Eventually we reached a big place with pointed gables and a prominent porch.

"Follow my lead," he said, rapping imperiously with a brass lion's head. A maid came, and Sin swept in, me in his wake. "I've come to see Samuel Leonard. And I'd like to know what kept him from meeting my coach." Skirts swishing, we took the hall until met by a plumpish person with too many ringlets set precariously around her head.

"Ah! Cousin Edwina!" Sin said with a barely perceptible curtsy.

"I *am* Edwina Leonard." The young woman didn't seem so sure. "You are . . . ?"

"But how could you not know? I am Penelope Leonard; your husband Samuel is my second cousin once removed. Cousin Penelope . . . from New York?" The silver-tongued master

323

might as well have told the befuddled creature he was Cousin Zangodork from Jupiter. "Surely you were informed in advance of my visit."

"Why, no, Cousin Penel—"

"That's impossible! I posted the letters myself."

"Oh dear, oh dear!" stammered Edwina. "My most sincere apologies, but I truly had no knowledge of your arrival. Or even your existence!"

"Can you imagine how dreadful it was, waiting there by the coach? Why, I'll have you know the impertinent driver traveled on to Hartford with my baggage still aboard!"

"Oh, my goodness! Samuel will not be pleased."

"Surely not." Sin pursed Pen's lips. "And to think I made a point of paying this courtesy call—I'm on my way to visit Uncle Harrison Leonard in Hartford." This, served in a tone to imply the Swoon Leonards country cousins of no importance. Brows lifted in hauteur, Sin gazed about. "I suppose we've no choice but to make the best. It's not as though the coach stops daily here in Swine—beg pardon, *Swoon*."

I thought I'd lose it. Sin was too funny—too cruel, but too funny. Edwina, embarrassed, ordered her maid to set up tea in the drawing room. (Speaking of maids, guess who dear Cousin Penelope introduced me as.) Sin yawned and bemoaned the strenuous coach ride, prompting our hostess to lead her guest upstairs to rest.

"We can find your maid a pallet in the servants' quarters," Edwina said.

"Never!" Sin took my hand and—audaciously!—kissed the knuckles. "Candice is far more than a maid to me. We are, indeed, like sisters . . . nay, closer."

Our hostess bobbed her head as she revealed a small but serviceable bedchamber.

"She'll sleep in the bed with me." Edwina's face turned to cake flour—the hue and texture of New England prude. Regarding her sweetly, Sin said, "Really, dude, no problem. It's cool!" Then we disappeared behind the door and gave in to hilarity.

"God, Sin, you are *so* mean!"

He plopped onto the canopy bed. "Only because there's no oxygen going to my brain," he said. "Come, release me from my stays, won't you?"

"Your . . . stays?"

"Corset, my lady. You're no doubt wearing such an undergarment yourself." He sat up halfway to swipe at me; I parried neatly. "Are you so appalled at my condescension toward our reluctant hostess? You mustn't be deceived by that innocent incompetent act. Edwina Leonard may be a little twit, but she's a passive-aggressive little twit."

I looked at him. "You *knew* her, didn't you?"

"Yes, Dice. I knew her. Not that I care to recount particulars for you."

"Not that I care to hear them!"

"Dice, please, I'm truly in agony. Come now. Undo me, and I'll undo you."

"I don't think either of us should get too comfortable." Our purpose here was imperative, and pertained more to the time we had left than the one we'd entered. "This isn't some colonial theme park, you know."

With a pendulum's arc, the mood shifted. Sin sobered, sat up straight. "Quite right," he said. "First thing I suggest we do is learn today's date."

Made sense. We'd left Swoon on an autumn's night and reappeared centuries later in summer; we had to allow some margin for error. "I'll go downstairs; maybe there's a newspaper or calendar or something." At the door I stopped, turned back, saw him with his head in his hands. "Sin, are you all right?"

He glanced up at me. "You think me a cad the way I behave, so cavalier, so callous. But it's only to avoid confronting our presence in this time and place."

"Oh." The syllable somehow scaled the huge obstruction in my throat. For we had come to witness a brutal, fatal beating. And do nothing. Absolutely nothing. Intervention was anathema—the upshot could change history. But stand by and let it happen? I couldn't even handle a gorno flick. Me and my bright ideas.

There, on the bed, swathed in green silk, sat a monster.

Pretty and pampered as my cousin Pen, yet containing all Sin's strength and rage, the enormity of his sorrow. Docile for the moment but with an untested capacity for everything that flew out of Pandora's box. So I couldn't help but wonder, as a queasy trickle spread throughout my consciousness, if changing history had been my monster's agenda all along.

XLII

It was the fourth of July. Small f. No fireworks, no red-white-and-blue big deal. Shortly past noon on this ordinary day, Edwina Leonard tapped politely to call her guests to dinner. A vegan's nightmare—beef broth followed by slabs of stringy, grayish flesh, plus a pudding also made of mystery meat. Sin and I pushed the ample slop around our plates.

"I must apologize again for Samuel's unfortunate absence," Edwina said.

"You needn't, really," Sin pooh-poohed. "We require no chaperonage—Candice and I will be fine on our own to tour this thriving metropolis of yours."

Our hostess was aghast, but we set out for town anyway. "I need to see Hannah," Sin told me simply. "I need to see her *now*."

My silence said I understood.

"You know, Dice," he resumed, "I've been trying to reconstruct this day, every word and moment we shared, but it's been so long. All I can recall is we passed the early evening together, and then I left. When next I saw her, she was dead."

Regret projected him. He walked the way you walk when going nowhere fast. Soon enough we made our first stop.

A farrier (a blacksmith with a specialty in horseshoes) and a knacker (who makes harnesses) often shared quarters, and so it was in Swoon. Sinclair had been a wayfaring stranger when he met Elijah O'Rourke in the tavern. A bearded Irishman with an Irishman's knack for stories, O'Rourke spoke of his poor partner who'd keeled over at the forge—the tale of woe convincing the young adventurer to stay. Now, passing the establishment in search of Hannah Miles, we saw only men—O'Rourke struggling over some stubborn hides and, across the wall, Sinclair Youngblood Powers with the tools of his trade.

"We've missed her," Sin muttered as we paused in the generous shade of a willow near the shop's open gate. He pointed to a bench within. "See there? My dinner pail. She'd brought it; now she's gone."

How weird it must have been for him to watch himself. For me, not so weird, not weird at all. Stripped to the waist, sweat delineating every muscle. Damn, he was hot. Literally. The forge, a crude brick oven with a giant bellows, spewed fire to melt metal into an obliging state.

"Dice, come away."

"Yeah, okay . . . in a sec."

Just then, a robust shout of "Sinclair! Sinclair!" as O'Rourke rounded to the farrier's side. Accompanying him, another man, as sallow and sinewy as the knacker was florid and rotund. "Look who's here! It's Patrick Marshall!"

Marshall! That sloping chin, those flinty eyes, an overall demeanor leathery and slippery at once. Instinctively, I stepped deeper into the willow's haven. "Give him a Patriots' cap and a beer belly and ta-da! Marsh's father."

"Yes, I suppose," Sin said distractedly.

"All right," I said. "We can go now." In any era, the dude skeeved me.

"No . . . I want to hear this . . ."

The farrier flung an iron rod into a water barrel. Steam hissed up like a flock of startled birds. Patrick Marshall went into his waistcoat for snuff. He offered the tin around, and all three had a snort. Then Marshall spat at the ground, fixed Sinclair with a beady stare, and got down to brass tacks.

"I'll be needing some nags shod by the morrow," he said, and spat again.

"I'm glad for your patronage," Sinclair said. "But there are others before you."

"Are there?" Marshall said, antagonism in his tone. "You're not hurting for customers nowadays."

"No, sir, I've plenty. But I'm not turning them away, either."

"Look here, smithy," Marshall said grimly, "they're not King George's horses. I just don't want no one coming back to me saying they were lame."

Now the blacksmith squinted at the sun. Now he took a turn and spat on the ground. "I assume you won't be bringing them round till nightfall?"

"That is so," Marshall said with his bent-wire smile. "Which gives you all day for the rest of your travails."

A deal, albeit an unsavory one, had been struck. I plucked the sleeve of my companion. Patrick Marshall was coming our way, and I didn't want his ugly ogle on me. How lovely we must have looked behind the peek-a-boo curtain of bowed fronds, the fair girl in her finery, the sultry one in common cloth. What man would not be drawn to our tableau vivant? Twisting his excuse for a smile, exposing gaps between errant teeth, Marshall stared at us. Sin stared back with Pen's eyes wide, as though searching for something, a morsel of memory, the crumb of a clue. It seemed as though Marshall might address us, but Sin's boldness must have abraded him, and he stalked away, muttering.

My love shuddered in my cousin's skin, and I put a hand on his arm. "Come on," I implored.

"Patrick Marshall," Sin said, more or less to himself as we hustled off. "Claimed to be a coper. Capper, more to the truth."

"Hey! Yo! Right here, next to you, Sin. You want to keep me in the loop?"

We slowed to a stroll, past the chandlery, the cutlery, the tavern. "A man who dealt in horseflesh was a coper," he explained, "but you called him a capper if his nags were stolen, or not worth the glue in their guts. That was Patrick Marshall. He wore the airs of an honest man, but he'd harness his own mother if the price were right. Still, who was I to turn down his business? For it's true—they *had* begun to go elsewhere, would ride a stumbling mare to the smithy in Chapin rather than take her to me . . ."

Sin steered me into the general store, a likely place to find Hannah. The assortment of wares—fabric and notions, soaps and salves—so fascinated me I couldn't concentrate on the shoppers, but Sin studied faces as his blue streak continued.

"Quite a brood he had, that Marshall, seven daughters, or was it eight? Wife died bearing the last child, that essential for lineal survival—the boy. One of the girls . . . Matilda, yes . . . went by Tillie." The words were spoken as if off a spool. "She and Hannah were the dearest of friends. Even when everyone else turned cold, Tillie was loyal . . . Tillie was true." Then he paused as though unsnarling one last knot in a chain.

XLIII

"We had a plan, you know." Sin was feeling revelatory as we ambled a path dividing fields and hardscrabble farms. "We'd scrimp and save till our child was born and then head west." He stooped for a stone, flung it at nothing in particular. "The baby was due in October. Come spring, we'd be off."

Was throwing rocks therapeutic? I launched one myself. It did nothing for me. "That was a good plan," I said.

"Do you think so?"

"Yeah, Sin. I really do."

Suddenly he grabbed my hand to lead us across the meadow. The field had a steady downward grade, mounting our momentum. Grasses grew higher, scratching our legs, threatening to tear our clouds of skirt. Flowers appeared in greater abundance—bluebells and buttercups, lilies and calendula, a kaleidoscope blurred by our increasing speed. Then two flowers rose from the bottom of the field, taller than the rest. They turned our way and put hands to hips, since they weren't flowers at all. Sin and I came to a panting halt, and we all surveyed each other for either forever or a matter of seconds.

Then I said, "Hey!"

The two girls regarded each other, then us. Queried one, "Hay?"

"Beg pardon, I mean, good day." What the hell, I didn't speak colonial. "My name is Candice Moskow, and this . . . this is my mistress, Miss Penelope Leonard of New York City." I tried out a little curtsy.

"Ah, good day! I'm Hannah Miles." Of course she was. Coppery hair and rosebud lips and baby bump. "This is my dear friend, Tillie Marshall."

Bashfully, Tillie mumbled "good day"—a veritable oration compared to my companion. Sinclair Youngblood Powers—paragon of palaver, the con man's con man, had gone mute beside me. He'd remembered this was the friends' favorite spot, and had hurried us here, but now he was speechless.

Hannah chose to ignore the discourtesy. "My goodness, what causes you to run so?" Her smile was precocious. "I do hope you aren't being chased by bears."

"Nah, no bears. Just a bad case of summer insanity."

Bug-eyed Tillie took me literally, but Hannah laughed, that silvery peal.

"Oh, I know such fevers!" she said. "Why not have a cooling wade in the brook?"

There was a brook, I saw then, sparkling over rocks. Tillie's washing basket was nearby, laundered items spread out to dry. "What do you think, Miss Penelope?" I asked.

A soft assent, and we sat on the bank to remove our shoes. Crystal cold water up to our shins. Bees and butterflies over our heads. Tillie still had work to do, and seven young siblings to mind, while Sin splashed off in the opposite direction.

"Please don't think my mistress snobbish," I said, assuming that's precisely what Hannah thought. "She's . . . broken-hearted, truth be told."

"Ah, that is a shame," Hannah said with a nod of empathy. As we waded and chatted, I felt like the new girl, eager to make a good impression on a charismatic classmate. Hannah really was . . . what's colonial for "cool"? In time we heard Tillie call out. Basket at her hip, she waved our way. Hannah and I quit the stream for surer footing.

"Ah, well, I'll need be getting supper on," she said. "It was lovely to make your acquaintance."

"Yeah—yes, you too."

"Haaaaan-*nah*!" Tillie called again.

"Fare-thee-well then, Candice!" The mother-to-never-be gathered her skirts and darted up the slope.

"Fare-thee-well, Hannah," I told her glossy tresses, then made my way along the bank. Here were my boots and Sin's slippers; I collected them and continued, as the brook bent and dipped. In due course I found Sin on the flat expanse of a high boulder, his knees drawn up, a cheek resting against them. I left our shoes and clambered up. We arranged ourselves around each other. For a while we watched the sun meander west. Then, just as inevitably, tears welled up, and they weighed so much I couldn't contain them. Sin, stoic, part of the rock, let them come and kept me close. I cried for him. I cried for Hannah. And I cried for me.

As I left a large wet stain on Sin's fancy silk, I perceived something going on inside him. A distant rumble, a volcano of the heart. It was quick. Almost a figment. I drew away, dry-eyed now. Except for the fact that he looked like Pen, he looked okay.

"I'm glad you two could speak," he said at last.

"Me too. She's amazing. But it should have been you with her, Sin, listening to her, laughing with her, watching the—"

"No." He said it resolutely, and laid a finger to my lips. "Not me. Not *this* me. Tonight, Hannah will have her Sinclair. I'm not him anymore."

XLIV

THE GROUND-GRAZING DRESSES HAD TO GO. DITTO THE SADISTIC lingerie. Fortunately, the dead presidents in my pocket had flipped to corresponding pre-Revolutionary British royals, so it was back to the general store for shirts, breeches, et cetera. We returned to the Leonard house and retreated upstairs to change.

"Ouch! Desist!" Sin took umbrage with my technique, but I had to comb out the pins and pomade responsible for that insane erection on his head. "Dice, that *hurts*."

"Sorry, but we don't want to be here all night." I got it undone and tied it, like mine, in a tail with ribbon.

"A couple of fine swains," Sin said, assessing our cross-dressed appearance.

"Swain," I assumed, was colonial for "dude." "Yeah, except for the boobs."

"Indeed. Let's keep the jiggle to a minimum, shall we?"

We laughed—nervous anticipation parading as jocularity. I cut us both some slack. The night ahead would offer no joy. Still, I mused for a moment on Sin, the way he held me on the rock as I wept. My eyes met his in the mirror, and he quickly put it down.

"Give me half an hour, and come at my signal." His manner was brisk.

"Wait—where are you going?" I wasn't inclined to let him leave my sight.

Without explanation, he slipped onto the ledge. "You needn't take this route, Dice. Simply slip out the back like any surreptitious servant boy." At that, he latched onto the trellis, descended with a few agile swings, and was gone.

His signal—it had to be his signal, or some deranged owl—came soon enough, and I crept down the hall, onto the stairs, and out the door. Another spate of hooting led me to Sin astride a caramel-colored horse. Beside him was another beast, without a rider.

"Meet Tawny and Thunder," he said, extending the reins. "Thunder's yours."

"Mine?!" She was dark brown with white knee socks. The way her long forelock dipped over her eyes reminded me of someone. "You have got to be kidding. I don't know how to drive a horse."

"You don't drive a horse, dear lady; you ride her. And you needn't worry. The name Thunder is meant to be ironic. The filly's meek as a lamb."

340

So why didn't he get me a lamb? "No way I'm getting up on that thing." Thunder gazed down at me with eyes like bruised black olives. "I mean animal. No offense."

Sin dismounted. "Dice, I know these horses. Tawny was Thunder's dame; your mount will simply follow her mother." He held out the stirrup thingee. "Up you go."

Bad idea. I ought to know—I've had a million of them. "Hey, Thunder," I said, patting her flank. She snorted in response and showed teeth the size of ice cubes. How did I manage this? By reminding myself none of it was "real." Not really. Oh, it felt real, really real, but I, Candice Reagan Moskow, did not exist in 1769. Ergo, I couldn't possibly break every bone in my body in 1769. Right? Right! Since next thing I knew the reins were in my fist, Sin's palm was on my ass, and I was in the saddle.

We rode.

And then we eavesdropped.

Pine stumps formed a rough-hewn patio behind the trim cottage. Twilight cast purple comfort as tree sparrows and mourning doves serenaded. The scent of jasmine was out of control. An ideal setting for a lovers' quarrel.

"Enough, Hannah, please. I must return to the shop."

"So you say."

"What are you implying?"

"Nothing at all. But you wouldn't even deign to come inside for supper."

"I shan't go where I'm not welcome."

"Then take me with you! I do not care that the room is small—*I* am small."

This made him laugh and rub her bulging belly. "Not lately!"

"Stop that!" she said, and laughed, too.

The tension bounced but did not break the strain between them.

"We've been through this. It's cramped up there above the shop, and the stink from the forge—it's no place for you. And I must work. We need the money."

"Money! It is all you care about."

"You're being unfair. I came to see you—but now I must go."

He cupped her cheek. She submitted to the caress but gazed beyond him. And after he mounted and rode off, she sat on a stump and had herself a think. Just a little one. Then she rose with determination. She was done thinking. She was ready to *do*.

XLV

MONEY, THE NECESSITY THEREOF. IT'S ALL MEN EVER THOUGHT ABOUT. But wasn't it unreasonable to leave the burden of acquiring money entirely to a man? Hannah Miles had made up her mind—she would do her part. Indeed, if what she'd gleaned through rumor were right, a woman with her attributes—one in particular—could amass a great pile of money while scarcely lifting a finger. So Hannah readied her pony and stole away from her parents' house. Her thoughts on what lay ahead, she had no concern for who might follow behind.

Hannah set off for town, then veered onto the road that skirted it. Intended as a secondary commercial thoroughfare, Emerson Street failed as yet to meet developers' expectations. Three buildings, unfinished, lay dormant. But on certain nights, so it was said, one of them came vigorously to life. Turning onto Main Street, Hannah hitched her pony to a post near the tavern, then scurried back to Emerson on foot.

Where we waited in watch, Tawny and Thunder nibbling brush. I didn't ask what was up. A crackling energy exuded from Sin—I figured I'd know soon enough. Then a white-capped shadow flitted into view. Flitted and paused, flitted and paused, flitted, paused . . . and vanished.

With a growl of a groan, Sin yanked on his waistcoat as if sparking some internal engine and crossed toward the buildings as fast as boots and breeches allowed. I was right behind. Unlike the white-capped shadow, he didn't need to pause and ponder; the boy made a beeline like he'd been there before. Through a side entrance he took us into an ambitious-looking box of brick. Torches flickered in sconces, directing us to a passageway. By the time we reached the staircase, I heard where the action lay.

No corner of the low, broad basement room wasn't in commotion. There was a bar along one wall, and a platform where a fiddler trio whittled an off-key reel. No one paid much heed. Music and liquor were adjuncts to the purpose of this place. Here, loud, anxious men threw darts. There, carved stones clattered in a bowl as bets were shouted and cash exchanged. Elsewhere, cards prevailed—contests of bluff and cunning.

A casino? You could have knocked me over with a hiccup. Though it had been a hundred-plus years since Thomas Hooker and company kick-started Connecticut, those Puritan roots ran deep. Gambling would be considered wicked. Which is why, I guess, it wound up here, hidden away to thrive, a moldering, nightshade bloom.

In our men's clothing and accoutrements, Sin and I walked among the gamblers without raising an eyebrow. It was full of men—white men, mostly, in upper-class apparel, but a fair amount of workingmen and military types as well. Remarkably, a black face, a red one, among them. Far less frequently, there were women. Sin steered me toward the bar and ordered cider. Not to be confused with apple juice—the shit was potent. Upon gulping his down, Sin bent to me, filling my ear as he scanned the crowd.

"Do you see her?"

"No." Leaning against him, I wished it were Sin's hard body and not Pen's pliant one. There was tension in the gambling hall that could erupt at any second. I tossed back more cider—liquid courage. "What would Hannah be doing in a place like this?"

"I never would have conceived it in a thousand lifetimes," he said, part angry, part awed. "But of course it's so simple, and so brilliant."

I trained my eyes on a nearby table, where a sole woman sat, self-possessed, among the men. Her hairstyle and gown were grander than ladies of Edwina Leonard's ilk. The man beside her sported a scarlet uniform adorned with medals; the two were clearly acquainted, possibly lovers, but the woman wagered from her own purse.

"I don't get it," I told Sin. "Hannah had money to gamble with?"

"No." He banged his tankard on the bar and left a coin, then elbowed me into motion. "She has not come to play," he explained. "She's come to—there! At the faro . . ."

An intricate game of cards and chips was in progress. And there she sat, between a blubbery gent in an outrageous wig and another soldier, this one younger, his jacket less encrusted with awards. Hannah wore an expression I recognized: the fake-it-till-you-make-it look. Jowls waggling, the fat man pinched her cheek and said something I didn't hear. Hannah rolled her eyes, catching those of the soldier, who gave a toothy grin. Finally the big guy plumbed his pile to make a deposit in Hannah's palm.

Not too quickly, not too greedily, she tightened her fingers, withdrew her hand. Expectation escalated around the table like heat. With puckered lips and upturned nose she let her gaze rove. Then her hand reappeared, rose to her temple, and swept off her cap. Down they spilt, those shining red waves, across her shoulders and along her back. A pleasured gasp resulted round the table, everyone leaning a little closer. The windbag in the wig reached out to fondle the sensuous currency framing Hannah's face—he'd paid for the privilege, had he not? Rearing back, she slapped his hand, then extended and opened hers once more. Laughing, her portly patron tickled it again with coins. After which, the game of faro resumed, and guess who started winning? As if there were a sliver of doubt. For any bold girl may step into a gambling house and present herself as the conduit to fortune. But there's nothing like a redhead to personify Lady Luck.

"You mustn't go!" cried the fat man when Hannah rose after several rounds, snatching her sleeve in a proprietary manner. The young soldier smacked the table, but Hannah gazed witheringly down her arm, and the bewigged walrus released her. Thus unencumbered, she began to glide among the tables, turning heads wherever she went. She was sizing them up, scoping them out, browsing for benefactors.

All Sin and I could do was keep tabs while Hannah worked the room. She'd sit at a table or stand beside a player, accept her cut, and wield her magic—the magic of compounded belief. No matter how sharp or jaded, all gamblers woo the fickle whims of luck. Everyone assembled believed Hannah held providence on a string, and so she did.

Soon enough, I noted an altruistic change in her choice of patron. At the game of stones in a bowl (hubbub, Sin called it), she approached a desperate soul who was losing sorely and didn't seem like he could afford to. She gathered the stones and blew on them. When next he threw, the poor man's luck reversed. The crowd hailed and huzzahed, but as the winner looked to give the girl her due, she had already gone.

Right around then I relaxed a little. Hannah and her blessed tresses had beguiled them all, and now she was dispensing charity. Who there could possibly do her harm? "She has them enchanted," Sin said, respectful yet rueful as we circled back to the bar. "To think that all the while I slaved at the forge, here was my lady, in this lions' den."

Two more quaffs were set before us. Yet as I reached for mine, it wasn't the heady tang of cider I smelled. I put down the tankard like it was diseased, only to find the stench now circulating around me, rank and dank, a cyclone of stink that was familiar, uncomfortably so. Vetting the hall, I found the source. Patrick Marshall.

He'd entered with two other men, his loud, loutish voice and clumsy swagger an indication that he'd been tippling. "Check it out." I gave Sin a nudge. "He's got you working overtime while he's out partying."

"What a buffoon," Sin said with tepid scorn.

In his estimation Patrick Marshall was more fool than fiend. Me, I wasn't so sure. The whole malodorous demeanor of the man. I strained to keep him in my sights as he muscled in on a poker game.

"Those with him, I've not seen before," Sin said. "Must be the lot he's unloading the nags upon."

Both men wore beards and the buckskins of frontiersmen. Sin nursed his drink, unfazed, his gaze alert to Hannah alone. But it wasn't long before Patrick Marshall began to lose, and not long after that Lady Luck, so generous in spirit, presented herself. After all, it wouldn't bode well for Tillie and her siblings if he were to fritter his money away. That prickly panic kindled in me again. I wove through the crowd, toward the table. The wolverine reek grew—I had the sinking sense it marked the beginning of the end for Hannah Miles.

"Mr. Marshall, good evening to you," Hannah said with a curtsy.

Miserably, the man looked up from his hand. "Begone, Hannah Miles!"

Hannah took a step back, puzzled.

"Why you spurn *la jolie jeune fille*? Marshall, *vous êtes fou*!" This from one of the (French, apparently) buckskin swains, who slapped his knee sharply. *"Vien ici, Mademoiselle!"*

Hannah stayed put. For the first time I detected a hint of fear. The other buckskin guy guffawed, the sound of a lobotomized mule.

"I've enough hard cheese on my plate," Marshall grumbled. "I don't need the bad augury of that bitch to compound it."

"You're being a fool, Marshall," the dealer confided from the side of his mouth. "The red-haired hoyden's been bringing fortune to all she smiles on this night."

Marshall coughed as though dislodging briar from his gullet. "Red-haired whore, you mean," he said. With a snap quick as a rat's tail, he pulled taut the front of Hannah's gown. "Pregnant, she is—by worse than a nigger, by an Indian savage and a bastard besides. Such luck as hers I can well do without."

This was not exactly news. Word that Hannah Miles was with child out of wedlock had gone quicksilver from tongue to ear. Yet here in this hazy milieu, where the upright went underground, it was easy to be magnanimous about such things. To err, after all, was human; to administer leverage over the odds, divine. Except now it had been pointed out, and the rules of the real world infringed. One by one the good folk of Swoon began to rescind their favor, and the shimmering flame of red-haired Hannah Miles was effectively snuffed out.

XLVI

EXCEPT SHE WOULD PROVE TO HAVE ONE LAST LICK OF MAGIC IN HER.

Tugging her dress from Marshall's grasp, Hannah spun on her heel to march off. Then, as if deftly avoiding a rusty nail, she retraced her steps. She wouldn't let him get away with this.

"In seeking to shame me, Patrick Marshall, you commit a far more wicked crime than I." She didn't say this hotly, or with much force; Hannah was matter-of-fact. "Yours is a crime against women, all women, and one for which you shall dearly pay."

Impatient eyes, pious eyes, judgmental, dispassionate, and ridiculing eyes alit on her from the poker pit. Patrick Marshall tipped back his chair to gawk derisively, too.

"You shall never earn a woman's respect," Hannah told him calmly. "Nor a woman's trust. Nor a woman's true love."

That twisted wire strip of scorn enlisted itself across his face.

"You shall long for this respect, this trust, and this love, and the unrequited longing shall be your plague."

Marshall folded his cards, fanned them, hunched over them.

Hannah would not be ignored. "Tonight you hold the queen of spades, Patrick Marshall—may she dig your grave and spite your kin forever!"

Maybe Hannah had peeked at his hand. Maybe she had a touch of the shining, or took a wild guess. All I know is now she did hurry off, coppery banner behind her. Sin watched her flee with a choking cry, as though he knew the hex had sealed her fate.

Instinctively, I reached out to him. That's when I encountered it again. A calamity. An upheaval. Like primordial jelly of boy, girl, golem, ghost tearing one another apart. Like sticking your hand in a bucket of maggots, each individual larva puking an electric shock. Like performing surgery with your fingers, and all your fingers are thumbs. I wanted to rip my hand away, wash it in lye, lop it off with a cleaver. Yet whatever roiled beneath Sin's skin made him so vulnerable, I couldn't let go. So, very gently, I applied pressure, pressure that promised, *I am with you. I won't leave you. I love you.* And whatever the turmoil was, it began to subside. And then it stilled. And then it stopped.

Sin turned to me like he'd just emerged from a fog. We looked into each other, saw there the same imperative: Hannah! Holding hands, not caring how we appeared to the denizens of the gambling house, we cut the place on the bias. No sign of her. Difficult as it was to imagine, much less enunciate, I said, "Maybe we should split up."

He regarded our two hands as if they were soldered together—a lifeline, an umbilical. But that wasn't so. "Very well," he said.

"I'll search upstairs. You go outside—maybe she's already on her way home."

"That's a plan," he agreed. "We'll meet back by our mounts."

We flew up the stairs to a wide maw of the main floor, and as Sin made for the exit, I called out into the gloom. "Hannah!"

"Hannah!" came the faintly mocking echo of the empty room.

I tried another name. "Marshall! Patrick Marshall, show yourself!"

Again, the unkind retort of my own voice. They weren't there. I made my way out to the emptiness of Emerson Street and crossed to our horses, tethered to a tree. Thunder lifted her head to me. Then I heard a short but piercing scream, and followed it to a sparse copse of birch. The pale tree trunks stood out starkly, but the figures inside were occluded under the cloud-filled sky. Only what was that, tossed between the shadows? A white cotton cap that fluttered and began to descend like a parachute. Before it fell to earth, the moon shed the clouds, and I could see all.

One buckskin boy had the pregnant girl pinned by the elbows. The other lunged for tiny feet, kicking mad as sparrows on leashes. Then Marshall started to manhandle Hannah, searching her as she writhed and cried out. He paused in his labors to crack a silencing fist across her jaw. Then he plunged into the pocket of her skirt and drew out his prize. A ladies' stocking bulged with coin of the realm—Hannah's earnings for her stint as Lady Luck. I could tell by the way he swung it that financial recompense was not the only payment he intended to extract.

I could not let this go down. I could not prevent it. Still, I drew nearer. Now I could make out snippets of what was said. One of the frontier *frères* insisting, "I'll have my way with her first." This said with a glinting hint of drool. Marshall demanding of Hannah, "Rescind the curse upon me, witch, or it will go worse for you." That said as he smacked the loaded stocking against his palm, producing a dull, percussive clank.

When I heard a ripping "Noooooooo!" from the opposite side of the copse, a ripping "Noooooo!" spewed out of me as well.

And when Sin sprang, nanoseconds later I did, too.

The next thing I remember was the distinctly unpleasant aroma of cheap beer.

Part IV

The Tears

XLVII

"CHICK FIGHT!!!"

Not a common idiom to the mid 1700s. Which could only mean a return to latter-day Swoon. Specifically, the Wolverine Tavern, where not much time had elapsed. A female fracas must've made a diverting novelty, what with all the wooing and screwing in town of late. One of the combatants was yours truly. The other—my blond, busty, and livid opponent—had me sprawled against the scarred oak bar. That was to be expected. The ninja act I'd pulled back in the birch would have kept Sin from saving the love of his life—naturally, he'd be pissed. While all around us, Wolverine revelers urged us on with whistles and jeers.

I wanted no part. Bruises from the Halloween brouhaha atop Libo's Gas & Lube had finally healed—the last thing I needed was a new decoupage of black-and-blues. "Please, stop—I'm sorry!" I swore to flared nostrils and flashing eyes.

My apology was declined. I could tell by the way I got flung against the pinball machine. Still, I pleaded my case: "Come on! I couldn't let you do it! I just couldn't!" I dodged a slap. "It was wrong! You know it was wrong!"

Finally, a response: "Fuck you, Dice. If I feel like doing a striptease, I'll do a goddamn striptease!"

This garnered approving howls all around but confused the hell out of me. Until I realized—chick fight, indeed—that it wasn't Sin pounding on me; it was Pen. Who, granted, had her reasons as well. Only if I was back in the twenty-first century and getting punished by my cousin—who'd evidently been in the middle of a burlesque routine when I'd rudely interrupted— where the hell was Sin?

No, not where. *When.* But of course I knew. And the knowledge filled me with more pain than Pen could possibly administer. I threw her off with a grunt. She stumbled in her high heels, stabilized, and seethed at me. Exploding out of a tank top, her normally sleek strands amplified, she'd achieved a new level of skank. Call it Barbie on a bender.

"You win, Pen," I told her. "You win, okay? You do what you want."

Tempted to express regrets that the Wolverine lacked a pole, I didn't want to instigate another round. The boy I loved was alone, adrift, in danger—I had to keep my head on straight. Thinking, *get me out of here,* I remembered how I got there, via the Cutlass with Marsh and Crane. Were those two still making out in back? That's where I headed, when a slow, rhythmic clapping began.

"Take it off, baby! Show us what you got!"

The demand jerked my metaphoric choke chain. I swung in its direction, and there was Douglas Marshall in full northern redneck regalia: Pendleton, Carhartt, Budweiser. No wonder Marsh was dead set against this joint—Cuckoo Pop's preferred hangout. Too embarrassed to tell Crane, she'd acquiesced to come, figuring her father would never catch her, since he'd be home babysitting. Guess she figured wrong.

"Come on, baby!" Marshall's lewd, glazed look was glued on Pen. "Let's see those tits!"

Others took up the term for that prominent section of female anatomy and made it a chant. A procession of emotions crossed Pen's countenance until, at last, the hot pink of humiliation settled there. I seized on that, pulling her by the wrist. Laughter hounded us to the pool table.

Marsh charged from a corner. "Goddamn it, Dice, you happy now?" she bleated. "Oh, I knew we shouldn't have come here. If my dad sees me, I'm dead."

I let go of Pen, who focused on the cue ball, a happily uninhabited planet on a green felt sky. "What's he even doing here?" I said to Marsh. "Shouldn't he be with your sisters?" Me and my inquiring mind.

359

"I don't know, I don't know!" Marsh said, tizzy mounting. "He must have finished the six-pack he started when I went out and just . . . just . . . left the girls by themselves. There's no telling with him when he's drinking. What am I going to do?"

I scoped out the muddy dim. There had to be an emergency exit—and this was an emergency. "Where do you pee in this dump?"

"Yes!" Crane piped up, glad to be of service. "I used the lads'—it's this way."

Behind a partition were two bathrooms and a fire door. We pushed the lever and once outside tore for the parking lot. Marsh ran to the Cutlass, Crane close behind. I glanced at my cousin. She rubbed bare arms and sniffled, her cheerleader jacket no doubt abandoned in the entropy zone of the barroom.

"Pen, I need a ride," I said. She hadn't uttered a word since we fled the catcalling crowd. "Okay?"

She wouldn't even look in my vicinity. I took that as a yes.

"Crane!" Marsh yanked the handle on the passenger side. "Come on!"

"Yes, right, very good," he replied. "Only . . ."

"Only what?" Marsh was angst to the nth.

"Only, ah . . . perhaps I shouldn't mention it; I don't want to propagate any ill will." His gaze jangled between Pen and me. "But whatever has happened to Sin?"

"Sin? Oh, he's all right. He's fine," Marsh insisted. "He's Sin!"

"Yeah, don't worry about Sin." I said, since I was doing enough of that for the entire Eastern Seaboard.

Pen and I trudged to her car. We got in, buckled up. She started the engine. Before she put it in gear, she turned to me, and I braced myself. Except she simply asked, "So you were with Sin tonight?"

"Yeah," I said. Why hide it? Why had I ever found it necessary to keep secrets from Pen?

"Well," she said, soft and fuzzy as a duckling. "What *did* happen to him, Dice?"

"I don't know." I closed my eyes. Then opened them, and proceeded to tell her what I did know. All of it. Absolutely, once and for all, everything.

XLVIII

WE WERE ON HER BED. BETWEEN US, A BAG OF CHIPS AHOY (AUNT Lainie hadn't so much as boiled water since the plunge). The bag was empty. The hour was late. And I was done.

"Uh," said Pen. "Huh."

I flashed on the last time this room had been my confessional, how I'd picked and chosen from tidbits of truth. This go-round I'd left nothing out. Maybe if I were completely honest, that would fix things—in the past, in the present, and (please, please) in the future. "Real mind-wank, isn't it?"

Pen nipped a cuticle. Her manicure was ragged, the red lacquer chipped. "Just to make sure I understand," she said, "it's like this: We're both in love with the same guy, who isn't a guy, but a golem—a soulless, animated blob of clay."

My fingers roamed the bottom of the cookie bag, reconnaissance for crumbs. I'd shoved mass quantities down my greedy tube but couldn't fill this void.

"And the reason he's on a vengeful mission to screw this town—literally—is some redheaded girl who got murdered in the eighteenth century. So the two of you combined extrasensory forces for a telepathic time trip in hope of learning the identity of the redhead's killer. Am I right?"

"Pretty much," I said. "Although you had a role, too. I haven't put all the pieces together, but the Wolverine was our gateway, and your presence there enabled Sin to inhabit your body in 1769. Don't ask me to explain beyond that because I can't. But let's be real, the geometry of this relationship has always been triangular."

Pen swallowed a giant marble. This couldn't have been fun for her. "And the last you saw him he was attempting to prevent the murder . . ."

"We were there to observe, but I guess he couldn't take it, or maybe he'd been planning to undo the deed all along; he's . . . hard to read sometimes. But I tried to stop him; I did."

"And that's when you came back."

"That's when I came back." Alone. "Only I don't know why."

"Oh, I do." Pen smoothed a wrinkle in her patchwork quilt. "That's easy."

I looked at her sideways.

"You came back when you came back because that's when I needed you to come back." She sighed. "Dice, I don't know why I went to the Wolverine—I just got in my car and went. I didn't even get loaded; I maybe had two sips of beer. For me . . . what he's *made* me . . . attention's my drug of choice now. I wanted their eyes on me; I wanted to drive them crazy. And I had them, but then you pounced out of nowhere, judging me—"

"I wasn't—"

"I know that now. You were doing what you had to do because our friend's father was about to, I don't know, lead the charge to gang-rape me or whatever."

I let that sink in. Then I said, "So you and me—we're good?"

"Of course," she said, and she meant it.

"You don't think I was . . ." Duplicitous? Deceitful? A host of unattractive adjectives jockeyed for position.

She shrugged. "Girls do stupid stuff over guys. Comes with the estrogen."

Pretty damn deep for Pen. Who at that point bent over her bed and picked up a shoe—one of the chunky platforms she'd worn to the Wolverine. She examined it quizzically, chucked it, and then went to her closet to slip on Crocs. "Come on, Dice."

"We going somewhere?"

"Yes," she said simply. "We're going to pick up Sin."

It felt like she lit a match in the cave beneath my rib cage.

We didn't have to sneak out. "I could throw an orgy in the living room; my parents wouldn't say boo," Pen told me. We got in her car and started toward town. "Emerson Street, right?"

"Yeah." I took in the empty night. "What makes you think we'll find him?"

"I don't think we'll find him," she said. "I know we will." She flicked her eyes off the road and gave me a sad smirk. "Maybe you're not the only one in the family with psychic ability. Maybe I'm a late bloomer."

Unlikely . . . but there he was, hands in his pockets, saunter sluggish, headed our way. Now there was sunlight and neon inside me, and puppies and kittens, pinwheels and confetti, and chocolate chip cookies, way too many. There was life inside me. He was back. He was here. In his own body, filling out generic Levi's and Hanes. Pen pulled over and lowered her window. "Want a ride?"

He approached her side. "I don't know," he said.

He sounded far away. I leaned over the console, looked at him. "Come on, Sin. Get in," I said. "You look cold."

"Cold," he said. "I am cold."

Pen drove to Daisy Lane, stopping in front of Number 12. She stared straight ahead at the twin spooks her headlights made.

"You going to come in?" I asked her. "Hang out?"

"No." She was very firm. "I need a shower. I've been slimed." Could be she really felt like that. Could be she just didn't want to be part of a triangle anymore.

"Okay," I said. "Thanks." I got out of the car. Sin sat. "Sin," I said. "Let's go."

He got out. Obeyed me.

Once inside, I said, "I'll make coffee."

Which I did, made it strong. Filled mugs, ample sugar and spot of cream. Sin stood there, stiff as the Tin Man. "Sin, sit."

I put coffee in front of him, took a chair, studied him. What was going on in there? Apprehensively, I reached out. Apprehensively, fearing that tumult of activity under his skin. Instead, just the cool surface of his able workingman's hand. His eyes were impenetrable, the pupils and irises fused.

"Do you want to tell me what happened?"

"I don't know," he said.

This was weird. This was Sin. Who had an opinion on everything. Who was not about ambivalence. Sin either wanted something, or he did not.

"Tell me." I gave instructions, and he took instructions. It was the way things had to be. For the moment.

XLIX

CLOUDS HASTEN ACROSS THE NIGHT SKY. THEY HAVE NO WISH TO witness the goings-on below. It begins as taunting—three men grabbing at a young woman's clothes and provocative hair. Yet the level of menacing escalates quickly, one of the men intent beyond the sport of rape. He twirls a weapon—white, fluid, a snake with a blind, bulbous, heavy head.

Such a tiny, delicate thing, held fast but hardly still, like a finch in the fist of a cruel child. She cannot fathom this happening to her—to *her*! She, who had always been lucky. She, who had done as she pleased, defied convention, laughed at the weather because, simply enough, she was she. Any moment, this will all prove a prank. Any moment, this will stop, due to, due to . . .

A redeemer! Yes! Leaping into the fray. But before her heart can pulse once, another intruder bursts in. Who's fighting whom? If the clouds could be coerced to watch, how befuddled they'd be. Astounded, too, when the last figure to enter the arena disappears like a candle flame in a sudden gust.

Her true redeemer remains. And isn't there something familiar about him? In the dark and frenzy, she doesn't flash on the young lady from New York she'd met by the brook, the one who'd been so high and mighty. Whoever he may be, he has the fortitude and courage of many, the wherewithal to vanquish three men.

Except . . .

Soil has always shared its bed with stone in this part of America. The reason farms fail here and quarries flourish, and fences are built for miles with stone upon stone upon stone. Tonight, a stone, a sizable stone, comes into play.

One ruffian finds the stone.

One would-be redeemer is brought down.

And evil takes up where it left off.

Until the clouds can run no more; until they crash and collide and break open as clouds are wont to do in summer. Meager branches of birch offer little shelter. The deluge scatters the scoundrels. It muddies the soil into soup and shines the stones like gems. It falls upon two bodies.

He is in one of the bodies lying on the ground. It's not his body, but he's in it. His true body rests in a stifling room above a forge, not more than half a mile from this spot. His true body has fallen asleep to a lullaby of snuffling horses. He's there in his true body, but also here, in this borrowed one. Rain hits the face; he opens the eyes. He gets to the knees. An ache throbs in the back of the head and surges forward like a cowl.

The other body is hers. He crawls toward it, and when near enough he can tell that she's in it. Barely. He needn't be gentle because it's too late, but he's gentle nonetheless. He cradles her. As to the body taking form inside her body, it quit a few blows ago, a few thrusts ago. Too much rupture, too much ruin. Now it's a thing. Now it's nothing. He cannot feel the life draining from her but knows it's happening and that he is powerless. She has to die.

Yet he is blessed, and here is why. This time she will not die alone. This time she will die with him. He is here; he is with her. If only she would open her eyes and recognize him, but she does not. Nor does she spasm or cry out or cough. She simply ceases to draw breath. Ceases to course blood. Ceases to be cognizant. Ceases.

Eventually, the storm breaks. The dawn arrives. The little town begins its little business. Someone comes along. The cooper's assistant, hurrying on foot, late for work, stops, gapes, even speaks. By then he feels this body thinning like fabric, melting like wax. The cooper's assistant takes off like a hare, and soon enough come others. They come and they gape and they even speak.

He waits, holding her body, until the farrier arrives—shocked, shaking, disbelieving. Then he makes the borrowed body rise. Awkwardly—as he still holds her body, and the dead are heavy. Holding the body of their dead love, he walks up to and into and through himself, passing her along, and comes out the other side.

L

Coffee, the miracle elixir. Caffeine and sugar hammered his bloodstream as Sin got up from the table. I said his name, craving the comfort of comforting. Yet as I murmured into his chest and stroked his head (discovering the lump of evidence left by the rock that felled him) he took no solace. He wasn't interested in solace.

"Thanks for the coffee, Dice," he said. Translation: *Kindly let go.*

I held on. Hoping, hoping, hoping. Extraordinary stirrings started up inside him; I was getting familiar with that curious factory under the flesh. Did he understand the disturbance or find it as mystifying as I did? Was he thrilled by it? Scared? Did he write it off as indigestion? To me it was a portent, but still I held on till the tremors subsided. Then he took me by the shoulders to move me, minutely, away from him.

"I must go." The dull, blank cast had left his eyes, replaced by a searing concentration. I'd seen that look before.

And I said, "Please . . . no."

"But I must."

"Then I'm going with you."

"Dice, you don't want to go. You don't want to see."

"What I don't see is why you have to go!" I was being a brat.

"This is what I came for. You know that."

I knew. But I'd been hoping, hoping, hoping, with the tragic truth out, that he'd have some release, some relief. I'd been hoping the truth would set him free. It only served to surge him on. Had I really believed he'd come back for me?

"No," I said. I only had one card to play. "Look, Sin, I've let you get over on this town because on a certain level I enjoyed it. These pretty people with their blond hair and preppy clothes, so well-bred and self-important, all their smug little ducks in a neat little row." This was my soliloquy, an aria absent of melody. "The only reason they tolerate me is because I'm related to Pen. But then you come along and do what? For starters, turn my perfect cousin into the slut of the century. Nice! Then you proceed to take 'em all down. Group grope at the homecoming dance! Lust-fueled fire at the old folks' home! Adulterous adults gone wild!"

I neglected to mention the good he'd done—Con Emerson's sexual reality check, the unlikely coupling of Marsh and Crane. "Who needs reality TV with Sinclair Youngblood Powers running the Swoon show?" I widened my stance, hands on hips—a pose. "But I still have to live here. Go to school here. Deal with these people on a daily basis. So guess what? Game over. You got me? Enough is enough is—"

"Enough."

He didn't roar or rage at me; he simply completed my sentence.

"Exactly," I said. "Enough. But I won't ask you to stop, or tell you to stop—I'm just going to stop you. I'll call over there and warn them. I'll call the police. I'll—"

Sin took me by the wrist, with control, barely a hint of stockpiled aggression. His other arm encircled, and that hand found my hair, fingers tightening to assure my full attention. "You'll do this, you'll do that," he said, calm as glass.

The calm got me, made me quiver. Still, I felt for him. As always.

"What you'll do, dearest lady, is fail. And I'll tell you why: You like to mock the people of Swoon, come off the liberal and liberated urbanite, yet your life has been every bit as cushioned and privileged as theirs. You, who've had every advantage, every luxury bestowed. You, who've sacrificed nothing, hungered never, lost no one. It is all you have that makes your efforts futile. You have everything, Dice, but it will do you no good against me."

With that he let me go. I landed in a chair. R.C., who'd been monitoring from the living room sofa, padded over and jumped onto my lap. She fixed Sin with a reproachful glower, something I couldn't manage. My gaze stuck on the windowsill.

Given everything. Lost nothing. That was his summation. Based on what? Deep delving of my psyche? Those marathon getting-to-know-you sessions we never had? He was six-foot-something of big dead wrong. All Sin knew of me was how I pertained to him. How he could sucker me, how I could serve him, how he could use, ruse, and delude me. Not that I blamed him. A golem's got to do what a golem's got to do. But he thought he wrote the scripture on suffering? That he was the only person who ever got screwed—hence his unstoppable flow? I loved him, I did, but man—what a tour de force of conceit.

I rubbed RubyCat under the chin, her purr imparting unity. Sin was juiced, impatient. I didn't look up when he sighed, and I didn't look up when he turned, and I didn't look up when he walked out the door. There I sat, fueling myself with feline affection, as he set off to do this thing.

Then I did what I had to do. I got up and went after him.

LI

Musing on Thanksgiving: Traditionally, our families traded off. One year on the Upper West Side, Momster bitching out the caterer. The next year in Swoon, my aunt pulling out all the stops with twelve different kinds of stuffing and napkin rings made out of hand-carved cranberries. This year—who knew? It was Lainie's turn, but who could blame her for not feeling festive. Sad, really.

It had always been my favorite holiday, all cynicism aside. But this would be the first Thanksgiving since a whole mess of madness. Better to do Thai takeout? Perish the thought! Turkey there must be, and gravy, an ocean of sweet potato with miniature marshmallow floatation devices. Even if I had to pull it together solo in the crummy kitchen of 12 Daisy Lane.

Call it a respite—contemplating a tryptophan coma as I pedaled through pre-dawn frost toward a destiny I could do without. Sin had no doubt "borrowed" a car (Pen's was easy prey) and reached his destination. Yet as I took the curve at Underhill, cringing upon passing the Wolverine, and bumped onto Stag Flank, I saw no sign of it. No, he'd park out of sight—no need to woo witnesses. As if anyone was out besides grazing deer. Still, hopping off my bike, I stashed it behind some trash cans. Better safe than sorry—though I had a feeling I'd be sorry no matter what.

Through the side door, onto a laundry alcove that led to the kitchen. All the lights were off; this was the gray world of a sleeping house. Dormant appliances hummed. I made my way to the living room, edging along walls and pieces of furniture before thinking, *Shit—prints!* Weaned on cop shows like I was, you'd think I'd know better than to get touch-feely with inanimate objects. I clasped my hands in front of me.

There was Psycho Dad, fetal position on the couch. I stared at him the way you stare at a highway wreck—revolted, respectful, with a little prayer that nothing like that ever comes crashing into your life. The tail of his shirt was out. His boots were still on. Except for empty beer bottles, the room was immaculate, devoid of toys, magazines, the random clutter testament that people peacefully coexist in a place.

Everything seemed copacetic. Which was all wrong. Where was Sin? Had he stopped for a hearty breakfast first? My boy would need energy to wreak havoc in this tidy house. As if streaming my thoughts, Douglas Marshall flipped over, boxed the air, then settled back with a snort, dream demon conquered.

I stepped away, not sure what to do with myself. I'd figured I'd find Sin mid mayhem and do what I could to get in his way. I hadn't counted on this limbo state. But cool, all right, this was in my favor—I'd wake Marsh, trot out some BS to convince her and her sisters to leave with me. Maybe my duty wasn't to obstruct Sin's justice with Marshall but simply to lead the girls to safe harbor.

A plank of light shone beneath the bathroom door. Water pounded behind it. I headed for Marsh's room, assuming she was showering, and flipped on the desk lamp so I'd be in plain sight. Weird that her bed hadn't been slept in. The spare, single pillow and thin blanket lacked the cushy qualities I was accustomed to—me, the girl who had everything. They invited nonetheless. I was working hard not to nod off when Marsh came in.

"Hey," I whispered quickly. The gasp that escaped her, the way she buckled at the joints and grabbed for the doorframe. Sure, I scared her—who wouldn't be scared by someone, anyone, who didn't belong in her room by dawn's early light? Only Marsh was already scared. The sort of scared no amount of scrubbing could send down the drain. A scared that might recede but never fade completely, a scared that lurks behind every minute of the rest of your life. That's the sort of scared Marsh was.

"Dice . . ." Her voice was threadbare. Her robe was not. It was fluffy, pink, and newish—and too big on her. She gathered it up at the collar. "What are you doing here?"

From the edge of her bed, I spun it. "The way we left things . . . I couldn't sleep, thinking you hated me. I wanted to say I'm sorry for—"

"It's okay, Dice," she said, her blurted forgiveness telling me that *we* were okay, but *she* was not. I looked at her, and she clutched the robe again, a gesture of hiding, of humiliation. That's when I knew. Not the specifics; if I'm lucky I'll be spared those forever. But I knew enough. Still, unbidden, rhetorically, my mind demanded: *What did he do to you, that depraved piece of shit?!*

Marsh began to comb her hair. She was all shut down, mum as they come, and I, no social worker, had no idea how to deal with this. Grab the gooseneck desk lamp, twist the beam on her, and expose the marks of abuse. That was the drama talking. Or just chill. So counseled my rational side. Victims often think themselves at fault for the crime against them—any question or outraged remark could be heard as accusation.

"Really, Dice, it's fine. You're fine . . . I'm fine . . ."

Fine, right—fine as cancer. What an effort it took to bring the comb up and down through those wet, lank locks.

"Only . . ."

That's it; go on. If I didn't ask, maybe she would tell.

"My dad knew I was in the bar last night." How clean she

smelled—glycerin soap and herbal shampoo. "I guess one of his cronies saw me, told him. Only I was so mad at him for leaving the girls, when he finally came home I . . . he . . . we had a fight." She put the comb down, re-cinched her robe.

"Oh," I said. "That sucks."

She held herself. "Because I couldn't comprehend how he'd do such a thing. What if something happened? So I told him so. I yelled at him. I . . . shouldn't have . . ."

"Yeah, well, what's done is done." A popular quote from the noncommittal phrasebook.

"But he was nasty drunk . . ." She quelled a shudder. "Anyway, it doesn't matter . . ."

I got proactive. "You know what? We should collect Will and Char and get the hell out of here. Go have breakfast at the diner, or go to my house—I want to practice my pancakes, you guys can be my guinea pigs. Because when he wakes up and you're not here . . . maybe it'll teach him a lesson."

Was Marsh even listening? I guess so, because she said, "Yes . . . maybe we should. Your mother's not even around this weekend, right?"

Right. My house as safe house. Once there, I could prompt Marsh to call the cops.

"Let me get dressed, then I'll wake the girls." She turned to a bureau.

At which point the front door opened as if by tornado. Enter the golem. Marsh yelped, clapped both hands over her mouth.

I said, "Shit."

Marsh lapsed into babble. I reached for her; she flinched. "Marsh, it's cool; it's just Sin, okay, he probably followed me here. He's—" More noise, a toppling, a crash. "Upset. Look, you just get yourself and the girls together, okay?"

She nodded. I went to see what the Dirt Crusader was up to. From the end of the hall, I had a fine view. The TV set was junked on the living room floor. Roused and riled, Psycho Dad began to uncoil from the couch, spewing curses. And Sin stood there, jangling things. Metal things. Leather things. He threw the bulk to the coffee table, retaining one piece, a stick of sorts. What *was* that stuff? Oh. Right. Ouch. Sin had evidently pit-stopped at the stable. Technically, equine supplies. In a pinch, implements of torture.

"Get up, Marshall!"

Sharp, shiny objects were affixed to my boy's boots. Spurs, I believe they're called. He applied them, with considerable force, to the surly figure on the sofa. This elicited a howl, then a demand. Douglas Marshall wished to know who the expletive was in his home, uninvited and attacking him.

"I am the face of your doom," Sin boomed theatrically. "And I am the end of your line. Unless the donkey in that field is your son—there is strong resemblance."

He sought to apply the spurs again, but Marshall feinted,

stood reasonably erect. His posture confirmed him as Homo sapiens, one of those Homo sapiens who believed the world did him rotten at birth, and grew up to hone a resentful, sneaky resilience. Douglas Marshall wasn't about to beg for mercy. He snagged a beer bottle and broke it on the coffee table. The jagged rim was a fatal smile.

Quick as a blink, Sin was on him with the slender leather stick that, correct me if I'm wrong, is called a crop. With a thwack and a roundhouse, he brought Marshall to the carpet, then straddled the man and yanked him up by the yoke of his shirt. I was wondering how much more I could watch when I heard a shuffle behind me. Little Willa in PJs and worn-out slippers. I swung and got to one knee, blocking her view, wondering how much she'd already seen.

"Is Daddy playing horsey?"

Too much. "That's right, Willa, you're so smart." Back on my feet, I shepherded her toward her room again. "They're rehearsing for a play. You know what that means?"

"Um . . . uh-huh . . ."

What was with Marsh? How long did it take to throw on jeans? "Well, then you know they're very busy and we can't bother them," I said. "That's why they're doing it while you're supposed to be asleep."

Another clang between the dirt devil and the parent from hell.

"But they're so noisy, how can I sleep?" Willa reasoned.

"I know, you're right. But why don't you pretend to sleep, like you're in a play, too? Then Marsh—Kristin—will be in and we'll all go have breakfast."

Charlotte was sitting up in bed. She assessed me critically and rubbed her nose. If ever there was a need for stuffed animals, this was it, but the Marshall girls had none. It was officially cartoon time, too—morning strafed through parted curtains.

Willa poked me. "Where *is* Kristin?" She looked at the floor to confess, "She and Daddy had a big fight . . . like he used to fight with Mommy."

"Oh, Willa!" My foundation felt as sturdy as a sand castle's, but I couldn't let myself cave. "Don't worry. Kristin's just fine." Stroking a lock of her restless night hair, I tried to keep the tremble out of my smile.

Bash, bang, boom, more turbulence from the living room. I told the girls to be good and stay put, then closed the door behind me. Next move, anyone? Douglas Marshall was execrable—a man who could harm his own child!—but he was accountable for his own actions only, not those of his ancestors. So I couldn't condone what dirt boy was up to in there. In fact, Sin seemed more brutally bent on retribution than ever. The saddest part was, I knew Sinclair Youngblood Powers, the *person*. I had laughed with that person, felt that person's pain, dreamt in the consolation of that person's arms. That, in there, that was a thing. How on earth could I put an end to . . . *it*?

When in doubt, stoop to female hysteria. I ran in, ranting, "Stop! Stop this! Stop!"

Intent on the more dangerous invader, Marshall ignored me, but Sin flicked my way, eyes black abysses, cocksure smile wide. "You could not stay away, then?" he shouted. "So be it—your presence brings out the best in me always."

I got the sense he was biding his time, drawing out the bout. Having waited so long, he'd want the extended version, the unrated director's cut. What the golem lacked in mortal soul he made up for in vicious humor and fluid style, almost stroking with the crop, then slashing at his foe. But Marshall was his own brand of monster. As for me? Nada. Not a speck of magic. Nor the assurance of the certifiably insane. In this mix, I was irrelevant. Futile. Just a girl.

So Sin threw Marshall against the wall and took a cursory survey of his gewgaws. He selected a what-you-call-it, the thing that fits over a horse's head. Just as he was shoving the steel bar part between Marshall's teeth, Marshall sank incisors into the pulpy heel of Sin's palm. Score one for Cuckoo Pops.

"Dice, did you see that!?" Sin was astonished. "Mofo bit me!"

Essence of violence soaked the air like a gaseous drug, speedy and woozy at once. It made my head spin—it and everything else that had transpired over the last twenty-four or was it forty-eight hours catching up to me. I braced myself against the wall, squeezed my eyes tight.

When I opened them again, Marsh had entered the room. *What is her problem?* I wondered, seeing as she was yet to put clothes on. She was still in that stupid robe. She had, however, accessorized it—in spectacular fashion. The juxtaposition between fluffy pink fleece and cold hard steel was striking. True, the clunky object seemed a bit outsized for her slim hands, but she held it straight, with assurance. Talk about dressed to kill. The overall look—impressive, iconic, and very, very deadly.

LII

THE GIRL WITH THE MOST GUN COMMANDED ATTENTION. BOTH combatants separated, stepped off, stood still. Marsh came between them. Pale hair, flint stare, and lunar complexion—a ringer for Andraste, Celtic goddess of warfare.

Could be Psycho Dad saw the similarity. "Shoot him, Kristin! Shoot the bastard! He's trying to kill me!"

The pistol was huge. Forget those streamlined, shiny semi-autos favored by thugs nowadays. This was a vintage model, a Clint Eastwood special. Marsh had it clasped in two hands, arms locked. Slowly she turned toward Sin.

He regarded the weapon with interest, as if contemplating potential effects. Could he be killed? What would come splattering out—blood and guts, mud and bark, or that ominous stuff that had been gurgling inside him of late?

"Marsh, come on, you don't want to shoot anyone." I actually said that, a standard line from a million schlock cop flicks. Equally funny, the wall no longer supported me; I'd moved to stand by Sin. If Marsh did pull the trigger and was off a little, she'd hit me. Only I remembered what Pen had said the night Marsh's mother went AWOL: "Marsh definitely knows how to handle a gun." Her aim would be true.

Sin said, "Can I see the gun, Marsh?"

She lifted it. Pointed it at him. Livid marks that hadn't manifested right after her shower staked claim across her forearms, jaw and throat.

"Marsh, you've been hurt," I said. "Why not put the gun down and let me see?"

"No!" her father barked. "Baby, give it here! Just give it to me!"

Arm extended, he took a desperate step toward his daughter. Only one. One was adequate. Marsh pivoted, lips pressed tight. She gave it to him, straight through the spleen. Which was a little low. As he was blown backward, she aimed higher, shot again, into his heart. Such as it was.

Then she let the cannon fall. She turned to Sin and me. "I shot him," she said.

Yeah, we knew.

"I guess I'm in trouble." Shakily, she made her way to the couch.

Then Sin and I exchanged a glance for about a millennium.

"Go," I said.

"No," he said.

Could I even begin to comprehend what he was feeling? Cheated, probably—to his mind, Douglas Marshall was *his*. To mine, if there was any justice in taking life, it had belonged to Marsh. Either way, the man was dead. What would that mean to Sin's mission? To Sin's very existence? The death room was for him a kind of purgatory; as long as he remained here, time was irrelevant and nothing else would happen.

For a moment we all observed it—the body, that is. It wasn't the first time I'd seen a corpse. Granted, this one was pretty grisly. Interesting factoid about bodies: In life, we obsess about our own and judge those of others, but when we're done with them we are out of there. The carcass on the floor was about as menacing as a candy wrapper.

Marsh made a noise—not quite sigh, not quite sob—from where she sat. I looked toward her, then swung my gaze to Sin. *"Go!"*

He held my eyes and promised them a thousand things until I felt them flooding, and closed them. At which I heard him swear to me, "Till soon."

I opened my eyes and went to Marsh. "Come on," I said. "You better get in there and chill out the girls—they have to be freaking."

Mention of her sisters made Marsh snap to. While she slipped into their room, I went into hers. Rumpled her bed and rolled around in it, plucking a hair from my head to put among the sheets. Earlier I'd affected a specter's presence; now I was planting evidence. Just in case. My hope for the moment was that Willa would forget the perilous horseplay shortly before the shooting. When Marsh and I reconnoitered in the living room, she was ready to call 911.

Everything unfolded with relative ease. Of course, Marsh did have a dead father and would carry the truth of his death with her always. But in practical terms the police bought our story of self-defense. That Douglas Marshall had pulled his daughter out of bed in a drunken fury to assault her. That I, the sleepover guest, was to be next. That Kristin Marshall, having suffered abuse at his hands for some time, couldn't bear to see it inflicted on another, so she wasted the freak with his own .44 Magnum.

There was no reason to doubt her, or the evidence of her bruises, and the vibe I got from the police presence was good riddance to bad rubbish.

Ultimately, the Marshall girls would be reunited with their mother to live happily ever after in a nice house with their nice soon-to-be-stepdad in the nice comparative metropolis of Torrington.

Only, that was ultimately. Immediately after the hoo-ha at Stag Flank Road, the girls were whisked off to their grandparents' place. With so much going on—all these official people doing official things—Marsh and I didn't even get a good-bye. I just watched her load into the sheriff's SUV with her sisters. She put a pale palm up to the glass, a still and silent wave.

Then I made my way home. Alone.

Soon. What an awful word. So ambiguous, so damn indefinite. Couldn't Sin have been more specific? As in, "Till tonight" or even "I just beat the crap out of a five-star creep, then witnessed his patricide—I'm going to Disney World!" Anything but "soon."

So I summoned him. Summoned hard and long. Maybe I was too exhausted. Maybe something was up with Sin, something that enabled him to resist my invocation. Maybe whatever, it didn't work.

Sleep wouldn't come, either, though I begged for it in bed, courted it on the living room sofa. Blocked, no doubt, by the image of Douglas Marshall—bullets going in, blood spewing out, the shock and awe on his face. I gave up, got up. The day was indecisive: maybe rainy, maybe sunny, definitely interminable. I prepared a grilled-cheese sandwich that I did not want and subsequently did not eat. To otherwise stay occupied, I surfed the net for T-giving ideas, did a load of laundry, practiced my solo for the recital.

Solo. Another word that bugged, but not for ambiguity. Just the opposite. How succinctly it summed up my lot. Not only was Sin a fugitive and one of my closest friends under grand-parental protective custody, my feline companion was apparently missing as well. The realization stabbed me.

"RubyCat? Rubes? Here, kitty-kitty!"

I wandered the house, calling her name, making that smoochy noise reserved for construction workers and cat owners. Dried-up remains in her food bowl gave me the guilts. Poor little furbag was probably famished. Ah, but she was a resourceful little furbag; once I watched her catch a mouse, torment it for twenty minutes, and then devour it from tip of nose to base of tail. Only the notion of R.C. out prowling didn't sit well with me. I pulled on a jacket and went outside.

Beyond the backyard were some scraggly woods. Tromp, tromp; beseech, beseech. Nothing. Beyond the front lawn was the road. Back and forth in both directions. Calling and calling. Nothing. My heart hurt; my head accused. It was getting late—my shadow as long as my dread. Had she run away? Was she lost? Did some bigger beast make a snack of her?

"Ruuuu-beeee!"

I trudged back to the house. To get on the phone, question neighbors for calico sightings. To make flyers with her photo and vital stats, plaster them for miles around. Still I called: "Kitty-kitty-kitty! Ruuuuu-beeee!"

A few yards ahead, on the other side of the road, I caught a flash. It could've been her. It could've been anything. I couldn't be sure. I started to run.

The truck came out of nowhere. No, that's stupid—it was on the road, right where a truck ought to be. A bright yellow pickup with fat wheels and fat fenders. It was too big and too bright but of course that wasn't true; it had every right to be that big and that bright. The only thing it didn't have a right to was my kitten. It would claim her anyway.

Whizzing past, stereo rattling tinted windows, on its merry way. Would I even find a bloodied clump of fur to bury? No. What I found instead was Sin, standing at the foot of the drive that led to my house, RubyCat wriggling indignantly in his arms. She jumped out, and took a stiff-legged trot up the drive. And me? I jumped right in.

LIII

WE WERE GOING TO MAKE S'MORES. S'MORES! GOOEY AND SWEET AND s'morey—right there in the fireplace. Serendipitously enough, I had the ingredients on hand. The graham crackers were kind of decrepit, but they'd be fine. Fine! Everything was fine! My boy was back—his "soon" sooner than I'd dared hope. He'd rescued my kitten from excruciating death. We were all snugly ensconced at 12 Daisy Lane. And I was ecstatic. Ecstatic!

I was only trying to seal the deal when I said, "So are you done?"

At the hearth, Sin sat back on his heels. "Give it a minute," he said. "It's kindling, wood, the chemistry of combustion. You don't just flip a switch and—*whoosh*!"

We'd thrown the throw pillows off the couch to form a cushy pit. I selected a small one to bop him with. "Shut up. I'm not talking about the fire."

He stretched out, addressed the rafters. "Then pray tell what are you talking about?"

I lay next to him, directing myself to the ceiling as well. "I'm talking about Swoon. Are you done with Swoon?"

He considered it. "Yes, dear lady, I am done with Swoon." Rolling to his side, he propped on an elbow and looked at me. "More to the matter: Is Swoon done with me?"

Avoiding his eyes, I pondered the beams.

"Something is . . . happening to me, Dice."

"I know . . . I've felt it." How nice it would've been to have the sustenance of s'mores before commencing this conversation. So much for nice. "What is it? Are you sick?"

The glow of his smile rivaled the fire. "Sick? Oh, Dice, no." With a finger he traced my hairline. Which I somehow felt all over. "Whatever this is, it's incredible."

Sin didn't impress easy. "Whatever this is" impressed him.

"It's not physical, though, or a mental aptitude; it's . . . all I know is if I could bottle it I'd be a wealthy man." His smile took on its lopsided slant. "Except I'd sooner give it away free. "

Free? Hmm.

Another touch, a glancing caress to the collarbone, and he leaned closer. "I'd certainly share it with you."

I'd seen Sin a lot of ways, but simply, purely happy—this was new. Unsettling, too. Something intense was in process;

"whatever this is" was deep. At least that's how it seemed to me, on the outside. "What does it feel like?"

"*Good,*" he said. "It feels *good*. A radiance. A warmth. An arousal. Alien yet in an elusive way familiar." He fell onto his back again. "I'm not describing it well at all."

"No, you are," I encouraged. "Tell me more. Is it constant? Erratic? Does it come at certain times of day?"

"More and more often." He took my hand. "Mostly when you are near."

He put my palm flat to his chest, and there it was, that formidable effervescence. I let it pulse against my palm. Then, shifting, lay my cheek beside my hand.

"It scares me," I said.

"At least you've not run screaming from the room."

"Sin, come on . . . after all we've been through?" Relaxing a bit, I could detect a rhythm to the rumbling. "Whatever this is" wasn't chaos—there was order to it, a natural pattern.

"It scares me, too," he admitted. "Mainly because it's so . . . so expansive, you know. Like I cannot contain it."

We rested a while. Then he said, "Sometimes it's all I think about."

"Yeah? And what do you think?"

"So far, so inconclusive. Except that there is a cost. Whatever this is seems to be . . . nullifying . . . certain other qualities on which I've come to rely."

"Like?" Now I propped up, gazed down.

"Like, for instance, I'd popped into the Stop & Shop for some Gatorade, but all I had in my pocket was a matchbook and some lint. Normally, I could . . . convince the cashier that was legal tender . . . only . . . to no avail."

I thought of my efforts to summon him earlier, also to no avail. "You mean it didn't work?"

"I mean it didn't work."

That was weird—or was it? Did he even need a golem's aspects anymore? Not to get all Pinocchio about it, but could Sinclair Youngblood Powers be turning into a *real* boy? My heart soared. Really, if this were a cartoon, my heart would have lofted me to the ceiling right now.

Then slammed me back to the floor.

Because another option occurred to me: "Whatever this is" was taking him, reclaiming him . . . killing him. I hated "whatever this is." Yet I felt it converting me, making me believe the truth or its inevitability. Whatever "whatever this is" was, it *had* to be. I wanted to trust it, at least understand it. Maybe Sin could share "whatever this is," a taste, anyway. By putting his mouth on top of mine.

That was entirely doable. I was fully receptive. The fire snapped, crackled, and toasted the room. His hand found the nape of my neck. *Screw the s'mores,* I thought. *Show me, share it, gimme some . . . kiss me . . .*

Only he did something else, and it was a shocker. "I really am a cad," he said, his smile so near, "the way I go on about myself—*my* past, *my* tragedy, *my* vengeance, and now my . . . whatever this is. I don't want to talk about me anymore." Lifting slightly away, he once again caressed a curl. "Dice, let's talk about you."

Deep, huh? "Whatever this is" actually put a dent in Sin's self-absorption. A smirk crept onto my face, corners softened by affection. "What do you want to know?"

"Everything," he said. "Anything." He gazed into me, eyes like uncut gems, that wonderful scent of apples on his breath. "I know. I shall ask the same query you've put to me on occasion: Do tell, dear lady, what brings *you* to the charming hamlet of Swoon?"

LIV

It's this culture — it's twisted. Unattainable standards of beauty. Money almighty as the stamp of success. An idealized concept of romance that has little girls who can't even tie their own shoelaces pining for the handsome prince. Ruby Ramirez was the poster child for that one.

"Can you just explain it to me? Can you make me understand? But go slow, in real simple terms, because clearly I am stupid, so fat in the head, so . . ."

On and on she railed. About? Some dick. Some dick I won't even gratify by naming. Dennis, okay, his name was Dennis, Dennis DeMarco. Bore a tattoo of Prometheus jacking fire. How about Prometheus getting his guts pecked out; I would've liked that. He was "the one." Again. Ruby Ramirez had more number ones than Mariah Carey.

Now here's Ruby opening her coat and hiking up her skirt in

an alley one winter's night. Bed head—ha! Girl got back to the party with brick head. And her eyes bliss-blitzed and her limbs all rubber. Only dot-dot-dot, along comes Valentine's Day with Ruby's ass on the cold, hard curb.

"But whatever," she said, straight bravado. "Plenty of fish in the sea."

True. No man shortage in Ruby World. There were guys around that day—the day that segued into that night. Girls, too. Seven of us, an odd number trooping up to her place. Not normally the party house, but Ruby's mother and the step-doctor had already left for the weekend.

"Vail," Ruby said. "My *mami,* the self-loathing Latina, ski-ing in Vail."

I don't know if Ruby's mother was self-loathing, but she was certainly upwardly mobile. The step-doctor was a cardiologist; he put a stent in the mayor. Her biological father was a janitor; he cleaned toilets in City Hall. Imagine the rungs in between, and Ruby's mother scaling them, an aerialist in stilettos. These days she swung that agility to the Colorado slopes.

The apartment sprawled out on the twenty-sixth floor of the kind of glass tower everyone on the Upper West Side that didn't live in one hates. Ruby lived in one but hated it nonethe-less; she was a self-loathing glass-tower dweller.

"Soon as I'm legal, I'm out," she said, grandly littering books and bag across barren surfaces. She directed the statement to this girl Irina Something Russian Unpronounceable, who was new. Everyone else was aware that "my aunt's going to hook me up in the Bronx, pre-war building that makes this claptrap look like Lego and Saran Wrap." Ruby was into architecture and design. She appreciated old things. "I'm talking gargoyles and shit." Ruby had a baroque bent. Gargoyles were most definitely her style.

So we did what we did: sat around. No alcohol, and only Owen Handlemann had weed, and Owen's weed stunk. Not in a good way. Ruby was in a pissy mood, so conversation skewed argumentative, more devil's advocates than a lawyers' convention in Dante's *Inferno*. I wasn't up for a snipe session. It had been a rough week—math test, drama club drama, not to mention dealing with Ruby's miasma over the dick. Perry Como didn't seem into it, either. Perry Como, just as an aside, was the name of this schmaltzy singer back in my grandmother's day, and our Perry, last name Como, had some sadistic parents. Everyone called our Perry Como Perry Como, never just Perry.

Anyway, Perry Como and I were chummy. Not that we really had the hots for each other, because if we really had the hots for each other and liked each other as human beings maybe we would've gone the boyfriend/girlfriend route. Because, yeah, sure, I wanted a boyfriend. Forget the flawless fantasy male who'd make all my dreams come true, I just wanted . . . someone. Someone to slide a finger through my belt loop, someone who thought I was pretty and told me so, someone to lose my virginity with and learn to make love to and not get pregnant by. Someone—but not anyone. The click, the vibe, the "get" had to be there. That was rare. Yet nonetheless critical.

So alas, my someone wasn't to be Perry Como. That had been established. On the few occasions he and I partook of each other it was goofy-geeky science-project stuff. We pressed each other's buttons to see what reactions we could elicit. Occasionally one or both of us hit the high note; other times we just got hot and bothered. It was always fun, in that empty calories, silly sitcom, abbreviated attention span sort of way. As I once heard a yoga instructor say: Yoga without breathing is just exercise. Fooling around with Perry Como was just exercise.

But we were bored. We excused ourselves, announced it.

Perry Como said, "Who's got a watch with a second hand? Candy's going to time me, see how fast I can undo her bra."

I informed him and the room at large that his stupidity knew no bounds.

Someone said, "You kids play nice."

It was argued whether or not I had inverted nipples; the consensus was no.

Ruby didn't care. She was haranguing someone about something; she was busy. Despite, or maybe due to, the speech impediment, Ruby was an indomitable debate-trix.

I'll spare you details about Perry Como and myself.

Fast-forward and here's Ruby in a full-on lather: Everyone had to go . . . *now*. I flicked lazy eyes to the window. It was dark, but this was February; it could've been midnight, or time for *Oprah*.

So we were leaving, and Ruby snatched my sleeve. "Not you."

Fine. Good. To go home was to wake up tomorrow, Saturday, February 14, without a valentine. Staying at Ruby's would take some of the suck out. I asked Ruby why she threw out the crowd.

She flipped her hair, flipped her hip. It was eloquent, the way she did that. It said, *I had enough of those people. I did not appreciate the way Owen was fawning over Irina—Owen has had a crush on me for the longest, so, what, now he's over me all of a sudden? Plus, we were about thirty seconds from Rashida going full gush about that prep school sweetie of hers, who I'm convinced is a pookah anyway. And you in the corner with Perry Como. Please. But mostly I'm just tired of fronting about Dennis—not that any of them even know about Dennis. You're the only one who knows about Dennis, because you know everything there is to know about me.*

I smiled. That silent testimony to our intimacy siphoned some of the suck out already. I asked Ruby if she wanted to look at menus.

She said, "God, no, because there is so much crap in this house. They always stock up before they skip town; it assuages their guilt."

She led the way to the kitchen. There was a walk-in pantry; we walked in.

"Plus, also, if I really pig out, my mother can enjoy disparaging the size of my ass when she gets back."

We tossed containers on the counter. Imported labels made an artful display.

"Although the thought of ringing in V-Day sober does not appeal to me."

Trouble was, Ruby's parents didn't keep liquor in the house. The plan we devised was to ring a neighbor's doorbell, explain we were making Baked Alaska and hoped to borrow a cup of brandy. A maid answered, and she was cool with collusion—she proffered Courvoisier and told us to take the bottle.

We hit another door, got another maid. This time we said baba au rhum and got a liter of Cockspur with just a tipple off the top.

Once again at Ruby's, we began to sup on cognac, rum, and chocolate-covered cherries. Somehow, a segue for Ruby to begin a new round of the Dennis lament, his failure to love her, and her failure at love in general. The girl was love hungry, more than most. Me, at least I knew from love. Maybe Momster and Daddy had little time for proper parenting, but they loved me. I was wanted. I wasn't an accident or an inconvenience or a disappointment. Ruby, her mother dropped out of school to have her; her father hadn't been around since she was on solid food; and the cardiologist gave her a credit card for her twelfth birthday—you get the picture.

She said, "You know what? We should make a love potion. To make us invincible love goddesses." She sipped cognac. She chased it with rum.

Now, this is when I might have raised objection. Because I knew everything there was to know about Ruby. I did. Knew, for instance, that when Ruby was hurting, she hurt herself. Not in any of the obvious ways. See, Ruby would consider it vulgar to flaunt documentation. Plus, she was vain; she had gorgeous skin and didn't want to scar it up. So she did other things, ingenious, impromptu things, like sticking wet fingers in an electric socket. Or tempting harm, sliding down banisters or skitching in heels.

Skitching—that's when you cling to the outside of subway doors.

Subway—that's how you get around in New York.

The point is, you couldn't say Ruby was into self-injury, per se. You could say, "Oh, Ruby, she so crazy!" and leave it at that.

Unless you really knew her. Like I did.

But what did I do? Giggled, that's what. Perry Como had left me with a gnawing emptiness and unrequited blips in my erogenous zones. I told Ruby I was game, and she looked at me all twinkles, then sadly shook her head. "No . . ."

No? Yes, no.

Because, "You are contaminated by Perry Como." She

swigged, gesticulated. "If we're going to do this thing, we must go into it sanctified."

I shrugged, commented that we weren't exactly in coven attire, either. That got her—dressing up was her art form. So we had a shower, anointed ourselves with aromatic unguents, and Ruby picked out clothes for us—although "clothes" is an overstatement, since all we wore was underwear. And jewelry. And ridiculous shoes. When Ruby deemed us done, I looked like an enchanting prostitute or a prostituting enchantress. From another planet. On acid. In a blender. Ruby, of course, looked fabulous.

It was on.

We lit candles. Chose musical accompaniment. Ruby got a pot, put it on the stove. A very low flame—mustn't burn the alcohol out! And for each ingredient, a line of improvised incantation.

Cognac and rum: "For the sway of intoxication . . ."

Chocolate-covered cherries: "For the strength of sweetness . . ."

Milk (fat free, but what do you expect from a cardiologist's larder?): "For the knowledge of nurture . . ."

A dollop of applesauce: "In homage to Eve . . ."

Just as our brew began to smell good, we veered away from comestibles.

"Flowers," Ruby murmured. "Nothing says female like flowers."

A massive arrangement wasted away in the foyer. We carried it to the kitchen. Ruby stuck her face in, bit the heads off blooms like some kind of rapturous herbivore.

By then we were pretty loaded. I had to force myself—champagne's a weakness and vodka goes down benignly enough, but as a rule I eschew the brown booze. Force myself I did, though. I kept up. I drank cognac. I drank dark rum. Cocktails the color of Ruby's eyes.

We exhorted a cabal of sirens, harlots, and queens—historical, fictional, mythical, biblical. Implored them to bestow their charms. Pledged solidarity. Damned the boys we soon would rule. We went a little crazy; we got a little loud. It was cathartic. It was fun.

I remarked that the potion looked rather disgusting. Ruby gleamed and splashed her fingers in the pot. She licked one clean, then offered one to me. I took a taste. It was . . . not awful. Warm and sweet and strange. The flower petals negligible.

"Mm, right?" Ruby said. "Almost done."

The master suite was done in muted gradients of cream and gray. Here we would find our final ingredients. Ruby perused the dressing table, selected a crystal flacon.

"Heads up!" She threw it at me.

Hand-eye coordination was never my forte, especially when drunk, but I caught the small bottle against my breasts.

Then it was on to the medicine cabinet. Inside, a platoon

of orange vials stood at parade rest. Dear old step-doc didn't believe in full fat or alcoholic beverages but he definitely had faith in better living through chemistry. Ruby perused.

"All right! Viagra!" She made further selections. Valium. Xanax. Adderall. Robaxin. Vicodin.

The voice of reason clamored—albeit from considerable distance. A blockbuster sex drug, okay, but how did the other shit apply to our transformation into boy magnets?

Fists full of pills, Ruby flitted back to the pot. I followed with the flacon, clumsy in ridiculous shoes.

Drop, drop, drop—in went the perfume. A grand an ounce; Ruby's mother had a penchant for expensive scent. From a million miles away, the voice of reason wondered if perfume was poisonous.

Plop, plop; fizz, fizz—in went the pharms.

That's when Ruby said, "Voilà, baby!"

She asked if I was ready. I tried to match her smile and must have succeeded. She hit the cupboard for a pair of delicate, long-stemmed vessels. Next, a big spoon, the sort you'd use to serve fancy dessert. Ruby filled our glasses to the brim.

Did I believe the concoction would make me a love goddess? Not for a second. This was simply something else to do with my partner in crazy since the fourth grade, the girl who knew me, who "got" me, who loved me, and vice versa, absolutely, ad infinitum, all down the line. Ruby *was* my someone. There was no other. Sister, soul mate, mistress, slave, all wrapped up in outlandish lingerie. She wanted to do this, and I was with her. I was *with* her. I was with *her*.

In other words, why the fuck not?

So we toasted, rejoicing in Venus, Delilah, Cleopatra, Lilith, the Comtesse du Barry . . . "And, oh yeah, to us!"

We clinked. The potion was viscous. I gagged, spat, giggled. Ruby chugged it like water. I tried again, took a major mouthful. It went down my pipes, splattered my stomach. Remarkably, it didn't rebel, come spewing back like a geyser. I put my glass down—on a shelf of air. It shattered between our four feet. The sound was far away. I gripped the edge of the counter. I needed to sit, no, lie down.

Ruby put an arm around me. She whispered something husky and funny and incomprehensible. Laughing, I clung to her. Crystal crunched beneath the soles of ridiculous shoes.

Then it was later. Much later. Morning later. I was on the sofa, and as though I'd gotten there via a vast desert. I was sweaty. Eyes felt glued together with grit, my mouth a pail of sand. The sun rose inside my head. People say, when they wake up with a hangover, that they feel like death, but that's not true. I felt like shit, but I felt alive. Very, very much alive. Because I was.

Ruby was not.

LV

IMAGINE A PAPER BAG FILLED WITH WATER. THE WATER IS A STORY.
The paper bag, a storyteller. The point being that eventually
all stories must be told. People simply aren't built to hold them
in. The Ruby story I thought was on permanent lock. I didn't
tell my parents or the cops or the shrinks. They extrapolated.
They conjectured. They had theories. I got a pass, because I
went into shock.

When I came out of shock, Momster and Daddy presented
a solution. Did I bitch? Did I moan? I did not—I packed. As
long as I could keep the truth intact and inside (I'd laid it out
on velvet, in a hidden cranial crypt), I'd go along with anything. Swoon. The moon. Whatever. All this time I thought
I'd sequestered the story out of respect for Ruby—what we
cherished, what we squandered—but the telling, when it came,
came so easily and felt entirely just. It had been a matter of

finding the right person to tell it to. Since a story, even a sad one, is a gift.

Sin responded accordingly. "Thank you, Dice. Thank you for telling me."

I said, "You're welcome." Then I started to cry.

Not very loud, not very violent—more like breathing, only wetter. It wasn't the kind of crying you quieted. Sin understood. There on the rug, amid the pillows, before the fire, he simply held me. Now and then, stroked my cheek with a forge-tempered knuckle. He let me do what I did, and continued to speak as if this—my tears, his talk—were the most normal thing in the world.

"I learned a lot. About you—and about me. How we're alike—and how we're different. Both of us suffered, but not at all in the same way. Because here's me, with my protracted, bumptious tantrum, deflecting my hurt onto others and in the end reaping only hollow retribution. And here's you, enduring with dignity, and with acceptance."

The best listeners listen between the lines.

"Then, just when you should've been rewarded with some semblance of peace, I come barreling into your life with my slings and arrows of obdurate stupidity. To abuse your grace and discount your kindness and spurn your counsel. And still—still!—you take me into your home. Illuminate me with your truth. Honor me with your tears."

At that, he collected a few.

"These are precious to me."

The ridge of his finger glistened in firelight.

"The substance of pure soul."

Right about then, in the clown theater of my brain, I bolted upright and shouted "Eureka!" Sin, too, bolted upright, and as I revealed my glorious, perilous epiphany—tears now the sappy, salty, proverbial tears of joy—RubyCat pranced around excitedly. There was even tinny calliope music. Whoo-hoo!

In reality, I curled away like a croissant, ignoring boy and cat both. Tiny, sparkling fragments of a puzzle had fallen into place. I had to muse on this, and keep my musings to myself.

Let's go to the videotape: That sunny afternoon of the autumn. Me, surrounded by earth and leaves and seedpods, the makings of my man. Me, fraught with thoughts of his tragedy, and how it mirrored mine. Me, liberally sprinkling golem guts with commiserative tears. The substance of pure soul? I think not—more like the Miracle-Gro.

From the start those tears were nourishment. Now their work neared fruition. Sin was amazed and aroused and radiant. His dirty tricks and naughty mind games had begun to fail him. Impossible, incredible, unbelievable, uh-huh—but no less true. I was pretty certain, anyway. Sinclair Youngblood Powers, boy-turned-ghost-turned-golem, was growing a soul. Unbeknownst to him. And with a little unwitting help from me.

"Hey . . ." His whisper stroked my cochlea. "Where'd you go, my lady?"

"Nowhere." I wriggled around to prove it. "I'm right here."

Still I strove to keep my thoughts from broadcasting across my face. Body, mind, soul—Sin was close to the triad. Just like anyone else. Except Sin wasn't like anyone else. Would a soul make him complete—or make him combust?

"Good," he said. "Because I've figured out what's happening to me."

It seemed he'd been musing, too. "Yeah? You want to fill me in?"

"I do. I must. Since you're so vitally involved."

My tears were over and my eyes were clear and my heart was open.

"Impossible, incredible, unbelievable as it may sound, I'm falling in love," he said. "I'm falling in love with you, Dice. Indeed, I'm almost there."

That's when he kissed me. Finally and fully and for the first time. And finally, fully, for the first time, I quit thinking. All I did was feel.

LVI

LOVE AT LAST SIGHT IS GLORIOUS. I KNOW THIS FOR A FACT. IT CAME in the fading light of a dying fire, as I woke from a fathomless slumber, woke smiling, wondering how two people could sleep all tangled up. Mm-hmm, he was still here—with me. "Whatever this is" was on our side.

Reveling in the sculpture we made, refusing to move, I took stock. Of the places I felt like honey—lazy and oozy. The places I felt like sugar—rough and sweet. The scratched parts and the strained parts and the stained parts. The warm spots and the cool spots. The urge to eat—vague, sort of crouching at the fringes. The urge to pee—that was insurmountable.

Movement, then, was a must. First a shoulder, next a limb, a deliberate, slow extrication, as if unraveling a priceless tapestry. I stood. I shook. How could I be shaking when I felt so sublime? I looked down. Neither one of us was wearing any clothes.

I walked through the house. I remembered. All the things he said. All the things I said. Somehow I'd assumed it would've been silent, except for sighs, the intermittent squelched ouch. No, we talked up a storm.

"Let's go outside."

It was his idea. "That's nuts."

"I know."

I giggled. "Okay."

The grass, pink under the moon and crunchy-cold under our bare feet. He held both my hands, held me away from him, and marveled at me—my shape, my skin—and I let him. He made me feel marvelous, so of course he could marvel at me.

A tire swing swung from the backyard elm; I got in it, and he pushed me.

"Your turn," I said after a few attempts to kick the stars.

"Thank you, no, my lady." Sin laughed. "I'm none too keen on swinging from trees."

We chased each other back to the house. We . . . resumed. All over the place. Ultimately returning to the pillows by the fire. Desire is a renewable resource. You cannot give enough. You cannot get enough. It's a circle. There is no end. You love each other. We said, "I love you." Over and over. Said it, sang it, whispered, howled. Then one of us insisted "shut up! shut up!" and we shut up. We communicated in other ways. I could understand his heartbeat, read his veins like a map. And he mine. And he mine.

Every phase of the experience had attendant contradictions. Like when he pinned my wrists to the rug and put the whole of himself against me, I floated free. When I tasted him, I also saw him—I saw what he tasted like. And when at last he told me he would hurt me, I said I was ready, but of course I wasn't. You understand the mechanics of it so you think you have a concept what it's going to feel like—you don't; you have no idea. It's that remarkable. You are like, "Ohhhhhhhhh!" You get it now. And you are changed.

I looked at myself above the sink. I loved me. I loved Sin. Everything else was irrelevant. I came back to him, and he was *still* still there.

"Are you awake?"

"Somewhat. Are you okay?"

"Very. Do you want anything?"

"No. I have everything."

I saw dreamy peace in his face, lips incongruously even, and eyes lulled by release. I saw his hair, spent across his forehead like an untroubled tide. I saw his hands, scarred and callused yet calm, the fingers inclined inward. I saw his chest rise and fall in easy rhythm. I saw a human being—my real boy—beautiful, content, consoled, secure, serene, and in love. That's what I saw when I joined him in the fading firelight.

Did I know it would be last sight?

No. I wasn't thinking that way. I still wasn't thinking at all.

Yet when I awoke this time, it didn't startle me to find him gone. I stretched out wide and languid, arms and legs extending as far as they would go. Where was Sin? Simply somewhere else, or nowhere else, done with the visceral, cerebral, emotional, instinctual, carnal stuff of this plane. Done with walk and talk and touch, with hunger and thirst, want and need. Been here, been here again, done here—off now, to the dust, or the spectral, or heaven or hell or wherever, whatever, comes next.

All I knew for sure is he was gone, really gone, not just on the porch. I didn't need ESP to know, or tarot cards; I didn't need no stinking magic. I didn't plan what I'd tell Pen. I didn't muse on what school would be like come Monday. I didn't wonder if Swoon would go back to "normal," with buttoned shirts and khaki pants and sweaters tied loosely at the shoulders. Thought was still a ways away.

I felt. A lot. Only I didn't feel afraid. And I didn't feel alone. Presence is ephemeral. Love, eternal. I didn't need Sin here to be with him. That's how it was. No surprise, really—we always had an unconventional relationship, he and I.

I lay there, just sort of spacing, till the cat came lumbering over the pillowscape to make a speculative request for breakfast. One of the many demands of the day, any day. I got to my feet, approached the hearth. The remains of the fire were powder white, without a hint of warmth, without a chance of light. Yet I folded the paneled screen and picked up the poker anyway. The braided handle fit against my palm, the iron tool balanced and weighty. I made a series of even stabs into the ash. A spark, and then a glow, as the embers flared back to life.

ACKNOWLEDGMENTS

With great thanks to the people at Pulse: Mara Anastas, Bethany Buck, Jim Conlin, Paul Crichton, Katherine Devendorf, Rob Goodman, Victor Iannone, Jennifer Klonsky, Mary Marotta, Christina Pecorale, Cara Petrus, Lucille Rettino, and most especially Anica Rissi and her magic pencil. Thanks aplenty to Meredith Kaffel for her faith, enthusiasm, and guidance. Thanks also to Rosemary Kassel Stolzenberg for the hot shot and the glimpse of a world so unlike my own. And thanks to Jason Shealy Stutts for knowing I could.

ABOUT THE AUTHOR

Nina Malkin is the author of three novels, one novella, and a memoir. She's also an award-winning journalist specializing in pop culture and lifestyles, whose work has appeared in the *New York Times*, *Entertainment Weekly*, *Real Simple*, and numerous other publications. Nina lives in her native Brooklyn with her musician husband and assorted felines. Find out more at NinaMalkin.com.

Check your PULSe

Simon & Schuster's **Check Your Pulse**
e-newsletter delivers current updates on
the hottest titles, exciting sweepstakes, and
exclusive content from your favorite authors.

Visit **TEEN.SimonandSchuster.com** to
sign up, post your thoughts, and find out what
every avid reader is talking about!

ATHENEUM

Margaret K. McElderry Books

Simon & Schuster
Books for Young Readers

SIMON
PULSE